D0903394

The Sudden Trees and Other Stories

Books by H. E. Francis

A DISTURBANCE OF GULLS

NAMING THINGS

THE ITINERARY OF BEGGARS

The Sudden Trees and Other Stories

H. E. Francis

Frederic C. Beil

Published by Frederic C. Beil *Publisher*
609 Whitaker Street
Savannah, Ga. 31401
http://www.beil.com

LIBRARY OF CONGRESS CATALOGING-IN-PUBLICATION DATA
Francis, H. E. (Herbert Edward), 1924–
The sudden trees and other stories / by H. E. Francis.
p. cm.
I. Title.
PS3556.R328H4 1992
813'.54—dc20 91-15541
CIP

ISBN: 0-913720-96-3

First edition

This book was typeset by SkidType, Savannah, Georgia; printed on acid-free paper; and sewn in signatures.

Printed in the United States of America

Acknowledgment is made to the following publications in which some of the stories in this volume first appeared: *Prairie Schooner* for "The Sudden Trees"; *The Sewanee Review* for "Joshua"; *The Montana Review* for "The Other Side of the Fire"; *Quarterly West* for "Walls"; *Four Quarters* for "Out There"; *The Ontario Review* for "The Impossible"; *The Greensboro Review* for "On the Heights of Machu Picchu"; and *The Southern Review* for "Mr. Balzano."

This book

is

for

Angel Díaz Albarrán

Contents

The Sudden Trees and Other Stories

The Sudden Trees

BY SPRING SHE was uncannily thin and stumbling frequently. And though her classmates, with a naturalness as uncanny, leaped to her and caught and straightened and supported her, even making comedy of it, his principal and fellow teachers and some parents insisted she be taken out of classes: she should be kept in the Home, first thing you knew she'd be breaking bones, there would be outrage and shock and trauma, and the children would never forget.

"But what of her future?" he said.

Breath sliced air. Faces froze.

"Her what?"

"Future."

Future.

There was a future—until there was nothing. Unless nothing.

"She'll spend it alone—in a bed. The state will send her to the hospital—to lie and do nothing but vanish—when she's unmanageable."

"She's almost that now."

"But not that," he said. "You see how the children help her—and there's only until June to go until the end of classes. She'd want to finish them."

But they were a wall of faces too wordless and still, eyes deliberately elsewhere. Oh, he knew they understood. How *could* they defend themselves but through staunch silence? They were parents, they paid taxes, they went faithfully to PTA. And wasn't it their town, their children's future?

But he could do nothing. Their unity was stone.

"If you could let it be natural," he said.

In two days, when she fell and tried to get up but could not, he asked Alice Dempsey to monitor his class and carried Rhoda out to his car and drove her to the Home.

The next morning he did not want to think her face, but in class the empty place—third row, third seat—gaped. The box on his seating chart was a grave. Absence cried out her presence.

When the children went yelling and shouting home and he said, "See you tomorrow, Alice," and waved down the corridor to Bill Brown, he went outside—and his breath caught: at the suddenness of trees, veils of instant spring gold glowing in the sun, the yellow burn of forsythia, and a warm weight of air that pressed at his mouth, nostrils. Off the road the bay moved with a glitter and heave that threatened to spill over the edge and carry him. This. And he went past his turn and took the old dirt road upslope and came abruptly onto a high flat rise overlooking the Sound, where the wind grew and the Home loomed barren. Its walls and uncurtained windows and long porch futile to sea wind, the great house looked hollow. From the playground below came shrieks and yells.

Inside, he did not look far. In the enormous hall beyond the desk where Ella Trask usually sat, Rhoda was standing. How tiny she was! A wind might whisk her off.

"I knew your car." She did not move.

He laughed. "You were right then. Well, you can't do without a history lesson, can you? Suppose—" He took her hand. "Suppose we do it in the little room. It's quiet and there are always gulls out the windows. I'll carry you."

"I don't hurt." Her voice, which in the chorus of class borrowed strength from the others, was as wobbly as her legs.

From the corridor Ella Trask called, "She said you'd come, Mr. Trueblood. Have a good lesson, Rhoda."

"Today Four B got to the hardest part, fractions, in math, and to India in geography, and a big battle in Africa in history. First for math. You ready? If I bought a quarter of a pound of butter—write it this way—and bread weighed—"

"I love fractions!"

Precocious, she had skipped third and usually left 4B behind too; and despite distracting cries from the playground and a tumble of children in other rooms, she did now. Her fingers moving the pencil caught the problems almost before his words fell—she was that adept. Her brown eyes rolled in quick thought, and the long brown hair rode over the table, flicked and lashed as she bent close.

Repeating names carefully, she followed through India. But in history, in the midst of Carthage, her hands had to hold her head in place.

"Well, that was a long long siege Hannibal went through

and *he* didn't do it in one afternoon. Why should we?" he said.

"Because Four B did, you said." Not to accuse. Fact was fact.

"That's because so many heads were working together. Sometimes that's fast."

"But it's easiest alone with you 'cause your head is much bigger and full of things." Though she laughed, her face stayed pale.

"Now we've got time for a go around the building and then your suppertime. On my back?"

All the next week was the interlude after school. She was confined to sitting, but when *he* (there was only one *he*, she let them know) came, by special permission it was her hour on the grass. Though they watched earthworms' probing mouths and pushing corrugations and girdles, she wouldn't let him ease up on her lessons. She would follow Hannibal. "I hate the Romans and love Hannibal and Hamilcar Barca! Ugh. Someday I'll climb the Alps, I'll plant a dandelion for Hannibal, it will bloom in the snow. You just wait." He let her crawl. Together they gathered a bouquet of dandelions to put in a glass on her windowsill, a yellow splash in the sun.

On Monday the bouquet was gone.

And Rhoda was not waiting.

"They've taken her to the hospital up-island," Ella Trask said. "But they'll take good care of her. We had to think of the children. They couldn't really bear it."

Bear it?

You did not know what children could bear. And forever.

At school Laura or Anne or Millie shifted roles, so losing Rhoda did not cripple their games, but after their cries and shrieks and laughter at recess, when they came in and took their seats around that dark center, the class asked, "How's Rhoda?"

"When's Rhoda coming back?" And Anne, out of the blue, said, "We all want to *see* her."

So, with permission from parents, a station wagon full, they made the long ride with gifts and his promise of a homeward-bound stop at McDonald's for hamburgers and fries.

You could see Rhoda's eyes could not contain—they darted from face to face as all spurted at once: "Listen you know Mrs. Berg hates games and scolded Timmy and Mill shoved Mary's head down the toilet she screamed and—" All the while her hands clutched the compass and hair ribbons and sketchbook they'd brought. Her own voice made a quiver softer than a veil over them. She listened so hard her eyes never blinked, even *they* listened: "Mr. Berry is sick and Mama gave me a birthday party and we went to the beach but the water's too cold to swim yet and Mary hid Mr. Trueblood's box of chalk and we all stayed in for recess and then Dennis squealed on Mary and—"

But how quickly they were bored. Their attention wandered to a nest outside the window, to the children in the other beds. Corridors—down, up—called. They pursued wagons and trays, tracked nurses. He was all voice and hands to tame them. But she—how in her stillness she blotted them up!

When he called time to go, everybody scrambled, leaped with laughter, sending volleys of "Bye, Rhoda," "So long," "Bye, bye, bye," making children in the beds turn heads, wave. Despite his voice and hand, his "I'll see you soon," her gaze turned stone.

Looking back, he saw she had not moved.

By the time they saw the big M blazing yellow arches over the trees, they were all screaming. Rhoda was virtually forgotten. The outing was over.

But Rhoda did not forget. Her presence startled: in his box in the teachers' lounge lay the letter with the jolt of her handwriting. She wrote in awkward clumps.

> Dear Mr. Trueblood:
>
> Tell the class thanks. I have all the gifts on the bed. It is cold at night but their gifts keep me warm. Sometimes it's dark. But there are lots of faces here. Mr. Trueblood we didn't finish Hannibal. Is anyone sitting at my desk? Tell hello to Miss Samples and Anne and Terry and . . .

He saw each face take its desk. The room filled. She had not left one name out.

After the last hour he read the letter to the class. They listened as if words stood Rhoda before them. Lines said special things to some—they emitted laughs, sighs, murmurs, but once he began reading their names, the tense expectation made them say "Shhhhh, *l*isten—" till he dismissed them.

But the letter did not dismiss him. At home he saw it when he lowered his books in halts and stares at the sea. Words stood in the waves: It is cold at night. Sometimes it's dark. There are lots of faces here. Blocks of words stood harder than glaciated stone. If his hand reached, it would touch words. Marie. He could not turn to her now. There was silence and the sea he had been maddened and consoled by when she left. He swore, I won't live with anyone else, I won't ever live with anyone else. She had turned life quicksand—not only by going, but despite all warnings, suddenly. Her going had told him that to her what was love was sex; what was companionship, time filled; what was hope, desperation; what was a dream of a long life together, a lie. She said, I can't live small town and be confined to salt water and your papers and books and sometimes a niggardly night's reprieve—to what? the same faces, same streets. I'm hemmed in—and Jesus, how can you stand it? I'm breaking, Darren. But, Marie, he said, this is my life.

Gone. Day after day, weeks, all he heard, relentless, in the beat of the waves was Marie, Marie, Marie.

He dropped the book and went out onto the deck. The sea was a great heaving. Waves beat, beat. He stared—all he saw was that face, stone, Rhoda sitting there stone—stared until he was sitting there, he was Rhoda sitting there, beating day after day— "No," he said, so loud it halted wind and sea in him for an interval. No. *Not* day after day after day—or what did it all mean?

He called Esther.

"Darren!"

"Esther, listen—I've decided to do something, and I may need your help, but first, don't think I'm crazy. You know me best, you'll understand, though I'm not even sure *I* do."

"Your voice is vibrating like wire."

"You know Rhoda Marsh?"

"The child you've just visited?"

"I'm going to try to get her."

"Get her?"

"Bring her here."

"To town? I don't understand."

"To my house. Keep her here."

"But, Darren— Do you know what you're asking for?"

"Yes. But no."

"You know she hasn't long. She may die there."

"Yes."

"Do you—oh, it's not your prime consideration right now—

but do you know what it will do to us—I mean, to your friends, relationships . . . ?"

"I've all summer free. I can."

"But—may I ask it?—*why*, Darren?"

"I don't know."

"You don't know why?"

"I told you—I don't know. But I must. Perhaps I'll find out why. Esther, *will* you, if I need it, help me, stand by my character, whatever this requires? I'll talk to Arnold Bingham—he's a fine lawyer—if there are complications. But why should there be? The doctors know her condition, she has no parents, to be practical the state will be glad of one expense less, they need hospital beds, so except for legalities you name the objections. Will you? You trust me, don't you?"

"Who more? But do you realize what it will do?"

"To all of us? But for a summer, one summer in our—her—life!"

"Well, I do have objections, but you know I'll help. You come first."

"Rhoda does."

"Well, Rhoda does."

"You're a prize!"

And despite his urgency, which Bingham echoed, he had not considered Rhoda's choice, he had assumed she would come. But Farnley, head of the hospital, had to protect. "You know rights these days, free will is public will or no will, and I, if I were Rhoda, would want to be asked. You agree, Mr. Bingham? Shall we all go see her together?"

In the corridor Bingham said, "You know what you're doing to yourself, Darren?"

"No." But his hand assured Bingham.

The presence of three official visitors alerted all the children, brought silence, all attention on Rhoda.

"You're blushing," he said.

"I knew you'd come, Mr. Trueblood." She was trembling.

"Mr. Trueblood wants to take you home to spend the summer vacation with him, Rhoda," Farnley said.

She did not once turn her eyes to Farnley.

"Yes."

"Well!" Eased, Farnley was smiling. "No doubt about that decision."

"Now?" Rhoda said.

"That's up to Mr. Trueblood."

Darren laughed. "Now."

"The nurses will dress Rhoda. Barbara, she's going home."

"Home?" the nurse said. "Oh. Of course."

When she was ready, he would have scooped her into his arms but for Farnley's warning glance: he was responsible for her now. He raised her gently. When word of her leaving passed down the beds, all sorts of nervous laughs and cries came from the others, and clapping. "Home!" "Come see us, Rhoda." "Have a swim for me." A few forlorn faces gazed, too still. Rhoda waved and for the first time a laugh, loud, broke from her throat. He felt it reverberate in her chest.

How she came to life! She slept in his brother's old bed in the room next to his, the door between open unless she wanted it shut—that way he could hear her any minute. But mostly he kept her at his side. She loved the spread of the Sound, especially when, roused, it thrashed at the shore below and swirled about rocks half the size of the house; and when it threatened to mount the cliff to the deck, she screamed with the thrill of it.

"Can I go down the steps?" Long wooden stairs went down the slope to pure white stones and then sand and water. He put on his bathing trunks.

"On my back?" But her clutch failed so he carried her. "Now, we'll take off your clothes and go in—"

"I don't have a suit!"

"Tomorrow I'll buy you one. Right now—don't tell a soul!—you'll wear pants in, okay?"

She buried her head in his neck, a huddle in his arms, and he walked deep into the water, and they bobbed awhile.

"I can swim. Let me."

He held her while she feebly flapped and kicked till, fearing her fragility, he gathered her up like a delicate web.

She helped him cook. "Hand me the package? That's a spatula. In that drawer's an apron—" In her attempts to move about, she would forget and when she toppled, vigilant as he was, he swept her up. "Must be grease on the floor. . . . That chair. Something wrong with your sole?. . . Let me see." But she said, "It's all right. I fall. I'm weak. You have to get used to that."

At such moments he wanted to stand in her place, in her thin body, behind those eyes—and see this house, sea, him. You made some adjustment. The body told you. You did what it told you. Did you know what the body was doing? He wanted to see from Rhoda, be Rhoda.

"And don't you worry," she said. "I'll tell you."

"Tell me what?"

"When I can't do something."

Some afternoons they would ride till she waned. "How 'bout an ice cream?" She would glow. But in her cup, hardly touched, it would melt.

Was she doing it for him?

When he had to stop by Dr. Spurling's, the M.D. shingle nearly stopped breath.

"Don't run off now. I need a word with the doctor."

"You sick?"

"Nope. Just need advice."

"You can go then." She made a deep laugh.

And Spurling confirmed: of course she would dwindle, bones could easily break, coordination go, speech go muddy, lumps and swellings appear, pain . . .

But could a hospital save? prolong? do more?

"You check with me for anything you're not sure about handling, the least thing, and at any time."

At home she said, "Hannibal! We didn't cross the Alps yet. We're stranded." She struck the table. Pain cracked her porcelain face. She gripped into laughter, bit, but he felt her pain dart up his own arm.

"Okay. Hannibal. But only for thirty minutes. Starting today we're having a schedule for what you missed, if you like, but only weekdays because . . . guess what's coming to the playgrounds this Saturday?"

Her eyes grew awesome. "Not—!"

"Yes."

She screamed, "The circus!"

Instantly he regretted saying it, then as instantly ashamed at his regret because she clapped and her eyes glowed so, she vibrated with excitement; but something in him did not want her to go.

Why? He was perplexed by his own probing, his own perplexity.

Half the nights she was awake—at intervals he heard her—until Saturday.

"It's today, and it didn't rain!"

By one she was nearly breathless with anxiety. She had gone over her four dresses—for him, happy because the blue was his blue. "Wonderful!" he cried.

"I'm ready." She yelped, pure joy, crawling about slowly on all fours.

"Stalking like that, you'll be joining the tigers."

"It's elephants I want to see."

"There'll be plenty of those."

All down the road she talked a blue streak, not one minute taking her eyes off things to look at him. Was she hoarding? "Down that dirt road're the best blackberry bushes!—you get quarts at a time, last summer Terry and me and Tina Lewis went, then we'd hunt things in the dump before they burned them all up, that's old Hinkelman's house, we steal green apples and he chases us and he swears to make you stop up your ears—"

In her excitement she was grinding and slurring words. Did she know?

"And did you stop up your ears?"

"No." She giggled. "*We* know all the words. Ohhhhh!" The woods fell away, sky fanned out, the big top loomed, colored flags galore raged in the wind, and the lot glittered with cars. "The whole town's here. Listen!" The band, tinny in the blow off the sea, came in spotty bursts.

Light in his arms, she was twisting, turning, waving. "Amy! Terry!" She called name after name.

"It's Mr. Trueblood and Rhoda!"

A crowd gathered around them at the entrance: Dr. Walker and Jenny, the Wardwells, and Charlotte Fay, half her classmates . . .

Nervous, somewhat annoyed, if smiling, he said, "We'd better find a seat," for it was bleachers catch-as-you-can; and they sat, but a wound opened in him when they said, "What, Rhoda?" "What'd you say?" "It must be the wind, but I can't hear—"

"Here come the clowns!" Red-white yellow-white motley atumble and berserk, leaps beatings falls screams whistles laughter. Confetti sprayed rainbows over the audience, in Rhoda's hair, everywhere. A joyful heat filled the tent.

She was not even blinking: trapezes swung in her eyes, bangles glittered, cycles flipped, lions leaped to a whip—with each act the wider her gaze. She reveled in it, sometimes in a frozen stillness of ecstasy. When she pressed close, he felt her heart quick quick quick against him; but when at last through the great flaps *they* appeared—"Elephants!"—she screamed. "Look! Gold and silver! Wow!" And the trainers glittered silver blue yellow red glitter, with batons—one touch and the elephants moved, surged, raised gigantic feet, knelt on front or rear legs; and when one woman lay under an elephant's foot, Rhoda's nails dug deep into his arm and she shrilled as the woman rose "Safe!" But when the trainers stopped the elephants and a man announced a ride on the back of each elephant for the lucky person whom a trunk pointed straight toward, alone she rose, she stood, her arms reached out—at once, as if the elephant spotted her, its trunk rose and pointed. "Yes!" she cried, but it came taut as a whisper. And the crowd around her shrieked as all the elephants pointed at their lucky chosen.

Down he carried her. Down slowly sank the elephant. He set her in the howdah. Slowly the elephant rose. Around the arena she rode, smiling, her hair asway as she sat, stunned with joy, as the tent filled with applause and cheering. Before the descent she threw him a kiss, and when she slipped down he could feel the hot palpitation and the thud in her chest. She could not speak, but she gripped louder than words.

Then the band struck up and clowns reeled into the arena, and amid final catcalls and shouting, it was over.

Not till they were in the car did she burst: "Did you see me? Did you? Did you?"

By morning she was in a fever, talking elephants and Alps and Hannibal. Hot and so dry, yet she pushed water and juice back, murmuring, "Nnnnnnn," and on into the second night, "Nnnnnnn."

She saw something. Something would not leave her eyes. ". . . nnnn . . . sark."

"What is it, Rhoda?"

He looked where she looked. He lay beside her, stared at walls, objects, following her hand and eyes, tried to think what she saw, how. The metal light disc made a dark shadow against the ceiling. If you watched long, it came down at you, it grew. ". . . nnnns . . . dar . . ." The sun's dark? He removed the disc and brought in a table lamp. She stopped staring at the ceiling, but kept up her mumbles Elephant Hannibal Terry Lee Anne till he knew he had to ease her, had to. It was the first time he must give her anything. The needle did ease. She slept. And when she finally closed her eyes, he felt a sudden hard choke that caught him so unaware it blinded him an instant.

But it frightened: she slept almost steadily for two days.

At night, straining, he could hardly hear her breath. By the night light he watched the sheets for the vaguest rise and fall of her chest—and stood long, looking, till reassured. Often she lay so motionless he had to sit on the edge of the bed or lie beside her to catch a sound or even the slight warmth of her breath.

Now he was learning her: the shape of bone, the thin skin, where it lay taut to ribs, taut over belly, vague blue veins, her dry forehead turning a pale translucence with the finest lines and lines down her cheeks, through her dry lips. Despite her small body, in the face so serious in repose, the expression of long experience, a woman was emerging. He pressed back the hair, surprised at how cool it was over the hot flesh. Her breath had a rancid odor, she expelled puffs of burnt chestnut, yellow smears he quickly washed. He came to know when each motion would come, could say It is time, and rise and go to her, as if she'd called. Awake or in half sleep she too responded to his motions, knew when to cling, roll, ease down with his hands.

Occasionally she would open her eyes, wide, still, unrecognizing. Was she confused? lost? disoriented? She would sigh back into that other world or let her head slump against him. Nights he lay with her, vigilant, fearful he might roll over, break bones. Her quiet throb slowed his own till her breath was his, her heat came from his body, the odor of her mouth from his.

When at last she woke fully, she smiled.

"You," she said. "You're back."

His throat filled with a rush.

He was cramped, but he picked her up and carried her onto the deck. "What a glorious morning!" The water burned, enough heaving gold to blind you.

That very afternoon Esther drove up.

"I've come to invade the recluse. Do you mind? I've something for Rhoda. A surprise. Do you like surprises, Rhoda?"

"Everybody likes surprises!"

"What? *Oh!*" She set the box down.

Rhoda's fingers gripped so hard they turned white.

The top shot off. "A kitty!" Fur leaped and veered, climbed, ran circles till their laughter exhausted Rhoda and the little ball found its way into the crook of her neck and finally fell asleep with her.

"You've been so cooped up, you must need an escape. Could I relieve you?"

"Relieve?"

"Well, it must be wearing."

Wearing.

"No." He realized how strange his view (was it a view?) must seem to her. She was, if nonchalantly, observing—in her own way, probing.

"We miss you, though we're aware you can't have anyone in. But don't cut yourself off too completely—you'll have to come back to us, you know. That—dreadful as it sounds!—is inevitable." She tried to laugh, but it was measured, testing.

"And she's holding the line?"

"We are, yes."

Esther's glance encompassed the house, conditions, arrangements.

When she was leaving, she drew his head down and kissed him full. She said, "I believe you've forgotten that too," smiling but considerate, letting her hand linger on his cheek, and then "Good-bye."

He shut the door, leaned. Why was breath so restricted all the while she was there? He was glad he had not moved the daybed into Rhoda's room until now. He set it against the wall so he could be sure to hear the least movement.

But that night all he heard was the kitten, its meow and purr, an actual bleat at times, overriding her sounds. And when he checked, the kitten was so close to her he feared it would block her nose or mouth, steal her breath, drain her warmth. And it was so playful and lashing, he feared for her eyes. You fool, you! Yet he resented it to jealousy; and with the kitten he felt Esther intruding, reminding that she was out there. So they made three here. She had set flesh between him and Rhoda.

One afternoon Rhoda cried out.

No, *not*—

But it was the kitten. It had drawn a long fiber of blood. Her arm was so thin the blood going out of her appalled him. He must stop it. He sucked at it, held his tongue there till it stopped, then washed and bandaged it.

She was petting the frightened kitten and murmuring to assure it, but when he said, "The little devil's got sharp claws," she set it aside and sank back on her pillow.

Waking in dark, she said, "I don't think I want the kitten."

He felt a leap of joy and, as quickly, shame.

"Can you give it away?"

"Yes."

"All right."

"Rhoda?"

He heard her turn over.

Afternoons she went back to modeling the clay he had bought. Because she could not walk now, he had set the armchair before the picture window so she could watch the people along the beach and the ships on the Sound. He carried her down to the sand to watch gulls and hunted shells for her collection, took her into the water and laid her on a blanket to sun until she slept, then carried her back up and into the shower with him or, if she was too sleepy, sponged her down.

An afternoon came when she said, "Can we read?" and he knew she could not go down. For the first time he knew walls, how quickly walls surrounded, how quickly flesh enclosed you, how you could move no farther than bones. And he felt frenzy at the thought: whatever you were, it was contained in those walls. All of it? He felt it, a mysterious prisoner, moving inside the flesh, trying every moment to break free. The kitten had scratched her and given it a fine split to escape through. He clutched Rhoda—too hard: her eyes widened, her breath rasped, though she did not cry out.

Angles hurt her now. She was comfortable only when she sat in his lap, slumped against him so long she was no longer a separate thing. She said, "I can hear your heart." Her fingers touched the throbbing in his neck; her own lay tilted, and he watched the barely visible pulsing in her throat. And after he laid her in bed, almost flat now, with a very thin pillow because bulges hurt her neck, he moved about the house, bereft, incomplete.

Soon she could not leave the bed and he feared lifting her too frequently.

"Read me more of your book. I like Rebecca."

She was too much bone, her head seemed larger, her neck too thin and long to support it. As flesh dwindled, her eyes grew and her hair seemed to thicken and spread. Long he would read *Ivanhoe*. After, he passed a damp washcloth over her, with his fingertips teasing the hollows and sinks he knew so well until she laughed.

She wanted sea.

"*I've* got an idea. Let's make the living room our bedroom."

"You mean it?" She wanted to help. She tried to rise but no bone moved.

He dismantled the beds and set them up so she would wake on sea, fall asleep to waves, though it was as much, yes, for himself. He would not stand the separation from her at night by walls.

Below, time mocked. It stood visible in the monolithic boulders. He could touch time. Yet with Rhoda there was no time, they lived a perpetual now.

But Esther brought time. Though she had been incredibly discreet in staying away, she phoned regularly. And she did help—by keeping everyone else away. "They understand." Her voice reminded: September was approaching, school threatened the world of the house.

"Don't you need anything?"

"I think not." His only venture out now was for food.

"I'd like to see you . . ."

"Right now, I can't see anyone."

"Darren, you'll be back?"

"Back?"

"To school. When the time comes. You wouldn't risk that?"

Risk?

"Of course. To school. But, Esther, it would be better—she's particularly sensitive to sounds—if you didn't call. Let *me*. Do you mind?"

"Well, if you *will* . . . ?"

How she put up with him was a remarkable tribute to her goodness, for he felt cold, distant, not really grateful for the protection.

"Rhoda?"

She wanted sun.

"Promise you won't move," he said, "and I'll be back in a jiffy."

In an hour he returned with a rollaway and moved her onto it.

Now he could push her out onto the deck and she could lie in the sun a while. She opened her mouth to catch wind, her hands reached to feel the flow.

And she began to tell him stories:

"There was a crab crying because she was lost in a field, and a hungry cat found it. The cat would have swatted her with his paw and eaten her, but he felt sorry for her and said, 'Why are you crying, crab?' and the crab answered, 'I'm lost. I can't find the ocean.' 'Well,' said the cat, 'I'm hungry and if you wait I'll show you my house and feed you, and then show you the way to the ocean if you'll show me your house and feed me!' 'Oh, yes, I will,' said the crab. So they went to the cat's house and they ate and then the cat led the crab to the ocean. The crab was very happy to see water again and the cat was surprised to see the crab lived in such a big house. He did not want the crab to see he was afraid of water so he followed her in, and the cat loved the crab's house so much he married the crab and stayed forever. And that's why we have fish with cat's whiskers!"

He wiped her forehead for the effort forced a fever and damp in her hair, which he would kiss, his lips wet with her. But she would talk now, talk tale after tale, a fever of invention—where did it come from?—poured out of her, a slurred cascade of words. Though her body hardly moved, her eyes were wonderful—large, shining: she saw stories, she was in them—somewhere beyond sea, beyond cloud and sky; and her sound, after, even when she slept, went on in him, a higher pitch, refined to thinness now.

Suddenly the stories ceased.

She sat silent.

In stillness her eyes, brown seas filled with worlds, would gaze long. They grew glazed. When he spoke, she did not respond.

Where was she? And if he touched her, the longest interval passed before her eyes turned and actually encompassed him. Then she smiled, so serene, with a calm look so comforting and assuring —she made him feel such a boy—and weakly her hands cupped his face. Her face was a woman's now, the wear of a lifetime, bones stark, stale skin, so little flesh, finely wrinkled. Surrendering to her smile, he would bow his head, and she would caress his hair. The breath, soap, dank acrid expulsion came into him. Since she ate almost nothing, "More?" he kept encouraging, "More?" for the yellow stains testified to how little came through her. Where did it go? She seemed to hold nothing, nothing stayed. What fed breath and bone? the voice that remained? heat? the motion of her eyes? What lived?

Inexplicably she wanted him, she sank against him; he held her until she eased into sleep, reluctant to let her go. He felt whole. What was he holding? He wanted what it was. He wanted to hold back what it was.

"Cold," she murmured. He set the thermostat up, for now was dog-days August. In the fields all the white potato flowers had long since vanished, the green life been drawn down into potatoes. Tractors sounded over the fields along the cliffs. Their sounds pained over her flesh. He quivered with her. The last summer heat lay a turgid body over the land and crystal shimmering over the sea. Inside, the least effort made him sweat.

And she sweat. He could not find the exact temperature for her comfort; she veered hot, cold, restless with starts and whimpers, for swellings multiplied, and lumps. When she reached for him, he raised her—so light, yet heavy with bone. Carefully he set her head—she could scarcely hold it up—against his cheek, and walked, sat, rocked, listening to her mumbles. She would of a sudden blurt, blurred, "Italy is a peninsula, it is in the Mediterranean Sea, it is shaped like a boot, the Mediterranean is a basin," a whole lesson verbatim; but it was her sound he listened to—it filled her hollow and vibrated in him; and her eyes he watched, expecting something, but he found she was searching his—and she smiled a smile filled with such pity. Did she know something she could not say? Rhoda! He saw an abyss in her, an endless fall—he wanted to sink down, know bottom. He was sure she did, sure she was going there, leaving bit by bit, sure she could in fact leave and return. She must carry him to somewhere in himself he could know—which in her stillness *she* knew—but not yet. Rhoda, have pity! But he was instantly ashamed, for didn't she have?

And he feared now—in darkness especially the fear besieged—that she might not take him there but go, not leave a trace. The thought roused a frenzy in him, but *she* startled: for her hand groped, her fingers touched his chin. "What?" she said uncannily, smiling up at him. And it calmed him.

Sometimes now it cost her to breathe. He must lie beside her. He must not leave her bed at night. The least break in her rhythm and his eyes flicked open. He whispered, "Rhoda?" A stir would answer. By aura of sky, light of moon, he watched the ridges of the sheet, straining to see the rise and fall. Like her, he was near collapse. He could not bear that she lie in the silence without him. He must touch her to feel her motion in his hands.

He fed her bit by bit. She would ask for nothing.

"The TV hurts." She bit her lips. He turned it off.

She gripped. "I feel things." Spurling had warned him he would have to be patient. There would be the unexpected. Should he call? But he did not *want* Spurling. He had even unplugged the phone. Feel things? If she could tell! She was listening to what she saw. Moments, she stared so hard, not blinking, he was sure she was watching something out there. He was afraid of her staring. Yet he was afraid to call her back. And when her eyes finally flagged and she returned to him, she said, "Where were you?"

Where was he?

"I was right behind you. I was with you all the time," he hazarded.

Now even her bones seemed to sleep against him, sink deeper into his flesh. And he wanted to enclose her. He would like to stand, walk, run *her*, be certain he held that motion, as long as he kept it it was his. If he wandered while she slept, her sudden whispers brought him back:

"Ssss . . . chool?"

"Yes, soon."

"Cat 'n 'y bed?"

She was wandering. He fibbed: "She's outside, doing her duty."

Despite the agony of her flesh, skin, swellings, he was almost afraid to take his hands off her now, fearful of *bereft*; and she depended on the strength in him. She was all eyes and hair. He combed it gently, not to pull at her scalp, let it hang soft, sank his face into it, drawing in the heavy oil. She lay docile.

"I'm cold."

But he had days since cut off all air conditioning because the sound needled her flesh so.

He lay close to her. "That's warm." Her head lay against his chest. "I hear you."

And he thought: I have never been so happy, not with Marie or at home or as a child, never. He could feel happiness running warm through him from her. He wanted to say it, if he dared say it, if she could know the meaning: you could touch happiness, you could hear happiness. And how could that stop? It would go on, it had to go on, he knew it would—

While she slept, he lay listening to the waves hush-hushing. He saw his classroom, all the children's faces, and Esther in her doorway across the corridor. The bell rang and the children dashed for recess, but they stopped— Rhoda had struck the desk and gone headlong. He bolted—

His eyes opened. He was sitting straight up in bed.

He heard the silence. His heart seemed to stop to listen. Then everything rushed.

"Rhoda?"

He touched her. Nothing passed into his hands.

"Rhoda?"

He stared into her open eyes. He could not believe the distance her eyes touched.

Rhoda.

For an instant he was seeing her from a great height: she was so small. There was almost nothing. Nothing.

And quickly she was close, she filled him, he could not contain her. The wrenching at his heart made him alive with pain.

Rhoda!

He wanted to tell her the pain she had left him.

And he felt an agony for what he had never said.

Had she known?

He bent over her.

"You're me," he said to her.

At last—after what hiatus?—he plugged the phone in and called Spurling.

"You'd better come. Rhoda's dead. And have them come take her. I won't be here."

He went out to walk the beach. Wind and sky moved, waves beat Rhoda, Rhoda, Rhoda. Water rushed over his feet, filled the sand, sank deep. It came with the rush of love that filled and sank far down in you, deeper than knowing—and unceasing.

He went through the days of the death, through stillness and ceremony and grave and nights of waves relentless against the shore, and Hannibal and the kitten, at last returning to his books to read those voices which would never die and to September and town, Esther and the other teachers warm with welcome, back to texts and chalk and the blackboard, the classroom empty but ready.

And to his place.

He went to the first window. He raised the shades. The room filled with the fire of morning. Green spilled, and trees, houses. The bay rose far off, shimmering.

He went back to his desk.

The bell rang and the children rushed, mumbling and shouting, to their seats.

He almost dared not raise his eyes to the class.

But he raised them.

For the briefest interval they were all skulls.

Then Jimmie Riley said, "Good morning, Mr. Trueblood."

And the air broke, the class chorused, thirty good mornings pealed.

When he sought at last the other place, the seat was taken: her hair gleamed gold and blue eyes glittered, and she had her hand up.

"I'm Ella Claire."

He mouthed it: Ella Claire.

He lined the other name through on his seating chart and wrote hers in its place.

"Ella Claire." He smiled at her.

"Now," he said. And surveying the class, he began.

Joshua

"CHURCH CLAIMED we'd have Philip's head before the Indian corn was ripe," his father said.

Head. Josh's blood stood still. A word could do that. You did not have to be grown to know that. Blood told you—be still, listen. He lay still on the scorched grass. Hot August burned down on his face, through his closed lids a great light.

The men were talking coats and scalps again. They were haggling, if friendly, under the shady maple, where he and his mother and father ate on sunny days, or sultry.

"The price to friendly Indians for each scalp is set by treaty." That would be the man Peleg Sanford's voice. "They are old terms. Promises must be kept. Of trucking cloth, two yards for every scalp. For every Indian live, two coats; for Philip's head, twenty coats; for Philip, live, forty."

"Forty!" His father groaned. For perfidious heathens his father begrudged such bounty. Forbes stood with his father. But they were two dissenters, no more. And three men defended.

"Recollect—the head would end burnings and all killings, Manfred," Sanford said. "Any number is little to give for salvation and some peace."

"True justice would give one of *us* Philip's head." Philip was God's devil and the Wampanoags his heathen horde, sent to make the colony choose right and goodness, and preserve them. For God, his father could hate.

"Who knows? Death by one of his own may be the greater justice—for betraying his father, Massasoit, and us." The Howland brother Jabaz' voice was coarse as hemp over hands; to hear Isaac's grated your throat. They were one. He knew all their voices. More: he would close his eyes to practice sounds. He could tell many a bird from the sound of wings, heavy or light; hear the fall of a leaf, down to a pine needle, fish bubbles in a stream; tell the moves of beaver, deer, squirrel, bear in the wood. His father never believed, nor his mother. Only *they* would. He was one of *them* sometimes with his fleet foot and stillnesses: he could become a tree; his body could disappear flat into the silence of pine needles. His mother restrained her anger at his dirty clothes. She was ever deep in water, scrubbing. Her hands were lye red. Sometimes, on stillest days, he could even hear, flat on his back in a field, the ticktock of the mantel clock that his mother had carried from England, and, far off, the bongs, regular, regular, "that marked something going," she said, "time going." Time had wings. They were cut in the glass facing, but what was wearing the wings, time, was not there.

"There is noise that Philip is about—at the Neck or in the

swamp, or on the Mount. This day, twenty-four hours, pray God we have him."

They were voices of men gone restless. They were not idle men, they would farm, but they would end fear—fear was that sachem who was a ghost, everywhere and nowhere, a wind moving. Philip.

He heard the shifting—they rose. Now he opened his eyes. In the sudden burst of bright their uniforms were stark, glowing deep blue, and clean beside his father's field clothes, dull brown.

Since the winter, all he could remember hearing when the men talked, in the house and working the field and whenever idle, was the great swamp fight and killing. Killing meant whoever he suddenly stopped seeing—a sudden nothing. Where a body would one day be in a house—Eldridge's father, Obed Borrow, the Beebe man, all four Moodys—*ping*, a shot, a hatchet, a knife—and then not. He could put nothing in the empty space. Where you could see somebody before, you saw through air. He saw the boxes and buryings, the people around the grave; he knew death, but it was the air you couldn't fill that his head saw that told him *nothing*, like the space between the wings on the clock, time. His father, she—when he asked—hushed him. "Spirit," she would sometimes make answer, "they are spirit now." So it was that: spirit. He would listen. This air must be filled with spirits, and Mount Hope, and the wilderness. When his ear learned, he might hear them. At the spring on the Mount he would press his eyes into the water to seek in last year's leaves gathering silt, in the still bottom or the moving water, what was living there, breathing—despite his mother's warning: "You don't go—never—beyond the last field or house, *ever*." His father put it in scalps. "Son, they would scalp a poor babe." He waited for the other words that would always come—"Perfidious heathens!"

"Shall we collect the women?" Sanford said.

The men's horses stood near the maple. He watched the tails flick at the horseflies. Mrs. Rowlandson's carriage and horse were close to the house. The Reverend had sent it for her.

The three women were sitting in the open, by the kitchen door, with his mother. They were shelling peas. He had shut out their voices to listen to the men and day. Now he rose to his knees. Even far off he could tell Mrs. Rowlandson. She was still bones, if not so bad as when they had ransomed her back. He did not want to look into her skull. It was all deep wet eyes and lips grim over her full teeth. On her first visit from Boston he dared not look more than a flick at her, but he could never move from her tale. She was made captive in winter and sold to Quinnapin, a slave to one squaw, dragged from remove to remove; she would keep her wounded little girl, dead—he shivered at the cold body—but the Indians did take it from her and bury it. He listened the way the men did, never tiring; they kept wanting her to tell and tell—to learn the Indians, what they could, every move and habit and clue, to help dog them, round them up, offer protection to turn them against Philip. And, but days since, their dogging yielded up 173, dead and captives, and Philip's uncle his counselor, and Philip's wife and son, and thirteen more. "Mary would turn your stomach with the food," his mother said; but he listened to how, near starved by the cruel and indifferent Narragansetts, she was cut off from their fires and food by the squaws, but for a now-and-again kindness if she made them clothes for a morsel. He saw her a dog scrambling for horses' guts, ears, a wild bird, a stinking bear chunk—each time she put her hand in her apron pocket, he waited for it to draw forth a maggoty joint-bone—yet she told how sweet all was to her hunger. Listening, he was preparing his guts to know surviving—what all the centuries the Indians knew. He too could live on groundnuts. Alone, stealing into the wilderness, he would watch them, food moving—beavers, rats, raccoon, a rattler. He would live in the wood. He would wait there for his secret brother. He would be worthy. All the colony knew Mrs. Rowlandson's story; it spread fast as Philip's fires. Eleven weeks Joseph, her husband, went trying to bargain her back.

"It was their worst winter. Cut off from their buried corn, they must cross into enemy territory for it, and I was their protection —from you, my own people," Mrs. Rowlandson said.

"And she all that time with the Wampanoags!" his father said. What he meant was: always close behind them was Philip.

"They write from England calling him *king*," Jabaz said.

"King!" his father muttered. "Because they've not seen such a kingship as savages boast."

"And is he kingly, Mary?" Jabaz said.

She thought. "He was not unkind like the others. He is middling size and brawn, yet seems large. I cannot paint likenesses, but I have done Philip's for the Volunteers, if it helps."

She stood, shaking her skirt free of fine green strings.

"Josh?" He woke from woods and stinking bear meat. "Say goodbye to Mrs. Rowlandson. She returns now to Boston."

She held out a hand.

He did not step forward, but nodded, raising his eyes, if not to her skull; and he saw the hand drop, bone too, and long.

"Good-day, Mrs. Rowlandson."

"God be with you, Josh." There was such singing joy in her voice that he did raise his eyes to Mrs. Rowlandson, if not, again, fully.

His father and the men seemed to delay. Perhaps he wanted the men here; perhaps they did not want to leave, knowing the noise about Philip. His father would seldom leave field or home, for the danger. The men dallied, reluctant.

"Let us hope for a sign," his father said.

"And soon," Forbes said.

"This night," his father said.

"God does not hurry, but is never slow," Peleg Sanford said.

"There must be a reason—he has not hurried, and Philip harrying us thirteen years."

Thirteen! A year and more longer than his own life. 1663! With eyes shut he tried to go straight back into time, far, with a groping; but it came *nothing*, clear as the space between the wings on the clock. He wanted to ask: Where was I then? For he would be somewhere. But there was Mrs. Rowlandson bobbing, and the two ladies.

"And not to know which village next," his father said.

Because it was fire they feared. All spring, relentless, the Indians came flaming Scituate and Bridgewater and Plymouth, and Plymouth again . . .

Till there was fire in dreams.

"So Benjamin is right—we must make a business of the war, as the enemy does." Major Sanford bowed to the ladies, mounted, and rode toward Portsmouth.

Mrs. Rowlandson and the two women took their places in the wagon. The men mounted. Shortly they were gone, but not long when his father's grip on his ear thrust him a shove ahead back to the potato field. "Manners, son."

His mother went silent.

"Get you your hoe."

On the way to the field he heard his father: "Ruth, prepare

what you two need for the loosing fort. If a sign come, I'll be gone, and it's small telling how many days."

There, at the garrison, was the idleness his parents loathed, and he. The place was a torture. The packs unloaded and the horses tied, his straw laid out with the boys, his mother gone with the women, each did his part—and it boredom. At home there was learning and work in the furrows; he could disappear when the woods, and his body, called. He could steal practice at running on toes to become wind, silent and skimming the ground, and keep before his own scent. He knew wind—what it carried—for *they* were back, they had come. Near the Mount wind carried smells down to him; he could pursue with no meanness, for all this was his—earth and home, colony and woods, rivers and the great bays. The Book said the earth and the waters. Listening, he could hear it breathe, and all which his eyes touched belonged. All last year he would steal to wigwams, new rush mounds like heads with straight yellow hair half emerged from the ground, calabashes, baskets, stakes in the earth, spits, squaws squatting and pounding the corn. His body stood in long stillness, his eyes drawing all like a mouth that would savor, then quickly be gone like a wind.

For a year-ago thaw he was bent to hunt sights on his own, and so went into the wilderness, and higher each time, hopeful of standing at the peak and, highest, see down between the two bodies of water. He took, from his training, his knife that his father gave, steel from Kinmer's forge and made just for him, so his father said, to fit his hand—he could not move with the musket. From thaw, the swamp and, higher, the rock and the ground and all bark were a madness of glitter that was moving. All was a rush and breaking of waters. The earth moved under his feet, rocks were wet, and water cold to the bone. He was wet but would go on. Never had he been so close to the top: trees thinned to scrub oak and fine pines, sickly in rock and thin soil; the gray outcrops were clean. And he came to the edge of great space, where the rocks, struck by sun, blazoned white till near blinding—his eyes watered, he blinked and he moved, but a motion of light stopped him.

A man stood high on a rock.

His skin caught the sun and glowed sun, as if flame, a miracle of light. His arms rose, and caught sun. From his wrists and his arms and his neck came white splinters of light.

So close to the man, he froze in the clearing.

He would fall—he trembled so—but he could not: a flicker and he would be seen and struck dead, not by an arrow or hatchet or knife, but by light.

The man's arms reached to sun; his eyes turned to suns. And in a great black stream hung from his shoulders, white birds sang in a silence; and flowers blazed white, and white deer, bear, and horse all alive in the wampum, and around his head, and a white star burned on his breast; and along all the black edges red hair ran like blood.

He watched the tips of the man's hands. He could feel the hands touching spirits, sending spirits between them, in a miracle of stillness, and he could hear his heart beat, and the heart of the other. And sudden, he saw: a man was a temple.

His heart knew he was seen. They stood and they stared. Nothing moved but the sun. It went low. Dark flooded the woods.

And then the man moved, and *he* did—struck by that motion as if lightning hurled his feet homeward. He ran till he came out long after and stood at the edge of the meadow hard by the farm, recovering breath, for he would not go panting in, and reveal too much. He was cold, but something was burning inside him, and he kept closing his eyes to hold it back, thinking spirits might leap from his eyes.

It was a bond and a covenant, this meeting and silence. He prayed he would be asked nothing, for how could he lie to his mother and father?

Praise be, they did not ask.

All the summer, when he could, he carried in leaves his own food that he hid and what grew in the fields and left all on a white rock, far down below the white rock where he had seen him. He would wait. Sometimes he saw and was seen. There were weeks without sight of the man. Some days he would race back in a sweat, against the time that he had, to find the food gone.

Then, in a quick instant, they burned all their own wigwams and fled. One day he studied the char. They left nothing but the spits in the ground.

But he waited, wandering back—in danger from the sly removes of the Indians and sudden wigwams—and watching, fearful not of *him*, but the others.

And all was reward in waiting: the Indian, his brother, was back.

Now he hauled the basket, heavy with potatoes. The sun was an hour before dark. He went back for his hoe. Ahead the wilderness made a darkness, and deep, where last sun touched birch and elm, sycamore, hemlock, maple, oak. He could not tell them how it thinned when you climbed higher, beyond the burned campsites where the Wampanoags had been routed, and how there was a clearing he knew, rock outcrops, stone ledges to rest on and survey all below. He dared not confess (*she* would say it was blasphemous) how he felt like Him looking down and holding it all, his: in the beginning, when no white man knew, was this place, and *they* were, and they were red, though whenever one was near he studied in vain for red skin. But for paint, and seldom, there was no red. They were earth. They were bark of trees. White walked the earth, but *they* were part of all things seen, and could become invisible while his kind stood proud to be separate and more than all they could tame and make theirs, all land and Indians, who could pray now, though his father would snap—and he did, in talk while they supped: "With a boy to work I need no pagans in sight, not even Praying Indians."

"Manfred!" His mother scolded, if softly, for she believed such Indians had seen the light, and so the Lord.

He had not seen the Lord, though he asked about Him. At night, reading their chapter together, his mother would tell him after she closed the Book how He came in white raiment, and a carpenter, and preached in parables . . .

"Like the Reverend Mr. Wilson?" Who preached till bone near broke from stillness and hard benches, sun died, and air went rancid with breath and body and the stink of old Mr. Rawson's mouth behind him.

She went on. But He was a light she could never make real. He had his own light now that he waited for in the dark of the woods or high on Mount Hope when the sun burst and fell through trees and made pink glows of the nerveroot and brought forth the lavender myrtles he would pick to take back to his mother for forgiveness. All the year, for long stretches of time, the Indian would not appear; yet suddenly he would come, sometimes with no squaw and no men. Then the boy shut off all he could his other senses, for his nose told—the pungence that bristled his nostrils on the vaguest of breezes would tell the man was there, somewhere close; and he would have to concentrate then to slow all his blood, which, exalted, might cut out all sound from his ears but its own.

"You, Joshua!" At the clip of the voice he stood. "Don't you start dreaming at table again." There was curiosity in the linger of his father's gaze. "You will look after your mother every minute, should I go, morning or night. And I will. I'm sure of it."

"Will you sell the Indians, then, after they get their coats?"

He hardly dared look up for the tiny hard musket balls his father's eyes would become. But he heard hardness in his voice: "They are heathens."

"But you said always to keep promises. And Mr. Wilkinson said there are men who have sold them to the West Indies for slaves and so broke treaties, and would they believe words now?"

"The boy speaks true as the Book," his mother said.

"There do come complications. But these are things of your elders."

"Would the Wampanoags sell me after I promised friendship?"

"To another tribe perhaps—in exchange for tobacco or spirits or some hunger."

"And are we hungry?"

"Josh!" his mother said.

But he was taught by his mother's example: you met eyes and no flinching, so did not have to speak. Yet it was truth his mother always told and he would avoid—but he *would* speak, and too much at times.

His father said, "The Narragansetts sold Mary Rowlandson."

"But only back to her husband, and for redemption pay, and they were hungry from winter and their buried corn cut off by us, she said."

"Josh, the devil's in you today," his father said.

"He wants only to know, Manfred. He was always the curious one."

"And old Caleb says Mr. Williams never had a day's hate for the Indians. He managed peace, and we need him," he said. "And I wrote that down. I could get it."

"No need, son," she said.

"Not every man is Roger Williams," his father said.

"Most men would be preaching, and not doing," his mother said. "And if every man were old Williams, it would change the world."

"Williams had Massasoit, but we've the worst of the pagans in his son. Philip would shame him, if he but knew. Nothing will end it but his head, living or dead. There is no changing that."

"You could powwow."

"Josh!" his mother said.

"But our men keep their talk to themselves."

"What does eleven know!" his father said.

"And when I am twelve, will I know more?"

"Josh!"

"Aye, son." There was half admiration, but a grudging. "And to be more arrogant and to dispute more. Now that's enough. Get you to bed. The sun is down long since." And from bed he heard: "What's got into him this whole summer?"

This night, as all August, was burning. You near died in bed as you did gathering potatoes and corn in the fields. There he would rest in the neighboring field, deep in mustard weed, or where bramblebushes cast shade at the wilderness edge—and told his father so again and again—so that if his mother called, sometimes in fear, his father would utter: "He's at rest in the weeds." Hearing that, he would flee till he reached his spring at the edge of the swamp, where the water never ceased from the rock, and a tower of stone rose against sky. He could bathe alone, and in silence. Each day, already too wet with sweat and his shirt and breeches and stockings asoak, he tore them off and waded in—it was cool, the water slow, and he sank; the bottom was slime and years of dead leaves, but quick he swam and sputtered in joy. And a week since, on the sixth day, he was lying on his back, afloat in a space between water and sky, his arms spread in wings, when the scent, bitter clean and real, woke him to now. He stood up in silt—and he knew. The scent came down the wind. *He was back*. And his jubilant blood surged till his head would break—how he thundered!—and all the water and ground and trees shimmered. Then he turned . . .

His nose had not failed. The man sat on his rock at the spring. But—confused, he stared—all the man's long dark braided hair was shorn close to the skull. But yes—the man—and the burning inside him said yes.

The man knew him. He raised his arm, greeting, but his face was sad and too still. He rose and stepped into the waters slowly and sank, thrashed and sighed, then went under. He too went under, and through the clear water he saw the form rounding and thrusting like a great earth-colored worm and saw his own limbs thin and white writhing as maggots, but he felt the thrust of water from the other, in a flow like the spirits that flowed from the light. Then he burst up, and the other's head rose. For a while both moved in the waters. Then he eased out and dressed, but could not leave till he looked into the face of the Indian, who emerged now and stood listening, then quick raised his hand *Go*. And his heart turned, but then he heard the cause: sounds over the crest, women's voices, and children's. Nearby they would stake out a camp. He raised his hand and streaked between briar bushes.

All the week he carried that moment. Were the spirits this fire that he carried?

And he was back in the woods, and in dreams, when noises woke him to darkness but no woods—it was thunder. Hooves! And then knocking and voices. He leaped from the bed—

But his father was quick to the door.

"Manfred, there's need for all ex-Volunteers—to hem Philip in."

"Philip!" He heard joy in his father.

He peered through the crack at the candles and his mother, wrapped, listening to the men. He knew Captain Church and Major Sanford and Captain Golding, but out the open door, by a horse, was an Indian.

"Where?"

"At Mount Hope Neck." By the Kickemuit, where he had seen Indians eating clams! He held his breath, not to be heard, and did not move, though he was sure of the quick flick of the Indian's eyes when he did stir the door. He almost missed Sanford's words for the thunder that was in him: he was telling, fast, how this Indian had deserted because Philip had killed his brother, and he too feared for his life, so he ran for Church and would lead him to Philip.

Church said, "Abiol Tripp thought the Indian was drunk the way he flagged and whooped for his ferry to cross to Sand Point and carry him over to find me. Abiol chanced it. Luck had it they found me."

You could hear he had ridden hard from the breathless clip of his words, and even in the dim candlelight their uniforms were darkened with sweat.

"Manfred, I give it to Golding—you'll serve him—to beat

up Philip's camp, and William at the right wing to ambush—"

Not an unfriendly Indian denied Church was the fair one. His fame went everywhere. Listening to him, he knew Church was an Indian now—he must think like one, telling how they must go now in dark and the company spread in two branches, creep on their bellies to the very edge of revealing and wait for first morning light, for discovery, before they cried out, fired, and fell on the enemy, with unceasing noise and shouting to confuse even savages with their own tactics—

His head was echoing cries and shooting in a time far ahead when the horses galloped and his mother snuffed the candle. So fast they had come and gone! It was dream? And if dream, what was the other? When was when? But he *knew* his Indian was real, and the men were real! Yet it was such a tumble of light and dark, and secret and hiding, that he feared it might erupt into words and confession. He waited for the sound of her feet, but saw she stood, a dark form against darkness, in the window, long, and was murmuring softly with the strain of a voice that would not break, and praying. He loved the language his mother said, from King James.

Then he heard the sigh of feathers in her room, and he slipped quietly back to bed, aseethe, and could not stop the run of his mind. It was there at Mount Hope. He should run *now* to his brother. Even in the pitch of this night he was sure his hand knew the bark and the width of each hemlock, hickory, birch; his feet their own path. But he must wait—she might sleep, but he . . . So quick came his blood, he was sure she would hear!

He sweated in the feathers, yet dared not toss and turn. His blood ticked with the clock. Three years it had never stopped ticking. "Because I wind it," she said. "If it stopped ticking, would time stop?" "No, Josh, it will go on, and always." He could not imagine *always*. "What is that?" She said, "What goes on, that you cannot see." But he saw she did not know, for she dropped her eyes. Black windows stayed black, but he strained for a sound across fields from the woods—but nothing, not yet the sound of a lark. With his eyes awake, dreaming, he saw fire, his father and Philip tangling and shouting, a hullabaloo; and a sight of blood made him start bolt up and clamp his mouth to hold back the cries—and keep his mother out of this room.

Gray came at last. He rose, rolled shirt, pants, and knife, and barefoot stole out the window, dressed, and went slow down the furrows beyond stalks she might not see through, then fleet into the wilderness. Vague sky made deep forms of the trees, black mounds of the rocks; but he followed the slants and chasms of gray, his fingers touching his way, and sometimes a dark glitter of water. He had never known *long* till now. He moved but time stood, things kept rising; if he strained, he felt blind, unless he guided by looking aslant from the way he would go. Then a channel cleared, the ground began damp, and softer—it was coming: high, a great gray clearing spread in the trees. He must reach the swamp edge and follow east to the river.

He had to find *him*. He must warn. In the man were spirits that moved. He had seen. He would save. But—how? For all the Wampanoags left would be there, the sachem's headquarters, all the men—maybe Philip himself—squaws, children: and the Volunteers coming—both would meet and kill and kill and take captives. Church, if he could, would make peace, his father said, and never break his word; but the government, *it* sometimes made lies of men's words and sold captives for slaves and shipped them to the West Indies, and might even send *his*—Nooo! They could *not* chain that light, not harness him like their Liddie in the field and flog him to work. *No!* He must find him.

But sudden his hands rushed to a hemlock to stop him.

He saw men.

He stilled, till his breath stilled, and he peered.

He listened: they were silence, not a move of a musket or man.

Day was ahead. The trees made the darkest of webs, till his sight grew and then he saw deeper: how the men—in pairs, one Indian with each soldier—spread far and separate and stood behind trees. Each man was a tree that waited.

They would strike with the light.

Slow, the ground rose, ahead lay the edge of the swamp, the water caught light from the sky. And suddenly a cry came, and a low flapping—his heart leaped—a lark broke the air, and all through the wilderness birds began to sing and warble, a bubbling of morning, yet in a great stillness.

Down here no man moved.

He wanted to streak with a cry to find *him* and warn that men would kill spirits. How did they know what they killed? But if he moved, at the least motion the men would shoot.

Not far ahead, stakes and skins rose, shelters facing east. The Wampanoags were sleeping, not a stir. Then a thing moved. It stood, and came stumbling toward them: an Indian faced all the woods and trickled his water, relieving, and stood staring at a tree—too long. A shot flared from the tree. The Indian fell.

A volley burst quick as nerves.

He himself fell to the ground between roots and watched, too stunned to move or protect.

But the Company kept place.

Awakened, the Indians shrieked and yelled, scrambling from

under the skins into the swamp, shooting in bursts and flurries, some streaking into the sun, some streaking straight toward the soldiers, who turned Indian now, all shrieking in a deafening madness, but waiting wherever a body appeared and at closest range shot and felled it and charged ahead, yelling.

But at once he saw *him*: he was the first man to dash—he leaped from a rock into the swamp in a run, near naked, pouch and horn leaping from his shoulder, his piece gripped—

You!

He thrust himself up and rushed into the open and threw up his hands, but a soldier appeared, then an Indian, in the space between him and the man. As the soldier aimed, he cried with a piercing "Noooo!"—the powder flashed in the pan, the soldier cursed and shouted "Fire away!" to his partner—so his own cry died in the sound of that shot, and another. His air choked. He felt the balls strike the man still as air before he fell on his gun, a lunge into mud, his face and his arms deep in mud.

Now he fell still on the ground again, part of the roots, his eyes hugging that body. He might die himself.

He almost cried out when the Indian touched the man's head. It was the one who had stood by the horse outside the house, the betrayer, whose brother Philip had killed. He let the face drop back into the mud.

"It is Philip!" In the voice there was vengeance.

Philip!

Almost he rose at the name. *Philip*. His blood burned with a pride and a grief. He should have known where the spirits would live. And a part of him thrust at his arms to reach out for the spirits that were leaving, to touch them.

"We must find Church," the soldier said. They left. And soon there were sounds, sudden cries, a shout—". . . escaping the ambush"—and a rush of Wampanoags back, tacking about from the sunside, straight in the tracks the soldiers had come by. . . .

He was alone, and with Philip. He wanted to go and touch, to draw him out of the earth where his head half sank, one eye, his shorn hair, and all the length of his body, the great thighs. And he grieved at such greatness naked in mud.

And it broke now—the jerks in his throat, tears—and his hands gripped at moss and his face pressed the damp green; and he muttered words, mouthed at his father and her for talk of the Elect—because he *knew*, he had felt, he had seen the light move. The man carried the spirits: when Philip raised his arms, he had felt their light touch him. He had seen them swimming in water. But the men killed him. They would kill their own spirits. But spirits lived. He knew. They were his. He would keep the secret, like God. He would never tell.

Philip! The cry broke in his throat, and his blood beat till his stomach was sick, and his head, with its throbbing.

They were coming back.

He heard far off the company rallying, and a great cry, like the whole army—*Huzzah*—three times in a shout. So they had told—it was Philip dead. And shortly they were tramping ground through the swamp back to the body.

"It's Philip," Church cried, and once more their cries, jubilant, broke the wilderness. But when they crowded about, there was awe, an instant's terrible silence, maybe a shame at so high a thing and a king gone so low in the mud, and themselves too, if they thought. But it was the briefest interval.

"Drag him forth!" That was Church—to some Indians.

They seized legs by his stockings, almost all he had on, and his waist, and dragged him from mire; but it was the hand his gaze fixed on—that great broken shape with its scars dragging the ground. They carried him to a dry upstretch. There, for what Philip had done, Church gave him their justice: let the traitor rot, bury not a bone in the earth. "He is nothing now."

What he had never seen, what he heard now, he would *not* look at. He could not bear, he shrank into the bark, yet his eyes imaged through the hemlock what the sounds told: the Indian executioner said some words to Philip's greatness, but meanly, and sank the hatchet into his neck. The bone cracked loud as a branch you stepped on, his own head ached at the blow, and the men roared.

Another quick crack—"Philip's hand!"—and the men roared again.

"You, Alderman— Your shot brought him down. Take his head and the hand for what profit showing them will bring you. And you men, you'll receive thirty shillings each, to the man."

He listened long, after, while they struck Philip's bones. You could hear each blow at the body—he was sick, but would not, *would* not vomit—and the lugs and straining, the chokes and rasps of the men, then how they bent down the birches with all their strength and hung Philip's quarters there, and let them swing and settle—four signs, and bleeding—for wind, sun, rain, and the birds.

He did not know how long till they were gone toward the village. He was not seen. Almost, so dazed his blood droned, his head sank with the weight of the hours. It would fall almost against his will—he had to be still too long, and when he moved he ached. He stood, but before he could leave the tree, the first sight of blood made him spew, he sickened and sickened till he was all a dry heaving. But he stared at the blood on the ground before he dared look up: he located the body, each of the four parts, dangling. They bled bit by bit from the sky, down the bark, on the leaves. He would cry out, but did not. He would *not* leave him there, no, never. He tore off his clothes, took his knife, and shinnied up the birch, slow, exhausted, choking at the sight, but cut one part loose, and clutched the tree hard when the flesh thudded below. Then he slid down. He cut loose the three more. Then he dragged them together, that body with one hand—and no head. He wanted his head. He could not bear that nothing. His mouth was choking. He stood there, exhausted and panting.

He knelt in the blood and smeared his own flesh with the blood, then covered Philip's body with old leaves, and lay down and packed his own body with leaves, and stared at the still stretch of sky between trees. Sun hung low between trees. His eyes closed, but sun burned through the lids. It moved and moved. His eyes beat with sun, throbbed till he heard nothing but the pulse and the throb where it came—tick, tock—tick, tock; he saw the bright, how it flicked— back, forth—back, forth; he strained, stared: in the space between ticks he heard thunderous noise; and he lay still in the box, the dark box, his blood beat to escape the black box. And down the space between ticks came the hand with its scars—it beckoned—he must reach between ticks, he must leap to the hand, his blood would burst free—and he leaped: the hand tore him through the space into a thunderous noise. . . .

He opened his eyes.

His face was buzzing with flies. Sun burned through the trees. The leaves caked his body. Was it hours he lay in that blood? No, sun had not moved down the trees.

Flies buzzed. The air was a madness of buzzing. He was covered with flies, hordes of flies, and bloodsuckers, ants— He looked at

Philip. His body was dark with the swarm; it was buzzing and quivering with life.

He went into the spring and stood staring: where the leaves fell away, the water turned blood and spread slowly around him, and thinned. He swam with Philip, his blood, the last time; then came out again white, and cleansed himself, and he dressed. Then he ran.

There was a thrush, and doves calling, and all along the way snapweeds and violets and tiny white pennywort and gossamer ferns on the dark sides of clumps. Each thing leaped live to his eyes as he ran.

He did not stop running till he reached the familiar fields, and he halted. They were too open and bright, too dry and dead, with scorched plants and withering stalks and no green but the weeds. He looked across at the barn—he spied Liddie's rump—and the shady maple and the house too unprotected from sun, but safe now from Philip. His father would return triumphant with the news. He dreaded his vengeance and joy, but had no fear of his father, who did not know the spirits.

He left the dark woods and ran up the furrow, for she would be waiting with her quiet and endless frenzy, his mother. He had brought her to danger. Hours since they should have been at the fort. But already he could hear her say, "Thank the Lord, O thank the Lord, Josh," and feel her warm hands, her bosom soft and sweet against his face; and he knew she would sit with him and wait without prodding for what he would tell. But there would be no word from his mouth, there would be nothing; he would keep God's secret. He heard even now in the silence the thunder of spirits that filled all the air.

The Other Side of the Fire

"JUST WAIT TILL the Fourth," he'd say, "and you'll really see something." My grandfather loved circuses and carnivals even more than the old minstrel shows he'd talk so much about.

The Fourth of July is still the biggest celebration in our town. Weeks before, announcements appear—of a carnival or Barnum and Bailey or Ringling Brothers, and band concerts and fireworks on the Common. And a week ahead the town begins to pile up crates and boxes, any wood, as high as a house for the midnight bonfire on the third, which burns back the dark and makes the Common bright as day all night long and glitters all red and gold and silver over the ready fire trucks. You'd think the whole town was afire. Gramp would let us use his little wagon to haul our few pieces of wood—everybody wanted to pitch in. That year Ben and I fought over who would pull the wagon, who load and unload the wood.

"Gramp, tell him!" I said, but he said, "Don't pick on your brother, he's younger. You take turns. You pulled it last time. Besides, you'll be hauling your own wagon one of these days."

"One like yours."

"You'll find out."

The appearance of the carnival was magic: on Sunday the Common was empty; and before you could take a breath Monday morning the whole sudden fantasy materialized under a dozen rainbows, flags aflutter and pinwheels spinning to dazzle even in day. I couldn't wait for night. I saw my grandfather couldn't either. There was something special he loved about carnivals.

"All right," Mother said, "Monday night and Saturday, but that's all. And don't you let him out of your sight, Pa."

The nearer the time came, the more nervous she grew.

"Now don't you be upset about the boy, Dorothy."

"What about me?" I said.

"If she wanted you to know, she'd tell you."

My grandfather had albino eyes and had to press his face close to things or squint to see far, but he could see forms, configurations, especially at night. In dark, when we were stopped on top of the Ferris wheel and rocked, he'd show where we lived—between Thames Street on the waterfront that my mother said was so low we couldn't go near it and Mount Hope on the far side of town; and the direct road out led to the capital, Providence, which all the ambitious people sooner or later left for.

"Why didn't you go there, Gramp?"

"Some of us have to stay to take care of you."

"Is that where the carnival comes from?"

"Carnivals are from nowhere. They don't have a home." From the way he said it, I could tell he knew about travel.

He rode with me on everything, the switch and chairplanes and again and again on the dobbies, holding me out till I got the ring. "You do it!" I said and watched while he sat on the outside horse, but with his bad eyes he never caught the ring one time.

Gramp saved the sideshow till last, the way I would save buying candy apples—one for me and one for my brother—till after the pink spun sugar and the hot dogs and onions that smelled all the air and watered your mouth. The sideshow was a long tent with a middle entrance and long platforms on each side; behind were long canvases with painted pictures of the exhibits: WORLD'S TINIEST MAN, THE THINNEST WOMAN, THE FAT LADY, GORILLA MAN, THE SNAKE LADY. It was enough to see the gigantic paintings alone to tease you in: you could see how people's eyes studied, the awe and disbelief, and hear the snide remarks of the dubious. But once close, listening to the barker, "See the lady wrap the giant python fearlessly around her thin body, see—," nobody seemed to want to leave, especially when he offered the extra special sight of a body with two heads "for one thin dime more. Step right up—"

"Got a good gospel voice, that man," my grandfather said. He'd know—he'd been a preacher on the circuit through all the outlying towns once, a long time before I was born, even before he'd come to live with my mother and father. I didn't know why he'd given up the word.

"You want to go in?" he said.

"Yes!"

"You sure? You're not af—"

"Not what?"

"Never mind. Give us two tickets here."

"And two for the two heads!" I cried.

He studied me some. Then he took out the dimes. My own dimes had long since vanished.

"Two of them."

Inside, my grandfather seemed at home, maybe because it was so dim—he saw and heard better in dark—or because he'd seen freaks a hundred times in his life. Each, separated by canvas dividers, was sitting alone with nobody to talk to. And most of the people didn't talk to them or to one another either. They looked, stared a long time, or gasped or sighed or ogled—or froze in wonder. One man did say to his little girl, "See! Wave at the man," and the girl waved. But the gorilla man's eyes did not even blink.

"Why don't they put them together, Gramp? Do they fight?"

"They're working. When they're not, they live together—in the trailers."

"What trailers?"

"Out back."

It was the snake lady most people stayed by longest, no doubt fascinated by her skin all streaked and blotched, a hard look here and shiny there, real snaky, and fascinated and petrified by her even touching let alone handling such a big snake. I watched it coil around her waist and one arm and then the other and around her neck and down. She looked hypnotized too, her hands all the while fluttering like real butterflies before the snake's head.

When I reached for my grandfather's hand, he was gone.

"Gramp?"

I saw his back. He was at the world's skinniest lady.

"Wow!" I said, but he didn't hear. You had to shout sometime. *Deef*, he'd say.

He stepped very close to the platform. I never saw so much bone, so long, and so thin you could almost see past. She had a very tall chair, special for her long back to rest against. Her head stayed tilted. She should fall, but she didn't. You could hardly tell she was breathing. She had such long black hair, parted in the middle, that fell below her shoulders to the skimpy red brassiere —she had matching skimpy red tights—and Gramp was looking up at her face: she had a lost look—far. Maybe that's what stopped him. I don't know why, but my grandfather set his arms on the platform and leaned forward. At his movement I saw her eyes flick, though her head didn't move the least, and then it did, slow as that other lady's snake, and as sure: it turned down, right to his hands. Then she looked into his face. Perhaps it was only a few seconds, but it seemed a long time they stared at each other.

"How did you do that?" she said. The sound, maybe because it was so soft and girlish, made him start as if he were bitten. You didn't expect them to talk.

Then she smiled. She had such quick pretty teeth you forgot her long bones.

And of a sudden, fast, he was telling her about the fire at sea— how he had knocked over the can of grease or kerosene in his ship's galley and caught fire and near burned to death, third-degree all over, almost dead, a white mummy for eight months in the hospital, till he came out almost whole again—but for those hands clumped like crouched spiders. He didn't tell her the best part, how the voice delivered him out of the fire: it spoke through the flames. It said Give me your hands, Tom. And he gave them. And they were his partner, Nate Coon's, hands. And they saved him. I could see him walking through fire. As he talked, she never took her eyes from his face. After, she raised her head high an instant—I don't know where she looked, up, but I could see her eyes gleaming—and then she smiled down at him again.

"I'm right glad you came," she said.

"Much obliged. Say thank you to the lady, Corey."

I said thank you, and she smiled that sweetness again.

He headed for the exit, and I had to call him back. "You forgot the thing with two heads!"

He gave the attendant the tickets and we went into a special little tent inside the big one, where a small group was gathered. On a table was a gallon jar with a baby with two heads floating like a dead sea thing, gray, here and there bluish. "It's a cheat," a man said, and the old man behind the table gave him a dirty look but went on telling the history of the pair. I didn't hear that because I was too busy, close up, examining it, a little startled because against the glass the heads were all eyes, big and flat as fish eyes staring out at you. It seemed unfair—that dead thing had four eyes and my grandfather two that could scarcely see.

The next day I told my brother everything, while his teeth stuck to the red candied apple I'd brought him, till he cried to see it all too. My mother said he was too young to see such things, and so was I, if my grandfather really wanted to know!

"Be sure of one thing. *I'm* taking Ben with me when I go. Did you see anybody, Pa?"

"Now who'd *I* see?" Even I could tell he was kidding.

But she was not. "You know who."

"Now don't get twitchy."

I couldn't stand the wait each day. If I couldn't go at night, at least—since it was summer and no school—I could go in the daytime, couldn't I?

"Alone! You're only six."

"Almost seven, Ma!"

"Almost is not seven."

"Now, Dorothy, it's a workday. How'd he be in town?"

"No telling," she said.

But the Common was only several blocks away. Though she didn't miss much, I did sneak off mornings; but in daylight nothing looked the same—no lights, nothing moving, you couldn't smell a thing or hear music, everything was scratched and worn, and paint was peeling even from the pictures at the sideshow tent. I sneaked past ropes and under tent flaps, but there was nothing inside but stillness and silence. When I came out the back side, there were those trailers all set around in a half circle, seven of them, and wash hanging from rope strung everywhichway; there were the freaks I'd seen Monday night and men and women looking like everyone else I knew, sitting around and talking. I was afraid I'd be caught so I scrambled, but when I ducked behind a trailer I thought I saw my grandfather.

I had whizzed so fast behind that I had to go back and peer around the edge to be sure. I almost called out and dashed to him, but then I saw he was sitting with the skinny lady. I almost mistook her for laundry because she was a long blue robe hanging there. She was listening with that head tilted like before—I wondered if she couldn't hold it straight up—and he was talking, he'd laugh and mull, nod and shake his head, his hands going as fast as his mouth moved. I was tempted because I knew I was missing a good story—he sure could tell them—and besides *she* might say something. But I shouldn't be there at all, and he was having such a good time he might be mad and even scold me and tell my mother—he didn't like me to do what was wrong, especially lie—so I ran behind the trailer and back down Church Street and home. I ran all the way. I wouldn't even tell him I'd seen him.

All the week my grandfather was busy. It was like this: my mother would call down cellar, where he usually hung out—he had his half, as Ben and I had ours, where most of the year he tended the furnace and in summer repaired toys for needy kids at Christmas. But no Pa answered. Suddenly he would appear spick-and-span—shining—from the bathroom upstairs.

"Why, Pa, you're shaved again."

"You're always yapping at me to." He ordinarily shaved every two or three days. I could feel almost anytime the sharp silver beard.

She laughed. "Not yapping, Pa."

"What do you call it?"

"Well, you don't have to get in such a huff about it."

"Huff!"

He would take his suit jacket he didn't wear much and slip it on, and he was gone again. Half the time even his wagon stood idle in the backyard. I felt cheated—I went everywhere with him; my brother wasn't old enough to knock around with me yet.

But he was ready Saturday; he would never break a promise—

"You not coming, Dorothy?"

"When Ralph gets home, we'll take Ben with us. We'll run into you there." My stepfather was in Taunton, doing insurance, so she had to wait.

I couldn't stand it till dark came. I could see the carnival light begin to spread a dome and the sky begin to lower over town. My mother handed him some bills and gave me some dimes.

"Don't go stuffing yourself sick, and don't be fidgety, you'll get there," she said. "And, Pa, remember—"

"Nobody'll get near him," he said, "not with me around."

This night he didn't take all the rides with me. I was mad for the Ferris wheel—I never would get over my passion for being suspended on top and surveying the whole world below—and Gramp bought several tickets and put me on—but alone! I felt a little afraid, but important and trusted.

"I'll be right here when you come down."

He was standing at the guard rope, but by the time I reached the top he was gone. I spent half the rides trying to spot him—in vain, but when the attendant let me out, he was standing right there.

"I couldn't spot you."

"I was talking to a friend."

The big event came at eleven each night—a woman would dive from a fifty-foot platform into a tank of flaming water. By then I was tired because we had to stand around waiting in a crowd which was growing and jamming. At the edge of the tank was a ladder which extended straight over us, all held taut by steel wires. We were close because of my grandfather's bad eyes. When the time came, he held me up so I could see. Suddenly there was a hooting and clapping—at the ladder the lady appeared, short and stocky, with the brightest yellow hair, in a red bathing suit and a white shimmery cape. She waved one hand in a half circle over the crowd, then slowly, firmly, began to climb—the ladder swayed, but her own motions blended with its rhythm. At the top she took off her cape, draped it over the ladder, put on her cap, and stood poised as a wild creature hearing a far sound. We waited what seemed a long time. The crowd talked and murmured impatiently, all expectant.

"Now what's she doing, Gramp?"

"Sensing the wind. You have to know the wind. A puff can kill. She didn't do it last night. Too much of a breeze."

"Did you see her last night?"

"I told you—she didn't dive."

Now she gave the signal. The tank burst into fire, a whack, and leaped high. I felt my grandfather's sudden grip. I looked quick at him: fire filled his head. Since his eyes quivered most of the time, the flames seemed to lick inside him, and I saw the burning fiery furnace. But the crowd sighed "Ahhhhh" because now the lady stretched her arms out, a still bird, a long instant, then let herself fall forward easefully. She catapulted straight down—I thought she'd hit us— and almost without a splash struck the water, the fire vanished, she bobbed up, latched onto the edge, drew herself out, and spread her arms to cheers and whistles and applause.

"Perfect!" There was wonder in his voice. After the crowd dispersed, he stopped and stared back, like listening. He was always listening.

That was the first year they let me stay up late enough to see the bonfire and fireworks. The band was still playing. At the heart of the Common was the square green bandstand jammed with musicians, their instruments gleaming, especially the cornets and trumpets, when the men stood up and raised them in a neat row. The town had lots of bands—Yankee, Italo-American, Portuguese, Irish; if it wasn't a big holiday, one or the other played, usually in some religious procession with mostly women in black, statues and priests, and always altar boys with censers spreading whiffs of tangy incense; but on the Fourth all the bands played.

After the last song, the crowd moved almost all in a rush—we were carried— because it was the big moment: they lit the bonfire to celebrate Independence. The flames leaped, swept, rose in a mad run, roaring, cracked—heat heaved, the pile made savage groans and thunders; fire turned every tree yellow, the ground, and buildings on all four sides of the Common; and every face was a fire. You had to back off, for the heat felt out for you.

"Come, Corey, it won't do to get too close." He really wanted to go—I didn't know whether more to escape the fire or to see the skinny lady—because he said, "Thought we'd try the sideshow again since it's your last chance. You care to?" I was tired and bored with the fire, yet didn't want to miss the fireworks, but I said yes.

The dark of the tent was a relief. I could tell he felt better because he suddenly perked up. My grandfather always preferred the dark—the dark cellar, his room, sipping tea in the kitchen after we'd all gone. "Pa, put on a light," she'd say, "you needn't save electricity." He'd talk to the dark, low. I spied, listening. Silences would come, and some words. He was always good with the word. "—I don't know why bad eyes, that's what is, but my own stupidity brought fire down on me—it was the one time I saw, and it was a voice, I couldn't speak, and I touched it with my hands, and the voice burned into my hands—" At some point he'd opened the furnace door and his head loomed against pitch, his face turned fire, his eyes burned, and his hair red—I couldn't move—and for the long moment he stared as unblinking as if it were Nebuchadnezzar's fire.

Inside, I went straight to the snake lady. I couldn't keep my eyes off snakes—I was always overturning rocks in Tanyard Lane and collecting garter snakes, which would turn up in my bed or pockets till my mother forbad a snake in the house or even mention of the word at mealtimes. Under the raw bulb, not very bright, the woman's snaky skin made a dull glow, but it was her eyes and the snake's that glittered molten.

Gramp was gone again, and I knew it was to see the skinny lady. Yes, there he was, only this time she was not still and staring far —she was laughing, her tilted head quivering, her hair ashimmer.

"You won't do," she said, and he laughed at her. "Cain't believe they're that hard." He had his hands held up for her to believe, and she was touching them. "Man, they are sure hard hands." Both of them laughed again.

"Say hello to the lady, Corey."

I said hello and she said something about my being "such a fine li'l gen'leman" in sounds half like the coon talk you heard brought up from Thames Street.

Sudden thunder made me pull at his jacket. "We're missing the fireworks!"

He said, "I'll see you, little lady," and she let out a high and clear peal so everybody looked, but she didn't seem to care.

"You won't do, Tom."

"How'd she know your name, Gramp?"

"She's smart, that girl." He chuckled.

Outside, the sky was exploding. New stars whiter and fierier and a million times bigger than my sparklers filled the sky and died; magic flowers opened, and butterflies; sporadic explosions cracked night, blew it to fire, and shivered the ground. At every new burst the crowd chorused aaaahs and sighs till a barrage of booms like an approaching army's deafened, catherine wheels whirled and hissed, giant Roman candles spurted and broke into galaxies high above, and when Old Glory spread like day over the Common, everybody whooped and hollered and screamed and clapped.

"That's it. It's your time, young man, or your mother'll be putting up a fuss."

First thing next morning the house was all life, for it was *the* day: half the state converged on the town. The parade usually began at nine and lasted four hours. It would march into town along Hope Street, right past our house, and back through High Street to the school where it had assembled. Right after breakfast, an hour beforetime, people were lining the street for a good place. Since our house stood on an embankment, we had an ace view from our porch, and a host of invited friends watched with us every year.

All week my mother had been alert, but now she was outright nervous, even vigilant, and insisted that Gramp keep a good eye out—I didn't know how, blind as a bat, he could do that and said so. But she said, "I'm talking to your grandfather."

"Pa, he and his family have more friends in town than you can shake a stick at. He's bound to be here, and if he's here, he'll be sure to want to see the boys, especially Corey."

"Who wants to see me?"

"Hush, Corey," she said.

"No telling. But he has a father's right, doesn't he?"

"No, he doesn't . He gave that up. You know better, Pa."

"He'd only want to see him."

"You can't tell what he'd want. People change. I've seen that, haven't I? Haven't you?"

He didn't answer.

"Now, Dorothy," Daddy Ralph said.

"Well, Ralph, you don't know."

"I should. You've told me often enough." But he set his hand on her shoulder.

"Well, he had the only chance he'll ever get. I thought I'd lost Corey when his father wrote to Ma he'd put him in a home if I didn't go get him. Wrote Ma!"

"Did he know where you were?"

"He could easily enough have found out. Wrote Ma! And you

know—she never did let me see Neal's whole letter. I've still got the one page she sent me. And me with no real place to keep him, knowing the court wouldn't let me have him unless I could account for a place and a living. They'd know I couldn't because Ma and the boys had Ben—had had him a year. My brothers loved Ben so, they didn't want to give him up. I had to work fast. Pa saved me. We got a place together, both working. Still, I didn't trust his father. I went to my lawyer and insisted a policeman go with us so I'd have witnesses and no trouble the day he brought Corey to that restaurant."

I knew then where she was: the day of cold wind, snow. The dark wood booths behind her came back, the grease smell, and dim lights, and the sudden sweet smell of Coty's powder I could always summon when she pressed my head into her fur coat, and *him* standing there, alone, saying "Goodbye. Mind your mother" as the four of us went out, her hand over mine, the icy wind smacking water into my eyes.

Band after band was going by, so after a while I couldn't hear them. You had to shout over music and the cheering and clapping for the Legion and police and Odd Fellows, National Guard, men on horseback—

"There's the governor!" Daddy Ralph said, clapping—it was just a long black car with the top down and a little man and a woman, smaller than my parents, waving from the back seat.

Great clusters of balloons floated down the street. Vendors with popcorn and candy strapped to their chests pushed their way along the sidewalk, and sun leaped off uniforms and chrome and weapons and instruments to dazzle any eye. What a morning! And the flags! American flags everywhere—people clapped every time and clasped their hearts—and plenty of Portuguese, French,

Italian, and Polish flags too. The Fourth was the biggest day.

"Say what you like," Gramp said. "Come the Fourth, I've seen those foreigners get so excited they'd fall down and kiss this ground they came to. And who'd do that anymore?"

When the parade had gone by, we went in to dinner. My mother called down cellar, "Won't you have some dessert with us, Pa?" He had a problem with his throat and couldn't keep his food down; he'd take tea at a special drop leaf by the kitchen window when he could have the bucket he frequently had to regurgitate into, so he didn't eat with us, though he'd sit to talk. But my mother never failed the courtesy of inviting him to meals. "Pa?"

But this day there was no answer.

"Who'll take me to the carnival if he's not back?" I said.

"You don't have to be there every minute."

"I do too."

"Corey!"

I pushed away from the table.

"You sit right there or you may end up not going at all."

"Now, Dorothy," Daddy Ralph said.

When the afternoon had begun to wane, Gramp came back. He was not pulling his wagon as he usually did.

"You sulking?"

I didn't answer.

"You got to stand on your own two feet sometime. You can't always be hanging after a man, can you?"

I shook my head.

"Tonight we'll all go."

When we did get to the carnival, it was late but July light, there were hundreds of people, the same sounds and smells, but the strings of lit bulbs needed the dark to blaze in. Ben wanted everything he saw, he grew tired and cried, and my mother and then Daddy Ralph had to carry him. Finally they found a bench free.

"I don't think I'll ever move again," she said.

But *I* wanted to—my heart soared with the Ferris wheel.

"Could we see the sideshow?" I said.

"If you want to," my grandfather said.

"Again! Hasn't he had enough of freaks for one week, Pa?"

"Freaks!" he said.

"Well, what *do* you call them? Take a look." Her hand flung at the canvas pictures far off.

"You can't tell by looking."

"I can," she said. "It's just your bad eyes, Pa."

"If yours are so good, you better look twice then."

"Pa!"

"Not a one but grew natural."

I was afraid she'd talk him out of going. "The skinny lady talks just like us," I said.

"Grew too fast. Was a beanstalk before anybody knew what was happening to her. It's the pituitary. She's from the South. Name's Eileen."

"Why, Pa!" My mother did a complete turnabout—she laughed. "You go on."

"Well . . . come on, Corey."

"I wouldn't let him out of my sight."

"They won't be too far," Daddy Ralph said.

"Look for us at the band concert," she said, still laughing, though she cried out after, "Pa, you watch him!"

Halfway to the tent I said, "You go, Gramp, and let me ride the Ferris wheel the way you did the other night."

He looked at me long—like when he'd scold or catch me in a fib—but he gave in.

"Three rides—and don't you move one inch from that ticket booth after, if I'm not here when you come down."

This time he was almost late: I saw him crossing just as I reached the booth. I was almost scared because I had a sudden feeling—a kind of electric shiver right up my spine—when I saw the man's back: it was all I saw, the back of a thin man not too tall, with dark sleeked hair, standing with the older woman. *Him* it came to me. I knew. I wanted him to turn, I wanted the face, but I grabbed my grandfather's hand and didn't answer when he said, "You had enough?" and pulled him toward the bandstand.

"Whoa! Since when'd you like bands that much?"

"There they are!" All the rows of wooden chairs were taken, but my mother had found a tree to lean against and Daddy Ralph had Ben asleep in his arms.

Maybe *they* had heard my grandfather's voice, for we didn't get far:

"Hello, Dad." The voice was so familiar I saw, quick, Benefit Street in the city and the backyard with the high stone wall that kept the hill back. By myself, my only game was to leap from that wall, so high my legs quivered from the blow long after. Then coons moved in, sudden big eyes staring through the first floor windows of that big house, scaring me to run.

My grandfather was startled for only a second, and then he turned, as polite as always:

"Hello, Neal." And he nodded to her, "Emma."

"Tom."

"You're looking fine, Emma."

But she already had me clutched close to her. "Corey!" I could smell perfume, nice too, and saw her bed she sometimes took me into when I'd stayed with her in the city. She studied me a little, smiling, my face between her hands—soft, that were little pudgy ones—and then she took mine in hers.

"Why, his hands are sweating. He's nervous."

I wanted to tell her I wasn't, my hands were always clammy.

And as suddenly they were all there together: "Pa!" my mother said, stiff this time, standing beside me.

"Dorothy!" my grandmother said.

My mother kissed her. She always liked my grandmother.

"Hello, Dorothy," *he* said, and nodded to Daddy Ralph.

"Neal," she said.

"How've you been?" he said.

"We're all fine."

"Say hello to your father," my grandmother said.

I wouldn't look at his face. I watched the crease and the shoes. I was dreading his hand.

"My father's here." I took Gramp's hand.

"Corey!" My mother latched Daddy Ralph's arm.

"It's all right," Daddy Ralph said.

The man my father kneeled then. "Hello, Corey."

"Cordell," I said.

He laughed. "Cordell." I wanted to hit. His word burned.

"It's all right, Corey," my mother said.

But I didn't move.

He finally rose and came over to me and held out his hand. I didn't give mine. He set his hand on my hair, and I jerked to one side. He didn't say a thing for a while and then he said, "Well, Ma, I think we'd better be going."

My grandmother kissed me and held me too hard and set her

cheek against my forehead and then let me go. I felt the wind cool the wet spot on my forehead.

She kissed my mother again.

"Bye." She waved to all of us.

I was watching his back.

"Nice to see you, Emma," Gramp said. And when they were gone, he said, "I never had anything against either of them. They were good to me."

My mother didn't say a word—that I heard—the rest of the night. But all the while I kept seeing the three-story building in the city and our floor I climbed the long dark stairway to, and the cot in the kitchen I slept on because my father and Louise had the bedroom and her boy Anthony the bed beside theirs. I knew every inch of the rooms and all the view of the city—I'd even sneak off and climb up to Prospect Park to Roger Williams' statue to see the statehouse and downtown below—because they left me all day while my father and Louise worked and Anthony was in school until there was nothing anymore I could play at in the yard because the watching eyes scared me and I wouldn't go down till Anthony came home.

The carnival was beginning to close down. When I grew tired, my mother said, "Time you were in bed." She carried Ben, and Daddy Ralph took my hand.

"Where's Gramp?"

"You'll see him in the morning," he said.

I was too tired to protest.

In the morning I woke before anybody else and went into my grandfather's room. He was not there so I stole down cellar. He was sitting in his chair, smoking—not in the brown flannel robe he wore mornings all year round, but in last night's clothes.

"What are you doing dressed up so early?" I said.

"I might ask you the same question."

Then, I didn't know what made me ask it, but as I was rubbing his chin—it didn't have the thick beard it had had before the carnival last night—I said, "Is her name really Eileen?"

He gazed at me a long time. "Now, when'd your gramp ever lie to you?"

"I just wondered. It's a pretty name."

With the carnival gone, I could go farther away, alone—to Tanyard Lane or Mount Hope; but after breakfast I thought he might like to go to the Common with me. I said, "Let's. You want to?"

I ran most of the way, but even before I came to the edge of the Common, I saw it was gone. Except for the charred remains of the bonfire, not a trace of carnival was evident—clean, far as the eye could see, like magic. I went to where the Ferris wheel had been, the whip, chairplanes: nothing. If it had not been for the holes where the stakes for the sideshow tent had been, I'd have sworn I'd imagined it all.

He came up, finally, from far behind me. He had his wagon.

"It's gone, everything."

He too gazed at the empty bandstand, the three schools like abandoned islands, bits of grass, acres of hard grassless ground crossed by cement walks, the elms, chestnuts. Some slight dust was blowing. Only the courthouse on the west side was busy.

"Now what'll we do?" I said.

"You go find your friends or I'll put you to work."

The Wyatts were supposed to be back—they'd gone away for the Fourth and missed the carnival—and I'd promised to tell them about it; but now I planned to tell one thing at a time, to hold them back, make it last. It would be days before I got it all out. I was learning from my grandfather how you told a story. "Tell me the end," I'd plead. He'd kid: "You may live your life out before you get to know the whole story, and not even then."

"Then when will I?"

"Wish I could tell you." He would squint hard, the way he did in winter when he checked the furnace and stared as if he were seeing something on the other side of the fire.

"Well, *you* better tell me then."

"Wish I could."

"Why can't you?"

"I haven't heard it all myself yet."

He would be too long silent.

"Gramp?" I knew he knew it all. "Gramp!"

"You run along now."

Wally and Georgie and I would play behind the garage unless Gramp was out; then we'd use the whole cellar. Ben and I had our part, but we preferred his—that side was not fixed up; there were slats and slits, the light in the coal bin was eerie, we could play ghosts and horror, though Mrs. Wyatt and my mother always scolded about our coming up so filthy with coal.

"There was the woman who dived into the flaming water." I described the woman and the ladder and the tank, finally the dive.

"I don't believe it. Her eyeballs'd bust right out of her head," George said, "or she'd smash, miss and go splat, or burn up or drown."

"She didn't. She dived and the fire stopped and she came right up."

"Then they cheated. Nobody could get that close to fire without burning."

"I'll show you!"

"Show us then!"

I was determined. I racked my brain. I rigged up a deep metal bucket with water and topped it with a thick layer of oil the way I saw Italian and Portuguese votaries burn lights with wicks to their dead. I had several small marionettes with a mechanical stage; one clown I tied to a string, held high, and let plummet—it shot way down under and leaped back fast as a buoy, and I jerked it up, untouched. "Just like that!"

"A puppet's not a person, dope! A person couldn't get that close to fire without burning."

"My grandfather did. He was in a burning fiery furnace, and he walked out alive, so there!"

"How do we know he did?"

"He said so—and look at his hands—and he never lies."

"Then *he* burned."

"But he did it."

"Well, why didn't *she* get burned then? I don't believe it. How close do you have to get to be burned then?"

I didn't know, but I poured more oil—it whooshed. I stared at it, stared and pressed closer. I'd show them how close you could get without being burned. My grandfather looked into the fire all the time and even if his eyes quivered he never blinked—and I wouldn't, maybe mine would quiver too. It was flaming, it was hot, some had spilled out and spread fire around on the cement, it flared at our clothes. I pressed closer and closer, it grew too hot, but I couldn't stop, I wouldn't, and Georgie said "Wow!" and Wally said "Don't, Corey!" and when I kept at it, he said "Stop, Corey! I'm afraid." I felt the searing and a burn and had to hold my breath or choke from heat and fumes in my mouth. And just then I saw the face on the other side—my mouth couldn't find the name—and my grandfather's voice snapped "Corey!" I must have tilted my head because suddenly there was an awful leap of flame and stink of burning. I never saw my grandfather move so fast—almost together he grabbed a coat hanging on a nail and swooped it over my head and scooped up a thick rug and threw it over the flames, bringing an abrupt dark that made me blind a second. He pressed at my head, then tore the coat free. My hair was singed.

"See, I told you! She'd have to burn up," Georgie cried, cowering against the stairs but triumphant.

"I don't ever want to see you playing with fire again, you hear me?" Gramp said. His voice was hard angry and trembly. "You hear me, Corey?" I stared at him. "You see these?" He held up his hands as if I'd never encountered them before. "You'll feel them if you ever do!" Talking, he clamped my face between his hands the way my grandmother had, only his were hard, they hurt, I couldn't move my head, but I heard his voice, and suddenly I knew I had never seen them—his hands were bones.

I felt like crying, especially with Wally and Georgie seeing it all, but I said, "I got close enough to see like you did, right into the fire, but my eyes didn't quiver like yours yet."

He gazed at me. They were quivering. Then he let me go.

Wally and Georgie scooted up the steps home. He clipped the fringe of hair, very slightly, and he never did say anything about it to my mother.

Monday a week she said, "Here's a card for you, Pa."

She laughed at the face on it.

"Not a thing funny about it." He could be as belligerent as I was.

He kept it in the inside left pocket of his old suit jacket he'd hang in the cellar near the furnace. He stuck that card in it. I saw him. He would take such things out now and then and laboriously inch his eyes over the words. After a long while he would shift the card or letter elsewhere to make a place for a new one.

It was a long time, years, before I saw that card. He was dead. I found it in the metal box among things his hands had saved for me.

There were five cards, not one, dated farther and farther apart, the way memories are, all of them signed *Eileen*. But that card held her face. When I opened the box, at the sight suddenly from its hidden place in me rose that other face, the image of my own, which I had denied that night with all the grim perversity of love.

Walls

AFTER HE RETURNED HE would tell his mother. He would say, I took Liz the silk stockings I promised her twenty years ago. Rain was beating down so he tucked them protectively under his raincoat and ran from the car to the office: it was a low building and white, everywhere white, but dingy—or it was the rain that grayed dingy and discolored, or the three days that it hadn't stopped and had seeped into him, his sight, and grayed the world. And it was cold, November cold, the first mean winter piercings, and he had driven along the stripped bleak gray of Long Island like going down the coast of his own life all the hours he was on the way, and along the river, deep gray, through the upstate mountains, long and gray walls rising and rising. The rain, relentless, and the off and on steaming up of the windows made him hemmed, feel he'd never break through. And when he had at last come upon the set of buildings, low and set in a clearing and down, in a valley suspended between mountains, he wondered why with a name like The Farm he had been expecting high, rising, a kind of tiny city rather than buildings which his eyes might have seen over, missed.

Heat, stale and too much, overwhelmed when he opened the door, and as he said, "I want to see Elizabeth Hardy," he was aware how the woman there stared at his hand on the package, which he pulled out now and held, awkward. Then she looked up at him with the eye of the public servant, demonstrating that absolute, impersonal knowledge that he was not Boyd, the husband, not Boyd Jr, not Andy, her other son, yet someone from time gone who had not been here in the two years so must be one who had discovered the facts about Liz and cared—he was too tired not to have cared, it must be evident in his face and stance and the voice weariness and tension. For he was nervous.

"I'm sorry," she said, "it's really too bad you have to go back out in the rain, but she's off the path left." She'd already reached for her raincoat. "I'll go down with you."

"No," he said, so abruptly it startled her. "You needn't get wet. It's too nasty."

"It's no trouble. I'm used to it."

"Please," he said between command and courtesy.

"Well, it's—" She wiped a window clear with her hand, and her wet finger stabbed at the pane. "—the second building. Her room's eleven. I'll call down. That way you can go straight to her." So there was a keeper. "But"—she caught him—"first, please, you must sign the visitor's log."

Mark Redgrave, 2:15.

He was asea then, in the gray again, and water came down, beat. He ran, eyes half-closed in protection, the packet thrust under and clutched. Inside the building, he jerked the coat off, shook water everywhere—a row of hooks on the wall—hung it, both hands suddenly dependent on the package. His scalp ran with water, and his neck, the collar soaked. And he'd wanted to look his best for Liz. Twenty years! He could still turn, run, get in the car and drive back and leave what it was, had always been. But the young Mark in him, in resentment at the very thought, rebelled, moved down the hall. He knew he had to see her one time in his life again.

He knocked and said, "Liz?"

There was a lull, too long. It agonized him. He raised his hand again, but her voice said, "I'm here."

He went in.

And before even the sight it was the scent, air damp here too but heavy with the lilac, not cheap now, which might have made this her room in his grandfather's house or at her aunt Mary's or in the tenement his grandfather had rented for Liz the first time she'd needed him. And then she was Liz, the form so exactly he'd known: sitting on the bed (she must have been sitting there, still, staring out the uncurtained upper half of the window and turned her head when he'd knocked), thin and unadorned, with the forever simple straight dress with no sleeves, flat gray, not the blue she'd always looked so pretty in, with her white arms: he could see all that now, even the simple slip-ons, though it was her head he looked at, and he couldn't believe (He thanked God for it. What had he expected?), but the same: long and angled bones with the sharp bony nose and eyes sunken a bit too deep but dark dark brows and lashes and the pitch hair, parted in the middle, that had hung long all her life, that swung, shimmered with a kind of thick heaviness when her head moved. He expected to hear her laugh and say, 'I've got such big ears, it covers them,' and see the light brown eyes smile.

"Liz!"

"Ohhh!" She threw her arms out—too thin, long—her head lolled, and back, and she did laugh, nervous, "You!"

He dropped the packet onto the bed and drew her up—so easy because unresisting, light, the loose dress looser with her standing tall, longer to him—and kissed her cheek, at which she laughed again.

"All the years!" he said. "I thought I'd never get here."

"Look at you—and so young!" She burrowed her head into his chest. "I wouldn't believe it."

Close, he saw the years in her hair, gray strands and streaks, greasy; and smelled the acrid odor which nerves emit. She was always nervous.

"You missed Boyd." She let him go now. "Boyd Jr and Andy couldn't come, he said, and he likes them to come just when *he* comes. What do you think of that? And me their mother." The voice was the same—nerves always vibrated her voice, reedy and tremulous, at the edge of breaking. He wanted to close his eyes to set her back then, but his eyes were on the keen rings in her neck—her neck was always too long, thin and too long. When she breathed hard, her collarbones stood hard, and her shoulder bones.

"He spent the night." Her eyes—beautiful!—flicked away. Her full lips—the other beautiful thing, though too pale—pursed, wet.

"Boyd?"

"Him. Yes."

Now he saw her two index fingers pressed into the thumbs, and nails all bit.

Photos had come to him and his mother, if always really for

Tom, his grandfather. His grandfather's bad eyes would press close to the photos or the magnifying glass: photos of Boyd, of that day they were married, a happy Liz, and Boyd tall, sunny, a blond cleanness beside her. Pictures would come after—of the first boy, the three of them, Liz alone with the baby; the second boy, Liz and hubby and the two, Liz and Boyd Jr, Liz and the boys. And the years grew.

"There they are. Boyd Jr sent it." One of the few things in the room—a frame, big and plastic with no glass—held the three: Boyd, a jaded sunniness now, vaguely bloated, but still edging handsome; and Boyd Jr, nineteen about, an image of the man twenty-years married to her; and Andy, sixteen or so, bordering dark, but not quite his mother's face.

"They're wonderful," he said with wonder. Boyd Jr and Andy.

"I wish Mama and Will and Harry could see them now."

'Aunt Mary's not her real mother,' his mother'd say, 'and Will and Harry are not her real brothers. Aunt Mary took Liz in when her mother died, but she's no real relation.' Sometimes now in town he would drive past the tenement house, three storeys, where he and his mother had visited. Aunt Mary's was the top floor. He'd loved the stairs, three flights strung zigzag up the side of the house with just a two-by-four handrail, perilous. He'd loved the danger. Aunt Mary, a great Irish hulk, had lived in her rocker, almost never descended the stairs until the undertaker finally carried her down. If she'd never moved, Liz had, moving up down, up down, a perpetual clatter on the stairs. 'Well, why *shouldn't* she earn her keep,' his mother'd say.

"They're never home when I go," Liz said.

"Go where?"

"To Mama's!"

How she leaped time!

"Do Will and Harry ever come to see you?"

"Who?"

"Will and Harry."

"Will and Harry!" She laughed, but bitter. "I get tired of picking up after them. What would I do with them? No room for my boys when they come."

He tried to unscramble time.

"They gave me this dress." Her fingers held the hem out—battleship gray that dulled her, sickened the face a yellow.

"They?" He wanted to follow in her head.

"They—" But to name stymied her. "The woman, the man out there."

"But I *forget.*" He retrieved the package from the bed. "I brought you something, Liz."

"For *me*? Ohhhh." She clutched an instant the thing to her breast and closed her eyes tight tight. "Ohhhh." Her lashes brimmed.

And he nearly spilled with all the years of her, bone deep in him, so far yet near, kid promises growing.

Then she tore at the paper, jerked—the six thin packets slid over the bed.

"Stockings! Silk stockings! I *always* always loved them." She laughed. She wiped her eyes. "How did you *know*?"

"Know! But—"

She laughed—she had broken plastic and drawn out a pair.

"I always promised!" There were the countless times: how she'd thrilled when he would say it, 'When I grow up I'm going to buy you something nice,' because aunt Mary never gave her money, not a cent, only hand-me-downs, and she sewed, sewed. And 'Buy me what? What?' she'd say. 'I'll dress you all up fancy and buy you *silk stockings.*' 'Silk stockings! Think of it,' she'd tell everybody, 'when Mark grows up he's going to buy me silk stockings. Aren't you, Mark?' There'd be the magic of her nervous fingers and the shiver over her and a reedy vibration in her weak chest which they'd once put her away for. That time, he'd visited her empty rooms; he could not stand the empty space she'd lived in. 'You spent too much time at Liz's anyway,' his mother'd said.

"Liz, don't you remember?"

"You!" She laughed, already on the edge of the bed, her leg out, sliding a stocking on, rolling it over the knee, up the thigh—too white, the white of closed in, stale air, no sun—a grub white. "Look! Oh, you!" But it was her leg, then the other, she tended and stared at and felt.

For a moment it was the time she was back from the TB place, when he would sneak away every day after school to the tenement his grandfather had moved into so Liz would have a place to go to. She was recuperated then, better, stronger, and ate, the TB gone. In a minute he would have to go home to his mother, and she'd say, 'You haven't been to Liz's, have you?—never *to your grandfather's*, always *to Liz's*. His mother had let his grandfather have a barrage: 'You moved out on me, Pa, so that *girl* can have a place to live, everybody talking about you. You know what they think, don't you, Pa?' But his grandfather'd told her, 'Gossip's gossip and knowing's knowing. Mary threw her out, the boys're afraid of the expense. Somebody's got to give her a home.' 'Why's it have to be you?' his mother'd said. And his grandfather silent.

"Liz?" He went down on his knees on the floor. In his old voice he said, "When I grow up I'm going to buy you silk stockings," and sank his head into her lap, against the flat of her belly, and felt her pulsing; and the hands touched his head.

Liz said, "Don't say that," though she was touching his hair. He wanted the fingers to press hard against his skull.

"But, Liz—"

"Don't say it!"

"But I always did. And you'd say, 'Mark, what will you buy me when—' "

"Mark?" She laughed, but so hard it was not laughter. Her hands were gone, her legs; he was bereft, on his knees; and she stood, still, and then made a quick move to the window. "They're always *telling* me things." She lashed the curtain, one panel, aside, and the gray and rain and countryside stood. "First it's Boyd telling things, then it's Boyd Jr. They've even got Andy doing it. Now *you*."

She turned to look hard at him, but through. How did you get to see what she was seeing?

"But, Liz, you remember when—"

"And when I tell the truth Boyd beats me. Just open my mouth and it's wham, he lambastes me one and won't let up, has to keep at it like a crazy man, but calling *me* the crazy one."

Boyd knew, everyone knew, she was always nervous, frail, at the edge. 'Enough, that voice of hers,' his mother would say, 'to make you grate your teeth. But to be fair to Liz,' his mother would add, 'Boyd presses his advantage, though she ought to know better.'

"And you know what? Driving me crazy that way too. Oh, I'd never tell anybody but you about Boyd."

You?

And when did she think it was?

"About Boyd?" he said.

"Yes, Boyd."

Boyd had appeared so quietly, at first a name he'd heard from her lips and his mother's, and then a thing inside her. Before he had ever laid eyes on the man, Boyd was a thing growing in Liz's belly that her hand half the day loved, touched, all her body content, and her eyes, teeth, lips wet and glowing, smiles. Liz's hands would take his and set them against her belly, and sometimes, later, it would be his head she would take and lay gently against her belly so he could feel the round hard weight and the beat of the blood of the baby inside him.

"Boyd!" Her stare stood Boyd at the door. She seemed to watch him enter the room.

"Last night?" Mark said, trying.

She turned on him, laughed, "My God! Last *night?*"

"You said a little while ago he'd been here."

"Said! Boyd—has—not—been—here—in—" She turned to find time in the window. All the gray and rain filled her. She couldn't remember. "Boyd?" she said, a break.

Boyd had made several visits to the tenement before his grandfather found out. 'Not in this place, Liz. Meet him anywhere outside.' The first time, belligerent, she defended shame, harder for the shame of it she would carry before the world.

Now she cried out. Her arms leaped up. She would strike the pane or frame or wall. But her arms stood, did not move. "He *married* me, didn't he?" But not till after it was a boy and Boyd had taken her upstate, far away, as 'his housekeeper' they'd said, what she'd been to his grandfather. 'You hate Boyd too, Mark, I suppose,' his mother'd said. Too? He didn't know whether she meant herself or his grandfather. He went silent. The agony—that Liz had gone—bit too deep.

"*Didn't* he marry me?" Liz said.

"Of course. He loved you." The word was an agony.

He was trying to follow her down her mind, how she thought.

"Then why's he do the things he does? And not give me a penny, never? And the kids half the time sick and no food on the table, no clothes, no oil for the stove, and winter and snow, and us in this crate of a cabin stuck so far out of town so all's you see is woods and no people. What life's this?"

She was talking years gone.

"But you got the boys through. They're fine. Grown. All set now."

"And *you* know how I did that—had to get him drunk for it, steal everything I could from his pockets, and got knocked black and blue for it. Boyd give *me* a thing! Over his dead body. Afraid —you know that?—afraid I'd run off, somebody'd have me, and I'd take the kids. A couple of times I did too, gone weeks and him hunting—but *you* know that."

He?

Through his grandfather's letters maybe. Her letters were always to his grandfather, Tom, private. *Dear Tom*. Her writing was up and down, straight and plain as she was—about her boys mostly or memories of when she'd lived in the tenement. There were questions about him, Mark, and the never-failing hello to his mother. His grandfather's eyes inched over her letters with the magnifying glass. If his mother came upon him like that, she'd insist, insist on reading them to him. Out of politeness and desire to hear, his grandfather'd sit silent, still, listening. His grandfather never forgot a thing, but he would come upon him bent over the table, rereading. He'd carry Liz's latest letter in his jacket pocket till the next one came. When his grandfather died, the letters were in a bureau drawer; now they were in his own. To see one brought Liz. One word and he heard her. Her voice was the same now. He could be standing in his own memory.

He began to wonder when he was.

"When Boyd ran off, I had to go to the law. The lawyer said they'd track Boyd down and get me and the kids something to live on. I never told you all the details— I couldn't, it was bad bad, the kids sick. I don't know how Boyd could— And they did track him down, too, but talk of squeezing blood out of a turnip! And he made good money, always did, but tight, and he'd sweet-talk his way out of things, but not with two kids, no—I wouldn't let that happen—"

She lifted up the whole gray rain-driven afternoon in her eyes, still, and looked at him, but he knew he was not there, not seen, whatever in her far sight, through him, she beheld.

Then it was Boyd she turned to—on the bureau, that photo —and said, a whisper pressed soft in her throat, "Boyd?" It was the cry, stifled, he knew she must have made, must go on making, a hundred nights and days all the minutes in this room.

He saw then how you depended. His grandfather must have been suddenly bereft—once of a wife, several times of Liz, and how many other times? If all of them went, what did you become?

Her fingers were gripping air again. "He'd better make up his mind—stay or not. Come and go, come and go, that's all he does. Well, I'll put a stop to that. Boyd!" As if he were somewhere about.

His mother'd gone to his grandfather: 'Now Liz has gone off and married the father of her child, you can come back home, Pa.' It was that phrase, echoed—*the father of her child*. Dubious. She had not counted on his grandfather's silence, the stare, the puff of his cigarette. She herself was alone with him, Mark; she would not marry again. 'Can't you?' Out of stillness, reverie, his grandfather replied, 'Best not act too soon. You can't tell how things turn out. Liz might need a place.'

"Liz," now he said, "you didn't tell me how Boyd Jr's doing."

She whipped back. "He's so *smart! Was* from the beginning. He's in college, Oswego. Boyd says he's doing fine. Boyd sees him, but I don't. He took them away from me, years now; not away—I mean in my own house turned them against me, said *things*—to my own boys—*things*, not a word of truth; said—every time I went off with the boys, or alone, and that one long time I ran away, months—said he'd put me away, said it all the time, 'I'll put you away yet, Liz.'"

"And Andy?" he said.

But there was cloud in her. She said, "And I was already put away right there at home in front of the boys, as if I didn't exist, and me walking around in that house with the three of them, shut out, shut out—do you know *shut out?*—like dark right in day. And I wanted to run or scream or kill, but waited to see what: I couldn't leave the boys, never. So you know what? He took them somewhere, weeks and weeks."

"I remember." His own words startled him because *from letters* read long after, he remembered, knew only her words. From that period had come most of her letters: the struggle was clear—Liz alone, winter, with nothing. Then was when his grandfather had gone away. 'Liz needs me. She don't say, but she needs me.' All bones he'd found her, and put her in the hospital. Then came one of the few letters from his grandfather addressed to him: *Mark, Liz is fine. You keep the house for me till I get back.* By then his grandfather had moved from the tenement. He had found a crate of a house, deep in shade, elms, and a quiet street of peace. But concerned, his mother said, 'You can't live like this, Pa': bed, table, a chair or two; eyes too bad to clean house right, to cook, clean, keep out dog and cats' hairs. 'At least give Mark your laundry.' She'd bring his special dishes—succotash, chicken dumplings, salmon croquettes. She didn't like to sit down there; she did not like the world of that house.

"Was that the time you were in the hospital, Liz?" Mark said, thinking from her words, his grandfather's letters, making himself that somebody, as if they were his own experience. Of course they were, now.

"Yes! And Boyd *used* that too—came home, jealous, raging, because you'd come to the house—"

You?

"—and he swore and hit—in front of the boys—called me names you wouldn't believe, Tom."

Tom.

He felt walls cracking. Skin. His own flesh a plaster breaking.

Who was what she saw?

"Liz—"

"Oh, yes, jealous—but *leave* me? Never! Not a cent of child support, alimony, nothing—that was why. And that's why he found the way, see?"

He listened—but with whose ears? He tried: if he could, he would see the man she spoke to; he would stand here in his flesh, the grandfather who had existed even before he was born, who'd carried part of him inside him and who'd already passed it on to the woman, his mother. Was that it? Liz was seeing the young grandfather he himself had never seen, the young man his grandfather had been when she was the little girl who'd moved to Aunt Mary's and first laid eyes on him.

With his eyes, head, he tried—but, scared, he broke in:

"Liz," he said, "what do you do all day?" in a loud, emphatic voice to break into her, though she was looking, very severe and straight, into the wall.

"All day?" She turned to him. "Do all day. Yes." She went to the window to show. Her hand flattened over it: "There. In the laundry with the women." She dared a smile. "They laugh a lot and make me." That building was the great dark complex, central, like a mound he'd seen in the middle of all the white buildings. Now, in early dark, early lights made a multitude of eyes.

"How long?"

"Four hours—in the morning. Sometimes it's afternoon, and then it's mornings."

And all day after, then what? He tried: you could sit yourself there on her bed in her place, you could see the wall and wall and wall and wall, you could see the photo, you could see Boyd, you could think *Boyd*, say *Boyd*, could get started with that word and go through your life, every bit of it, again down to now, you could begin again then, you could begin again, there were the years, how they started the day you got a sight of him and went on and unfurled to this moment, you could say *Boyd* and begin again, you could try to reach the other side of the wall of your mind and hit *Boyd* and start again, over and over and over and over, and you could never stop beginning.

Was it that?

So she would know who was inside the walls: it was the photo told her, that made Boyd for her there: she could stand before him, confront him, and be Liz. And if you took the photo away, who would she be then?

But she could not escape the photo.

He saw now how it could drive, craze.

"Yes, you, Boyd Hardy," she said to it.

For a moment he, Mark, was not there. And then when he

was—when he moved—he startled her. She quick laughed, but bitter, to herself, said, "Brought them in."

"Who?"

"Them." Her hand, her eyes, stood them there in the gray wall of rain. "His women. Brought them right into the house. He didn't care. No respect. He had it all fixed in his head what he'd do—get me out, put me away, let the state pay, and him pay nothing, and could do what he wanted then—he did anyway. Listen: in the middle of the night, to wake up and find him lying in my own bed, right beside me, going at it. And why wouldn't he let me go. Because he wouldn't. Whenever I left, he'd come get me, start all over."

His grandfather'd written her: *Liz, there will always be a home here for you. You will always be safe here. I will allow no man to cross this threshold.*

She had escaped, but her heart returned to the boys, and then her body. That once, Boyd waited, relentless, till she succumbed. Maybe Boyd did not know he was not Boyd without her.

"I won't put up with it, I told him. I'm not having you touch me after *them* and give me some terrible disease."

And how many years of that till she'd been brought here?

"But, you know, sometimes like a miracle he'd be my Boyd—come into the house, say, 'Liz, honey, we're going for a drive.' We'd go down the road, under trees, far, in a field, and it would be love, the first day, the first time—"

Love: what it was.

She was abruptly too young.

"—and then go the long way back, around the road with the green valley between and all the white buildings and stop. 'It would be a good place for you to stop and rest and get away from things, Liz. You could rest there,' he'd say. '*You*,' he'd say, and five minutes before it was *we we we*, but with me it was *always we*. 'I want my house,' I told him, 'I don't care what it's like, it's where *you* are, Boyd.' Since the day he came right down the street out of the dream, there never *has* been a single man, nobody—*you* know that, Tom. You're the only one really knows, Tom, no matter what anybody ever thought."

She clutched him too quickly, and held. "Tom!"

But he wanted to be Mark. How would he know when he was Mark?

He held her. Her head lay against him, her odors strong in him, inside him all a nervous leaping throb from her. And she damp. So thin.

The rain would not cease. All the gray stood unchanged outside, only darkening now, hazing beyond.

"I could find him. Take me with you, Tom." It was a bolt. She was charged with it, gripped, glowed, waiting. Then, fast, she left off him and flung the closet door open. "Oh, I won't take much room. That's all I have." There was another straight gray dress hanging on the door hook, on the floor a pair of black slip-ons. All. "Please, Tom?"

Who he was. What she made him.

"It's Mark," he said, too gruff.

"What?"

"I'm Mark."

For a moment her face, wrenched with confusion, the eyes wide, the face near shapeless, confused him. His blood tugged. "Liz—"

Her gaze faltered.

"Liz?" He wanted her sight—clear. Her lids brought a veil down. But when she raised them, the eyes went wary. "Liz—?"

"Don't do that!" she cried. "Not you too." And then she laughed, but hard flat as a shield thrown up. "Like everybody else. What're you trying to do to me?"

"Liz, it's really me." But he did not know. How did he know if she didn't? She could make him that.

And then it was the photo, sudden in her sight, made her as suddenly laugh and turn to it. "Oh, Tom, Tom, you *know* I couldn't leave. Don't even ask me." She caught up the photo and sat on the bed, Boyd and Boyd Jr and Andy clutched close under her chin. "I have to wait." She smiled. "Sometimes he comes back, my Boyd. I know he will." She seemed alien to all the gray afternoon.

He said nothing. In him he tried to travel the distance her eyes were on, down time: Was it in the dream: Boyd coming over a crest . . . ?

It was the moment. He had to go *now*. Wherever she was—where?—he had to leave her in that time.

He caught the last hard bone of her face, the long hair cocked, the still mouth moist and the traveling eyes, the whole of her hunched too thin on the edge of the bed, then shut the door behind him, closed his eyes, and stood, listened: nothing. And all the white corridor was still. Outside was darker now. He took his coat, passed the windowed office wall, where the woman smiled and wrote something, his time of departure perhaps, and he went out. Immediately it was cold—the rain, cold, smat—but he did not put the raincoat on. The mountains rose deeper into the sky. Rain so confused ground and mountains and sky that he felt he stood at the edge of an inverted precipice. And the earth where he crossed to the lot gave way, sank, soft mud. He slid into his car and sat, soaked, feet caked, and held the wheel until his own heat, breath, on the panes walled him in.

Then he drove—back down the hours, it seemed; back down the hours to drive upstate; back down where, at the end, his mother would be. All the battering, steady, would not cease, nor the windshield wipers' insistent click-clack, going back down: It all unfurled now—the farm gone, the valley behind him, the rise of walls which soon tapered, drifted behind, and the eternal wind of road down toward the city, edging the city, where the lights grew, over the river bridge, past sea, over flats, back down the coast, darkening, dark now, to that town, a few still lights on the edge of the earth, and endless darkness.

And he knew—he saw, he heard—how it would be when the headlights threw the house, garage, into focus, when he put them out and went in:

She would be reading in the living room. She would be ready for bed early, her night face pale, old, cleared, not the morning face that came out bright, made up, ready for day. From her he would know. She would see him: he would be what she saw.

"You missed your supper."

He would say nothing, so long still, and her hand would rise to her face.

"What's wr— Oh—" She would laugh, but nervously. "I'm ready for bed."

"I went to see Liz," he'd say.

"You what?" She would be clearly dislocated.

"I went to see Liz."

"But—" Her face would fester with it, with what it brought back. "After all these *years?*"

"I took her the silk stockings I promised her twenty years ago."

"Silk stockings!"

He would go to his room, he would hear her drop the book, hear her breath strenuous as she rose, her robe chafe as she followed to the door.

In the closet was the suitcase. It would not take long.

"What're you doing?"

There would be nothing to say.

"I want to know what you're doing. Where are you going?"

"I'm going to get married."

She would moan—from wonder, shock, disbelief, hurt.

"You're *what?*"

"I'm going to get married."

"Married! And how do you figure that? To which one? When?"

"The world's full of them."

"And where are you *going*? Where?" She would thrust her hand under her breast, against her heart, and clutch.

"To a motel. I'm moving. I'll get my things later."

"What's come over you? Who do you think you are?"

He would collect his shave things from the bath. She would follow.

"What're you doing?"

"I'm going to get married."

There was nothing more he would need to take.

He was startled now at even the thought of the completeness of it.

"Mark, you come back here!"

She would moan.

"I'm going to get married," he'd say.

"Mark!" she'd cry.

"I'm going to get married," he'd say.

Out There

"I HEARD your father last night, Wilson," the dean said.

"My father?" Beyond the corridor the quadrangle froze green. Against the sun he could scarcely see the dean's face.

"A great lecture. 'Where a man lives.' You certainly come by your talents honestly. But didn't *you* hear him?"

The pines by the chemistry building, spires of green, quivered.

"But I never knew him."

"Never?"

"He died when I was a baby. I'm virtually an orphan. My mother brought me up." But he faltered, watching the lie settle in the form of a sparrow high in the pine. *Abandoned, but at least I've got his name.*

"That's hard to believe! Why, he's the spit and image of you. And your name a foot high at the old Civic. You're sure?"

"No," he said—too rapidly, but laughed.

"Obviously!" Dean McCullough laughed with him. "Too bad

you can't hear him anyway, but he's off to Emory tonight. Well—" He shook hands. "Have a good summer in Spain."

At the Humanities exit, the blazing lawn made the quad rise in a quick sea in his vision, like the Sound at home. He blinked it serene. Why *home?* Sun gripped his head. He was so tired—steeped in the degree too long—but sometimes the buildings seemed to dissolve, trees sink, the earth fall away.

He crossed the quad in a hot inundation of pine. Helen was waiting. "At Holly's Grill," he murmured aloud, because he *drifted* so. The least movement hooked his eye. He halted. *My father?* Did moments lie like objects waiting around certain corners to confront you at critical times, as if by design? For faces intruded; they fought the day; his head followed them—his grandfather, Joseph K, John of the Cross, Quentin, Felipe II, Ivan Karamozov—to Moscow, Hades, Castile, Yoknapatawpha . . . *No, not now.* Grimly he set his eyes on Holly's Grill.

And there was Helen solid as truth behind the pane. She waved. He ran as the light turned red.

"You just made that one," she said. He slid into the booth, laughing, feeling his skull reverberate.

"You're sure keyed up." Her hands touched his. "And why not? Tomorrow at this time—oh, David, at last—we'll be on our way. A week with Mom and Dad and—"

But he was staring at her hand. His own crept over it. "Tomorrow?"

"David!" she cried with such a pitch of apprehension that he jerked. "*Now* what is it?" He looked into hard, hurt eyes.

His own eyes palpitated, she was talking from a long way off, and perilously a corridor opened. He said, "Dean McCullough—"

"Dean McCullough? He's on *leave*."

"He saw my father."

"Your *father*? David, you're not going to start *that* again?"

"Start what? What?"

"And on the day before we leave. Please, David."

"He said he was the image of me, the same name." There was a billboard with his own head.

"That doesn't mean a *thing*, David. There must be thousands of Wilsons."

"But only one father."

"Don't look that way. You should *see* yourself!"

He felt sorry for her—she was afraid—and touched her cheek.

"I'm sorry, Helen." But his gaze wandered over her shoulder, beyond.

"You are *not* sorry. I know you. You think I don't remember?"

Once he had holed up in a cheap hotel in Dubuque, calling every Wilson in the directory; and once he had been gone a week, scouring St. Louis for a man he'd never known. But he had a right to claim that other flesh, hadn't he? Oh, no, Helen would have none of that. "You don't owe him a thing. What'd he do but abandon you? If you drop your work and pop off at every clue, how'll you get through prelims?" And she was right; she finally did get him through the Ph.D.

"I know what you're feeling, David, but—" Her voice pulled. "We're free now."

Free?

"Dave . . . ?"

He was not used to such urgency in her. She managed food, rent, extra books, pleasure—by watching. And she had patience, seldom mentioned marriage, and never directly. Only the sight of children made something in her halt; a glaze—to ward off pain?—

shielded her and rapidly she channeled her excitement, vagrant over Boston Brahmins, Emerson, the Transcendentalists, though at times she would halt to look back.

"You won't be satisfied, will you, David? Not till you find out *he* doesn't want you. Then you'll come back. Well, I won't be your mother and father too. I'm *Helen.*"

"Not *here,* Helen." For the waitress interrupted, a quick acrid odor. "Nothing," he told her.

All the way to the apartment Helen's silence accused. Heat clutched his head. Once inside, she drew the shades. "David, not this time—you wouldn't?" she whispered, kissing his mouth, cheek, ear, drawing him down. "Please?" But somewhere in the shadows, across a meadow, a dark thin post of a man was calling, a voice reached after him into the woods, where he was lifting rocks for garter snakes he liked to collect. He ran out of the woods into sudden sky, through the swamp of purple iris to dry ground and islands of forget-me-nots and over the brook where he caught frogs. The man's arms stretched out to catch him.

"DavidDavidDavid," Helen moaned ecstatically as he leaped into his father's arms.

He fell away, but Helen clung, whispering, "Promise, David. Hon?" whispering into slow sleep. But he could not speak; he would not belie the sign from the dean. *And last January I saw Kohoutek—like a herald.* His heart soared ahead with it. In the next apartment time struck the quarter hour, *Go go go go,* nine times echoing his decision. He got up and finished his half-packed suitcase. Then he closed himself in the bathroom, feeling a coward—but he dared not wake her, she would find a way to stophim—and wrote *I'd stay if I could, but I must stop feeling suspended. I want to know the reality I came from and what I belong to.*

Go to Spain. Sell what you want when you come back. Remember: We decided no obligations, *but don't think I'm not ashamed. If I weren't, I'd wake you. Maybe my shame's the measure of how deep the other is in me—nothing else is real when that presence overwhelms me. I seem to become someone else. My imagination comes so alive! I can't describe properly what happens inside me then. Maybe that's hell—being trapped in feelings you can't communicate. I want to share, but I turn to stone then. I don't know how long this will go on, but I can't put you through that again. Forgive me. David.*

At Trailways three men and a woman were sitting still as islands, one man with his arms hung, mouth wide in sleep. All the years gray heads had called his eyes. "Keep it up and you'll be on one wild goose chase after another," Helen had said. He was relieved when the bus pulled out, but he felt his betrayal of her. He saw her lying alone, blurring into the anonymous dusk. *I can't help it, Helen. Can you imagine what it is to see someone pass and be suddenly impaled by the thought that he's part of your own body?*

One Fourth of July when he was a boy, a woman came to the front door. Something walked on his heart: memory knew her from a time when uncles had milled about, when he used to eat with her and sleep in her bed—his father's mother. So he hid in his bedroom.

But his mother shadowed the doorway.

"Your grandmother's here. She wants to see you."

"I don't want to see her." He wanted to cry from fury, yet he moved forward. She was standing far in the parlor, small and round and dark in the sun.

"Don't you remember your grandmother?" Already her pudgy hands clenched his fingers, thick fragrance seeped over him. "Why, his hands are sweating. You're nervous!"

No no no, they're always wet.

"We came to town for the parade. He just thought he might see his son."

"Not here," his mother said.

"Would you like to go with your grandmother—just for a little while?" the woman said.

"No!" he cried. "No!"

The woman's voice was filled with energy, her laughter infectious. She talked with his mother. They seemed to forget the man. And he was glad when she finally left. But why had she left the room so empty?

"Helen," he'd said, "listen: after she left I spent the whole day on the Common—there were thousands of people there—and once I *knew* my father was behind me. I turned around: he *was* standing with his back to me, slim and straight as in the photos, with sleek dark hair. I wanted to say *Dad* and touch him. I was afraid and sweating and wanted to cry. I hated him for not turning around, but when he moved, I ran—Can you understand that?—I ran all the way to the woods and stayed till dark and the sky got white with the bonfire a mile away. Then I decided to go back, swearing *This time I'll go right up to him, I will.* But I couldn't find him. I've never been so close since."

Until now.

Far, Atlanta made a golden dome warding off the dark. *If my father is there. . .*

When he stepped off the bus, a subterranean cold swept up the passage, his heart gripped, a dark cold corridor came, someone was calling *Felipe,* he was standing in the Escorial. But who were all these people? He wanted to turn on them: *What are you doing here in my palace?* But the tower clock struck. It was time for his devotions: he fled up the stairs, past the pilgrims, through the cloisters to his private chambers. The bed he had just crept out of was unmade. Gold light poured through his little window above the *altar mayor*. He fell to his knees to pray. Below, candles burned gold; a smell of stone and wax and incense, damp tapestries, smote. His place in the choir was empty. He closed his eyes. *O my Father, I am sick with longing. My body clings to this place, but my soul leaps to you. Forgive my vanity. Accept this my tomb and palace and monastery, and forgive my errors for this my beloved Spain. And, O Lord, do not ease the pain in my body that makes you ever present. Let my soul grow large feeding on this my dying body. Let my bed reek and the air give back my own stench that I may be ever mindful of Thee.*

"Move it, man."

"What?" He was on the escalator; it ran into the waiting room gleaming around him.

"You're blocking the way." The man heeled his suitcase aside.

Atlanta, he said to himself, *Atlanta.*

Outside, he told the cab driver, "Emory University." On the street were hoards of pilgrims. *You fool!* His throat made an absurd little laugh.

"What?"

"Nothing. It sure changes. I was a student here,"

The city was higher, stone burgeoned into sky, walls drove the eyes upward.

They followed his old way: along Peachtree, turning at the Fox, down Ponce de Leon past the fruit stand, the joints, Sears, the Church of Christ, where they'd called him *Brother*. At Manuel's Delicatessen somebody would be playing the pianola. A dank breeze flowed through the tunnel of leaves. Far, a choir was singing. They wound the way into Druid Hills.

""Left—the Student Union."

"You sure know your way."

"I got my M.A. here. It's home."

The Union lights were on but the doors locked. He couldn't be too late! But a wide strip over the billboard read CANCELLED, leaving the top of the lecturer's head and half his name, son. He tried to tear the strip, but it was glued fast. *No, not again.*

He went directly to the Union desk. "The lecture—what happened?"

"The speaker had an attack in Alabama. They flew him to Chicago."

"But I've got to see him."

"There's a refund. And we've an address if you want to contact him."

"Address?" His blood halted.

The boy copied it out.

"A hospital then?"

"His home, I think. By the way, you're not Mr. Wilson?" *No. He's my*—He felt a bone in his lungs. "Yes."

"A woman called long distance. She said to expect you. Her name's—"

"Helen. . . "

"Say, you psychic? Helen Riddle. She said the agency would refund your travel ticket in care of your old address, unless you'd changed your mind."

Was she finally swearing off, or was it her way of loving, even now?

"Do you have a room? I'm an alumnus."

"I can just make it."

He reserved a morning flight to Chicago and bathed, but

throbbing with the Trailways trip, he walked the campus. Through dark trees lights blinked from the hospital, dorms, library. Up fountained memories of Pike parties, field trips, soccer, the apartment . . . Soon he came to the depot: those rails went north to the sea where he was born. Waves rushed into his head. The dark whispered.

"Here?" a voice said.

"What?" he said.

There was a brushing, a leap of face from the shadows—so familiar!—and a boy drew a girl quickly after him. Ah, to leave his skin and be that boy! But he went back. Lying there on his old campus, he felt younger, as if Helen hadn't happened yet; and such a yearning came into him that he hardly slept.

On the plane he was nervous and tired; his eyes seized the least shadow. On the train west to DeKalb, the suburbs tore dizzily, cornfields poured through his skull, shadows flagged; and he felt such a pulling *back*. At the DeKalb station, still a drab whistle stop, his direction was certain. He laughed, hurrying into this terrible familiarity. 422! *Yes*. How could he have forgotten that number? He'd lived there: a two-storey white Thirties frame house, renovated, a picture window where he'd read on winter afternoons. His legs felt splintered, but he gained the porch and rang the bell—its sound took his breath.

"Mrs. Bulgarov!" The door filled with that heap of flesh.

"David!" Her mouth sucked his cheek. "Why you didn't tell us? Papa! Girls; Such pla-sure!"

"Home." He was bewildered giddy by so much joy.

"Always your room's waiting," Mama said. "We never rented yet since you're gone. Always we said, 'David loves pita. The smell's bringing him beck.' And I made pita this day!" She let out a series of high pitches.

"And why you come DeKalb?" the old man said. The eye burnt from hot metal in the Chi factory still squinted, but the other glowed a clear dark sun.

"I'm in Chicago for an interview—just for the day, but I couldn't resist—" The stairs called to his eyes.

"See, Papa! What I tell? Not write, but like son to us. Mara, take bag upstairs."

"*No*," he said with quickened laughter, already ascending. "Let me. I can't wait to see my old room." But there was nothing there, only himself in the old mirror.

Mama called, "You come now. We eat pita." She was telling them, "David came to door the first day with two eyes only; then one day comes downstairs with glasses. 'Why hiding?' I cry. 'Where's David?' Such good times! And now finished all education? Good! We celebrate. Wine? Beer? Whiskey? Papa!"

They made him tell all. The afternoon ebbed. Dusk thickened the trees. The girls' eyes admired.

"And that girl—Helen, *yes*? See, Papa!" Her arm pressed warmly. "I'm glad. You never regret. And empty house next door waiting for our boy."

"Waiting for me?" Afternoon light etched white crypts in the vacant house beyond.

"Sure. You get job, marry, live here. Is paradise to marry. What more? Eh, Papa?" Her laughter scaled the chandelier and fed Papa's and the girls' and his own: for his head reeled, bobbed—with the wine, no sleep—their voices echoed down corridors. Surely it wasn't real. Not *now*—*was*. But he couldn't blink them away. *But how'd I get here? I'm looking for my father.*

"Excuse me." He went up to the bath. His frenzied hands went through the wallet—for that address. Pine Street, *yes*, but *Knoxville, Tennessee*! He couldn't wait. He must leave, now, *now*.

Downstairs he told them, "I could stay forever in this good house." How he wanted to say *I have a family—in Knoxville*. But there's somebody. . ." His hand went—out there.

"*Hel*-en. What I tell!"

"Helen," he murmured. In the graying deeps outside, he could conjure no face, nothing of Helen. *Mama, I feel sometimes on the edge of a precipice poised for the longest flight*. Papa and the girls held him, reluctant to let him go.

"When you come again?" Mama's eyes shone black with farewell. Her voice lamented *Never*.

He finally stumbled off—"Bye. Thanks"—back to the depot, to Chicago, back, back—His still self glided along beside him in the pane. Wires, houses, lights went through him. And on the plane, a star straight out palpitated with his own heart; his bones wanted to reach through his image and touch that light. Helen would fly to Spain, astronauts reach into another orbit, and everywhere things made milkweed spurrings upward. "*But Helen, why such despair in the moment of falling, when such frenzy only the moment before?*"

"*You silly. We're animals—and then some. We wouldn't despair if we weren't, would we? But let both be together, can't you? Remember 'Fair needs foul'? Who can keep up one without the other for long? Isn't your memory good enough to tide you over?*"

Memory?

"*Sometimes I forget who I am, Helen.*"

"Because you have such an exceptional faculty for feeling into somebody else."

"How'd you know that?"

"I've seen you steep yourself in all that transcendent literature, and I love you— Remember? And that's why you need me—to tell you who you are. I'm the straightest way!"

But over his desk hung St. John's words: "Take care that you always choose not the easiest, but the hardest way . . ."

In Spain, in the Carmelite monastery of Toledo, he saw the cell where they had imprisoned St. John of the Cross for trying to reform the Order. The guide said, "If you want to see what the poor *padre* lived in for almost nine months, *adelante*." So he went into the dark hole—ten by six with not enough room to stand, and no windows or light or air. "*Así*—like that"—with the door shut. Darkness. Silence. Damp cold stone. *Juan*. For that instant walled in, he lay in Juan's flesh; someone was calling from a far place. He strained, listening. . . My name?

But the stewardess intervened. "Knoxville . . ."

He sat the long black night out at the airport. Once outside, the morning world gripped: Kingston Pike, arcades of trees, Ayres Hall on university hill, downtown high on Gay Street, the mountains going beyond. "Here!" he cried to the driver. But *why* here? The brakes pitched nervously. The Court was a horseshoe-shaped building. Old Mr. Waites, nearly too fat to move, would be sitting in his armchair overlooking the campus. He took the elevator up to third and rapped.

But it was a woman, gaunt to a shadow.

"Oh—" Walls gleamed clean beyond. "I roomed with Mr. Waites here." Then, the walls had been drab, a sullied maze through mounds of undusted objects, old Waites's personal archaeology.

"Mr. Waites, I'm afraid, died some years ago. I'm sorry." Cautious, she inched the door to.

Down. The suitcase plagued, this burden he lugged everywhere.

Pine.

"Taxi!"

Straight to Pine.

"What you think of *that?*' the driver said.

422 was gone except for slab steps, a hollow in the earth, and the severed backbone of a chimney!

"Should I wait?"

"No, no. Maybe the neighbors know." And that *was* the address—clearly. Could that boy at Emory have blundered?

The neighbor had been watching from the window.

"I'm looking for the Wilsons'." *For my father.* The words unsaid, hung like absurd furniture in his eyes. "But I've made so many mistakes, I've looked . . ." The man grew wary. "Oh, I'm not a bill collector. I'm a relative."

"Ah. But I never knew them, just he's from Pennsylvania—you from there?—and that property's gone for sale 'cause the owner's in the hospital."

"How'd you find out?"

"The agent who put up that sign."

"Thanks. That's a great help."

The taxi was waiting. "I've been watching. Figured you wouldn't get far. Where to?"

"Ultimate Realty."

The agent was wary too—and disappointed—when he told him, "I'm not here to buy. I'm a relative."

"Then you ought to know Mr. Wilson's sick—very."

Very? His eyes throbbed, and his temples.

"He went into the Harrisburg hospital—to see a famous specialist there."

"I must find him." And he *would*. He had enough money to get to Harrisburg, some over—and then? He didn't care. His blood thrust at his skull: close, yet so infinitely far.

By the time he boarded the plane he was so tired, tired, his body sank limbless, his mind numb... Far off was a singing—he listened—and footsteps, hoards of footsteps; the organ, the choir, burst forth. Yes. He rose, feeling very ill, but urged to review his handiwork. *For you, O God, this monastery of San Lorenzo.* He went through the throne room, following the pilgrims down cloistered corridors, down, down steps damp and cold to a circular room. Who had built this room? *I Felipe did not. It was water and mud.* But now marble and jasper, niches with gray marble sepulchres; and he read the names of kings there, his father's name—and Felipe II, his own! How could that be? And abruptly, at the odor of his living flesh, he turned; his hand, long and thin to his own sight, felt his way up the damp wall, back, up into that sound—How it came louder, louder! to his bedchamber, which he could no longer bear to leave for any time, and down on his knees. He dropped his head, fever-ridden and hot in his hands. The incense and wax could not eradicate his own stench. *O my God, protect my daughter, forgive me my sins, do not deny me, O Father.* Against that cloth harsher than sackcloth his forehead chafed his arm.

His arm jerked. "Your lunch," the stewardess said. His head

woke full. Food throbbed bold with sunlight. Jet air rushed through his skull. Serene, the heaven settled around him. Catapulted through stillness.

Where is my body going?

Into me, you fool!

Helen?

David, I want your baby—but with your consent. You don't have to marry me. Just let's have a baby, or what else is love for? When do we stop lying, after all the education and facts and history and knowledge of death: a baby's not a mere disconnected happening, darling, but still a miracle and a real live event like you and me in the continuity of things. Why be two more simply screwing ourselves into meaningless oblivion? Oblivion means. You talk about the paradox of dying into somebody else so that you can let go yet still be here. But why do you resist that?

Because. . . But no word came into his mind.

Perhaps the answer lay down there. Below, the Susquehanna made a brown coil through the green city. In the descent, a membrane slipped down over his ears. His head vibrated.

Outside the hospital, in the last sun leaps of forsythia, bloodbursts of salvia crowded into his head. He halted to let his blood ease, then gripped the suitcase and mounted the steps. Inside, white streaked everywhere; the odors were pungent.

"Wilson?" he said to the gray lady at the cardex, feeling a fool when she said, "We've two. Both *Paul!*" She laughed, but he felt pinned. "Is he young?"

"My father."

"Then it's 313 west. One's a boy."

313 west.

He felt foolish carrying his suitcase. The elevator parted on a bright, empty way. For an instant his blood lurched with the motion, and he closed his eyes: dark corridors extended, a quick subterranean wind came as the elevator closed. His legs trembled but he followed the black arrow down the corridor. He pushed 313 open.

Two bodies were lying in a blaze of sun—the near one young, the other old. He approached the long body under the sheet. The old head hung back, the mouth open, lips dry; the eyelids lay limp in the sockets; sun gleamed along the wet rims; all the skin lay close to bone; a bolt of white hair grew from the skull. From the rotting teeth, the hole and dry tongue came a foul odor. Too old! Why wasn't he younger? *Why?* He wanted to pound that flesh into the right face; he wanted to raise that body up and shake life into it. Instead, he covered his eyes. *Where do I go now?* But when he began to retreat, the man's throat scraped. He stared into that mouth. The tongue lapped.

Suddenly the eyes opened. They fixed on him. They stared so long that he thought, *He's dead.* Yet he dared not move. Then the head rose: sun drove into the man's eyes; they went blue and deep. He drew away, but the man's hands clamped his wrists. His heart bolted. "You came," the old man wheezed, "you!" and smiled, his wet eyes raising the light, which broke and spilled down his cheeks. Who'd the man think he was? Now the old fingers shot up to his collar and drew him to his chest and began to weep; the dry, warm hands moved over his hair and eyes and mouth. He heard the breath in the man's chest and felt the warm bones; and all at once his own fear and disappointment and despair welled up, and he clutched that frame. "Yes yes yes," he cried, "me!" And both of them wept with all their hearts.

"What?" In the next bed the young man sat up. "Nurse? Nurse?"

In a moment a nurse came.

"What's going on? What are you *doing* to him?" She tried to part the old man's fingers. Still they clutched, impervious to her —until, finally, he fell back exhausted. His eyes closed, but his lips were smiling.

"Look what you've done," she cried.

He rose and backed off and took his suitcase and fled.

"Do you think it was the son?" the young man was saying. "Who else would cry for him like that?"

But that *You* echoed in pursuit down the elevator, through the foyer, outside, where it was growing sunset, hard white clouds edged with dying crimson. Cool wind came. Still he felt those warm hands, the pulsing too rapid in his blood, and in the sky. *You must stop this.* But he could not obliterate the deep sea in the old man's eyes; and he saw his own Sound, the Point, all the Atlantic, and beyond; and he yearned for it. *Yes, go.* The house was there waiting. His mother had said, "After I'm gone, it will always be there when you want it."

He turned to look up to the third floor, where the old man was lying. He wanted to tell him about the town near the tip of the island—"the end of the world," his mother'd say—where he was born, where the air always held sea, where wind carried morning up from the east and "Nearer My God to Thee" from the Episcopal Church tower and the first tatters of darkness and all the seasons, where on clear days you could see to the very edge of things.

I am too near home not to go. Years I have not been.

He would not let up now, but go on to the end.

All the way, tunneling through the Pennsylvania dark to New York and trundling along the battered Long Island rails, he felt he was willing the train home. But there was the haunt of Helen's voice: "You fool, you! Don't you see I'm the only way?"

Way?

Then why did his father beckon always ahead, over her shoulder?

"And where will all this take you?"

"When I find him, Helen, I'll know."

"And when you do, you'll think of me, but you don't know how bitterly. Remember that. "

The train was so slow! It stopped at brief islands of lights, stations of the past more distant as the train recovered his island. He was so close. Surely that house, with the son returned, would draw his father back at last. Maybe he had *been* and the neighbors would bear witness to his presence. And he wanted to hurry, to bear witness before the old man's eyes went out. Perhaps he should have waited with him! But the old man was here; he felt his breath in his ear.

The first glints of light appeared, land narrowed, water encroached in black glimmers. Ahead, the waterfront materialized like a town undersea. The train lurched, wrenched a cry from the rails, and halted on the dock. The town was too real. He could not believe. *Back*. But how far did you have to go?

"Taxi!"

He wanted to recognize the driver's face, but it was a stranger's, though the man's gaze halted on him when he gave the address. The sound of that address from his own mouth startled him. *Home*. A fine ringing ran through his head.

Through the village, the taxi lit a way past the traffic circle and the potato fields and up to the edge—the Sound appeared and deep infinite darkness. Clean, damp night air poured over.

"The last house."

"You're sure this is it?" The driver took the money.

"Sure? It's mine."

"O-kay."

The taxi backed out and dark fell whole, soft with wind; and fine stars of light emerged from the Connecticut shore. *This*. He could walk blind to this house, he knew it so well. But his legs faltered, and he groped for the gate, hanging broken, and nearly tripped—the cement was broken too and uneven—and mounted the stoop to the front door—it swung so easily—and went in, knowing it was empty, years, waiting. For him? Wind swept through broken windows; waves struck the sand below. *Empty*. But he would fill it. *"Never. Not without me, David. I'm the only way."*

He dropped the suitcase. In darkness he roamed from living room to dining room and kitchen; then, taking his suitcase, he went up the stairs, stopping at last at his own room. He could hardly stand, but his blood was alive with the place, his head raced—too fast. Stop, *stop!*

His eyes grew accustomed: out the window were the cliffs, the width of sand below, the sea merging with thick, endless dark. *The house of my fathers*. Empty. He had nothing but the suitcase. He sat on it. His head drifted. Dark corridors opened. *Felipe? Juan? Who?* His head jerked. He stood, this time grasping the casing. His gaze tried to fathom it, encompass the whole dark. And for an instant he was still in the hospital, gazing into the old man's private sea. Was *he* looking out on this too? His head pulsed with the waves. How far back did you have to go? Into every nook and cranny? Down onto the shore? Into the sea itself finally? He must know. He succumbed to the wind inundating him, aware that in a moment he would be asleep, but not before he made up his mind to stay. He would make something, he would wait here, wait. Surely his father would come.

The Impossible

THE IMPOSSIBLE was not to cry out. If his mind chose not to, his body had its own impulse, disconnected, it seemed, from any will. So he discovered two selves, one which pain hurtled toward unknown regions, whetting an infinite desire, another whose cry hurtled back into this earthbound body lying under white in his own bedroom, with the bay beyond a sheen of white blazing into his eyes.

Sometimes he saw himself sitting at the desk again, where the seizure had come: another of those sharp pains which paralyze the entire nervous system for an instant. He had always expected the relentless inevitability of pain. It had come while he was sitting staring across Peconic Bay at Shelter Island a summer afternoon *en mezzo del cammin*. But this time the pain did not cease, but gnawed, begetting multiple pains; a burning flush and then dampness followed; in his vision a galaxy of sapphires sprinkled the sky, each palpitating with enormously dense brilliance; and the sky glowed the deepest cathedral of blue toward which he was drawn in irresistible rush. His heart strained. Pulsings filled his mouth. The pain was so great he cried out. The cry startled his own ears and he tried to look around to see who else was there— He slumped. And when he opened his eyes, he was lying on his back, the sky was a close white purity, confusing, until he saw Sara's worried face suspended over him. Of course: he was in the hospital.

But at Sara's insistence—because she respected his own—they had brought him home, away from that clinical whiteness.

"There, darling," Sara said now. "It'll be gone in an instant."

"Nnnnnnnn—" He did not want the needle. Did—not—want. If it killed pain, mostly it drowsed him, dulled his mind, garbled his tongue, but—worst—fastened him to the room and the view: the bay, the near edge of sand, the rim of Shelter Island, richly green, and the stretches toward where the Orient light would be, miles away.

"Would you like me to read to you?" Cheerful. But her lines—heavily made up to conceal the deepenings, the darkening skin under her eyes, the finely ribbed rictus—bespoke her own sorrow. For him she concealed it.

". . . ssss."

She read—wonderfully—the famed confrontation scene between Lord and Lady Dedlock in *Bleak House* (proudly *My own pupil,* he thought, seeing her front row seat in his class at the U).

But the injection blurred— He tried to sort out the landscape from Dickens. Worse, her voice grew heavy, a pressure too close. All his senses had become too acute: subtle smells were pungent; the vaguest light, nearly infinitesimal motions commanded his eyes. Yet he lived to reach out through his senses past the room, past the Orient light. He inched out, prodded by promises. If he was still himself (Sara'd brought his desk sign home, RONALD GOODMAN, PROFESSOR OF ITALIAN LITERATURE), even in tranquillity when under sedation, he was discovering a new creature: no matter where in the house they were, he knew what Sara or Mattie or each visitor was doing, and that was the beginning—far, a brush of feathers dusting, the tin lid of Sara's Mum set down, a rub of flesh, a sigh, a chafing curtain, a knob turned.

But, stilled, he went further: because he was lying flat so much—though Sara'd hired a hospital bed so he could view the bay and beyond—his ear scooped in sounds over the close topography of the constant pillow, feeling them: after-motions of heat and rain, swells and shrinks in the shingles, insects crawling, chafes of a bee in a peony, the fall of a grain of soil.

"Do you hear, Sara?" He described them to her. Her eyes marveled at his expertise, satisfied that something held him with such life. She'd even come to ask, "What new have you heard?" not patronizingly, but with the deepest curiosity, her own eyes sensitive to each change in him. She wanted to share—go with him as deeply as she could.

"There are times," he told her, "when your voice touches my body, sinks in, and flows. Your perfume falls on my skin heavily. I'd never experienced synaesthesia before."

Pensive, she scowled. Taut in her anxiety, she rose and left. From far off upstairs, he could hear the catch of her crying.

Early in his illness there were visitors: faculty, administrators, town friends, and—more and more—students. They did not stay long; they stood in the doorway, talked from the living room—the discomfort he knew of his odor, which, so steeped in, he was seldom aware of, except through them. When they left, he was startled at his relief. People he had loved—Cal Grove, Jan Eckhardt, Jeff and Al Walton—came to be interruptions. Sometimes even Sara, whom he'd felt he could not breathe without, intervened: it was not that he did not want her there to share, but that he had begun to cross a threshold he couldn't describe.

That motion had first happened as he came out of sedation, before he had quite reached the upper limits of a sea he was lying under, the outer limit of all the universe he knew. He eased into waves of sounds toward whose far source a muted, almost unheard note teased him. Without, it resounded within; and he had the sensation of looking down into his own chest, entering, and going deep into the beat, down, deeper, until at the end he experienced a sound absolutely unknown before—it filled his mouth with the taste of flowers, washed its perfume over his eyes, swayed all of him toward it; impelled with greater speed the closer he approached, he strived, reaching, opening his mouth to draw it in as if without it he would die—

That was the moment his body began to scream.

"Ron Ron Ron, what is it?" Sara held him gently down, lay him back on the pillow, but she glanced out the window.

His eyes couldn't get it all in. He—

"No no no no!"

Why did she ignore him? He saw the gleamed needle; his angle shifted his face to the wall; then she set him right, the thing done, and returned to sit by his bed.

So he was a prisoner of the room. He tried to rise, grumping sounds. *Why* did you pull me back? Don't you know where I was? He'd told her a hundred times since the first real pain, "No needles. Let me have my pain." And, in fact, she did try at the beginning, tried to let him endure what *he could stand*—her words—but then *she* could not: her face came, stood above him, pummeled like a mashed pillow by his cries, despair driving her hands to her temples.

"Ron, I must. I can't stand it. You can't."

But he could. *Could.* His mouth tried to tell her. If she didn't listen, she would hold him back from— But he couldn't find the words. Yet *she* did: "Is that better, darling?" He cried out *Nooooo,* but only a moan struck his ear.

Mattie, smiling with her sweep and swish, yet quiet—on toes sometimes—widened his view by pinning the ecru curtains back, shifted the dust, tucked and arranged, leaving him a strong weight of lily-of-the-valley and acrid armpits preparatory to the scent of Sara, airblown Clorox and sweet flesh.

And Dr. Waters materialized: he would come so nonchalantly out of the window like the last shadow of night from the far morning, grip his wrist for pulse with such firmness, laying a quiet wave of smells from his hands suit bag on his body the remains of kitchen bathroom office family patients: "That's fine."/"A little color today."/"Quite an improvement."/"Your wife's some nurse!" His voice came down the tide. He himself eased into a soft sea. Far off a wall rose over which he knew was that other sea: only pain could leap him up over the wall. Why did they deny him that? "Just so long as he doesn't feel anything painful."

Oh, Sara, do not be merciful. You must learn real mercy. I know you can't help it, my darling, but look into my eyes. Can't you understand what I'm trying to say?

When his head rolled into clarity, he said it, "No more, please," and she said, "They hurt a second, darling, but they're such a help." And he cried out again, "No. I want—don't you understand?—

want my pain," and "Yesyesyes," she said, fleeing to the kitchen—to call Dr. Waters again—she couldn't fool *him*—for more medicine, *surcease from sorrow,* yes, he *knew,* could hear every word she whispered: "I think it's affecting his mind. Oh God help him, he never talked this way before, he's so brilliant, nobody was ever more brilliant, and to see—"

"Sara! Sara!" *StopyoubloodygoddamnedfoolI'mnotcrazynotyouunderstandandIjustwant*

At once she was beside him, for one brief instant trying to yield, not give him anything, let him go through it, let him clutch her hand, feel the wrench of his own teeth, tautness of muscles never used now, stiffening even of his bones, see the old rigidity under the sheets turn writhe bolt (water soft as air came warm over his eyes; his body sank easefully down; above, light grew; and as flesh drifted down, the fine form of his body, shimmering, rose out of itself, answering the sound of light, so sweet on his tongue and melodious that it persuaded him, drawing his little light into its great flame; and so great grew his desire that arms and legs sang, every hair on his head singing with the light touching, and his fingers reached—

But his desire turned to anguish. The wall rose. The light vanished into sudden night. *Agggggg.* Water bitter as salt filled his mouth. He fell back into the dark body below and opened his eyes, his mouth shouting for light desired remembered lost), and then his body stopped writhing.

SaraItoldyounotto

"Sara . . . ooo," he said.

"I *know,* sweetheart." Her eyes were filled, but she smiled. "I'll make your favorite potato soup for lunch. How's that?" She was gone. She would be back filling him a spoonful at a time. Her black hair and oval face would bend close: *Loved that face—but dark now, hiding sun, in the way.* Why didn't she move? *I loved you, yes. Love, yes. But now—* Sometimes in her green eyes the light glimmered and through her head he was sure it was coming—he reached, but the eyes came down, kissed. "I love you, darling," she murmured. *No no no no.* He wanted to grip the light through her eyes, go. She clutched his fingers, but softly and set them back down, with her Camay scent, against his chest.

"Sara—" Why was his voice so hard for his throat to catch hold of? "The wall is like the breakwater in the bay. I almost get to it. I can't get over the breakwater. When you give me the hypo, it throws the wall back up."

"But you feel relief, don't you, dear? It's too much struggle."

"Nooo. Couldn't you help me, Sara?"

But her eyes went blank again, veered to the window, her chin quivered, and the newspaper. No smile could keep the unwept tears from sounding in her throat.

"You wouldn't have me go against Dr. Waters' orders?"

"Yes! *My* orders. I'm your husband." She loved him, didn't she? Would give all, her life even, for him—had told him so. Now now *now*. "My life," he said.

But "Myra and John Wellek are back from Bermuda," she read, her eyes inching down the paper, "and there's still talk of that silly bridge from New London to Orient Point. Think what it'd do to our lives here. There'd be so many new houses this end of Long Island'd be a beehive."

Moments, when she evaded, he felt he hated her—ashamed, *ashamed,* but his animosity rose: he wanted to strike her, Dr. Waters, Mattie, visitors, it—whatever kept him from *that,* over the breakwater. *What have I done to be kept from it?*

In the darkest moment of night, when his lids slipped so quietly upward and the dark softly touched his eyes, he waited, thinking pain, conjuring. But how gauge time when he did not know how long he'd lain here, slept, drifted since the last injection? His head tried to fight the drift, but slowly succumbed, sank—then abruptly bobbed. *Try.* He did try to swim above the dark. He had to get to the surface, where it would all sear, burn, and, as it did, give such impulse to his desire that *it* would leap free over that wall and *see (My life dedicated to the idea of suffering. . . . Not now to destroy my work before in my own flesh I know what, in the study of literature, my intuition has made into the most significant book on the meaning of suffering and death, the relation between the sensuous and the spiritual, in Dante. Now in the dark wood of this life, perhaps I am Dante himself for one moment. I come before I die, through my dying, to verify all I have said about physical suffering transformed into meaning, sure, so sure that I stake all on it).*

My life.

For he knew—he would not lie—he was dying. He had so little time to discover—and tell Sara. But would she *be* there at the right moment? His heart throbbed, blood resounded in his head, the sound palpitated in his eyes, and, above, a great rent came in the sky, burning his eyes to water which flowed down over his body, and with a speed that almost took breath he felt himself leap into the light with singing, his mouth opened wide, filled with such speed that he could not hold the music throbbing nor hear the beauty and wanted to shout it out shout *shout* reaching over the wall for his hands his body his mouth ears eyes to touch it

screaming

"O GodGodGod, help him." Mattie was holding him as gently

perhaps as she could, but *down. Why are you holding me down?*

screaming at her

and sank sank into black dark, gone the wall.

Sara's hand barely touched his forehead with a comforting damp cloth.

"No fever. Dr. Waters is delighted at that. Mattie's made some of the best whipped spinach, soft as down. You always love Mattie's specials."

Such a pretty yellow dress, trimmed with white, white beads, tiny earrings white too. Her skin had color, not much makeup, green eyes glittering with life. He could see how something moved in her skin, making warm. Her hair was so thick and springy, clean. All clean smells she was, coming into his nose, down. He could not stop looking at her skin, fine hairs, pores, even drawing her arm up and staring.

"What, dear?"

"The mirror. Why'd you take the mirror?" The top of the bureau had been removed.

"We did it for the light—much too bright when the sun comes up, and with the shades down the lights reflect much too sharply from the other room."

"Bring one."

"Bring?"

"Mirror!"

She brought from her upstairs dresser her mother's old hand mirror.

"There! Let me tidy you up for—" Her voice was chipped at the edges.

"No. Give me." But *she* held it: he leaped to himself abruptly, halting his words: he stared like their shocked cat when it met its first mirror. *Who? I do not know the mouth eyes nose hair, nothing, the skin hanging, bones. Mine?*

He looked up at her eyes he did not recognize now with the apprehension in them.

He laughed. She was so startled that the mirror slid sideways, taking him. He supported it back.

"Time for your—"

"No," he said. She would not take the glass, not yet: he wanted to be sure. *It's the not me of me.* He said it to her: "It's the *not* me of me."

"You're all you, darling. You know better."

He felt he glared, but she was smiling. Did nothing happen to his face? Where *did* it happen then? He stared at his image: yes, the eyes. *My eyes. To watch with—but to look where? But the rest of me? I do not know him.* When he closed them, when far off nib-blings of pain began to drive up into him, toward his heart head, he saw fast vibrations of light calling; sometimes the note made an almost voice he strained to hear.

The mirror was gone. She too. The room rock-hard stood: the tall bedposts he'd knocked against in the dark so many times; the bureau with gleams of brush and pincushion bottles stoppers; pictures (her mother, his); the gold frames and the one Van Gogh sun he sometimes thought (you fool you!) was the other sun he went into mornings, remembering it was night; and the window frame, ghostly curtains wisping beckoning; and sea sun Shelter Island and all air space blue gray black rain; glass glinting sometimes to hurt his sight.

Into his eyes came Dudley Wells, his little nephew, Sis with her husband, Jim Wells, Uncle Henry, Silas—*What were they all . . . ?*—and "Just stopped in to see you, nearly the whole family—*surprise*! Aren't you delighted?"—filling his eyes; and Silas took his hand, said, "We'd not have missed you for the world. Your aunt's not well—always troubled with that sick stomach. You'd swear she's pregnant—at fifty-eight!" laughing, all the others laughing, and Sara raising him up, cranking the bed so that the room became another, new the angles, and his eyes explored, forgetting, and then struck their faces in the doorway, all of them, their voices too near to be theirs, shrieking inside him so loud they echoed in his head. "It's hard to keep your voices with your faces," he murmured. They talked smiled laughed at that. Humoring, yes they were.

But under, he knew, they felt pity, though to him—he could see it, hear, feel—over them lay pity; and when Sara sank him back carefully and all his body ached with the motion and he cried a sudden pain, he threw over all their faces confusion, and he felt for them, he sent his hand out to them, pitied them for pitying him, for needing to, having to, life making you pity, poor people.

But his hand, his pain, scared them. They withdrew with awkward discretion, humbled. In the kitchen—he heard their voices scraping him loudly—they returned to forgetting, to *now*, life, this, eating—Sara's banquet for all of them, because they came far: *to see me, they came far.*

In the afternoon they returned the quiet to him. The car drove toward tomorrow. The sound took itself, and them. They left him to never.

He smelled dark coming out of his flesh. In that dark the dark wall rose, ridged faintly with a brightening. He slipped down the darkness, toward. And entered the bay easeful as a fish in a glide. He shot ahead in spasms as if through a hand squeezed over viscid scales. He reached the base. The wall was up. A giddy joy scintillated his whole frame, impelling. He heaved arms at masses of drift, thrusting himself up, knowing the wall would sink down past him and he at last leap into vision: "It will be the meaning of all suffering to have acquired the ultimate justice, eternal, through that very suffering: breeder of knowledge, pathway to light, revealer of wisdom. No one more dearly demonstrates, in delineating the finely wrought levels of Hell, the necessity of suffering in accordance with choice as its consequent revelation than Dante in *The Divine Comedy*. But it is the human mind, reason—as Dante by his own self-examination in the Dark Wood shows—which, calling on all its powers in the midst of apparent sin and suffering, can avoid that direct Hell now as well as then, by willing into the depths of the senses, absolute lust, and out of the destructive vacuum, the pit, let that knowledge of destruction be the illumination. Such men of double awareness as Dante are rare. But—like the poet who can become the initiate into the highest wisdom—Dante penetrates through the darkness light. There are those who may know and reveal." In his lectures he did not say *I am one*. His very premise written into this book bespoke that he had chosen—been chosen for—the path: *I will go the way and I will reveal because I will know*. When suffering came, he would not deny; he would purge through experience and utter, if possible, for Sara or whomever to reveal that what he had written from intuition now *was* so, the fact of his suffering and revelation would prove it. He knew. He would let them know what he found. To this end the sufferer had not only to accept his pain, but to direct it, watch, and reveal where it led.

He had expected the end at the biblical three score and ten, not at thirty-five.

Swifter than light, his mind swam through infinite air.

But—it could not *be*!—the wall rose.

His arms strived, his; he tried to double his pace, but his muscles began to ache; he was sweating fire, burning with it; multiplied aches shot into all his limbs; his eyes shuttered dark; and glimmers of light, an outward palpitation, drove inward through his lids so that his heart swelled, thrust against his ribs, cutting breath— He cried out; the sound rent his own ears, drove back into his body; even his skin burned with the sound; he could not bear it.

He surfaced in sweat and white glare burning. "Nnnnnnnnn-nnnn," he moaned. The room settled around him.

"Sara!" Straining to rise, he farted. He smelled the inside of himself coming over. His hand was streaked with come. He had wanted her to hold it. On his chest, close to his eyes, each hair loomed into bay and sky over the window.

Instantly Sara materialized.

"Where were you?" he said.

Didn't she hear? She kissed his forehead then. She sat, patting with a towel his face, neck, chest. "There. Dr. Waters is coming in a little while." Now she had no makeup on. Sorrow, making age, ate forward. Wrecked, he saw, she slumped, trying, holding up. *Do not scream, do not,* every line, the darkness in her face, urged.

He saw his narrow huddle under the sheets, angles he had not known before. *Bones. Mine.* She was so careful in lifting him. Each wincing made her eyes dart fearfully. *All bones. Fearing to break.* The rag chafed his legs loudly. He wanted to protest. Breath thundered in his head. His eyes rose to her. "Can't reach," he said. "Must." For the light over the wall paled even the bright sun on the bay. Sara had no idea. He must tell her: *If you let me, I can reach it. When the pain comes, it drives me so close— Help me.* His eyes filled—she rose and drifted high off, but when he blinked she settled in her chair beside him.

His mouth groped, empty of words. She dampened his lips. ". . . sssss" came. Wanted to tell: *Listen, Sara, the body is the way or why given the senses?/Justice the duration of the soul through the battered flesh, without which no salvation/I know/Didn't Dante, both the man and the character, descend and experience such sympathy that his body could not endure, he fainted out of it—because of it—into vision, led by Virgil, Beatrice, St. Bernard, as he leads me/I'll find out, Sara, and show you the way, but do not cut off my suffering/My grandfather said Pride goeth before a fall, but pride is the way too, a man must be proud he is a man and bears all/He is entitled to justice if he is worthy/All my life I have prepared for this mission, I must know, and you wouldn't take it away from me, you and Dr. Waters and medicine? Why won't you let me have what's mine? I have almost touched/You bring me back/Don't destroy me, Sara, listen to me, listen—*

He rose. His elbows thrust him up, the room turvied, Sara came down.

"Oh, Ron. What are you *doing*? Careful, darling!"

Her arm came under. His head her breast struck, settled. She was murmuring, her breath not her words crying; a drone through her flesh filled his ear; the bay pierced his eyes, but no pain pierced. All calm in the room fell over him blue as sky, the wind waved, Shelter Island entered. Trees struck by light stood in the doorway. *Ahhhhh, Dr. Waters. Reverend Burnside.* A forest behind. Who? The doctor wanted to take him from her. "No, no. He's comfortable. Aren't you, Ron?" His mouth locked. Her chest, vibrating, thundered in his ear. "You see?" she said. Dr. Waters filled his eyes, divorcing the room. Reverend Burnside was saying words, but his own mouth was speaking to Sara against him. Were words mere sympathy entering her flesh? She didn't hear.

She held him. The doctor let the room fall back, the light blazed into him: he closed his eyes. "Oh, no," Sara murmured. He opened them. He heard her lungs catch. And he felt a lurch in him, but no move came over him. He cocked his head, but only his eyes cocked: they caught the three of them. He confronted them: *I am dying, you took my pain, I feel nothing. I'm waiting. I want to tell you what it is.*

Somebody, one, said, "He's going."

A cry broke from Sara. She clutched. And he cried, *Nooooo, not going until I know, my pain you give me, my hell; no man lives without hell, all life hell to make him know* and he actually rose, his body lifted from her breast, it tilted, throwing his gaze up at them *Where, where my suffering? Why did you take my salvation from me?* and fell back. The doctor's hand picked his up, Sara whispered wordless whispers, and he saw the light, the bay, sky move away a quick distance and the room darken and his blood cried *No*, a quick terrible dark dawn in his head, blinking, *No*, and tried again to thrust up, a little gasp came, nothing more, no movement, and the trees grew dark standing there, light flickered, he was sinking, a fall, *No*, and one was saying words he knew, church surrounded him, open earth and flowers, dark suits and crying, and he fell far from the window, his hand rose to grapple for the sill, and with an abruptness that startled the room blazed so hard and close and clear that each object pained with itself, light so filled his head that no darkness was, knowledge like an object struck down the others, light sending swift as a voice through his mind, bearing the hollow, terrible in emptiness: *never to know*. It came with such awful revelation that his chest throttled with words, his hands gripped at Sara to tell her *This, my punishment, the worst suffering—*

not to know, and agony worse than any flagellation besieged him, for he wanted to tell her.

He opened his mouth.

He began to fall. Long arms flailed out to latch her. His mouth opened to tell. *Never to know,* he said. *Agony.* And the terror of that realization was so overpowering that the realization itself pervaded him like joy. But *not able to tell her?* He opened his mouth. The doctor was bent over. He looked at the doctor and Sara and Reverend Burnside. Not to know. Is a man such a paltry thing as that? *Am I such a paltry thing?*

". . . m . I . . . sh . . . ing?" his mouth said.

Listen, Sara! He summoned up all his voice. He hurled it up the blackening hole toward the light where her face was as he fell. *Never to know.*

The hole sucked his words down like a sink.

Had

THAT ROOM was large, filled with sun, with many people sitting, monuments of stillness, a few in a walking drift, one man weaving with some speed among the isolates, intent.

"You wouldn't believe anything could sit so still," Had said. Through the pane, over Rolfe's shoulders, he saw the male attendant set a hand on a woman's shoulder.

"There's Hannah," Rolfe said with hollow joy. The woman's head looked factually across the room and he stood up and followed.

"I've been all my life on the water," Had said. On the *Annie B* you could always hear sea. It never stopped. Here, feet whispered over linoleum, then silenced. The sun on the waxed floors was so still. You missed waves moving forever under you.

The door opened—rancid air poured out—and Hannah stood there an instant before the attendant gently edged her forward. "Your brother's here to see you, Hannah." He said to Rolfe, "You can have her an hour or so," and went into the sun.

Hannah's smile was not for her brother, but for Had. Her hand went out.

"Pleased to meet you," she said.

He was fifty and a bachelor and her neighbor all his life.

Blunted, he said, "Hannah," but took her hand. Strangely, he could not find her. Her dress was straight and gray like her hair, and her face now.

"Yes." She turned to Rolfe, who said, "Sis—" but her gaze had already sidled into air, off right. "Aunt Marilda nearly finished the quilt but she had two missing patches, red ones, to balance the two red on the left, and didn't know what she'd do till my cousin Ted said he'd get her two—and came up with them almost then and there! But a second later Mandy tore into the room screaming 'Ted cut those squares right out of *my* quilt!' and headed right for Ted with her scissors. Marilda's fit to be tied. Just look at her!" Her shoulders turned, the arm lunged but struck the pane to the room beyond, and she cried out.

Rolfe quickly cupped the hand and held it paternally. "Now look what you've done, but it's fine." Her eyes widened, and she set her head against his. "Come on, now," he said. "We'll take a walk. You won't believe it's so green out."

The tap on the glass had stirred a man and woman sitting with their backs to them. They turned almost in unison. The four eyes caught Had's hand, which had instinctively touched the spot Hannah had struck. Between his fingers, shielding, he stared back at them.

"Had?" Rolfe said. He and Hannah were moving down the blinding corridor.

"You go on. Have a good talk. You'll enjoy that. I'll be waiting in there—" His hand told *Reception*, but his face went closer to the sliding window. Inside, the man, his curiosity perhaps satisfied, righted his head in frozen stillness; the woman initiated the same action, but halfway her head halted, cocked wide an immobile expression, and fixed her eyes hard in Had's direction. She rose but stood there, staring at the space from which an instant before he had displaced himself. What was she seeing?

For a long time he watched her until he felt ashamed. "A private thing," he muttered. Yet he couldn't draw himself away.

She was about forty, too thin but with a breast fullness and a vague roundness of hips thrust forward, impressing a slightly balled stomach into cloth short enough to show her knees—they looked somehow young. Thinness widened her cheekbones and jaw; dark straight hair, cut clean a little below the ears, narrowed the face somewhat. Now even her hair hung motionless. How could she stand so quiet and still be alive? Yet she seemed moving. He could not fathom that: moving but still. Then he saw it was her throat—cords and muscles were going tautly. They held his eyes. Strange: What was happening? Suddenly her throat seemed still and the floor moved like a sea under him.

Then she took a step toward the glass, mechanically, and stopped. She gazed where he'd been standing, her pupils making not the vaguest motion, then went closer. Her right hand rose, touched the pane, and rested there; then very slowly her fingers traced a pattern, traced, kept tracing. Fascinated, he followed the fingers. This close he saw her clear skin, strangely unlined eyes, lips smooth but not young—a face suspended in tired innocence from life, left waiting. All her energy lay locked in the dark focused eyes and in the unbroken ritual of the fingers. They made a soft chant against the glass.

The fingers went on for a long time. They were making a face.

Was it on the pane or behind? He was tense, all his muscles pulled. He wanted to move into her vision. Suppose he did stand directly behind and set his face under her fingers?

He made the move.

Nothing happened. But he was right: her fingers outlined his head. Yet her eyes saw beyond, indifferent to his face. He wanted to be certain. He swayed his head. Her gaze did not follow. He couldn't believe he wasn't there.

Again he froze, following the undeviating pattern of the fingertips, the rigid prison of pupils. This time he couldn't tell how long it went on—ten, twenty, thirty minutes? But his eyes burned, dry from not blinking; his vision faltered; he swayed, charging his muscles with a network of fine pain. He had so long looked into her that he was afraid to stir, yet—*did* she see through him?

He stepped abruptly aside.

Again nothing happened.

"I wasn't even there," he said aloud, feeling forlorn—but why?

Then, as abruptly as his own motion, her hand halted; it hung inert and silent against the pane. He waited. He was about to withdraw when, as if sensing, her hand jerked away with a speed that arrested him. Both her hands hunched up against her breasts, loose as paws; but her gaze still riveted beyond. The spasms came back into her thin neck, subtle under the skin. Long she stood like that; and he stood, dependent on her, long. He began to tremble with a far-off sound he could scarcely hear; it grew; it shivered him to his bones before he realized the sound was coming muted through that glass, a cry from her barely parted mouth, "Nnnnnn-nnnnnnnnnnnnnnnnnnnnnnn," such pure agony that it hurt him.

"Nnnnnnnnnnnnnnnnnnnnnnn," she wailed.

Jesus!

His own mouth opened to let her pain out.

He was sweating.

"I'm afraid," he said. He had never said *I'm afraid* before. Afraid of what? That woman made him afraid. He would not forgive her for making him afraid. In the throes of his shame, she came at the window. She pressed close to the spot she'd never taken her eyes from. Her hands cupped around the place. By then other sounds penetrated—doors, footsteps, squishing. Dark, from blazing sun, came two figures; the door opened; quickly her sound burst full pure agony into the corridor. He jerked, closed his mouth, startled that the sound was really in that other room. The door closed. Fast they seized the woman, whose arms winged out, reached at the glass, clutched air. She stiffened, so they raised her between them from the elbows and carried her, rigid, out of sight. The cry died.

His throat ached. He couldn't believe she was gone. But—close—not a sign of her. "What happened?" Only rank air lingered. He held his breath. He didn't want to breathe her; but it was all that was left—it made her real. Where had they taken her? He strained his eyes left: they must have gone through the far door into forbidden regions. Despite the figures sitting or milling about, the room had an emptiness. Yet he felt: carted off like that, she might reappear anywhere in the building. He tried to blink it all away, but when he turned, two figures approached, black against the burning afternoon. He went cold. No, *not*—

"Had?"

Rolfe and Hannah!

"God, Rolfe, you gave me the willies." He laughed loud. Clean pleasure flooded up.

"Hannah and me had a good talk," Rolfe said. Hannah stood like the other—straight, arms hung, as tall, as thin, the face washed colorless, but the eyes a silent channel—except that Hannah was smiling. "Pleased to meet you," she said. Her hand touched out, bringing a brief shock of cold. She kept smiling, but her eyes were dead.

"I'm very glad to see you, Hannah," he said. Where was she?

"Had pulled you out of the old Boys' Hole 'cause you couldn't swim. A good thing, too, or you wouldn't be here now," Rolfe said. "We owe him a lot."

She was still smiling when an attendant led her back to the ward. Had watched the thin angled bones under her dress. He'd known Hannah all his life, but was Hannah just a thing in his head all the years? Who'd Rolfe think he was visiting every week? Maybe it was just his old self Rolfe was going back to see.

Outside, fresh air came in a welcome assault, but intensified the odor he carried in him. *She* was in that odor. "Smelled like a—," he said aloud, with instant pain and guilt. Rolfe said, "What, Had?" "Nothing," he said, but bars, peanuts, came to mind.

In the parking lot the late sun glinted over car tops like white-caps but all too still. He wanted the wind and roll, the deck's sway that his legs met with a balance, not the hard world under his feet.

Beyond the hospital, sun fell through the trees, darkening them, reddening the sky. They drove away, east, where the dark had already begun to rise over the land.

"I sure would like to take her home," Rolfe said.

"Who?"

"*Han*nah."

"Home?"

"To Laura and the kids. But they'd not want her."

"Not want Hannah?"

"What's with you, Had?"

Ahead, trees thick with leaves settled deeper and deeper into the dark ground.

ii.

The *Annie B* was dredging when the squall came up.

"Had, hold the winch fast!" Bojarski shouted. Behind the mate, the darking sky was coming fast, a quick wind driving rain. The *Annie B* rolled, heavy with the skimmer haul. Had signaled okay.

"She'll pass in no time," Farley cried from the rail. Mick and Jeffers were watching for the dredges to come up. Farley closed his eyes, thrust his face up, and opened his mouth to catch the rain good. Had laughed.

"The hold's close to full. With luck we'll be back in Greenport tonight," young Mick said. That meant two or three days at Helen's Place, guzzling, blowing his share of the catch.

"You line old Had up with something. He needs a little," Bojarski bellowed, standing waist-deep in the hole. He raked the skimmers, clearing for the final drop from the dredges.

They had been out eight days now; a full hold and the prospect of booze and women tonight roused their spirits.

"What you do in that shack of yours?" Mick said.

"I got me some secrets," Had kidded. They knew he didn't drink. He was not much good on land; he liked sleeping in the ship even in port.

"Well, you're sure keeping them to yourself," Mick said. The crew, all younger, went on that way all the time; he liked the banter. He'd been the senior long years, and sometimes he thought he did not know anything but sea and men. Far in him, though, was his sister—single, dead at thirty, ten years now—and his mother, dead years since. His father he almost had not known. The old man had always been "out there" in the sea he had drowned in; but at strange moments Had felt the old man near him, as if he breathed his father in the sea air or touched him in the water or in the skimmers. Strange: he was the father—to Loretta; and when he had not been his mother's support and companion he couldn't remember. Yet the thought of his mother and sister irritated like cankers on the tongue—he couldn't explain it. They had been intervals between sailings—warm rooms, beef stew, clean smells, sheets. He had thought his return was the joy that filled an emptiness in their lives. Always he went to sea expectant, he returned expectant. But life was the time between. And the boys—why did they race ashore and race back so?

"Had—let's get with it!" Jeffers shouted, laughing. "Jees—he's back in town already. Look at him, fellas!"

Had kept the winch going. The creak and scrape came clear, the wires pulled taut, the ship shifted subtly under the weight. The dredges were surfacing. At the rail Mick watched for them to hit. Jeffers, ready to hook the chain net, stood legs astraddle. Bojarski leaped up out of the hole.

Far were edges of thin light. But deep into the horizon Had was seeing the house his mother had left to his aunt Addie. Well, if that's what his mother had wanted . . . But why had she done that? She had given away his place to go. "Addie's old, you're young," she'd always said. After she died, he would stand in its darkness waiting for some sound, waiting for something. Now when they docked he would go to his room at Bella's and close the door and sit in darkness and look out at the night sky.

The ship lurched, the dredges ceased pulling against water and hit air: the great nets rose, loaded with skimmers; water dripped black with silt, the shells gleaming wet. Warm, cleaning rain in a fast downpour sleeked everything a muted shine. The winch whined, the strained wires creaked as the load halted over the water, swung out and back, tugging at the ship. The three moved up to guide the drop into the hold.

"Watch it!" Bojarski called.

Mick grabbed at one net as it swung away from the side.

"Goddamn it, watch out, Mick!" Bojarski shouted.

But Mick's grip broke. His left arm caught the edge, he hung from it dangling between the side and the dredge.

"Had!" Bojarski leaped forward, Jeffers closed in from one side, Farley from the other. By then the great weight of skimmers had swung back, crushing Mick against the ship. One arm shot up. In that interval Had released the winch, Jeffers grabbed Mick's arm, Farley drew the body up as chains and skimmers fell away in a momentous splash that bucked the ship aside, it rolled into the waves and rose, Farley and Jeffers lost footing, slipping over the deck with Mick's body and then holding fast.

"Don't move him yet!" Had cried. He kneeled beside the boy. "Thank God, he's breathing!" Mick's chest moved: he was crushed, a great stream of blood gushed from his mouth and nose, rained back into his eyes and hair and ears, neck. His throat choked. Now they were afraid to move him—it was on all their faces.

"Jesus, he'll choke on his own blood," Farley said.

From the pilothouse the Captain streaked across the deck. "Turn him over and take him to the bunks," he said.

"But his bones—," Jeffers said.

"The bunks?" Farley said. They looked at each other, but they moved.

"On the floor," Had said.

They kept Mick face down till the blood lessened, then turned him over. Had cleaned his face. Mick's breath came in hard rasps. In the midst of it the engines whined, caught, and putted. "We're heading straight in," Bojarski called down. The room was hot, humid, terribly close. Had felt the others hovering too close. "Get out, can't you!" he muttered. He stared at the boy. He felt each rasp tearing inside him; he wanted to breathe for him. *Live,* he wanted to shout, *live.* "Mick?" he said. But the boy made only hard faltering scrapes. Had shivered. He wanted to touch the boy—help. But how? If he dared lift even an arm . . . No telling how many bones were broken. "Mick?" he whispered fiercely to the crushed face. "I did it, Mick. I'm responsible," he said. The boy groaned deep. "It's my fault. I didn't let the winch go soon enough. I should've known. *I* did it, Mick." He could feel Mick trying to breathe. Now the head tried to move, but something was wrong —Mick couldn't move it; then the fingers made weak efforts, but nothing happened. "Mick?" Had said. The breathing fluttered, came to silence as if it had stopped, then burst into a low agonizing groan which faltered, shifting pitch, and became a deep wail.

Then Mick opened his eyes. He looked straight into his. They did not flutter or shift or blink. They stunned Had; he could not move. Mick's face struggled in pain. The cry reached a thin high pitch and stopped. The chest jerked. Kkkkkkkkkkkkkkkk throttled in his chest, and his head twitched. Then Mick was still.

The painful grimace remained there. The eyes did not close.

Had was trembling. He was sweating.

"Me." He stood up. "My fault." He was talking to somebody who wasn't there.

He felt a hand on his shoulder: Bojarski's. Where did he come from? He wanted to tell Bojarski, No, it was not the dying, it was Mick's eyes . . . But he went up on deck. The air assaulted—and the clean rain; but in him was the odor, that stench. No, not— He turned to the rail, looked into the water, up into the dark sky, breathed deep. But the smell was strong, and no matter where he looked the eyes were there.

They were the woman's eyes, hers.

He did not even know her name.

iii.

Had sat by the window in his room. The wind pressed warm at his skin. He listened. He gazed out there. He felt something in the sounds coming through the boards of the house, something from the ground they had all gone into—his mother, father, Loretta and aunt Addie, Mick. He had seen them all under; but he was still here, and he felt a familiar thing was trying to get into the room.

He went out onto the porch. The air was a strange golden, it stung his nose, quickly yellow down clung to his navy shirt and jeans, the blow through the new spring leaves brought whispers from a far distance. He harkened—not the sea this time, not waves, but a sound beyond them. He stood stark still, straining. His fingers tingled with a sound, it grew closer and closer, louder, till it filled everything, throbbing—he wanted to touch the sound, a cry in the trees, eyes; and the first thing he knew, his hands were in the air, reaching— Then the sound stopped; it was still, too still, like a breath before speaking, and he heard nothing, only *himself* throbbing: and then the rustle, wind, voices down the street, cars . . . He was back.

For days he had sat in his dark room, waiting for a call that had been coming fifty whole years, maybe more, from a place he didn't know. If he missed it, then what? Did you just go into the ground? The thought stunned him. He had a terrible fear of missing it. He wanted to run.

He went down off the porch. "Had?" Bella called from inside, but he kept going.

He headed straight to Rolfe Humphries'. It was a mile from the village. He walked fast. He did not think of anything else. His eyes he kept intent, directly ahead, yet he was shocked when he arrived at his old house, next door to Rolfe's—for he had seen each house, unobserved all the years; had seen fences, flowers, birdbaths, shrubs, mats, everything. His own house—only last month it hadn't bothered him—jarred now: gone to seed, unstained, fallen shingles, peeled trim, spring rioting in the yard. The Ranhams, renters for years, had left it in bad shape. The FOR RENT sign was stuck behind a broken window.

"Rolfe," he said, "I need to borrow your car, bad."

He was not surprised when Rolfe studied him. "Had, you're not looking so good."

"I got a thing to do. I'll be okay. What say?"

They'd been near brothers all their lives. To avoid speech, he turned and glanced over the fence: in warm weather his mother was always in the garden, turning back tomato leaves for worms. Within, Loretta would whisk past a window, cleaning. Were they *in* things? But morning sun poured into emptiness. The house had a space through.

"Here you go!" Rolfe handed him the keys. He didn't even ask, Where you going? How long?

"It means a lot." *Everything*. He was almost afraid to look up at things, the sky. There was still a humming.

"I'll see you when you get here," Rolfe said.

sound did catch in his throat. Rapidly his hand took hers; and though she didn't react, he led her toward the sun parlor. Nobody was in it. "Berenice?" She watched. "Come. Sit down." He sat. Cautiously she sank into the armchair facing him. It must have felt good—her hands glided lightly over the arms, and she half smiled. Morning sun struck her teeth very white and ribbed her lips a pale pink, and light seemed to pour from her. He saw himself dark in her eyes and realized she couldn't see his face for the sun, so shifted his chair. Her hands went right to his face, almost touching, tracing his head, his eyes, nose, mouth. He froze, feeling warmth from her hands. "Berenice?" he whispered softly. Her hands stayed the least second, then repeated the gestures. He was nervous. "Berenice?" Then he pressed his face right against her hands, gasping at her touch. "Ahhhhhhhnnnnnnnnnnnnn," she moaned, her lids flicking swiftly, her mouth crooked. Then he clasped her hands, but she held back, rigid, and he clutched fiercely when her head turned to the side, though her look cocked warily. Fearing she'd break free, he said, "Berenice, *lis*ten. It's me. I came with Rolfe—to see Hannah. You know Hannah, don't you? And you saw me behind the glass. You remember, don't you? I never *saw* anybody before. You got in my head, and I couldn't get you out. On the *Annie B*—that's my ship—I kept getting a feeling something's with me, only couldn't think *what*. Nothing was the same, I couldn't figure it: was like the sky's pressing down and I couldn't breathe—and all the time it's you in my head only I didn't know it till Mick got it—" Her pupils moved. Mick! And he pressed close, he talked right into her eyes. "It was my fault. I didn't let the winch go, I killed him or he'd be here now, I had to watch him die and couldn't do a thing. He was trying to tell me something, I swear he was! And when he was gone, his eyes kept looking at me. And they followed me on deck, they came right through the sky—I couldn't stand it, but I *wanted* them too—I don't know—*wanted* . . . Then it was like suffocating: her, her, her, I said. *She's* blaming me. I have to find her and tell her *I* killed Mick."

He sank down on his knees, clutching her knees.

"I had to tell somebody. I knew you'd understand. You're the only person in the world'd understand."

He dropped his head into her lap.

"You were close. I could feel you. Mick moaned and I heard your mouth, it was you. I was right here beside you—I'll do for you, Berenice, I've got to do for somebody, I'll make it up, I'll never forget Mick all my life, I won't—" The words came in a tremble, he shuddered and heaved, his chest ached. He wanted to cry. He couldn't go on—because he felt her quivering, her hands touched his head gently with soft warmth, and she raised his head and looked down into his face. There were tears in her eyes.

"Person," she said. "Person."

iv.

He did not leave for three days. Every minute possible he spent with her. At the motel her presence kept him awake; he saw her in the dark. He could not wait for day.

He was sure she knew him: change had come into her, a musing gaze and nostalgic smile as at memories not quite materialized, and she liked resting her hands on his cheeks—she would hold them and look long. What did she see?

He talked long monologues on end, he who had never talked, who had spent a lifetime listening and watching. And he was still watching—every flicker of her.

"Berenice, you know Greenport? I was born there—we all were, Ma and Pa and theirs and theirs too. Swamp yankees we are." He made a gleeful chortle. "You know what *they* are? That means roots there, from the beginning of this country. My aunt Addie was mad for family—I got papers. But it's the sea got me. You never see it? *Sure* you have, but not *my* sea. I'll take you in a rowboat to Pete Neck—first, to make it easy; maybe even teach you to row—think you'll like that?—and crab. We'll catch our own and eat them, save money that way. We'll be needing every cent we can get our hands on. I only got a little in the bank—and what the skimmer haul is each trip out, I get my part; it's up and down. My mother gave Addie the house; I sure could use it now. A room at Bella's is not much, but I know some places'd maybe come dirt cheap, maybe the old house—"

All the while her brown eyes watched; they didn't go through him like the first day. Thank God for that.

With quick familiarity the nurses jibed:

"He stays away years and now thinks he's a patient himself. Wants a bed here."

"Got me a bed but nothing in it," he jibed right back. All the nurses, repeating it, echoed the little nurse's laughter.

"You wearing our patient down?"

"My own talk's wearing *me* down."

"Where've you been so long?"

"My life's at sea." He heard it out there, big and deep behind them. Whoooosh. Whoooosh.

"You some kind of fisherman?"

He laughed. "You'd say so, I guess. We dredge for skimmers. Know what they are?"

"Lots of things I don't know, Mr. Ames."

"What?" His heart constricted as Berenice's eyes shot up at her. The nurse noticed it too.

"Say, you're doing real good with her," she said.

"What'd you say?"

"I said you're doing real—"

"No. What'd you call—?"

"Person," Berenice said. He turned to her.

"There! *She* knows who you are," the nurse said. "You should've come home a long time ago."

"Didn't—" He dared not say *he*. "Didn't anyone—? Who did come?"

"Poor soul. Who'd she ever see but *their* visitors?" Her sweep encompassed the others, beyond the glass. All the Berenices, waiting.

Quick, he said, "You got her record."

"In there—," the nurse said: down the hall the door said RECORDS. "But being's you're one of us, I'll see what I can do." His body was cold with it. He feigned a laugh. "You're straight from heaven," he said.

"Pearson Ames," he murmured with wonder.

"Person," Berenice said, smiling. For the first time her hand gripped his, almost painfully.

Bluntly the nurse said, "But—you're supposed to be dead."

"I don't feel very dead. You don't think I am, do you?" He laughed, but his heart struck; hard, separate beats rapped at his chest.

"Her sister said so. She committed her. Juanita Lewis—from East Moriches. But now she's dead—over a year. And no other relations, but maybe some in Wise, Virginia—they're from there."

He must remember everything. The floor tremored. A cold

colder than ice crossed his flesh. He looked behind—but out there sun blazed a golden sea.

"Look at her smile," the nurse said. "I'd like to know what she's feeling. Bet she thinks a miracle happened."

Pearson Ames.

Who'd *she* see? He wanted to go inside her—to see out with her eyes. But he could only set himself before her and see his reflection and all the land behind. What did he have to do? He rose.

"Person!" Her nails cut. A look of fright twisted her mouth.

Gently he loosened her fingers, caressed her cheeks. "Shhhhhhhh." He led her with him.

After, all through the interview with the doctor, he held her hand, the blood easeful, sitting before the desk, feeling like two people the whole eternal hour: one watching Berenice's narrow fingers in his, warm with pulsing like the cliff swallows he used to catch in his hand on the Sound bluffs; the other listening, wanting to tell Dr. Brighton the truth. But the doctor kept on talking:

"And not very responsibly you disappeared one day—simply ran off, Mrs. Lewis said. Dead. Or missing. Gone. Like that." The doctor snapped his fingers. Mick. Far. Out the window darking trees netted the afternoon sun. The light throbbed. He glanced down: that hand! He was startled joyously by her responding pressure.

"Her sister couldn't know everything. Nobody does," Had said. "You can't tell what's happening inside a body, can you? Like her —just look at her."

"No denying that. And she certainly takes to you after all this time."

"Why shouldn't she?" He was almost belligerent. *What am I doing?* And Bella's came to mind, and that empty house, and the bunks where no woman belonged. But the warmth pulsed into him—he didn't want to let her hand go—and as the doctor spoke words he yearned to hear, "And she just might talk, though the blockage, whatever actually happened, is the result of the worst shock," he felt he held another chance—at what? He didn't know, but he stood, trying to hold still, but his blood surged so.

"You hear, Berenice? We're going home." He drew her close.

"Person." Her hand fluttered up and settled peacefully on his chest.

"Send in Nurse Rawlins," the doctor said into the intercom.

Berenice had been there so long they'd kept only the envelope with her name—it contained a gold wedding band and a tarnished locket on a chain. He waited till he got outside into the car before he slipped the ring onto her finger. It was getting late, but the late sun glinted on it.

"Got to stop by the motel, pay the bill, Berenice, and pick up the Gillette I had to buy. Ninety-eight cents!"

Free at last, they headed into the darkening east. The dying sun cast thin pinnacles up the pines. He drew air deep in. "Smell that pine, Berenice? You do it. Get some wild roses and honeysuckle." She imitated—again and again, and laughed. "Mmmmmmmm-mmmm," she uttered.

"We'll go to Bella's tonight, and in the morning I'll see if I can get the old place. It sure can do with some fixing, looks like."

They streaked into the dark; the night washed warmly over; town after town, islands of still white fire, came and went.

"We're almost there," he said with a sudden catch of fear. *I'm responsible. She's mine.* He was overwhelmed with a feeling of joy and pain: he saw his mother in the kitchen, Loretta in the window, but the sights made him feel empty. He touched her hand—

it was so cold. And suddenly she started to cry. She lay her head against his shoulder. "It'll be all right, Berenice." Under his hand her own was rubbing her ring. Night light made her tears black as bits of rain. For one instant he closed his eyes: sea came in, the *Annie B.* He felt the rain, Mick was trying to speak— He blinked the sight away. He felt afraid. Suddenly the night seemed endless. He'd never find his way to Greenport—they would go on and on, lost like this, not knowing where they'd end up. But they struck the rise into the outskirts, the road dipped and the town lights glittered through the trees.

"There she is!" He was relieved at the musty cool rush of sea, pungent salt and fish from the flats. She leaned forward, eyes wide.

He drove straight to Rolfe's.

"I'm back, Rolfe." He gave him the car keys. "I sure am obliged to you."

She stared into trees.

"Rolfe, I want you to meet my wife, Berenice. Berenice, this is Rolfe, my friend I told you about."

Then, without a word, he led her down the street.

"You'll get used to walking, the town's not so big, and you'll know it in no time. It sure is warm. Come on. We'll stop by the diner and then go home to Bella's."

v.

He laid out for two weeks, and every once in a while—puttying a window, painting, setting out garbage cans—he would turn with disbelief to assure himself she was no figment—there she was, working with a rhythm and regularity which awed. When she baked without recipes, he said, "Where'd you learn that, hon?" Watching him eat, she'd laugh.

And all his words, years of words, silenced on the *Annie B*, flowed out: "And you know what my pa did?—got so mad 'cause I said, *No school*, he threw the dadblasted hammer at me! That's temper for you!" Day and night he talked, talking even in his head when away from her, storing up what he'd say when he got home.

Except for a few needs, she seldom made a sound. No matter. She was here, though he wondered what was inside her, waiting for him. Besides, he was sure the day would come, and he'd know. But what if he were at sea and didn't hear? Wasn't it *his* ear waiting for her words? Worse—what if she left? The more he thought, the more he feared: suppose he missed it?

And one day, hacking away at the field grass, the wind waving the tassels, he stopped right in the midst of work: a cry stilled the grass an instant, transporting him to that other sea, before he said: "Berenice!"

He ran. Withdrawn against the wall, wide-eyed, she was watching an enormous spider. He killed it. "There," he said. "Aggggggfrrrrr," she uttered, the most she'd ever said.

"Why, you— You!" he said, embracing her. And she touched his sweaty forehead, his damp hot shirt, and clung close. But he was still unnerved by her cry. She drew his hands up and kissed each palm. It drove Mick's eyes away.

"Person."

After his years of solitude, the town was startled at the sight of the two—and pleased, and wondering. He felt them look at him in a new way, and he rose to it: the old salt in him gave way to a new man, quick, energetic, still puzzled a little by his name *Pearson;* but he *felt* the new restless motion, and an increase from her too, without even glancing at her, knowing her presence, the deep brown eyes and half smile close. Yet occasionally at night he woke, startled at another's breathing, with sudden fear at not being alone, someone was in his room, his bed, inside him—and then with a rush he recognized her regular, trusting sound. Yet that sound was not enough: he put on the light to look close at her: the slack skin, the pores large here and there, fine tiny dark hairs in her nose, and thin red webs under her skin, faint pin-points of oil, hundreds of lines in the pale lips, the corners damp; and he breathed in the natural odor of breath and skin. His fingers slid over her dark clean hair, ran along the hairline, traced the nose, chin, lips—until she opened her eyes, at first with a brief void, a distance she couldn't cross till her eyes met his face and settled cautiously on it. Where was she traveling from? In those brief instants he wanted to go *there*, to her. "Berenice, why don't you take me with you?" But he was glad she was back; he crooked her into his arm. Yet when she said, "Person," he felt closed out in the very moment he was drawn in. This Pearson Ames, what *was* he? Maybe *he* was Pearson Ames all that time, waiting for her. When he turned out the light, she went back into dark distances, the same dark he saw in Mick's eyes, descending around him. Lying there, he hit on his plan: he would go where she was. When the time came, the *Annie B* would be the way. He would surprise her.

Now each trip out on the *Annie B* he grew restless. The boys kidded: "Suh-matter—nothing to grab ahold of, Had?" "You horny old bastard." "Wish I had me some steady stuff." And now the familiar bunks were mangy, the walls smeared, the sweat and dirty feet and rotting shellfish stank. Years he and the boys had gone out together on the ship, but suddenly they were not boys. It startled. He had never reckoned it before. And they were alone, even off the ship, and dirty and smelling and not caring. And where did they go? To Helen's Place, to beer and any loose woman, the bright sun around drawn shades the morning after, the world throbbing with a big head—and then the *Annie B* again, skimmers; then a repeat— How many times in life? He felt sorry for them. Is that how his mother and Loretta had really considered him, Hadley Wilson, all those years—not able, or too kind or hurt, to say a word? He felt sorry for them too; and thinking of them, he saw Berenice alone in that house.

She was sitting at Preston's dock when the *Annie B* got in.

"She's sure faithful," Zac the clothier said. Her constancy struck pride in Had.

Zac's wife said, "She sits there all day." But the tone appalled—the first time anyone had used it: *poor thing* was in her voice.

"All day?" Had puzzled.

"Comes mornings and don't leave till dark. She hangs there like one of them gulls. I don't know what she eats."

Had felt his heart pound; tears nearly blurred his vision.

He took Berenice's arm and scooted her off.

"Berenice, that true? You come and sit all day that way? What for? Honey, you can't do that." He was trembling. A quick passage like nausea went through him. "You've got to stay home, hon, and wait for me there." The image of her sitting on the dock hurt and shamed. But in a minute her hands touched his face; she laughed, slipping her arms around him and clutching him joyously close. "Person," she said. "Person." He felt maybe he had been Pearson Ames all his life, waiting for her. And he could not say another word. He kissed her. "You! You! How'd I ever live before?"

She came to be a familiar sight at the dock. The town pitied her. Their pity made him indignant, and when he dared scold her, his tone, not his words, brought tears. The reprimands catapulted her, sitting right beside him, into distances. He might as well have been back on the ship.

Yet each time he did go back, the thought of her at Preston's gnawed at him; he wanted to protect her from *them*. But other thoughts ate at him as well. Suppose, in desperation, she took it into her head to look for him elsewhere? And always he imagined she might make some utterance—at sea he'd miss her words.

Summer passed, the flowers fell away, October came, leaving only mums and the late September red roses stark in the browning yard. By then his hair, always light despite the graying, was sun-bleached and long, a hard glow against his weathered skin. He was spry with a restless energy. Work on the house kept him moving. "See what you do to me, Berenice?" And on ship he'd say, "You try it, boys." "She sure done you good, Had," Jeffers said, amazed, "slimmed you down some." "*Lean* we used to say." Had felt a self-satisfaction—doubled at this moment—for he knew his chance had come: off the Virginia coast, an engine conked out; they were headed into Norfolk. His nerves quickened. The coast came—remotely familiar territory— though he had never been beyond the city. Far back, weeks, he knew he was going. He had planned on this trip when the time came: he was going inland.

Both engines had to be overhauled before they could leave. Repairing would take three days, maybe a week. He told no one his mind. He had never left the ship before; but he might never be so close again. Once he'd never have suspected he'd go that far: if he should miss the *Annie B*, he'd take the train back. But what would she do if the boat came in and he wasn't on it? Still, he was fixed: back of his mind was the town—Wise, Virginia; the instant the Captain said Norfolk, he heard the nurse, "An old sister from Wise, Virginia. That's where she grew up."

The only way to Wise was bus. He settled back to watch the gleaming city drift into dark, but the rhythm soon lulled him to half-sleep. Through vague lids he saw the man next to him, the disembodied face with wet eyes.

"Where you going?" the man said.

"Wise, Virginia."

"Wise! That's my hometown."

"You going back?"

"Been *years* trying to get back. But I'm always falling on bad times."

"I had a stroke of luck. Ship's engines went—out of Norfolk. I've prayed to get to Wise."

"Think you will?" The grimace caught him off guard. Was the man laughing at him?

"*Yes* I will! Got to. Everything depends on it."

"You're looking for somebody?"

"How'd you know that?"

"You won't find him."

"How'd you know it's *him?*"

"A man with a woman problem's got a look about him. You have. But you won't find him there."

"How come you're so *sure?*" Irate, he said, "He *lived* there. So'd Berenice. Somebody'll know them. It's not been that long."

"Don't say I didn't warn you—" The man laughed.

"Well, you're so smart—where then, *where?*"

"Nobody can tell you that," the man said with a forlorn note that suspended Had's anger a second and goaded his curiosity. "Nobody but me," he added in quick recovery.

"*You!* What right've you got? Who do you think you are?"

"Pearson Ames," the man said, turning full face on him.

"Pear—!" Had's voice died, half terror, half joy at the revelation. "You!" Several brittle short laughs broke from him.

When he leaned forward, he met frantic dark eyes gleaming wetly; the night was in them; he was falling into dark and he reached up for the face. "Mick!" he gasped as his hands struck the cold face.

His eyes opened. He was in strange country. It was bright morning. The light smarted. Blur fell over his eyes. A mountain came up ahead. The road was dark between high walls sunstruck far up. Gradually light came down, spread over the valley walls, the road narrowed in treacherous hairpin curves down.

Had was lost. He was used to seeing out—clear and far—on the sea or over the flat Long Island sands, not used to up, being confined between high walls. And behind each wall that sank away loomed another, far, which hung there long. The mountainsides looked blighted—browned meager stubs, holes like eroded mouths, and shrinking frame houses set on piles thin as insect legs, still but for thin black smoke above the tin roofs. Heaps of fallen stone, rusty soil, and blue-black wash fused, smearing the green. Up, the sky was promising blue.

By the time the driver called out "Wise," Had's anxiety had risen so that he turned instinctively to the man—not there, of course—then chuckled, muttering aloud, "You fool, you!" and suddenly was standing in a drift of oil darking the air. He couldn't get used to the ground or the mountains. Here, the earth seemed to have hardened into gigantic stone waves.

At the bend he stopped at a grocery.

"What for you?" The old man squinted with morning. He was dirty and unshaved. The store smelled rancid.

"I'm looking for Pearson Ames."

The man fixed on the floor.

"No Ames I know of in this here town."

"Well, maybe not Ames, then—but married to one. Her name's Berenice."

"Hmmm." The man was really watching a boy sling clumps of dirt across the street. "No Berenice neither—"

"Yeah, they are—" He had not seen the woman behind the counter, a stick of a thing, bone, with a wet mouth. "Least—was. Kin to Laird Riley. Laird been dead a heap of time. Berenice—she got took away—" Her hand made a quick arc. "—yonder."

"Took away?"

"Got her a husband. Ames, you say? I cain't remember. From the Navy—wartime it was then." That startled: a seaman? World War II Navy. Could be, without even knowing it, he'd been near Pearson Ames. "But then she went—don't know why—but her sister come back. *He* run off, they tell it. How come you to forget sich of a thing, Raymond?" Her head cocked expectantly.

"Is the Riley house still standing?"

"Like as not."

"Which way?"

"You want to see it and nobody in it? Now why'd a body do that?" This time the man moved outside to point the way up the road. "They's a broken well."

Had smiled.

"Say—you kin?"

"Not by blood. Much obliged."

The old man flicked his hat genially and disappeared, a moving smear behind the window front.

So Ames was not from Wise, but yonder. Swept off her feet by an outsider, was she? But what *was* Ames? If he could only know—

But *why*? What did he want of Pearson Ames? He had Berenice, didn't he? But no, he didn't—not *yet*, or why'd he *be* here? Still he had never felt so close to discovery. . . .

The house was two miles up the road—no mistake: there was the toppled well wall. It was a shotgun cabin, the supports still straight, but porch and roof sagged, all with the bleached look of dead boards; it sat at the head of a dirt way, rutted and washed away. Up here, a cold wind came down. The stripped trees whistled, boards rattled, but sun struck a desolate warmth over the bare gray. Someone had left a washboard out front, rusted down.

Inside, the two rooms were dark and empty except for some broken glass, loose planks, a makeshift sink, dirty rags and lovers' refuse. Tacked to the wall over the sink, a piece of mirror caught one eye and the half of his face. He looked out each window, then left. Before going down, he stood on the porch. Riley. Berenice Riley Ames. She had sat here, perhaps in this very spot, the sunned boards warming her bottom and falling on her head and shoulders, with this pure air sharp in her, and a sight of the road, infinite distances over layers of treetops into the high horizon. He glanced east, where morning made everything black against the bright sky; then below at the sloping walls, branches and brambles, sharp green along the thin dark rivulet following the gutter. Everything was so sharp and dear. It was strange: he had thought it would be all pain to find Pearson Ames or her relations or this place. When the old man had said the house was empty, his heart gave; but in this desolate house, empty of people, there was life. He listened: the wind made a quiet churning, the water made whispering, the boards shifted, the heat moved over him. He wanted to know it all. He strained to catch everything, fearful he might miss a part of what she had lived. He let her world sink into him. He must remember everything, yes. He had to hold it in him and carry it all back to Berenice.

vi.

They pulled into Greenport at night, but the figure was huddled black there. He leaped onto the dock and dropped the line over the piling.

"Berenice!"

She fell hard against him with choked joy.

"Honey, you're so cold! Don't you know—" But her mouth and hands touching quick cut him off.

"You devil, you! Now you come on—" He led her aboard. "—and sit right there till this work's over with. You know the boys . . ."

He couldn't wait to tell her—but wouldn't let the secret trip out to the boys—so gassed all the way home:

"I got to *Wise*, Berenice. I went all the way, saw every bit. You know where the highway forks and the big generator is? I took a right by the sign says W. B. Peckham on the bend. Right off I saw the well and the rock cliff and there it was—Poppa and Momma Ames' house and sister Juanita's and yours, Berenice honey. Why, I expected *you* to walk out the door then and there," not even stopping when she said, "Mmmmm," and laughed. Encouraged by that enthusiasm, he kept at it: "You remember the grocery? The old folks're sitting behind the dirtiest window! Couldn't but just see SALADA TEA across the front." And Berenice stopped short. ". . . kkkkkkkk," she said, "kkkkkkk."

"Yeah, that's it! MacCready's Grocery. And the mountain's straight ahead, and two sycamores by the well, all pines down the dirt road."

Did he put it in her sight?

He sat down at the kitchen table with paper and pencil and drew the Riley house, then a view from the porch. She clapped hands to her breasts, rocked and chortled. WISE he labeled it. Her wet eyes said words her tongue wanted to say—he was sure she understood everything. She took the pencil and sat a figure on the porch step— where he'd sat—and pointed to herself; then she made a crossed stick on the road. "Person," she said. Now she fluffed up Had's long hair; with fingers wet from her tongue she damped his hair and flattened it. He licked his lips. "Person." She laughed, convulsed. In the mirror he looked at the man with the long hair flat over his forehead. "Your Pearson's back?" he said.

In bed her fingers traced his face, neck, shoulders, all down his body, and when she whispered, "Person," he trembled with what was happening. "Yes," he said.

He was not long at home when, the next morning, a knock came. Berenice squinted darkly. Through the glass was Ed Pall's wife.

"Why, hello, Libby," he said, somewhat blunted. Years he hadn't seen her. Berenice shrank. Had *she* seen her before?

"How are you, Had? Why, how good the old house looks! Good morning—" She nodded to Berenice, whose gaze widened bewilderedly.

"Not Had—Pearson."

"Pearson? Since when?"

"Pearson," Had insisted. "My middle name." He laughed.

"Well, Had—Pearson. I'll get right to it. I came to talk to you about—"

Berenice obviously caught the cast of voice, rose—intimidated and nervous.

"My wife, Libby." He caught Berenice's hand. "You stay right here, hon. It's fine."

"But it's precisely not fine," Libby said. "You're aware what happens when you're not in town?"

"Happens?" He drew Berenice close, apprehensive.

"She goes down to Preston's dock and sits there day and night."

"Day and night?"

"She never leaves. What she eats, where she sleeps we'll never know. God knows it's cold enough. She'll freeze to death, Had, when winter comes, really comes. Besides, anything could happen to her these days, the town's not safe the way it used to be, hippies all over, dope in the schools, the Riverhead jail too full. We're trying to clean up the streets. The women at the church want to get up a petition—"

"Petition! Against her? A peti—"

"To *help*!"

"What do you think she *is*? She's my wife, damn it!" His stomach palpitated, half fear of what they might do, half shame at Berenice's never leaving the dock—and knowing the truth of the danger. They'd dare!

"I came to let you know. It's not right to leave her that way. We don't think it's humane—"

"Humane!" he shouted. "Stop talking about her as if she's a—"

Berenice whimpered. He was clutching too painfully.

"Nobody knew at first she was ill."

"Was was was!" he shouted, releasing Berenice. Her throat rasped now, frightened as much by his outburst as by Libby's staunchness. "She's my *wife*. Now get out."

He slammed the door behind Libby, watched her get in the car and drive off, cursing her and all her kind, and raged with constrained fury, wanting to break, smash, but dared not scare Berenice more. "Honey?" She was throbbing like a frightened rabbit trapped into immobility before the blow. "Nobody's going to hurt you."

All night long and for days after, he felt Libby's presence; wherever he turned, he expected she would be there, accusing. She bore some familiar and insistent thing he had known all his life. Something in Libby he feared. "Not this time," he muttered, and when Jeffers stopped by to tell him the *Annie B* was scheduled to leave at five the next morning, he'd already made up his mind to tell the Captain he'd be staying on solid land from now on.

"Or sure as hell those women'll get you—us, Berenice. Once people get onto a thing, there's no stopping them. They mean to do good, I know that, but there's something hard goes with it. Maybe they don't even know they're mean and enjoying it." It was something in him too, close as wind and sea and sun. How did you separate such things? "But I'll stand between, hon."

His staying home was her transformation. His presence nourished her, she did blossom, but more than a rounding out of flesh it was an effervescence in his company. The sight of him relaxed her anxieties. She eased into cleaning, baking, sewing even, with the first snows insisting she put on pants and, though he wouldn't let her shovel, accompany him—she made snowballs and threw handfuls of pure white dust at him with childish glee.

He had been sure he'd have no trouble getting work.

"I lived here all my life. They all know me." But, short of the boats, what could he do? The fish packers employed women cheap; the skimmer shop had openers who'd been there years, never added any the way business was; after Labor Day the tourists went and half the town closed up till spring; the shipyards and lumber companies were in a bad way. There'd never been much business in town anyway. Construction was the only thing —but it fell off in cold weather and, besides, it would take him out of town—and then where would Berenice be? For a while, before the cold set in too bad, he tended gardens and lawns, and did general repairs; because he was an all-around handyman without work, people paid him cheap.

Now she went everywhere with him. She would not stay home. She became a familiar sight at the edge of a lawn, outside a gate, eating sandwiches on the job or sitting beside him in the diner at noon. Then the jobs decreased—with the cold, they said—but he knew it was because of Berenice. People—a lifetime's people—looked at him different again—far, cold, now. Even the boys from the *Annie B*—whenever he ran into them accidentally, for they never visited—had the aloof quiet voices of self-conscious shame or guilt.

In November, when Kunicki the gravedigger was laid up with pneumonia, Had pleaded and the Town gave him the job digging graves. People driving past the cemetery grew used to the two, him digging and her perched by the accumulating sod at the grave's edge. But that work was sporadic and at fifteen dollars a hole he had to do several jobs to keep up with needs.

They were shadows of each other, seen picking over Saturday remains reduced for quick sale at the A&P, walking along the back road, digging on the flats for a few clams, netting for crabs in the crick, or watching the boats at the docks. Though people were distant, they spoke to Had and smiled as if marveling at how inseparable they were.

Their greatest pleasure was beachcombing. Always they found so much that he took to carrying a burlap bag. Inevitably an object would catch her eye—driftwood, a bottle, a starfish, a discarded handkerchief; after, she scrubbed the new possessions, displaying proudly the results. She would dash along the sand, amazing him with her speed, her arm thrust up in celebration and her laughter jerky with excitement—and at times tore back to him with such animation that the impetus nearly struck him down.

"You little devil, you!" He squeezed her till she cried, "Perperperper," struggling, and he was sure she would break into speech. *She's going to tell me.* But she leaped away, her eyes riveted on a new lure. One day at the Point, where she was running far ahead, she buckled to her knees. "Berenice!" he cried, but she made no turn. He raced, gripped with fear. "Berenice!"

She was holding a dead gull, its head pressed stiff against its breast, the feet hanging in hard limpness.

"Ah, so that's it. Berenice?" She was wailing softly. "Berenice?" he said several times, wind thinning his voice. She cuddled it, crooning. "Hon?" Then she held the gull out to behold, and turned her eyes up. "Perperperper," she murmured. Her eyes glittered wet, and he saw the endless space in her, for the first time the little earth colored islands floating in her; he wanted to go deep into her, on and on. He drew her up, close. "I'll never let you go, never." But her throat made a protest—for the bird crushed between. "Let's bury it." He moved toward the water, but again her sound halted him—she pointed away from water. "Where it's dry?" She nodded. Behind a rock he scooped a hole and lay the gull there; she covered it. "Let's find our burlap," he said, but she gripped his arms, her eyes wide, her mouth wet and serious, and hung to him and kissed him, kissed, kissed, her skin all hot damp. "Here? Here?" he said. She chafed his face, burning against him, making her sound, and nodded, urging him to go into her on the hard, dry sand.

vii.

By midwinter he could not pay the rent. The town was settled into its usual winter slump. Except for scarce gravedigging there was little odd work. On one of his stops by, old Tull said, "You could go on the Town, Had." And Had's pride reared fiercely—a man strong and with conscience and responsibility? "I couldn't do such a thing when the boats're making their runs." Gloom settled darker than the overhanging storm after Tull had left, his final words still ringing, "What else can you do?"

"*What?*" he said to Berenice, without explanation.

When he'd find full jars—string beans, tomatoes, pears, apples—and freshly baked bread on the back stoop, or when Rolfe himself and Laura came, he knew it was not to humiliate, but simply the intimations of worry and friendship. If he and the Humphries did not see much of each other since Berenice, they understood; and they knew he would accept nothing more than courtesy gifts to Berenice. Nor would Rolfe step beyond the natural limits of their respect.

But when the worst came, he set his pride aside and went alone to have a talk with Rolfe.

"You know the answers," Rolfe said. "They'll always take you on the *Annie B.* but that'd leave her alone. Or you could get out of town—to a bigger place—or—you know the last thing—" Rolfe wouldn't violate, even with words.

"—send her back," Had said.

And his bluntness blunted Rolfe. "You mean, you've thought to do it?"

"Never one time in this world. Never!" *Back*. Berenice behind glass? Good God! His nostrils twitched. A sudden odor came. Berenice roaming in that foul smell and him in Bella's dark room, and all the sky and the big sea out there—and nobody ever to see her smile and eyes, or touch her, or hear the sounds she makes? He knew every little meaning now. Back? A void dark and deep and endless spread.

"Well, you asked me," Rolfe said.

"Sure, sure. I guess it's only real when somebody else says your own words to you. You can't kid yourself then. But I won't leave her alone, and I can't go to a big place, cut her off from everything." He feared the city, all the faces. "But those women—" Those meddlers were no longer just people he'd always known, but rumors, alien faces, respectable indignation. "They'll be back. They always are." Outside, the wind shrieked against the shingles; the stripped limbs clacked; far, the sky was pale and the ground frozen barren.

"What choice've I got?"

"No matter what you do it's the same—she'll be alone."

"Less I stay with her no matter what."

"And starve," Rolfe said. He did not mention the other—welfare—either.

"Not likely," Had said, though now, with no money for rent, the house itself was a threat, too big, useless.

But for some time he had a notion. That afternoon he took Berenice along the back road. About two good miles out of the village was a small shack set back off the road, neglected, nearly reclaimed by bushes and scrub oak. Trees made a natural web around it.

"Belonged to old Gus and Effie, brother and sister, great-aunt and -uncle to my mother—by marriage. It's all tied up, the heirs out west somewhere. Come on." He made way: inside were two rooms, empty except for a split kitchen table. "Don't you worry about windows. I'll put glass in. There's some I'll take from Gus's coop out back. He kept chickens. Think we'll be okay here? We got enough'll easy furnish the place. That's the bedroom, this's the kitchen. We got the old oilstove. Put an oil barrel out back plenty full— What say?"

She went outside, stretched her arms to the trees, laughed. Yes, she liked it. She sniffed, suddenly holding her nose with one hand —the outhouse! Her mouth tried to move. "Wise? *Wise?*" he said. Exultantly she threw her head back, revolved—as if embracing it all, her disbelief reassuring him. At last she belonged. *Now,* he thought as she said, "Person, Person." Her arms grappled for him. Somewhere inside she was traveling. But she did not speak.

"We'll be moving right away." They would have to use oil lamps and candles, but they'd be alone and free out of sight, and the place was rent free.

Still, he didn't tell her the rest until after they'd used Rolfe's station wagon to move.

"Now, Berenice, you have to do what I say, hon. Listen—I figure one trip, a week, maybe ten days—now, now, don't carry on so, hon—just this one time on the *Annie B,* and we'll have enough money, several hundred dollars, to see us through till spring. How 'bout that?"

That night they made the excursion to Wise; he drew for her, expectant as she became fervent, at times intense, her mouth distorted into silent speech. He prodded: did she remember the day he came up the dirt road, Pearson Ames, looking for his woman, how they'd sit on the porch with Momma and Poppa, her sister, and see the neighbors coming from town . . . ? And he observed the motion of her eyes left, aware of the triggerings of her mind, her reflexes, waiting for the moment—

"Remember now—Pearson'll be back in a few days. There's plenty of food. You stay here, don't let anybody in, and don't go far— Hon, you listening? You stay *home*, and Pearson'll be back soon. Just remember: Pearson loves you." Her eyes lifted to him, her mouth made a sound of painful wonder. She gripped him to hurting. "Love." That word from his own mouth startled. "I never said it to you all this time, did I?" What was it? Love—maybe it's how far you'd go for somebody. He held her till she fell asleep in his arms, then carried her to bed and lay watching her sleep.

In the morning, just as he'd intended, he left at four without waking her, to walk the three miles to Preston's dock. At the boat he wavered, but already the dark morning edge on things, thick salt smell, planks clunked underfoot, the lap of water at the pilings brought his sea legs back nostalgically. And it helped when Bojarski said, "Get your ass aboard, Had. We've been waiting long enough." The Captain and the boys accepted him home with an occasional slap on the back. And once Jeffers said, "The missus like Greenport?" and he said, "Happy as a lark," with a glad soaring at the question. Not long out the old relaxed seaman talk came back, "Getting much, Had?" "Man, you know Wanda from over on Fifth? She'll tear the asshole right outa you."

When he was fully back in the routine—working the winch, loading the hold, raking—he doubted he'd ever left the ship. Mornings, before the fog burned off, gazing into the shifting wraiths the prow riled up, he sought her image; but the veil lifted, revealing nothing but far reaches. He felt she did not exist, had never existed but in his mind. And he wanted to turn back at once, go ashore, find her, prove—but he was trapped, stranded in the everlasting sea. And once, headed into Montauk in deep fog, he murmured on deck, "Berenice, where'd you go?" startled that the face appeared, its rapidity frightened him, he stood straight up—not hers, but a man's. Mick's. "Agggggggg," he gasped.

"Why you sticking to the rail like that, Had? It's poker time."

Bojarski!

"Poker?"

"Yeah!"

"I'll watch. I'm broke."

"Suit yourself."

Bojarski went back to the bunks; the opened door sprayed light, doubled the darkness. With the boys playing their game, he felt the isolation: she was out there, beyond darkness. What was she doing? Was she all right? And Mick's eyes—Bojarski's really—hung in his head, accusing. A heavy guilt for having left her descended. I'm trying, Mick, honest, he thought.

The cold drove. Actually it speeded their work. Always they went at it night and day, but now an instant's interruption and the cold penetrated. Ice hung stiff from the wires.

"Jee-sus!" Farley would cry. "Freezing my balls off."

"You'll get them thawed out at Helen's Place," Jeffers said. They could all laugh now—the hold was nearly full; they were about to head in.

The morning was clear. The instant the *Annie B* hit the harbor, Had spied Preston's. His heart leaped happily: she was not there. Yet, strangely, her absence palled.

The Captain gave him a small advance. Next morning they'd settle—enough cash so he wouldn't have to leave her all winter!—so he was on his way. He bought some chocolates and one red rose—she loved a live thing so—though he pinched at the price.

Snow had come down and frozen, patchy and dirty. He passed out of the village and through the woods. The winter trees were ashen against the sky. In the sparse fields the January hardness made hard clunks underfoot, sound went far, even the air seemed frozen.

Berenice must have heard him. Her hands and part of her face appeared vague through the frosted pane. He ran.

"Berenice, honey!" he cried, opening the door. At the window she turned and rose with a great effort to leap forward to him, her arms stretched, "Ahhhnnnnnnnnnnnnn," she wailed, the sound rang horrendously loud in the room, and she fell.

"Berenice!" He dropped to his knees. Her head rolled against him. She was burning up. She was hot through her clothes. Then the air struck him—the room was icy!

"Christ! The stove's out."

He lay her on the bed, bundled the blankets over her. The bottle was empty. He went outside and filled it. What had happened? Did she forget? pine? get sick and too weak to lift and carry the bottle?

"Berenice? I had to go—you know that. You promised you'd take care and, honey, I know you didn't go anywhere. That's a good one, you are—" And while the stove warmed and the air slowly turned tepid, he talked, talked, moving from the bed to the stove and back, "Honey, I know you hear me, even with your eyes shut. I know you're tired from waiting. But your Pearson's never going to leave you again, he promises—"

But she did not open her eyes, not move, not sigh even. Only the quilts over her chin rose and fell uneasily with a peculiar irregularity that frightened him.

"You in pain, Berenice?" She did not open her eyes. He thought, Where is she? Where's she going?

"Berenice!" He sat on the quilts. "I'm going for a doctor. I'll get Rolfe. He's got the car. Now don't you move. Promise! I'll be right back. I'll cut across the fields. It's not far. I'll hurry. Be sure and don't move."

He struck out toward Moore's Lane. His steps made raps in the air. His breath tore in white bull spurts, sounded like someone behind. His heart thumped. Two cars careened along the backroad—his arm shot up—but neither paid heed. He lunged through the dark edge of woods and came out a few minutes later opposite the drive-in theater. A car was coming. Thank God! He hailed it.

"Had? What you doing in the woods?"

He hardly recognized the man—Walt Mitchell from the old icehouse.

"Listen—it's my wife. You get Rolfe Humphries, please. Tell him to bring Doctor Kennedy right away—to Gus's shack. Rolfe knows it. Tell him he's *got* to. I'll go back. We'll be waiting. Hurry."

"Sure thing, Had." The car gunned.

Had's eyes were cold, filled. He ran.

He did not stop until he closed the door and saw she really was lying on the bed. He was sweating, his clothes steeped; the smack of heat and the oil smell stifled. On the floor was the rose. He put it in a glass. "For you, hon." He pulled up a chair beside her and waited. Rolfe would come. Rolfe would come right away. He wanted to take her hand and make her *know*, just by his feel, that Rolfe was coming; but he dared not disturb the blankets. Keep her warm. He tucked the quilts tight. How small she was! He'd thought of her as delicate, but never small, not frail. She looked thinner.

A great shaft of sunlight was pouring through the window, over the foot of the bed, over her feet and his grandmother's patched coverlet, over the dust on the floor, into her empty shoes. The sun was filled with moving motes drifting. Through them he saw the far woods, the stripped branches dark against the morning. Everything was so silent. There was no wind. Occasionally, over the blacktop a car whined. He could still hear her breath, going more naturally now—and then came a quick flurry. He strained: chickadees!

"There's your birds, Bern. Hear them? They came for their feed."

He got up, made some crumbs, and tossed them out the kitchen door. The birds swooped down, unafraid.

"They think I'm you, Berenice."

The sun crept higher over her. "It'll warm you, hon." Again he sat on the bed. A strange little push and pull agitated her breath; her chest lifted and sank below the still shoulders. He listened so long that his own chest filled and emptied with hers, a single sound in the room, and all the while her nostrils moved, widening and narrowing like night moth wings. He bent close: on her skin a light gold down glowed stark in the sun, on her lips line after line in a strange network, glistening tiny pores. Her sockets were too brown, lines there, but rounded, filled, for her eyes were puffed so the dark lashes sank deep into the swollen flesh. He touched the lids lightly. "Berenice, honey?" The skin was hot, oily; it sagged off to the side under her brows, like his. He traced the lines over her forehead, the hairline, the edge of her ears—there were hairs there too, and a sheen of wax—and her chin, mouth, nose. His hands were learning her, teaching him every crevice and nook and line. He felt her heat, the pulse, pulsing with each breath—and bent closer: swollen, fevered, her face had grown round and full as his. He said, "Berenice, where've you gone? Where's my girl?" He stopped tracing, absorbing the face that looked too full. "Berenice, where you gone?" he cried, wanting to open the eyes and find her. "Where?" His hands embraced her face, clasped it between them, hot. His air suddenly tore into the room with anguish, a terrible rasp, as if he couldn't catch his breath—

She opened her eyes full. The pupils were dark and wide, a web of red around them.

He gasped—at the same time her body wrenched with far air, broke with rasping. It was *her* rasping he felt—in his hands.

"Berenice!" He was filled with fright.

And he raised her head—her shoulders raised stiffly with it—wanting to hold her.

But she stared. She opened her mouth. He saw the dried phlegm, bad holes in her teeth, her tongue glide over her dry lips, the dark hole of her throat. Her mouth opened wider. She struggled. A sound—*kkkkkkkkkkkkkkk*—scraped deep in her throat. Wet came over her tongue, ribbed her mouth, but the sound was dry. His heart beat—*thud*—hard. Now. She was going to make it at last. It was a miracle. "Pearson's waiting. Say it, Berenice. I'm waiting, honey."

Her eyes strained, her mouth made indistinct whispering, opened and closed—more, faster. Her hot breath touched him, soundless; flecks spat over his face. She made a ferocious struggle —her tongue rose, curled, twisted; her mouth pursed, spread, flattened—her body rose with the effort of it—and a furious sibilance came, a rush *ssssssssssssssss* touched him. In his hands her blood pumped violently. His heart beat with her.

"Berenice?"

But her arm tore from the quilts, reached past him into the sunlight, her cry scraped, and stopped. He stared into the wide eyes gazing through him. They were terrible. For an instant he did not know whose they were. Then he clutched her close, pressing—

He sat holding her body until the car door struck loud and Rolfe appeared in the doorway with Doctor Kennedy.

"She's gone," he said.

"I'll take care of things, Had."

"I was just getting to know her," he said. He did not look at them. "She went."

He stared at her body and got up and went out and left them with her.

He crossed the potato field and the back road toward the bluffs and came to the Sound. The waves struck with a hard regular rush against the shore. He went down on the sand and stood there and raised his arms and opened his mouth and yelled. But the waves killed the sound. Then he kept walking.

In the morning he went back to the *Annie B.*

The Healing of the Body

HE HAD NEVER KNOWN such persistent sun. All day sun burned into the room. His windows in the pension looked out over the patio, and except at siesta, when it was as silent as death, there were the sounds of the house—its aches and breathings, the clatter in Cati's kitchen, the orders of Doña Elvira, the patrona; the oily insinuating voice of Rodolfo, the hairy wretch who passed as her husband and whose touch she could not resist, as the moans from their room both afternoon and night too evidently testified to. He knew now the hours of the eight other pensionistas, who came, who went, their meanderings. At times they were, with their strong Latin voices, a noisy lot, and he could have found a more genteel place, a small residential hotel, but no rooms had captivated like these on the second floor, bright, with a small bath, with bed, bureau, and desk and chair—but, best, French windows which opened onto a balcony over the patio. He could see beyond, over grapevines, lush glicina climbing the walls, the great palms on the Plaza de San Martín and the city buildings beyond, and, left, a glimpse of the precordillera, the blazing white of snow on the farthest reaches. And such sun! When he had asked the criada, "And rain?" Matilde's high pitch made a volley of laughter. "How's it going to rain in Mendoza!" Perhaps five, ten days a year it might rain. Wasn't that why he had sought out this país de sol y vino, Mendoza, with its aire puro and the water pure and cold channeled down from the melting snows of the Andes two hundred kilometers to this oasis in a near desert?

"Because I need rest, sun, stillness, and a graduated physical activity—walking, swimming, playing bowls, sunning, whatever, but gradual—" He had told Doña Elvira: "a kind of general exhaustion."

"Ah, you North Americans, how you go at it! It's a wonder you don't all collapse."

"Well, these days we don't all go at it," he said.

At once Doña Elvira had taken him into the dining room—in pleasant weather the patio—and introduced him, already the honored guest, who would be too spoiled, yes: to Don Bosco, a retired government clerk who, even with his cane, could barely haul the enormous stomach, which resembled the shell of an armadillo sucked against him; old Señora Amelia Redondo, once of the Teatro Colón, in the better days of that opera house, "cuando Perón," a soprano in the chorus, as it turned out; her daughter, Nélida, already a waspish spinster fading but not from a lack of desire to escape Mamá; Jorge the rack, showy clothes on a bone stick, who spent so much that he was constantly borrowing, whose large teeth were a perpetual devilish white glare which did not allow his lips ever to meet; Anita, an attractive middle-aged woman, who claimed independent means; Hector, who traveled for a sindicato petrolero, secretive, quiet, dark, perpetually into a newspaper; Andrés, without books a student, so handsome and carefree that all the pension accepted as his mother the rich older woman who visited him each week and as his "buddy" the sleek preener with the new Renault.

His body baked. He felt sun touch, gently osmose, deep, penetrate his vitals, bones; the floor, furniture, walls radiated its heat; he drew sun into his lungs. His only nightmare was that he might awaken one morning to no sun. He let it take him until he felt he himself was the sun.

He was so exuberant over this city, the sun, the dryness, that he walked the streets, went to all the plazas. Afternoons he sat listening to the waters released by the city into all the acequias, as the waters trickled around each tree and flower bed in beautifully wrought canteros—like the bloodstream of a great body he was traveling through. He would occasionally return to the pension at noon, but always for the siesta and the evening meal.

Encouraged by the increasing distance he managed to walk each day without taking a trolley, he decided to venture through the park. He took a trolley to the gates on Boulogne-sur-Mer. He would spend the morning in the park, have lunch there, resting, and then spend the afternoon at the zoo, which was set along a path winding higher and higher up the cerro called the Hill of Glory with that great bronze woman, Liberty, breaking the chains of tyranny from her wrists.

He made it to the foot of the statue. But his lungs thugged, thugged and a sweat all over his body made his clothes pull with each motion, and bind, and he had to sit. He rested, though his lungs took long to ease and his blood to calm a bit. Far out, though he would swear he could touch them, white edges of snow lay like soft down pillows on the precordillera. On one side of the cerro was the great amphitheater, the teatro griego. And in a press of dust below lay the villa miseria, a cluster of adobe squares topped with tin, with rags leaping over window openings and little dark streams of smoke and dozens of tiny forms moving about, a blight on the beauty of Ciudad Universitaria nearby. But just below him on the slope, grew little pink and white and yellow enamorados del sol. He reached down to draw one into his hand, a tiny yellow face.

But his blood did not settle. And when a taxi arrived and let out its tourists, he asked to be taken down to Las Heras. They wound down the caracoles, down. How the air smat, filled his mouth! He could not get enough. And with the speed, the bars of trees were thrown down in dizzying flickers, and when the taxi reached the Café Gom at the corner of Las Heras and his own street, "Aquí," he cried out, "bueno, gracias," and paid. He was not prepared for the hard tile when he stepped down—and faltered, but he went into the Gom. "Té con limón." And when his tea came, his hand embraced the silver teapot as if it were sun itself. How the heat pulsed into his hand, flowed. He laughed aloud.

When he left the Gom, music filled the air. He halted—it was coming from the boys' school—and listened till the song was over. In a few instants the boys came filing out, the priests shepherding till the boys broke free, streaking around him. He was impelled by them to the corner, his, where he was left bereft, suddenly weak, his legs faltering, and when he looked up, on the sidewalk before the pension was the man who sometimes hung at the curb. He halted, disguising his weakness, feigning interest in the acacia, supporting himself with one hand against the trunk. He dared not raise his eyes, dared not admit such weakness, but he stood and, abruptly, walked—if too fast—without deviation toward the pension, hardly able to control the thudding of blood in his head. But he reached the steps, touched out for the wall, missed—his hand struck air—

But he was suddenly caught, suspended, and drawn up. The strength! Those hands straightened him up, held him firm. "Can you manage?" "Yes, yes." But his legs buckled, and before he could object the man had lifted him off his feet and with one arm held him while he rang the bell. And before he could protest, Matilde was crying out, "But, señor! Dios mío! What happened?" and despite her look of resentment at that ruffian, she was leading the way up to his room and crying out, "Doña Elvira, que venga enseguida! Quick! The señor!"

Doña Elvira came scurrying. Quickly they readied his bed. All the while the man said nothing. He stood aside, watching.

"Señor?" Doña Elvira was clearly dismissing him.

"And how can I thank you?" he said.

"A sus servicios, señor," the man said and left.

"Un rufián! No haga Vd caso, señor."

"But I would have fallen, Matilde. What luck he was there."

"Not luck," she said. "Es un tipo de lo peor."

Now alone, he was aware of that man, how he was always at the Gom or at the curb outside the pension: not too tall, but thin, with—yes—amazingly large hands hanging from jacket sleeves always somewhat short. It was that, now he thought it, the disproportion—the enormous hands which had caught him and lifted him up so lightly. He recalled the form, yes, but the face had been shadow.

He did not go down that night but Matilde brought him his supper tray, a red rose on it—"from Señora Amelia. I don't think she believes the señor is married." The singer was always preparing, if allusively, a life for Nélida (and herself). "She will be shocked when your señora arrives." Matilde's laughter, in imitation of the exchorus singer from the Colón, broke into soprano notes.

"Matilda," he called as she went down, "por favor no breakfast."

And he slept through despite the far sounds of the kitchen, which he usually woke to, till late morning when Matilde's voice, firm with a hard anger, reached him. "No es posible, atrevido!" and "Sí, sí, atrevido!" Whatever it was, she came with her usual streak, up the stairs to his room, energetic with annoyance; she usually fed on minute flurries.

"It's *that* one again, señor."

"That one?"

"Sí—the man from last night. He wants to know how the señor is. Atrevido!"

"Did you tell him?"

"He won't have it from me. He wants it from the señor's own mouth."

"Then you tell him to come at noon. Tell Doña Elvira to set a place for him."

"Set—! But, señor—" Her face said contrary to all rules, not possible.

"Tell Doña Elvira to set an extra place for a guest, Matilde."

"Sí. But—perdóneme Vd, señor—does the señor know what he's doing?" He could see that, despite her "reprimand," there was something in the order which pleased. "Hacen así los norte-americanos?"

"We'll find out, Matilde."

But it was Doña Elvira whom he had to confront.

"Pero, señor, it simply is not done. And what will my other pensionistas think? This is a respectable house."

"Ah, Doña Elvira, it is simply a gesture for his help to me. I'm sure they'll understand that, just as your own generous nature does."

"Perhaps . . ." But she went, confused.

"You wouldn't want to see me ungrateful."

"Well, if the señor insists."

Dressed, he went down to the street door.

"So you're the one who kept me from falling," he said. "Come, they've set a place for you. But—nobody knows your name . . . ?"

"Evaristo Vargas a su servicio." His voice was deep, tunneled, but not loud.

Because sun blazed down so in the patio, the tolda was drawn over the tables, a gay yellow and white striped canvas whose shade deepened the crimson in the baldosas.

"Buen provecho," he said to the group gathered at the long table, at once aware of Doña Elvira's discretion in setting apart a table for two, wine and bread ready. "Señor Vargas, my fellow pensionistas." They nodded in turn, but it was the men who cast their eyes to their plates; the women—Nélida and her mother, Doña Elvira, Matilde, Anita, even Cati the cook—whose eyes, with the rapidity of rapacity, took in the last detail. In fact, for the first time he too could look at Vargas, who stood amazingly self-assured. He was virtually indifferent to them; his gaze, passing over, seemed almost not to see them. He was badly dressed, but neat—black trousers and black belt with a large silver buckle, an old brown tweed suit jacket worn at the sleeves, a dark green woolen shirt.

The pensionistas immediately went at their talk, noisy as usual.

"Siéntese."

Vargas sat opposite him at the small table.

"Servidos—" Cati set down the first course.

Now there was the confrontation with the weathered face—a heavy mass of hair, wavy, well-groomed, very thick brown, which seemed to deepen the already sunken eyes, so dark a brown they appeared black, very prominent cheek and jawbone, and a thick skin deeply sunned. He grabbed the bread at once, broke it and stuffed a crust into his mouth, and like a host poured two glasses of wine. "A su salud," he said. Then he hunched forward on his elbow and stared across the table at him. "And now?" He laughed at his own candidness. "And, now, as we eat, perhaps we get to know each other."

"Yes. You can tell me—what you do, where you're from, maybe all about this Mendoza I don't know yet?"

"I? I am nothing, señor, a nobody. I have no trade—any trade, perhaps, which needs me, or I need, on the spot. If I'm from this city, it's because I'm here now. I don't, as a fact, know which place I'm from—I've been all over the República—but now, this day, it is Mendoza. You think that a bad way to live?"

"Enviable!" He laughed, struck the table—called to himself by the sudden silence he brought to the other table. He nodded in apology. "But you make it sound not only natural, but so easy."

"Easy, no. You can starve, be without shelter—except in a place like Mendoza, where there is so much sun, it is dry, you can sleep almost anywhere without misery."

"And you do all that?"

"What else?"

"With no home, family, job, friends—?"

"Not for the likes of me."

"Why not?"

"It's not meant for me."

"But you make these things—you choose them."

"No, I don't think so."

"Then *what?*"

"You just have to know what you are."

"And you know."

"How am I not going to know?"

He laughed, and for a moment his presence—the hair quivering, his eyes catching the burn of sun, even the teeth, the red and dark deep of his open mouth—absorbed the room. The other table grew silent again. He was so at home there; the others seemed strangers—they were all eyes on him; his legs aspread, his arms resting on the table, he seemed so much bigger than he was. The hair made a dark froth at his neck. Health vibrated wet over his lips, teeth. In stillness he was constantly in motion.

"And you're never sick—from bad eating? no sleep? nodding?"

"I can't afford to be sick. My body is tough, hardened to this life. Who could want more than this Mendoza sun and air? It would keep anybody healthy."

"I'm counting on that."

"But you must get exercise, the mountain air, plenty of our good Argentine beef. You have been to an asado? to the mountains? You don't know the provincia?"

It shamed him even to think, I've lain in my room except when walking.

"I've walked, even overdone it." He smiled.

"But we must do something. We must go one day to Potrerillos. You'll never be the same after. Now—" He took an apple from the fruit Matilde set down and put it in his pocket. "You've been very good to ask me to eat with you, but I must leave you to your day." He addressed the other table, a slight bow of his head to the women. "Adiós. Buen provecho." Even Jorge succumbed to his gentility. Only Don Bosco firmed his lips and stared at his plate.

At the door he said, "Gracias" again and started up the street.

But he could not let Vargas go so easily: "But Potrerillos!"

The man halted. "You want to be taken to Potrerillos?"

"Why not—if I haven't seen anything of the province yet?"

"Then we take a driver or rent a car."

"Yes—that. We can take our time then. And the asado?"

"If the señor trusts me, I'll buy what we need at the mercado."

"Of course I trust you—" He handed him a thousand peso note.

"Tomorrow—for the afternoon."

"Perfect."

"I come, then, at eleven with the auto?"

Don Bosco, who had the room nearest the front door, was just sighing slowly along the corridor on his cane.

"Señor," he said, "forgive an old man this intrusion, but *cuidado*! That one"—he hissed it—"es un sinvergüenza."

He could say no worse word about anyone.

"I'll watch my step, Don Bosco, thanks."

He went up to his rooms, but light, spongy he felt. Why was that? That he could let go? someone was going to take care of him? he could put himself into another's hands? Not once in his life had he succumbed to such an impulse. And what would Margaret say to all this? Need? Why, from the moment he had met her, he'd assumed—almost to the point of drive, knowing how she must have expected it—all decisions, not merely to please her, to give her anything she wanted, but to demonstrate his own nature, the strength of his will, which could make of their marriage a success, free her by supplying all her demands, demands he knew she would not voice, but which she expected from him, a fountain of energy which would not fail her, *would* not—and he had driven, *had*, hadn't he?—till there was no end to the habit of his obsession. Yet something was wanting. He felt how she suffered from it, grew thin and tired until, worried, he too grew thin and tired, nervous, because he could make nothing come from her, could not rouse the fountain he knew was in her to stir and replenish his own so that he could go on, on— "Why, Margaret, why?" he had dared, when she turned away from him, to the wall. "Because I've never been able to touch you where it could move you," she said, "make *you* who must be under all that." "But who am I?" "Who! If I knew! Because you've never driven *me* to know. Do you realize what that means? Together, we're—ultimately—alone." "But I've done all I could, I'd do anything—" "It's not *anything*, or *if* it's choice—I hate saying this because we've suffered these years together and that's love, a kind of love, if not the deepest thing—perhaps we chose too consciously, we *aimed* at marriage with each other, we *knew* it would be right, and what does *know* mean and what does *that* mean, *right*? Anyway we did it, we even believed it was right—for them out there? our people? But instead of growing, and *that's* the measure, something's dying, we've brought waste in our ignorance and inexperience, because we *thought* too consciously, we couldn't have said that; but when you *feel* parts of you dying, not moved to anything, dulled, sometimes barely alive enough to ache, oh yes ache, for what you can't put into words,

great low stars. Left, the long dark ridge of the precordillera burned a knife edge of white.

Margaret was coming sooner than she—or he—had planned.

> —because it was wrong of us to be so logical (again) and let you go so far away without—what should I call myself?—a nurse. I know you when you don't have proper food and rest—your energy, how you'll overdo. So I've planned on leaving in two weeks, the twenty-seventh, so will be there with you in Mendoza through the spring—beautiful, the travel agency tells me. Surely it will make all the difference in the world to how we feel, once away with you from the nightmare of work and the lightning life we (you) live here. I arrive at Ezeiza and will spend the night in Buenos Aires. I fly to Mendoza from the Aeroparque at eleven a.m. on the twenty-eighth. If you don't feel up to being at Plomerillos airport to meet the landing, you know I won't be put out. I'll take a taxi to your pension. Are you sure you want us to stay there? You make the place sound third rate (preparing me?), though the boarders sound like fascinating types.

But he was somewhat disappointed. He had not grown acclimated yet, had not grown into a pleasant idleness or fully learned the city so he might meander with her as if it were his. He wanted it to be *his*, to take possession before he laid it out for her, though he did want her to come, but to see him in this self that was just beginning to be born, open to the world around him. He wanted someone, a witness, to know what was happening to him—and who better than Margaret, who could measure his growth in the deviations from what life she had known in him? And he *did* feel like new, this instant felt the soft warmth of walls, a second skin, the burning winter fire of the palm spikes in him, the upward rush of darkness touching, but with it, too, the treacherous early night chill, which he must watch against. He shut the windows and lowered the persiana.

He did not go down at nine for supper, but showered and went to bed early.

But he was restless, and he watched, surprised that white covered the floor, filled the room—not moon, but snow—and he rose to walk through it, he had to get to the crest of the far mountains, where the sun drew him, guided—lured—at the same time blinding, sending a long dark shadow down the center of his vision. He advanced and each time the crest was in sight and he moved toward it, the dark form loomed, struck and darkened his vision with a thrust of pain. He gasped—as if it had struck his chest—and awakened. Again. Again. By morning he was exhausted, but he must get up to wash and breakfast. The rufián was coming. The thought burdened—he should not go with him, yet he yearned to be taken somewhere, carried, driven, even if merely jostled into a sleep, though really he wanted to be awakened—be—break at last into the life he had denied himself. Wasn't that what he wanted to tell Margaret, and she him? But where was that life? What?

At breakfast he sensed a new animation—familiarity. He sat by Señora Amelia, and Nélida sat opposite him, more direct, less coy this morning, as if assured of his attention. He didn't feel so distant from them, and the student, Andrés, asked his advice about a trade school (his mother had come, urging him to be useful), and the government clerk, Jorge, with vague intimacy knocked his shoulder gently when he set out for work, "Adiós, señor," so that the current set him peculiarly alert, at odds. They would want something? They saw he was susceptible? Especially Matilde, whom he generally tipped by the week, hovered more closely. Only Don Bosco, at the head of the table as usual, went through his fixed conversational routine—greetings, the morning paper's news, a political tirade against the Argentine military, its flippant government coups, inflation, lack of economic progress, humiliation before the dollar; and when he left, the only variation, almost unnoticed (or was he too hypersensitive after a fitful sleep?), was "Cuidado, eh?" so that he remembered the hiss and his *Es un sinvergüenza, señor* of the night before.

But Vargas came—promptly at two he struck the knocker.

"A '58 Buick!" He bellowed his joy. Weighty chrome, black, an ugly sturdiness. And with pride Vargas let him in.

"No, no—up front."

Dios mío! The back seat held a great covered laundry basket, wine—a damajuana!—and mineral water, soda. "What more?"

Vargas laughed. "It has to last until late. It will be dark when we return." He sat comfortable, his jacket off now, a clean white shirt open at the neck; he seemed long and thin without his coat, wiry and sturdy, hard. He was happy at the wheel, and he rode the highway well.

He himself felt all excursion. "What air!" The warmth from the open window pressed an invisible hand over flesh, through the hair, the sun a dazzling madness through the acacias. Outside the city came an endless dry barrens—gray, ashen, brown—only now and again green, where in a glimpse of the near dried riverbed glittered last weary waters.

"The petroleum flats, YPF," Vargas said—derrick after derrick erect against the sky.

Now past the foothills, walls rose, steepened; they followed ridges, ravines, the road pockmarked and bumpy, here and there stretches of green, a house by a drying stream, cattle, a village—and suddenly great breaks, vistas of sky and far peaks, and there—"Mire Vd, señor"—a great white tip highest in the sky—"Tupungato"—as if a cloud had fallen and settled there forever in frozen stillness.

"Allá, señor!" There. Far off the road meandered a stream by an enormous willow and some large rocks. "Perfecto!" He pulled the car off the road; it bucked and veered over the rough ground, billowing dust, then came to a halt near the tree.

In no time Vargas was unloading. "No, no—ande Vd, go. If you like, pick up what twigs and wood you can find for fire. There are matorrales, clumps, but careful, don't confuse the sticks with snakes." He gave a sly smile.

Vargas laid table on a flat rock, set stones to hold the cloth down. There was a pleasant wind down the slopes to this rather high valley, though with sun overhead the ground gave off quickening heat and made crystal shimmers over the landscape. He lodged bottles of wine and water between rocks in the cold stream and built a mound of twigs until the fire finally caught and he could set chunks of wood on.

"It will be a while. Vino!" He poured. Sun spread wine like blood over their hands. "What better—sun, air, wine."

"You love this life, Vargas?"

"Not this life, señor—life. Life!"

"And you don't want to make anything of it?"

"What would you make of it? It is what it is. You can't change that, so live it."

"But you want nothing?"

"Like?"

"Something solid—land, house, a place in life—for family, for love, security, respect—You know all the words."

"Sí, but *words*. Not? You don't need so many words—if you listen to your body, it tells your head what to do."

"Perhaps."

"But sí, señor."

"And you can live with that—that way?"

"I'm here—living, enjoying. And you—not?"

"Yes. It's wonderful, but for me this is an escape from my world. I was sick. I'm recuperating. It's not, in a way, real."

"Not real? You're not feeling this sun, rock, earth? What's your hand doing in the water? And not seeing sky and mountains, Tupungato—so beautiful? Not real? Then I ask you what's real? I didn't finish the colegio, I'm just an ordinary man, perhaps even stupid—I think not—but I ask, and I do not joke, what is real to you, then?"

He faltered. His hand dripped.

"Ah, you see—if you knew, you could say at once. Isn't that true?"

"Perhaps I'm still figuring it out."

"That's why you are here, then, in Mendoza?"

"Maybe, though not intentionally for that. A rest. To get my sights straight, we say back home."

"You came at the best time, spring, except for the viento sonda, when the winds come down from the mountains and stir up the tierra so the air is pure polvo, dust that blinds and gets inside you till you think you're made of dust—it maddens the blood, presses at the brain, some people go mad—"

"I'm glad you told me. I'll seal myself in my room."

"Nothing escapes it. You find grit in your sheets, shoes, clothes.

You can't keep air out. But when it's over, the world is pure—you can see as far as God, as if the eyes have been given new sight, señor."

"Then it's worth being blinded!"

"Ay, look at the fire—perfect for the beef! I'll mix the lettuce. Take more wine. That's a perfect rock to sit on."

"But you've been here before!" It suddenly struck—how he moved about this terrain with such intimacy.

Vargas laughed. "Where haven't I been before?"

Whether the air, the wine, sun, nothing had ever tasted so good. "I've gorged, I'll die stuffed to the gills."

"That's what the siesta's for—such moments. Allá—a perfect place under the willow. A blanket!" He had one folded in the trunk.

"You've thought of everything."

"That's not my job today?"

"Job!"

"And it's yours to rest?" He laid out the blanket. "I'll clean up and take a little walk."

"In this sun?"

"Mire, Vd!" He flailed a sombrero of mimbre. "Mi contrasol!"

Briefly he heard the sound of Vargas at the stream, but he could feel himself drift, fall, thinking how he was lying here in a strange country with absolute abandon and trust, not a care in the world, floating, floating in a warm, warm sea.

A spray woke him and the great dark shadow flicking wet hair—"Vargas!"— standing over him, naked, dark and long as a tree in the sky.

"A good dip—be prepared for icy water—and you'll feel the blood leap. Don't worry. We're far from the road and nobody sees but maybe the goat—allá!—" Very high, on nearly vertical ledges, goats were foraging. "—and maybe herders—who cares?—when they come."

While he undressed and inched into the slow-moving stream, Vargas dried and dressed; and when he emerged, struck cool by the mountain breeze, then warmed by sun, Vargas said, "Acá, señor— You stretch out and turn over." He lay on the blanket, and Vargas came down, straddling, and he felt the hands, so enormous that they covered his shoulders, grip and press, grip and sink, drive into his back more firmly with each grip, so that he nearly cried out with the pain of such pleasure. Then they moved down his back to his buttocks, thighs, calves; then, so lightly, easily, the hands turned him over and worked up over his legs to his chest and arms till the blood was one burning flow and his breath easing steadily, till Vargas thrust himself back on his haunches, drops of sweat flicking over him—

"There! A workout. What you need everyday. You'll be scaling the walls like those goats."

"My body's never felt so alive. Gracias, Vargas."

"And now maybe an hour's sun—you're already turning brown from your time in Mendoza. We'll make you a pure indio. Then you dress, we go down to the aguas termales so you can see at least where to take the natural springs, hot from the center of the earth—the great cure."

Vargas himself was a burnished brown, the dark hair over chest and arms natural shadows, and his head soft shimmering black. Such health! he envied.

"Take—" Vargas split the muskmelon.

For a brief spell they sucked at the tender orange flesh. Vargas buried then what he could not burn and left all neat. Except for the wet-down charred wood vaguely smoldering, no one would have known they had been there.

They drove down past the bridge to the hot springs—the mountain walls rose, the ravines deepened, and, though it was not really late, night, so early in the mountains, began its dark sea. Only breaks high up admitted great pours of light, though the road grew gray.

He should have been exhausted, and part of him was, but a great vigor coursed through him, energy which threatened to spill —a long-forgotten feeling so new again that he laughed.

"Señor?"

"Nothing. I was thinking how you missed your calling—doctor or male nurse or social worker."

"I missed no calling." Serene, serious, his eyes delved into the narrow road with its potholes, treacherous in shadow.

"Ah, you have a calling?"

"Sí. Every man has a calling—if he will know it." His voice was edged with pride, and light edged his profile hard against the mountain stone moving past.

"You believe that?"

"But absolutely—or they, the world, couldn't go on."

"And yours?" Where they were descending onto the arid flats, the great oil derricks reappeared, black against the blazoned last sun.

"The señor would not appreciate it."

"Yes, tell me the truth. You have one?"

"You think you want the truth?"

"Of course."

"People think that till they know it. They wish, after, to change it, but can't take it back."

"But only if ashamed—"

"And why ashamed if it is true?" Quickly he gazed at him, so direct, so candid, the last light luminous in his deep-set eyes; and he saw himself dark in them against the sun, and with the harshness of stone too.

The car, following the curve, suddenly lost the sun. The air turned quickly cool. Far, where the derricks stood, sun turned their tips fire.

"A man can't be ashamed of what he is, even by nature, born to be."

"And what *were* you born to be, Vargas?"

"What I am, señor. I tell you, as you insist, straight." Pride, stone in his voice, returned—not defiant but zealous. Vargas, as if to let the stone fall properly, looked straight at him. "I'm a thief."

"Thief!"

"You see—it shocks."

"Because I don't believe. Because—look at you here with me now. What are you stealing?"

"You think it's always clear what somebody steals?"

"But you're paying your way—working—right now."

"Because you can't know how the mind works. You'd have me describe how I go about it?"

"I can't see that you're going about anything."

"Since you're not a thief—" The observation gave him great pleasure. He was seriously playing now, trying, teasing. "You don't have the habit. It is—built in, a way of life, a way of being. I told you: I was born to be a thief."

"Who taught you such a thing?"

"My own nature."

"That's not possible."

"To be completely—completely—honest, that is the only thing

possible. So it's to be expected you don't understand. You're not a thief, not enough of a thief."

"Then you'd claim I'm part thief!"

"Every man, sí, has his moment, steals something—another person's dignity, maybe; a little joy, honor . . . But a thief is bent fully toward that side of his nature. It is his obsession. His food, drink, sex, goods, whatever—come from it, are associated with it; but that pleasure—need, you call it—is first, always first."

"That's destruction—will lead straight to it. You can accept that destruction?"

"You are sure it's that?"

"Can't you will against it? Are you telling me you're trapped—by some destiny you can't avoid?"

"*Not* trapped is what I tell you. To be trapped is not to know, or not accept—then is misery, the worst misery. To accept the way, the way you are, is to go into yourself, find every corner of that—you'll laugh—gift, whatever gift it is, and begin to know what *happy* is. I can tell by your face you think me mad—don't you?"

"You make me wonder what madness is. You give up everything to steal?"

"But I get everything! I get everything, señor."

"Respect, decency, all the real connection with the world—you break them to get the things you steal?"

"Things. You've seen me with things, señor? Maybe you haven't understood a word I'm saying. I thought you would." He looked genuinely downcast—not sullen, sulky—with a vague sinking—in his voice, eyes, mouth even—of despair. "It's the life that grows in me when I'm going each time further. I can feel how I'm pushing, pressing out because I'm being—don't laugh—true, not lying. You can't, I'm sure of it, imagine a thief daring to say not lying and mean it?"

"It's hard to."

"And not to understand?"

"Not understand what you steal."

"Perhaps it's like most things: what you really take, only the taker knows, and that is all he needs to know."

"You are telling me?"

"I've told you."

In the precordillera, the last white ridge of snow gleamed and went out, peaks and sky turned endless gray. The lights of Mendoza rose, glowing, and spread, a great night bloomer against the darkness. When they finally drove down San Martín and onto Las Heras, though he was tired, his mind ran, the flow in his body set into motion by the day did not want to stop.

"I'll return the auto," Vargas said.

He was reluctant to let Vargas go. It struck with real force now how it was the first time he had really had company, shared, since his arrival, weeks now—since Margaret.

"What do I owe you?"

Vargas turned, looked at him long—till he felt embarrassed. Was the man feeling pity for him, shame? Was he hurt?

"What you have to give."

Balked, confused, he said, "How much? You set the price."

"I'll return the auto," Vargas said, this time forlorn. "I hope the señor does not feel the day was wasted, and will feel better."

He was dismissed. It was that.

"Buenas noches, señor."

"But—you won't come back? There will be another day—"

"If you wish. I am at your disposal. You know where to find me. Adiós."

He stepped down. "Adiós, Evaristo." He watched the Buick drive off. The pension light burned feebly. The hall was empty. The rooms would be empty. He did not want to go up, but if he did not, there would be the dining room, the clatter, and the battering of voices, and tonight he did not want that. If only Margaret were upstairs. Well, he would go up and write her.

When you get here—soon—you too will feel what a Mecca of sun this city is. I feel a primitive yearning here. I could worship. You'll love it, if I am any judge—I feel strangely and completely permeated here. At times I can feel a million pleasant pinpricks in my flesh, as if I were a broken bone that is beginning to knit. The pension is a fascination. Types, you say! Oh, I know you won't like it immediately, but when you get used to old Don Bosco lugging his weight around on a crutch and a bad leg, and my opera star (chorus girl!) who has her eye out (you may have lost me by then to Nélida—or do you still have me, or I you?) for a husband (I think she could be coyly ruthless, the object being married or not, if one gave her daughter the slightest side-glance of intimacy). The two single ones, Jorge and Andrés (kids, obviously) they know Amelia's limits and, besides, have their own playthings, or *are* somebody's plaything. Doña Elvira has a lover, who poses as her husband, all of which, if it weren't within the (socially) accepted (centuries!) framework of a Catholic tradition, would simply be like living back in the States, all under one roof. You'll be a welcome part of the menagerie, as I have been—a novelty, a still unknown quantity. You may take all the mystery from me when you show yourself, but until then there's room for faith that I'm available. You know the game. I write to keep you in mind—that is honest, and I wonder how it will be to have you here, how you will fare with this new me who is growing under this sunbrowned skin. We'll see. Alone here, lazy, I feel like a thief—

He stopped. Suddenly he wanted to go down, to mix.

"Ah, we'd given you up!" Señora Amelia cried. Nélida nodded.

"And your trip?" Doña Elvira said. "How much of the province did you see?"

"Potrerillos."

"What beauty! And you didn't get as far as Tupungato?"

"Only a glimpse."

"But you must go the limit!"

"What *is* this, Doña Elvira! Tupungato! Until he goes into the high cordillera, the real heights, sees Aconcagua and reaches the pass with the Cristo Redentor between our beloved Argentina and Chile, he has reached nothing. Tupungato!"

"Ah, Don Bosco, you'd counter eternal peace if there were such a thing! The señor can't enjoy one day's beginning outing to Potrerillos?"

"And who claimed he did *not* enjoy one day's outing? You make me out a revolutionary every time I open my mouth."

"Sí. And you weren't a revolutionary?"

"Pero—years, years ago."

"You see, I *was* right."

"Señora—Don Bosco— Whatever point of view you take, your Argentina's wonderful, and I want to see, to possess, it all."

"Precisely that attitude!" Señora Amelia said. "Possess it all." Nélida nodded.

Anita the beauty, till then silent, merely assented with "Sí, possess" and, glancing at Andrés, laughed teasingly.

"Bitch!" He rose, seizing the remnant cheese, but not hesitating to glance too knowingly from her to Hector so that she dropped her eyes as her laughter rose insistently higher and he went off mustering almost inaudibly, "Bitchbitchbitchbitch."

Nélida hung her head in embarrassment.

"For a decent girl, such an environment, señor." Amelia patted Nélida's hand, which cringed and withdrew.

"A wonderful environment, señora—perhaps because I'm from a country where so many restraints have been removed that the modulations which bring joy and insight are going. Restraint is sometimes the best measure of joy, love, friendship, passion—"

"But I've never heard the señor speak so much!" Doña Elvira said with—feigned?—awe. "Or so well. Such a bubbling of castellano."

Matilde trilled. "Because he is becoming one of us. What more?"

"Who would wish that on him, with what he has in his country?" Rodolfo said.

"Chancho! Always it's money money money with you, eh?" Doña Elvira pressed with low voice and a genuine accusation.

"But what he has in his country," Matilde, romantic and a mediator, said, "will soon be here, verdad?"

"My wife will arrive on the twenty-eighth."

"And I can imagine the señor's anxiety." Señora Amelia's eyes set fixedly on him. "You must be very lonely."

"Loneliness is a much exaggerated state, señora."

"Oh? My husband—it has been eight years—I don't think it is so exaggerated. No, Nélida?"

"Hardly, Mamá."

They rose.

He was left alone with Jorge. All through these meanderings Jorge had been leaning against the patio wall, listening, his eyes on him.

"So, Jorge?"

Jorge raised his brows, smiled, and left too.

Matilde cleared the table. "But, señor, you touched nothing."

"Sí, touched nothing. Hasta mañana, Matilde."

For three days he hardly left the rooms except to read in the patio while Matilde was upstairs cleaning. "You are ill?" Doña Elvira asked. "No, no." "But we have a fine doctor, señor." "It is no doctor I need, simply sun and isolation."

Now, lying in bed nights, he became aware of the sounds of the house, a great body with one breath palpitating its rhythm under moon or dark, heaving its foul air and drawing a fresh flow from the mountains, responding to the shifts and sounds. The house made familiar, he seemed to penetrate it, enter its flow, become air itself crossing hallways, down corridors into rooms, till he knew whose doors, which body moved: Amelia's weeping, muffled, and the whispers of Nélida, the rhythmic MamáMamáMa; Nélida's own static visit at four to the baño, a glass lifted and lowered, the interval of a pill, and then the pull of a chain (a facade?); the stealth of Hector as his door hushes to, his testing of Anita's door (never locked), the quick opening and closing, no word but the quick gasp from Anita as Hector takes her with a relentless rapacity, then slips back to his room, leaving redoubled silence; the throbbing engine of Andrés's lover's auto, the cut off, the long doubly loud hiatus, then the slammed car door, the front door inched shut, Andrés's feet on the baldosas, his room door, the rush and gulp of the toilet; Jorge entering by two, noisily clicking along the corridor till Doña Elvira from her apartment off the patio whispers in what is nearly a shout, "Jorge! Maldito que sea!" in her zeal waking them all for a hazy instant perhaps, but, as if tired, waking Rodolfo, so that, between Don Bosco's tearing snores, they murmur, and breath drives with the reach and moans of passion again.

But he penetrated now the house till their rhythms too came to penetrate his own flesh, his body became the house, the motion of the house, so that when he lay waiting for its rhythm and his expectations were blunted, broken, he could not sleep, the blood would not flow smoothly, but rushed and slowed, his ears rang with it, his head ached as if clogged. He was separated from it.

It was the time of the moon and when he rose to open the windows and go out onto the balcony, all the city would be stark light and shadow, two cities, one of searing light and one of shadow that lay under—and two of him. He felt his whiteness stark and bared, naked in the moon, and that shadow he cast, which moved, clung, but apart. Why did even his shadow annoy him so?

The cool air drove him in. He drew the blinds to cut out moon and flung himself onto the bed. But vague light still penetrated—it spread, as he stared, over ceiling, in the mirror. He felt cold; even the bedding felt cold. He turned, turned till the blankets slid away, till annoyed—he'd worked himself into an anguish, he must get up, he flung open the windows again, let the moon in—and he wanted to go out. Foolish! But he had no schedule! Why shouldn't he walk the night, walk off the moon, walk till sun drove it off? He dressed and went quietly down, through rasps and sighs, and let himself out with the slightest click, and stood free under the veil of new foliage burgeoning overhead against the moon.

He crossed the Plaza de Chile and went down San Martín street—all dead but for a car now and then, a straggler, a kid huddled asleep in a doorway, several men stretched out on the dirt under benches on the Plaza de España, where the Moorish tiles caught the moon in a dizzying pattern. The dogs were out, strays mad to forage, who in day skulked away from people in the baldíos, wastes where they would sit as if in groups, but each isolated, sunning, waiting for night to go on the prowl.

He walked till the sun began to turn sky a greenish light over the precordillera. The street cleaners were out. At the mercado central men were splashing and sweeping down the walls. A block from the pension, at the Café Gom, workers stood crowding the counter for quick coffee. He sat at a table and ordered an espresso and a medialuna.

Vargas was standing at the bar, talking to two others, though he was gazing at him. Didn't he ever sleep? Was the man always vigilant? His dark eyes, in those shadowed pits, seemed to fall on him—but did they?—as he went on talking to the two men, seedy types with rather voracious eyes, restless thin bodies, nicotined fingers. Were they partners, a team?

He was furious with himself: what had happened to his thinking?

He paid and left, and went back to the pension.

"Dios mío, señor! We were frantic. You weren't in your room. Nobody had heard you go out. I'm glad to see you." Doña Elvira eyed him with wonder.

And all through breakfast the others treated him warmly,

cajoling, his night exploit suddenly adding a dimension of intrigue to him, no doubt. Even Nélida gazed with a kind of enchantment. "Who can resist the beauty of Mendoza at night?"

And seizing his moment to thicken the ambience, he laughed, smiling into Nélida's eyes. "Ah, yes, who, who, Nélida?" so that, mystified, that shy flower gave way to a release of nervous laughter, which Señora Amelia and Doña Elvira and even Matilde echoed until Jorge threw up his hand and went off to work. Don Bosco settled on his cane and went to ready himself for the morning gathering of old men on the Plaza de San Martín.

He was tired, yet, stretched out, he could not sleep for the sounds of Matilde and Cati clattering, their voices, sinks and showers, and traffic trundling outside. When he did half-doze, it was to see darkness, a pit glimmering deep below, a dark eye with a white center toward which he was moving—his hand reached out to protect himself from the surface of that dark eye— A terrible ringing halted his descent.

"Señor?" Matilde rapped. "Alguien le espera."

He rose. Light splayed the pit.

"Who?"

"The other. Ése."

He caught the condescension of *ése*.

"Un segundito."

He heard her descend, and he rose, flung back the curtains, washed and slipped into clean trousers and shirt, then went down.

Evaristo Vargas.

"Buen día."

"Buenos días."

His shirt in the dim hallway startled with its whiteness, his skin a dark shadow under, his hair pitch, but his eyes glittered with the vague light from the patio windows along the corridor.

"The señor was looking for me." He said it with assurance, such confidence.

"Seeking you?" His blood thudded. He felt distended.

"Sí. At the Gom this morning."

But he had been walking! pressing the night on, though it was true he had desired speech, company. He was beginning to realize the continuity of his days with Margaret, her presence, the unspoken dependence on instinct, how it was in silence that speech went on—in the head, heart, through the body. When it ceased, the body had to find it in another. Could you prevent its response? Could you help but seize it?

Perhaps he was too slow to respond, for Vargas said, "I was mistaken," but then added, "I don't think so."

He felt trapped by the other's assurance; it was so easy to give way and let the other's confidence carry him; Evaristo had the habit of still eyes, which would not move from you. But he did not feel free to answer. Instead, he said, "Perhaps since you know the province so well, you're willing to be my guide? It would be convenient. I'd waste more time venturing out alone."

"Then you want me to come this afternoon?"

"Today?"

"Not?"

"Yes. Perhaps we could go farther—to Tupungato?"

"That would require a full day, but we could go to the baños at Villavicencio— you could soak up some health—if you don't mind losing the siesta. We can arrive justo, justo for an afternoon workout."

But when, on the dirt road, they wound up onto a miniature plateau, a flat terrace high in a valley, which was at the moment perfectly sunned, "Evaristo," he said, "stop here. I want sun more than the baths."

Evaristo was a climber, agile as a goat, at home on narrow ledges.

"Venga Vd, señor." Evaristo led him a goat's path up, up, the valley falling steadily away with a treacherous threat as he rounded rocks, rising, one foot constantly higher, till he would not turn back unless he reached the ridge and gripped and looked over —and *behold*: ridge after ridge, endless, futile.

"What illusion, eh, señor?"

"Yes." All illusion. "But I've never been so close to the sun." He lay absorbing the hot ground, feeling it molten.

"Come—" Evaristo stood over him, a colossus alone against endless space. "Take off your shirt, trousers—everything, and let the sun touch every inch of you. What is worse than a body too white? You don't want to remain a maggot?" He threw his head back, laughing, a dark sun in the sky.

He was undressed. "Now, relax—" Evaristo straddled him. "Why do you shudder? You think the criminal is going to hurt you? Are you so afraid? I haven't secured your confidence? You haven't known me long enough, that's it?" He laughed. "And what is it—to know, señor?" And his hand gripped his shoulders, those enormous hands covered, encased his shoulders—he quivered under the touch, again not believing how gentle—and the hands rubbed slowly until the muscles, stimulated, were afire with the flow; rubbed down, a firm, ever-increasing pressure, extending, down his thighs—and then, miraculously, as at Potrerillos, the hand slid under him and turned him so his body blended with the earth, turned heat to the earth; the hands blended with his bones, they sank against the earth beneath.

"Aye, Evaristo, you ruin me. I'm destroyed, destroyed!"

"In a month you won't know yourself. You'll think you're a stone broken off the mountain. What a man needs is all here in the world—walking, climbing, swimming, hot springs, sun; he doesn't need to invent it."

He leaped over the rocks. A goat, frightened, charged off, but not far from it, a ram stood poised, motionless, its horns aglow and challenging in the sun.

"Evaristo, where are you headed?"

"Down."

"Wait."

Evaristo let out a bellow, two, three times. "I leave you to find your way down." He leaped, veered, jumped with the speed of a creature born to the slopes.

As the days went deeper into spring, they ventured farther out into the province—to San Rafael, San Luis, Luján, Alta Verde, an ever-widening circle. Evaristo was filled with enthusiasm and knowledge about places and Argentine history. They ventured to San Juan, the neighboring province. "Sarmiento sat here, his mother here." It was the dirt patio. He sat under the fig tree himself, like the great Sarmiento, under the greeny flowers. They crossed the miles of flat scorching sand and dust; and then always in the afternoon they would stop somewhere, he would be made limp by those hands, which it seemed were moulding him. Now he was dark, and his teeth flashed so white in his mirror that he laughed at his own new self, thinned and hardened. After Evaristo rubbed the oil in, he would lie sleeping the siesta; he'd then scrub free in a stream or the aguas termales or a public bath in whatever city. He felt himself emerging. He would laugh abruptly as if to burst with what he drew into him from the earth, sun, those hands. "I'm going to be a new creature, Evaristo, because of you. You're doing it."

"No, señor. It's the sun. Our Mendoza does that."

What, he thought, if *they* back there could see! Thorne and Addison and Telliers, who had worked with him, his parents, Margarita. Margarita! How would she know him, for never had he been this—never dark and hard—yet that was only part: there was the other who was forming in the chrysalis, whose body lay open to sun and earth, which was developing invisible hands that wanted to touch sky and mountains, reach, reach— At night in bed he felt them, invisible tentacles, moving like a plant's groping across the floor, over the balcony, down, out— He laughed, seeing his own tentacles draw in everything, absorb Don Bosco, Anita, the entire pension, streets, plantains and acacias, this city, moving toward the precordillera, the altiplano, over the Andes and toward the Pacific, drawing all, all, along inside him.

Filled with joy, he was sure all the pension could hear his laughter; and he was two people, one watching the other, who delighted him. And one September evening when the night spring air lay thick as flesh against his earth, so thick it seemed to take breath into it, he heard steps outside his door. Someone whispered—

He was not expecting Evaristo. The knock came, but no voice followed.

"Who?"

He flung open the door.

He was stunned. "Margarita! You!"

And she was stunned. He saw she was stunned. For the briefest interval she was not sure, did not recognize—the voice perhaps, but not *him*.

And then he laughed. "You didn't know me!" He clutched her, kissed, and she gave way, almost as if not quite convinced yet he was not a stranger.

"But what happened? You're early. You weren't due for two weeks or more yet."

Now she settled against him. "God, you scared me! I had the nightmare feeling I'd come to the wrong pension, wrong city, wrong man." She sat on the bed.

"Thank you, Matilde." She was standing there, rapt in their union, as blunt as a tourist. He shut the door.

"Ohhhh." Exhausted, he saw, she fell back and stretched her arms out. "So terribly hot. I'm sweating. I hate sun."

"But you look marvelously untouched by it."

And she did—impeccable. Surprisingly, not a wrinkle in her robin's egg blue, perfect her makeup, fresh. He understood why Matilde gawked, fascinated with this untarnished perfection.

"Why didn't you write or call or wire you'd be early?"

"Because it was either rush or stay home. There's the airline strike in New York, scheduled for today, and it did happen, so they reported in Buenos Aires, and I didn't want to risk being stranded. So I booked for yesterday, and here I am! You were right—what a drab place. Quaint, yes. But couldn't you have done better?"

"The food's wonderful. If there's anything about people on a limited budget, it's they know where they get the best food for the money, so why not follow them? And you'll have gossip galore. Our apartment's quite private, yet the pension's a family—for company, and you can leave anytime—"

"And since when did you crave company?"

"To ease the dull hours without you."

"How Latin you've become! You were never—never—so gallant, darling."

"I'm not now."

"You're parading a good show."

In a moment Matilde and Cati had brought up the luggage, Cati surely to gawk too; she stood too obviously taking Margaret in before Matilde had to call her. "Ya voy." And he did have a moment of pride in how Margaret looked before it turned back on him how quickly his judgement reverted to *home*. Why care how she looked! She was here.

Surely because curious about a pension he would so defend, she asked not to be taken out anywhere but to eat here and *know the house*. Isn't that what Spaniards said?

There was certainly a flurry in the dining room when they went down. Jorge, Andrés, and Don Bosco, even Hector rose; all the women nodded, smiling excessively; Doña Elvira, all grace, having swept off her apron, which she clutched out of sight; Matilde and Cati ravishing her clothes.

In English Margaret said, "Hello. I'm so glad to be with you all," which charmingly embarrassed and impressed them as if they were guilty of not learning her language. Actually, Margaret knew a few Spanish words, very few, so at first it would be lonesome for her—she would require him most of the time. "This night we sit apart, but from now on we'll join them at the big table when there's a place, so you can learn the language."

"Are we to be here that long?"

"I hadn't thought. I'm so used to it."

"Well, darling, there *is* business. Todd can't do it alone—forever."

"Alone! He's dozens of department heads. I'm not sure he couldn't disappear, as I have—and for months, like any North American—"

"*North* American!"

"—and find out that business had gone on the very next day as usual without him."

"Sorry, baby, *your* home, as you very well know, has lost the fine art of honest labor—a fact you must put up with."

"Because they've lost the dream. You can't have a great nation without a true and great dream—unless our nightmare of a car or two and a swimming pool in every yard, and leisure first and then work, is a true dream."

"A dream that's made you."

"Yes, and look at me."

She bent close. "Yes, look. You're," she murmured, "unbelievable. It startled me at once. *I've* never seen you so physical. It confuses me. What I fell in love with was that spiritual blue that was constantly dreaming past me."

"Then you fell in love with my *place*. My dream was of that."

"*You* haven't lost that, have you?"

"Not the dream. Maybe the place is here."

"Here!"

"But you haven't seen Mendoza yet. Every day I'm here, Margaret, I feel closer to the physical place, so right. When I'm lying or walking in the sun or breathing sun in the air, I'm so conscious of it touching me that I feel if I could stay still long enough I'd feel roots in me grip down, send fine shoots out of my flesh, and I wait, wait for the sensation of them breaking through my flesh and growing out—"

"You'd look a fool decked out in green."

"Don't laugh at me. It's—what shall I say?—a kind of marriage."

"It's not that I'm laughing. I'm being realistic. Why wouldn't I?

If that's marriage, what am *I* for?" She was staring into the mirror, but he saw she was waiting—and out of its depths he felt the distance. "You've never taken me there. You've never let me into that place—"

So already they were back in New York, they were sitting there in the apartment, there were drinks and talk, drinks and talk, they were exhausted, he could not leave business, she could not leave her glut of *arrangements*— They were, in an instant, back to that, were they? How could it happen so quickly? Breathlessly, the long gap closed, you had gone to Argentina, you weren't in New York but New York had come to you, brought its air, ambience, closed off this city—

He flung open the blinds.

"Perhaps—because I saw it, but only in my mind, and hadn't touched down on it yet—couldn't, Margaret."

"But I *am* here now, and something is happening to you."

"Yes, and you haven't even seen the place yet."

"From the air it looks a desert, arid, as far as I can see."

He dared not say *With what eye? I can't give you the eye.*

He said, "It's a virtual oasis. There's a poet here who calls it the *Venecia vegetal.* You must succumb to this Vegetable Venice, Margaret, and maybe we'll flower?"

"You'll show me how? help me?"

"I'll do all I can. You know I will."

And later, before they slept, she said, lying beside him, spent, "You *are* someone else," with wonder, with a queer gratitude he had never known in her before and which he lay thinking about—how it battered, that queer gratitude—"different," she said, and she lay close, her body close to him, against his back, resting, genuinely resting against him.

He awoke to voices, familiar—Matilde, then Doña Elvira—a hard rapid muddle, before he remembered Margarita lay beside him. A rapid knock jolted him and at the same time that Matilde said, "El hombre está, señor," he thought Evaristo! Matilde called him *El hombre* or *El,* never *un señor* or *Evaristo* or *Señor Vargas.*

"I told him *imposible,* señor. La señora Elvira tried to drive him away, but he insists he works for you and only you can send him away. He's waiting. La señora told him the señor's wife arrived last night, but he still insists on being dismissed by you."

"What is it? Who?" Margaret was sitting up, her hands having automatically drawn the sheet over her breasts, her negligee, so that he laughed.

"It's only Evaristo."

"Evaristo?"

"Send him up, Matilde."

"'Send him up?"

"Sí, Matilde."

In a moment Evaristo was at the door.

"Don . . . ?"

Margarita was standing now, in her robe, but except for the most impersonal recognition that someone was in the room, she glanced, if formally, at him.

"My wife is here and we will all three go. Perhaps we could go the park, to begin, and we can have an asado at the Restaurante Azul and you, if you prefer, can entertain yourself—"

"What?" Margarita said. "Did you have plans?"

"I'm arranging—"

"No, no, we must do as planned. I want to fit in exactly to your life here. It's *you* who knows what you need."

But she had stepped closer almost instinctively, with a restless glance over him, down him and then hard at the dark face, the deep eyes, the mass of black hair—and then too long, with disbelief, at the hands hanging so naturally loose and still there. And he knew that Evaristo, with whatever indifference or courtesy or nervousness or fear, was aware that she was watching him, and for an instant he felt sorry for the man caught in such a situation of discomfort.

But Evaristo did not take them to the park.

"You're headed toward Tupungato!"

"Your wife hasn't been to Potrerillos."

"So he's a tour guide?"

"Not exactly, though I believe I've turned him into one." He gave her a day by day history of his travels with Evaristo, difficult because with the wind filling his mouth he had to talk loud while from time to time Evaristo would very quietly comment from the front seat in his pleasant, rather deep voice, which carried. He found himself an intermediary, translating till Margarita or Evaristo would cast eyes at the other in acknowledgment, in a wordless interplay which struck him as so comic he laughed outright—"

"Are we that funny?" she said.

"You're like two characters bobbing and turning in a silent movie." The image struck them so they laughed together.

But translating was palling, tiring, and they all settled into observing, until he shouted when he recognized the willow: "Allá, Evaristo!"

"Exactly, señor." And he pulled off the road exactly as before and made the bumpy trip up to the little plateau down which the stream near the willow ran. But it was hotter this time with the first dust in the air, and the earth was burning.

"The sonda—the hot winds and tierra—will blow soon."

"But where are you going?" she said, with something of fear, as Evaristo went off.

"Oh, he won't leave us—it's for firewood."

"Then let me—" She went off with him and, after a while, it startled to hear her laughing; it would be Evaristo's ten words of English, perhaps.

After, when, having eaten and rested—he began to undress—Margarita cried out, and it startled him too, realizing her embarrassment. "But you may too. He'll think nothing of it. I'll send him off for a while if you like."

"You can be seen from anywhere—" Her arm scooped-in infinite space. "—And I couldn't possibly with a stranger."

"But Evaristo is one of us."

"One of *you*. You forget I've just arrived. I'm your wife, and I'm still—if vaguely—foreign *and* civilized."

"Not civilized enough! Oh, come on, Margarita—or at least sit there while I get a workout. You can't believe how you could become part of the earth the way Evaristo massages."

"I'm not so sure I want to be part of the earth."

It did not embarrass Evaristo at all to rub oil into him in front of her.

"It's something *I've* never done," she tried to explain to Evaristo. He nodded—he understood—intent nonetheless as always on his task. But she watched his hands; she did not take her eyes off his hands, stunned by the size, no doubt, and the contradictory motion of gentleness.

Feeling the coursing initiated by those hands, he sank away—

Voices woke him. Laughter.

Evaristo was in the river—gleaming. He was talking to her.

"I can't understand five words he says," she said when she saw him sit up. "He's been muttering all the time he's been in the water and no telling what pearls of wisdom I've missed—criollo wisdom, isn't that your word for it?" But plainly she was enjoying the sight of Evaristo so naturally sloshing and splashing, turning like a seal at play. "But he's certainly enjoying himself."

"And you're not? You'd have liked something more sophisticated. You're not disappointed, are you?"

"Disappointed! With that view? And everything new? Give me time."

But he did not give Margarita much time. In the ensuing days they explored the city, its surrounding areas, each day venturing farther out into the terrain, the series of towns like oases in the gray-chalk-brown spread of earth, where there would be sand, then tierra, then rock, matorral, thickets gone brown only beginning to give way to vague green. Now they knew Challao, Maipú, Luján and Cacheuta, Las Heras and once had gone as far south as San Rafael and even north to Uspallata, green willows and poplars stark against the snow, where steeps began and deep gorges promised danger and there was a high penetration of snow beyond. "Peligro?" She had acquired a vocabulary quickly, impressing Evaristo, who joyed in anyone's flattering his native tongue.

"Es guapa, su señora."

"He says you're quick, a worker—guapa."

"I work at what I want."

"When didn't you?"

"Look—a train!"

"It's the international train." It was moving very slowly along the low slope, dark and insistent as a serpent.

"And where do we go if we take that direction, Evaristo?" She pointed—hard into the mountains.

"He says to the high limit between Chile and Argentina—to the Christ of the Andes, Cristo Redentor."

"Y Aconcagua," Evaristo added.

"The highest point of all the Americas—you can see Aconcagua."

"And you've seen it?" she said.

"Not yet. The snows are just now thawing in the lowest regions. The roads have only recently been opened."

But she must have decided then because back at the pension, pensive, she said, "I want to go to the Cristo, I want to see it, I've never been high in the mountains, I can't imagine even seeing with my own eyes the highest point."

And he too wanted—more—because it was becoming *his* place and more and more his body wanted to extend, absorb it all as part—nor would he be satisfied until he held it all—inside him.

And so she waited, and he, and it was a mystery to him to see her—for it was strange, it was irritating too, to see her so set, at times quietly trance-like, *gone*, while she was in the bedroom, at meals, where she seldom talked at table while he and the pensionistas rattled on like a family. He saw she was apart and waiting; this time he felt it had nothing to do with his having been sick, with North American business, with work and stress—and in a way he was glad that something obsessed her, that she had a desire he knew but did not yet understand, for she would not talk of it, and he felt her urgency must be so different from his own, though she would now and again say, "Is the pass clear to Chile?"

"More and more. The landslides are ending, señora."

"And how does the train get through?"

"There are tunnels and sheds in the worst areas—it burrows and sometimes waits—and when they are sure it can plow through, it goes on."

"So I must burrow and wait, Evaristo?"

"He says the señora must do what everyone else in her situation does."

She laughed. "In that case I wait and then I put myself in your hands, Evaristo, to get me there."

"I will try not to disappoint you."

But the following day he disappointed them both.

"Está el hombre," Matilde said with her usual distaste for Evaristo. She always accompanied him distrustfully to the room and, if they allowed it, she waited to see that he went down and directly out. Evaristo himself finally said to Doña Elvira, "How did you ever find such a guardian of honesty, señora? She's a treasure anyone would be proud of," and from that day Matilde—still reserved and rigid in her requirements, though at heart romantic (as she had never married, but brought up her sister's children)—carried off that little treasure, which deepened her smile and quickened her step whenever he arrived, and occasionally she would utter to the cook, "He's a sinvergüenza, but he's every inch a man."

Evaristo said, "I'm not expected, I know, but I must go away for a few days—three, five, perhaps two weeks—and I wanted the señor to know."

"What? Is he saying he's leaving?" Margarita said.

"Sí, señora. I leave."

"But—" Her gaze challenged him. He did not flinch. "What will we do? You must tell him—he's been invaluable, indispensable."

Though he too felt forlorn, felt as if those great hands had suddenly released him to air, a void, he said, "But for a few days, two weeks, we will do what we did before, Margarita. What else? We may even get used to it," though why he said it he did not know, for he felt as if he were falling, giving way—

"Negocios?"

"In a manner of speaking, business, yes." Evaristo gave not the least glint of self-betrayal.

If business, business. He knew, if he did not know specifically, that to Evaristo it was business. He did not question Evaristo's words. For a long time he had not once thought *thief*.

"Then, when you return."

"Adiós. Hasta luego, señora."

Now the heat began. Subtly it pressed, a weight, the air growing almost a fluid hot sea that lay still over you. "Ayyyyy!" Cati or Matilde burst out against it, wanting wind, motion, but the still sea hung so that he and Margarita scarcely wanted to leave the pension. "You go," she'd say, near naked, daring to catch what vague breath might ease over the city. And when they did go out together, they sought shelter, quickly worn by the drive of heat, your breath pressed back into your mouth, building up, building—a great dry womb which held the stale hot air rancid with scents (flowers, people, buildings) turned odors—till children cried irritably on the plazas, mothers impatiently shouted at them, dragged them after them; lovers flopped on the benches; and only the old men sitting there in their black suits and berets, clutching canes, were happy basking motionless, bombarding the plazas with their talk and laughter.

Worse, at the pension, since Evaristo's leaving, the pensionistas, playing on Evaristo's success with him and Margaret, began to make overtures, innuendoes of assistance, service, subtle guises of friendship, even intimacy. Jorge would drive them anywhere, only drop a word. "But you've not seen the Museo Fáder yet?" Señora Amelia had a friend who could arrange a visit for the hour of their convenience. "Ay, señor—" Andrés pressed—all charm, his natural Latin beauty aglow in his *claros* eyes and perfect oval face, his boy's suggestive sprawl. He said in English, "I take where no turista have chance to go." And only Don Bosco was immune except for the joy of company: "I invite you to 1515—for an aperitivo, Don, with your señora—no?" But it was Matilde who intervened most of the time, saved them, with her muttering, her appalled glances, her overt slamming down of knives and plates on the tables, and, unable to refrain at times, with out and out admonitions to Jorge and especially Andrés: "Maleducados! Tempting the señora to corruption! As if anyone didn't know your nights! And dragging from sleep to meals, meals to sleep, sinvergüenza! Yes—you, you, you! By comparison that other, el hombre, is a saint—yes, a saint!" And Andrés retorted with "Because you want them all to yourself, do you? Is that it, eh?" until Doña Elvira, fearing the loss of any one of such good-paying residents, reduced Matilde to crying in the kitchen by threatening within hearing of everyone to fire her, thus satisfying them, though they all knew Doña Elvira would never part with Matilde.

He and Margaret decided one morning to take a bus to anywhere, on whatever was leaving, for the day, simply to ride, ride, forget the heat, see— They went to the station, TAC. There was a bus south to San Rafael, but, no sooner out, they were stifled, the windows were down, the air hot and the blow of tierra blinding, the passengers thrust the windows up one by one to keep grit out, there came an awful odor of feet, breath, but, worse, the bus stopped at every tiny cluster of stucco and adobe. By the time they reached San Rafael they could do nothing but find a restaurant and sit outside under the canopy in the growing heat. Margaret drank wine, though he had frequently enough warned her about the effect of the heat and the altitude, while he drank Campari; and soon she had the predicted headache—she was annoyed, there was nothing to see but one more bodega in this wine country, though since it meant being driven around, she chose to go, and there they gave them wines to sample. "It will surely drive away my headache," she said. "Or madden it," he said. "You *would!*" By the end of the bodega tour, she was all abrupt laughs—he knew the sign: fed up, a pitch and crisis, she would begin to want to go home to the States, plague him, if quietly, when she wanted her way; but he preferred her with the shell removed, so raw and direct: *Do you or don't you?* The only return to Mendoza was a late afternoon bus. "My God! Sun—forever!" And the town was deserted—siesta time; they retreated to the rancid olive oil darkness of the restaurant, exhausted by the time the bus finally came. Halfway back, he had to ask the driver por favor to stop, his señora was sick; he helped Margaret down, where she vomited on the dry ground by the bus. All around was nothing but dry earth, though far off there was the green shadow of the valley they'd been too hot and tired to notice. Back in the bus, she drifted into sleep, her head slumped against him. He realized how relieved he was—he looked at her, the soft, unblemished skin, the lips pressed to a pout, the tangles of honey hair; too innocent she looked, only the reek of wine, the worst stench from the breath, belied her sleeping innocence—yes, relieved, though he was ashamed at the thought: relieved of his irritation, of her as yet unspoken desire to leave, which he saw coming in the

—ah, how beautiful Mendoza is then." She burst into a peal of joy, spreading her arms as if it lay spread—she could see it—there out the window before them.

Margaret lay in bed three days, blinds darkly drawn, at times dizzy, nauseous, or sleeping, sleeping—perhaps she was shedding skin, sloughing the old life, in darkness protecting the new soft skin, letting it gather texture and strength and deeps.

But she was not. "If only it would *rain*—just once!" she cried and Matilde said "*How* is it going to rain in Mendoza!" and went off into her gale of laughter, though her hands sympathized, making Margaret comfortable.

"If only I were somewhere it rained—"

And he sensed that she was escaping—she would sleep it out, sit, hold, bind him in until he consented to go home, and then it would be the same: "*You* wanted to return just as you wanted me to go."

While she slept, he was drawn outside by the perfume of glicina, took walks, sat afternoons listening when the carefully guarded waters, stored from the melting snows of the Andes two hundred kilometers away, were released and flowed through the acequias, poured a great stream of glitter and life through the city, coiling into every cantero, around trees and flower beds, breeding an oasis of green, flowers, palms from its dry flesh. And the sound made him want to go up to the high mountains, to the pure white snow and the cries at the heart of silence closest to the sun, where it burns the snow into cold water that flows down into the valleys in a vast web over the dry earth. He stared at the cordillera, longing for that sensation—to be caught in the burning and transformed in substance, flow with that motion of waters. Feeling his blood quicken, he laughed aloud. He would tell

Margaret. Yes, he would say, It's time, let's go the limit—to the Andes, the border, and your statue, El Cristo Redentor.

But when he arrived at the pension, he was startled at noises in the apartment: Margaret was sitting up in a chair and there was the dark form against the sun—

"Evaristo!" He almost reached out to verify—but no, no illusion.

"Just back," she said.

"Sí, de vuelta," Evaristo echoed.

"We thought you'd abandoned us for good."

He wore a suit this time, black, the perennial white shirt, no tie—and new shoes.

"How could the señor think I'd abandoned him?"

A catch in his own throat kept him from answering. But Evaristo seemed to notice how he examined his clothes and, as if sensing his thought, said, "An old suit, but—perdónenme—a jacket bothers me." He removed it.

"Ah, your trip was successful?"

"Shorter than I expected and, sí, successfiil—though perhaps not in the way the señor may mean."

He felt Evaristo's honesty—and disillusion with him?—as evidence of the naturalness between them. He would intimate nothing of Evaristo's secret.

"But, Margaret, coming up, I heard you—you've really learned to talk a blue streak in Spanish."

"I think Evaristo and I have established a common ground, though it costs: he promises a Spanish word for an English word. And he's just promised, if you don't mind, to drop me at the baths for an hour—he'll wait—and bring me back. It might just bring me back to life, he says."

"If anyone can do it, Evaristo can." His hands lay clumped, earthen on his knees.

"Entonces, media hora, Evaristo?"

"Perfect pronunciation, Margaret!"

"Perfecta, señor!" Evaristo laughed.

He was grateful for Evaristo's return—the house expanded, tension diminished, nerves calmed, though the pre-summer heat, an unceasing presence, did not let up; and he was glad for the momentary respite, the isolation from Margaret. At meals in the pension her absence gave him a vague detachment when, under Don Bosco's lizard lids, the eyes focused too meditatively on him, or the women were filled with carefully phrased inquiries about the señora. "All the way to Villavicencio every day? What devotion to her health!" "And the awful turns up those terrible caracoles in an auto? I'm frightened to death of those whiplash roads."

Those roads. Alone, wandering, swimming in the park—he had an associate membership in the Club Azul—when Margaret was off, he pondered more and more those roads into the mountains. They were deeper into spring now, and the high snows were melting. And he grew impatient with Margaret, wanting now to go—as she had wanted—to the border; but Margaret *would* go to the baths every day. "They're doing me wonders. I've never felt so well, and you may lose Evaristo so I'm taking advantage of him before you do lose him." After her little siege in bed, she was lithe, open to any activity. She did not like the pension, and perhaps she was trying to intimidate him into moving by avoiding it except when she must return, by leaving him alone enough so that he would long for her constant company and so move. She sloughed off his desire to go to the mountains. "They'll always be there, won't they, darling?" It became a series of postponed tomorrows; in fact, it was Evaristo who assured her the trip was easier the later in the season they went—because of the snow. "Besides, the winds have not come down yet. You don't want to run into the viento blanco up there —you would not survive." And he *had* heard of the white wind, grit and snow frozen and hurled by the driving winds till it battered walls and penetrated even stone.

And as if Evaristo's mention heralded them, like a heaving hot ocean in torment, spring winds drove at the city. Standing in the street, he could not believe—the mountains had disappeared. A great gray-brown sea rolled over the desert, rising higher and higher, spreading till sun vanished, sky went; the dense air thickened to a brown fog that whipped and smat and beat so that inside the pension you could hear tierra swat stucco and tiles, trees, earth itself, till you could barely see close trees and houses, sidewalk, ditches. At night you had almost to come upon a lighted window to detect it; only on the main streets, where all the businesses were lit up day and night, did landmarks guide you. But an instant away even the most familiar object deceived—you could lose yourself a few yards from your door.

"Impossible, Nate," she said. "We're stranded." Margaret and Evaristo were at Villavicencio. "It came up so suddenly. Fortunately the hotel was not full. We can't drive fifty-one kilometers in this smattering sand."

"Of course not. You must stay until it's all over. It may be days."

"But there isn't a thing to *do* here in this weather."

"Live—and wait."

"You!"

Those who ventured out wore handkerchiefs over their faces.

They moved like the blind, feeling their way slowly. Autos moved with dim divorced eyes through the sandy sea.

Wind and tierra came as relentlessly as a castigation and cleansing—as if to drive the sick and dying to the grave and the guilty and weak mad—for the pressure of heat was unbearable. Inside the pension, the viento sonda transformed the pensionistas. Every door and window was closed, sealed, but sand made its way into the finest cracks, over floors (Matilde worked constantly with her kerosened mop, pasando el trapo over the baldosas and parquet); sand settled into clothes and food—nothing, not even the bedclothes, was free of it. Dust clung to hair, coated the skull, lay in the comers of eyes and mouth, inflamed eyes and throat. The blow and heat and pressure made the pensionistas irritable; they smoldered, lashed out. Jorge and Andrés and Don Bosco went at it, Doña Elvira screamed at Matilde and Cati and they at each other; Amelia and NéIida confined themselves to their rooms and wept. There was no place any of them could go to escape; and the pressure came down like hands gripping their heads till people wept, cried out, became ill, and in the city some actually were driven mad or died. "Ayyyy, you don't know the viento sonda. Vicente Gómez went mad, Lorenzo Abal committed suicide—" Histories, legends, the old stories—now he believed them.

It lasted four days. After, the pensionistas, the city, lay exhausted, laden. As it came, it went—suddenly winds ceased, there was a great silence, and then a long slow sifting and drifting down. Over.

Then the rains came, as if by design to clear the air, to cleanse the city, to bathe its body and carry the filth into the acequias and back out to the desert past the asparagus fields, past frutales and viñas. . . .

Sun penetrated the earth. Each flower, each cantero, every palm leaf stood sharp, isolated, dean, every object, wall. You could see infinitely—each ridge and striation of the precordillera, the far white peaks sharp as blade edges blazoned. So clear, all seemed to have moved closer.

Matilde and Cati worked, clattering in camaraderie, and laughter filled the pension; doors banged, street sounds echoed, the canaries sang; pure sun and air and especially the waters—ever moving, bringing the suck and tear and rippling of joy through the city—bred new life in everything: glicina doubled its perfume, the alpine violets opened, the little enamorados del sol spread pink and white and freshest yellow—immaculate.

Margaret and Evaristo returned—immaculate too. The maid at the Hotel Villavicencio had washed and pressed their only change. "Oh, God, simply to be able to *move* again!" she cried. "And you should *see* Villavicencio—overnight transformed."

"As you are?"

"I?"

"Yes. You're as bright as a flor de la montaña."

"Darling! Mendoza is making a poet of you. You never before—"

" It's light, the sun. I've never seen so much—so far, or close."

"Sometimes too close deceives?"

"By now, we should know better."

"Yes, should." She played with Cati's newest canary. It would not sing for her, but it flicked gold sun.

But Margaret herself seemed to sing, reverberate with the energy burgeoning Mendoza. All the pension laughed at her rapidly increasing vocabulary, her charming blunders, flattered by her unflagging devotion to speaking.

"Pero qué graciosa su señora!" they told him. "Qué encanto!"

"You should think of going back," she said. "Things can't go on forever without you."

He was startled at how menacingly that other world, which seemed to have vanished, loomed. Long nights he had no longer heard the rush of machines. Even she had made not the least mention of the factory, computers, parts, metal deliveries, research. And of course she was right, though the very thought brought dark skies, rain, turned his body white skin, sank sun—

And that night the machines came back. He saw himself standing on the sands, the endless arid flats at the foot of the precordillera, and listening, waiting for the sound of water flowing down from the mountain, walking toward the sound of waters, but what he heard halted him. He listened, not believing; it was the sound of machines; the machines were here, louder and louder, closer— And he turned and ran, his arms outstretched, and he ran straight into one, and screamed when it gripped him.

He woke—to sudden silence.

"What's happened? What is it?"

Margaret rose, dark against the moon.

"Nothing. A dream. Too many of Cati's ñoquis, I guess."

But he was afraid to sleep again. He watched the moon, slow, shift bars over the floor until he heard through the open window Matilde and Cati moving about in their rooms over the kitchen, across the patio.

Now a strange hiatus set in. Margaret wanted to lie in the sun, to meander alone, a whole day at a time?—"Don't you always say it's a perfect paradise?"—at the zoo, at the amusement park at Challao . . . "Don't worry. I know my way about alone now—you've seen it all—and I want to absorb what I can before I leave."

"Leaving! Leaving. Why do you insist on driving that home to me? *I* know we must leave. But must you keep goading?"

"Oh, Nate, it's only that I want *you* to make the most of what you still have here—and each of us not to waste a minute. Don't you see?"

"Quite honestly, I don't."

"Well, darling, one day you will."

So he could go on delving this city, could go back, as he had before Margaret, walking alone, walking till he knew every street, every departamento—until happily exhausted, sweating in sun, feeling the fullness of his lungs and all the brown hardness of his body. And he knew now he could not leave without going to the border—to complete things.

"To see the Cristo," he told her.

"Yes. But we *can* go now. The avalanches—*aludes* Evaristo calls them?—that come in spring are surely over?"

"It may be the end of us if they're not."

"You don't know how funny you are!"

And always he passed the Gom, thinking to see Evaristo to arrange for the trip to El Cristo. Evaristo must be off on one of his ventures or he would be there as regularly as before.

But Evaristo arrived one morning to ask if he could be of service. Margaret had succumbed to the charms of Andrés, who had invited her to tennis in the park. "But you do something, darling. I leave you in Evaristo's hands."

"I know a hidden place where the río Mendoza is deep and even in the daytime the señor can swim without a soul around."

It was a steep valley, its deeps filled with green—willow, acacias, poplars.

"How you love this country!" Evaristo said.

"Yes. It is a crime—" Both laughed spontaneously. "—to leave it. Have you ever thought of going to my—or another—country, Evaristo?"

"Many times. Business would be fine there."

"Then—?"

He was silent, sad, sitting on the bank, hulked over himself, embracing his knees, dark as stone there.

"Such melancholy at the thought? Surely you don't fear you won't find a living?"

"My living I carry with me, as the señor knows."

"And my wife knows?"

"Not unless you've told her."

"You don't think I'd say anything?"

"I trust you with my life—you sense that. What do women understand of this bond?" Evaristo's deep eyes seemed to close apprehensively.

"Who knows what a woman understands?"

"If there's love, I suppose that's understanding?"

"And you love señora Margarita deeply?"

He started at the name—not Margaret, but Margarita—coming from Evaristo.

But love? He had not thought *love* since his arrival; he had thought *sun, life, body, time, peace.*

At his hesitation perhaps, Evaristo said, "Forgive me, señor. It was not a question I have a right to ask." And you could see he was truly sorry, with a hangdog shame, and he looked away to the far cordillera. "I myself don't know—truly—what it is to love, to love really."

Because you're a thief. But he caught the words back in time—and with shame too.

Evaristo had his eye. He could not look away, could not, without betraying the humiliation he felt at being trapped in his own words—

"Because I'm a thief. You think that? You're thinking that. *I* know. *I've* thought, trained myself to think, how the world thinks. You wouldn't believe how a man thinks such things. Oh, to believe as the world does, that *finally*, no matter how intelligent, the one who steals is stupid. Because they don't know what a thief is."

"But you're justifying stealing?"

"Never stealing for its own sake—like some thieves—not incurable lust. Not for a code, no. I don't mention how the world needs us to justify itself either. But a code for me, for this self, yes, because you know, señor, I discovered—and I was young, young! nobody would believe how terrible was my reality, but it made me —I discovered I was *every minute* watching, *alive*, never one second dead: oh, yes, maybe filled with fear, apprehension, dread even—but never resting, all my senses alert, sometimes (very many times) in a kind of agony which made me—it was the next great discovery—understand their suffering—because I knew them, because I kept looking and saw and did not lie about what I saw, *would* not. I saw what it is, this world we build—lies, señor, lies—and who would spend all his life on what he knew to be lies?"

"And stealing's not a lie?"

"Sí sí sí—to them. But not, not to me, señor. It is what it is. I stare it in the face every day—my own face."

"But you can't help it?"

"I *can* help it—sí! What *are* you? I ask. A thief, I answer. *Born* to be one—yes, I believe that. And *how* to be one? I ask every day. Never betray yourself you're anything else. Oh, that, I know, is no virtue—" His head rose. Sun leaped wet in his eyes. "But neither is the other, to be something else—honest in their terms, honest to satisfy the world, and to give it your best—think of that, señor, to give your *best* to a lie—for them who proclaim the lie a disease. Or can only what they call the diseased truly call the disease by the name, eh, señor? And who has the disease, the thief or the ones who will not admit their own thieving, the ones who know the thief in their own flesh, but free themselves by making him *their* lie, eh?"

He could feel Evaristo's breath close on him, the great hands move close to him—he shrank from them, inside himself.

"You don't answer."

"You knew I wouldn't?"

Evaristo did not cease staring, nor did the hands rest.

"But silence—that is an answer too?"

"You answer your own questions."

"I've always done so. Mi madre, she taught me answer your own questions honestly and you'll come as near the truth as most men—you might even get the answers. What do you think of that? And mi madre, she was a poor, ignorant woman.

"She doesn't sound so ignorant."

"I use the world's words, señor. She saw, mi madre, with the eye of light."

Now, in his sight—he was staring at the willow—the way his hand half rose to green, she might have been standing within hands' reach. Light burned over his hands.

And quick, transfixed by the light on those hands, he was afraid Evaristo, who had never spoken so much, would stop. He was afraid of his words—they burned—yet he was afraid the spate would stop.

"She—mi madre, mi madre—"

The sound compelled him to Evaristo's face. His voice was

struck by light. He heard love, the first time he heard love in the voice, and it made his heart fill an instant, burn. He almost uttered.

"Mi madre was a thief."

"Your mother!" All his training must have leaped into motion.

Evaristo laughed, but not at him; it was the tender laughter memory evokes.

"Mi madre stole me."

"Stole you?"

"Sí, from the Hospital Emilio Civit."

"And she told you?"

"Said I was sent from God—but never, when I was old enough, kept it from me. 'Why would I hide it from you,' she said, 'when you're the one happiness of my life He sent me? To hide it would be a lie, and lying would deny my happiness.' Think, señor, the one happiness—and from stealing, and never repenting even in the eyes of God. 'God must mean what happens. I would risk it a thousand times over,' she'd say."

"How did she keep you up?"

"You mean did she steal—for life?"

He nodded.

"Never once."

"But—"

"Because she was not by nature a thief, señor."

"By nature!"

"By choice, then, but if something more than the head chooses, so—the heart. You don't believe—who could expect it?—when you *know*. Oh, I know, you'll say: if you had everything, money, all, you'd never have stolen. That is not true. She, *she* gave me all I needed to live, without stealing—poor, yes, but she gave, every minute of her life gave, and worked for everything: for this love.

She had to steal me to get the one thing to make everything worth it—or nothing. Nothing, señor. You do not know *nothing?*—how it is a grave around you when you are walking, eating, breathing. You look as if you don't know me. I scare you?"

"Not scare—startle. You've never spoken before. It's—an avalanche."

"But I upset you?"

"It's too much at once."

"Because you've never stolen anything? Have you, señor, never stolen anything?" The voice compelled—close—and the face close. He was conscious of the physical waiting, the suspension in the man. He looked now into the dark eyes, which would not release him.

"No, I don't think so," he said.

"Never? Nothing which did not belong to you? of any kind? something you maybe couldn't even touch? All things to steal are not things you can see. You're sure? Not one time? Not one desire?"

"Desire?"

"Sí. Anything. Once. To make you seethe with joy, after, with pain too, but that you couldn't undo—never, and never want to?"

"I don't know."

"Never?"

"I don't know. I *don't!*" His own voice, breaking, startled. It drove the dark eyes back. The willow and sun leaped up where Evaristo had been, for he stood.

"I get too serious. Forgive me, señor." At the same time Evaristo gripped his hand and drew him up to full height so abruptly that he felt Evaristo's breath in his face, his chest chafed his, his heart beat in Evaristo's hand.

"We climb a while now?" Evaristo released him and, without

waiting for an answer, leaped over the rocks and wound up narrow ledges, calling down, young joy in his voice, "Que tenga prisa! Hurry!" harrying pleasantly his slowness. In no time, high above, Evaristo stood throwing his arms out into the light that emblazoned.

"You're a goat, Evaristo. Cabra!" For he himself made his way clumsily in Evaristo's footsteps, heaving breath by the time he rose under him.

Seeing his difficulty, "Grab my hand," Evaristo said. The wall was steep, treacherous, and he feared losing balance, but he reached— Evaristo with one easy draw raised him up.

"Dios mío!" he cried. For beyond, the valley opened, the world thrust up, spread—vast, clear. Ridges rose one after the other, hard white edges of white that looked soft as cloud. He was standing on a high edge of the world, which fell away—below, the road, the stream close by, a serpentine edge of green, great fallen rocks everywhere, and goats scattered in singles and pairs. Yet despite the peace, the air was violent, cool, and pressed; at the same time sun blazed, penetrated.

And suddenly he wanted to see the high cordillera, must go as far upward as he could into the space that pressed against earth, let his body feel the weight of infinite distances. He must go to the frontier. Perhaps then he could go back. Back! The thought of North America gloomed. The wind became a great whirr of machines echoing in his head, drowning all else. He feared the devastation.

"What is it, señor?"

"I don't know."

Evaristo set his hands on his shoulders.

"Terminará. It will end."

"Will it?" Wind whipped their voices thin. "Evaristo, we must go to the Cristo."

"As soon as you wish."

"And Margarita, she too wishes it—" And he saw Evaristo smile, perhaps at how strange now the new word which sprang so spontaneously from him.

"Sí. She has told me. She's ready. And the mountains are ready to receive us—the season of violent winds and the worst avalanches has passed. It's safe now."

"It's strange to hear you speak of safety."

"So you don't forget our talk?"

"I don't forget."

"Because I must always take risks, you mean?"

"Don't you?"

"The end is everything—what you take, why. The greater the gain, the greater the risk. After, when you have it, you know what it cost you. Think what it cost my mother—to know every day she might lose me, they might discover the thief, they might come, someone might prosecute, jail her, and always *when*, which instant, day, hour— Worst of all, señor, someone might—yes, steal me!" He let out a great bellow, but it was no laugh—it was filled with pain. "Imagine her fears—the agony. But do you know, it *made* her, that agony, gave her character—would you believe that?—so kind, such love. She understood—everything, everyone. Such heart! *Doña Flora!*— They would come with such problems. *Doña Flora!* To talk, simply to hear the wisdom pour from her. I think mi madre knew, yes—not to understand is to steal too."

"And now where is she?"

"Dead, señor. She went to the peace of the provinces—the dry earth of La Rioja, under perpetual sun. And you know how she died, señor? Listen. I'll tell you a woman—eaten day by day, from the inside rotting, and the body shrinking to nothing, and agony, and the sores you wouldn't believe—and no hospital, she would go to no hospital but die in that adobe patio, crammed with our few possessions into a corner of the patio, with a tin roof and walls around her. She would crawl out into the sun in the morning and lie there all day, wasting, and you know, señor, she'd say to me, 'Don't ever believe what they say about the great things, my son. If people knew I stole you, they would say, *See,* she's suffering, she's paying, God's punishing her, she's getting what she deserves. But they're wrong: if this is to pay for what I've done, it is nothing, I'd take ten times this for what I've done and still be glad, there's no punishment so terrible I would not be glad to bear for my joy in you, you.' *Me, me,* señor! To carry such a memory. Do you know the joy? And the burden, yes. Never to betray that woman. Always to know I'm the only one who carries her, the truth of her, in my heart—"

And he was staring—at that woman? Was she standing in air, sky, the far mountains? His hands quivered. The sun rose in his eyes but did not fall.

"And now in mine."

"In yours. Sí, señor."

At the thought he tremored—it touched marrow. He grew apprehensive. Why had Evaristo told him? Why now?

"We must go down, Evaristo."

At the pension Margarita was sitting with the other pensionistas on the patio, still in her tennis outfit, surprisingly natural in her talk despite her crippled Spanish.

"Andrés is easy to talk to. He's such a charmer—and that's not your forte, sweetheart."

"And the game?"

"Andrés *let* me, I think, take two sets."

"We swam, then climbed a little. Evaristo insists on making a regular goat of me."

"Speaking of climbing, do we get to Chile before we go on back?"

"The passes are clear. We can go anytime."

"With Evaristo? Surely you don't prefer one of those tours!"

"As you will."

"But you're rankled."

"I am?"

"Or tired."

"That, I suppose."

"Nothing else?"

"What else could be wrong?" But now he was rankled, perhaps at her starkness about leaving, which he had resisted putting into words, or at the complete lack of regret in her voice. Well, why should he expect regret? He, not she, was pinioned by sun, bound by earth, and—what?—burgeoning; he dared not say recuperated—that too much suggested imminence: for what could keep him then? what excuse or excess? He felt more burgeoned at the moment since all the way back from the río Mendoza in silence he was with Evaristo's mother. She would not leave. He knew she would never leave. Evaristo had given her to him. And now the giving gnawed in him: Why me, who will go, never come back, never cross his way again? Never? Well, wasn't it the beauty of travel that it eased the self open, made it discover hidden seeds, which pressed through mind, body? At the same time nothing made the ephemeral more visible, the evanescence of worlds gone, with the awareness that what is palpable is already going. The hand rises but in an instant what it reaches for is out of touch—then all blood cries out against its going.

So the time for going to the alta cordillera came at last.

"And are we ready then?" Margarita said. "I'll get the lunches. Doña Elvira's packed the drinks. She's been a marvel."

"So have you." And she had, tirelessly concentrating on everything: Would Evaristo be sane enough to rent a good car? What would they need for overnight? For six or seven hours each way was simply too exhausting to do in one day, and there was the hotel at Las Cuevas, or the hotel, if they preferred, at Puente del Inca— Staying would give them time to rest, wander, get the feel of the high cordillera. They could stop and loll where they would. And she was excited, all too nervous, very responsible, so that he and Evaristo had to laugh. "I'll pack the trunk," Evaristo said. And in no time, Margarita in a flurry—he'd never seen her like this before—Margarita laughing and embracing the women, all the pension was excited about nuestros amigos los norteamericanos going to Cristo, waving from the doorway, Doña Elvira shouting long out of earshot as if they had forgotten something.

Past the arid flats, the cement factory, the land rose, low walls began to rise. The auto billowed bowls of dust. Soon they were taking the twists and turns, caracoles, up to Villavicencio. "Look! Where Evaristo and I were stranded when the sonda came." The red tiled roof of the hotel rose against the barren brown mountain wall.

The road descended, followed the river into a long valley of green, everywhere willows, poplars clean, grass stark; and a great canvas sign spread BIENVENIDO A USPALLATA over the dirt highway. They stopped at the inn for tea. Evaristo insisted on staying with the auto.

"Let him." The air, so clear, with an electric crispness, seemed to inebriate her. Inside, a great stone fireplace was burning bright. Her eyes darted over everything, charged. She captivated the manager. "Killing condors *is* prohibited?" A great black and white wingspread, an ominous eye. "And was the rug made by Indians? Quechuas? Are there many left? Do they come down from other countries? Bolivia! They don't really follow the railroad tracks all that way! Whole families? From country to country? Unbelievable!" And she thanked him profusely for the chat and took it back, almost verbatim, to entertain Evaristo on the drive to Polvaredas.

"Sí, the Bolivians blow with the winds—where food is, they must go."

"How terrible!" Margarita said.

"They're not alone in Latin America—in the world, I suppose."

"Men have always done it, whole civilizations," he said, "depended on the earth, followed the seasons. Think of the layers of us in the earth, over the continents, and undiscovered yet."

"Took their chances," she said.

"Of necessity," he said. "It takes plenty to uproot. Habit is vicious, if beneficial. Perhaps, despite the upheaval, it was the only way to bring themselves back to life. I'd like to believe uprooting's a trick of nature—to awaken us. But who believes in our own basic nature anymore?"

"I do—," she said, "in mine and yours and Evaristo's. *We're* moving, aren't we? *We're* going—if it's not to *eat*—to Cristo, aren't we? Why would we? Vacation? Did you really come for a vacation? You certainly wouldn't be living in Doña Elvira's third-rate pension even if you had started out simply to rest. Something—beyond vacation and rest—happened to you, didn't it? *I* don't know. You got hooked on the life here."

How could he tell her there were flowers in the heart that could not stop growing, that would respond to sun, seek sun, split flesh?

"Well, you did, didn't you?"

"Or impaled on it."

Hooked herself, she would not let go. "And if I hadn't come, there's no telling how soon you'd have forgotten *that* life, me—simply left us there abandoned. Wouldn't you have? And then what would have happened? I shudder to think. I had to take it into my hands."

But he was watching how the valleys were deepening, gorges beginning to steepen, walls straighten, how snow dominated the sky far ahead—

"You're not listening."

"Have you forgotten *him?*" Though Evaristo did not seem at all disturbed at their tone.

Her eyes widened—he himself grew large in them. "Him!"

"Well, his English *is* limited—"

"Oh." She sank, relieved, laughed. "Evaristo—" She touched his arm. "Forgive my crudeness, crudeza. Hablo español ahora—okay?"

"Don't think anything of it, señora." But you could see he was pleased at the concern. Something in him seemed to spring alive, all the muscles, then relax—in a great breath. His hands too relaxed their grip on the wheel. Had their interplay actually disturbed him?

"Miren Vds!" Near La Cortadera Evaristo pointed— Against the mountain wall was the skeleton of a cow, bleached ashen, clean—standing whole, leaning as if it were simply resting, waiting.

"Frozen suddenly in a storm long since. This is the region where begins no respect for life," Evaristo said. "A man must know the cordillera or keep out of it. Only the animals know, and even they misjudge, sometimes surprised too soon to escape. If we all had the wings of the condor!"

Somewhere there would be, always, the birds waiting for the flesh— All along the way now, at intervals, were scattered bones, skulls—until the snow began low on the slopes, clung close to the roads, and falls here and there, and streams running with a dizzying glitter. And sun, high now, moved the shadows.

The way became treacherous, the road unpaved, pin thin, twisting close against the mountain walls, edging steeper ravines. Twice they had to stop, hugged against the slope to allow oncoming autos to inch past theirs. Beyond Punta de Vacas they halted at a curve slightly above a tiny plateau, where water flowed about monstrous fallen rocks, into a pool which spilled into a ravine below. They stretched and walked, but the tug of desire for the high climb made them impatient. White walls rose ahead, a blinding glisten of purity, the waters rushed louder now, the snow edged the road. Despite September sun, the spring air bit, deception. When almost at Puente del Inca, Evaristo stopped, where a narrow break in the mountain opened on peak after peak, and beyond, over them all, the hard, gleaming loom—aloof, serene and, yes, proud—towering, a white still fire—

"Aconcagua," Evaristo whispered.

Even naming it did not violate its purity.

"Your only view of it on the way."

And he wanted, wanted that peace—if he could only touch, immerse himself, in it; yet he knew, silent and still as it looked, a howling maelstrom of winds must be seething about it. Through the gap came rushing cold as if to warn of its presence. When at last he turned away, Aconcagua loomed under his lids, rose through his skull. He stared, silent, all the way to Puente del Inca, until the Inca bridge caught his eye—a great natural arch of yellow brown red gray clays spanned the ravine, where the waters, dammed at that great generator, plunged, heaving over the earth, down, down until finally flowing into a gigantic conduit that lay like a primordial serpent over the earth, bearing the waters he had heard in trickles and rushes through the acequias of Mendoza.

Margarita was asleep.

"It's the wine and the air at this altitude. Best to cover her. We won't be long."

As they crossed the bridge to the power plant, louder and louder came the rush of waters: a great white glide spilled, plunged in steep falls down the gorge, so loud that the ground, the stone of the mountain, vibrated. When they went into the plant he felt the floor quiver, felt the immense machine hum till his body hummed. They came out onto a platform under the falls. The noise assaulted, the air seethed mist, the mountain seemed breathing—he was caught in the throbbing heart of this stone, which spurted into the sunstruck air explosions of iridescent light, confused, near addled, his senses. He would dissipate in this chaos. The silence must be like this. He would reach out to Evaristo, but cried out when Evaristo touched him. Startled too, Evaristo spoke. No word came. Evaristo pressed his lips to his ear. The warmth of his breath, the brief touch of lips, the hand on his arm—and the word "Impresionante!" restored him to himself. He nodded, but Evaristo held his arm—he felt through his arm the quiver and throb from floor, stone—and thrust him to the edge. "Mire Vd!" Evaristo's mouth, Evaristo's nod drove his eyes down where a ledge, insistent liquid ice, glided into deeps made invisible by the mist churned up by that cauldron.

Why? He did not understand. What did he want? My life—he wants my life?

"That is what you go back to, señor."

"What?"

Back to? Home?

"This is our life, señor—that." That tumult? The power thundered, made itself felt in spray and mist—they were damp with its life.

"The thing frightens you, señor?" But Evaristo *saw* he was afraid! He was ashamed he had mistrusted him. Evaristo drew him close an instant. "Ay, señor. you have just cause. We come out of such madness, we go back to it."

"That—?"

"Do you never feel when you are still, doing nothing, that seething—how it threatens to take your mind down unless you do something to hold it back?"

With Evaristo close to his ear, he was aware now of his own seething, his straining not to miss a word.

"But sometimes you want it to—"

"Yes! But it is this, this—you *must* not. You must hold it back. You must make it do what you want."

"Do?"

"Only then you know who you are. How else can you live?"

Be who you are? Live?

But what was Evaristo trying to do? What did he mean? Again, instantly he feared, then resented, the close wet eyes, the warm breath, the hands on his shoulders that thrust him to the rail to face the falls— He wants my life! This foreigner, thief, dares— And at once he was ashamed, for surely Evaristo was trying to say something, do something for him, and he, *he*, could not fathom.

He stared into the thunder and churning, the mist, mystified. But at that moment Evaristo released him, words died, his mouth was empty motion, and all was reverberation. Evaristo flagged and they went back up the stairs and even the noise seemed silent and soothing, an escape.

"You two!" Margarita came running over the bridge. "I woke blinded by sun on the snow. It scared me. Look at you! You're both wet!"

"It's only surface—from the falls. It'll dry fast in such sun."

And sun blazed off the walls, so steep as they moved toward Las Cuevas that at times the white hung in shadow, a menace over them. Margarita grew excited as they approached, thrilled by the gigantic peaks, close now; and Evaristo became more talkative, laughing, telling incidents of the mountains.

"But I've not seen one llama or guanaco, not a living animal," she cried.

"We'll let *you* loose," he said.

"For a condor to swoop down and steal off," Evaristo said.

"What condor? I don't believe you. Everything's dead up here. How could anything survive?"

"Look," Evaristo said. "Always there's a way—"

Her breath caught—left, in the valley they had come into, lay a whole village: red roofs merry in the sun, a great hotel against the far side of the mountain, its windows like laughter in the sun, a great stone ledge hanging high over it. The only point higher lay in the western pass; just below it, the Gendarmería and a gate marked the exit from Argentina. There the road began its twists, its caracol, up to the border and Cristo.

"You must go the last kilometer on foot, difficult because of the altitude you're not used to, or ride up with the tourist van."

"Oh, we can't stop now! We'll go to the top, then we'll come down to the hotel, have dinner, rest, and tomorrow—" She seized snow and flung it, a dazzling dry glitter—it burst in white dust over them—and began a free-for-all till they could no more. "Stop! Stop!" he cried, but she wouldn't. "I—started—it—I'll—finish—it!" she cried, lightning upon him, a thrust of snow down his back, her wet hands over his face. "Stop!" But she was lost in her zeal, prodding, pressing, till he suddenly seized her—"Margaret!"—and shook, not understanding, and shoved her into the snow, where she lay laughing hysterically. Evaristo had turned away. Now he said, "We should begin the climb. Afternoon sun goes early in the mountains."

Above, the peaks glowed, a cold white rising, serene.

Margarita started to run.

"No, no, Margarita!" Evaristo cried. "The gendarmes will let us through as tourists. We drive up to just below the Cristo, park, and go the rest on foot."

Past the Gendarmería the road up was barely passable, the car inched along a narrow way, taking the steep winds. At last they came to a break—a level area surrounded by peaks, like the broken edges of a great cup, and in the clearing rose the Cristo. And how pathetic it was! Its robe emerged from snow, its arms reached from snow. Despite its great size, it was a lonely, paltry thing alien to the barren of peaks that spread over the far side, down, into Chile. It stood lost there, like a thing forgot. Its base was covered with ugly plaques and mementos. It stood like a cheap gigantic metal toy some Amazonian child might have left for the smiting winds and snows and rains to beat at and wear and reduce over the centuries to come till it would be part of the earth again.

"Look—Chile! It's Chile, Evaristo!" Margarita cried. And it *was* awesome. Below the peak, the white ridges blended into dark brown stains, great stone teeth bared and rotting.

"The train goes down there—see." Evaristo's finger traced the serpentine.

But his own arms rose like the Cristo's: the end of the earth! as near sky as he had ever stood on earth—and yet nowhere, as far from it as ever: closeness was all illusion—approach and it receded. You thought your breast would touch the heavens, but you touched nothing, yet sky was all around you. No wonder the Cristo's outstretched arms! Mercy? Pity? Despair? A silent cry? And he felt for even that ugly metal statue thrust up out here, this poor little gesture left as men's tribute—to what?—defiance? This brave futility! And he felt for them, for them all—for Evaristo, Margarita, himself—that they were left to cry out against the brevity, the taste that yearned for fulfillment, for breath etemal—for this, now.

"Qué pasa, señor?"

"Nothing. Nada."

Margarita came up behind.

"That statue spoils everything," she said. "Men! They have to leave their little marks everywhere. They can't leave real beauty alone, can they?"

"Why, Margarita, you sound so like me that you embarrass me with my own words. Did *I* do that to you?"

She laughed. "I knew a little bit about creation before I met you."

But it was Evaristo who was captured by the statue.

"Y qué, Evaristo?" he said, if cynically.

"The worst thief of all," Evaristo murmured.

"What did he say?" Margarita said. "Thief? Him?"

But he was watching Evaristo's face, which turned now to him: it carried Christ down, and for an instant it seemed to lay the words on him, let them visually weigh, penetrate. "Sí, the worst." There was pain and bitterness, but not admiration.

And Margarita said, "Why did you say that, Evaristo? Jesus a thief. What a thing to say! You're a little mixed up, aren't you?"

"I think not."

"But what?"

"Anyone who steals life from us is a real thief. He stole our thought from this place. He set this place last. He wanted to live out there, faith to prove out there; and he did it so convincingly for himself that it destroyed life for—ayyyyy, how many! You must steal *for* life, not against it."

"Steal! But I don't understand what you're saying at all. Slower—despacito, por favor."

And she did not—his Spanish, a rush, and slurred, must have escaped her.

But following them down, watching Evaristo catch Margarita as she slipped, steady her with his big hands, he listened:

"Because a man has only a few real things in this world—life itself and the woman and some love, children, people, and a place—if he can have them all—and to take any of the joy from them now, here, or make us ashamed to live full in them, that is to be the worst thief. They ought to give that statue back to nature, clean and beautiful with nothing to mar its perfection."

"I've never heard Evaristo go at it so. Have you? Evaristo, you're so full of life today. What's riled you up?" She seemed to bask in his energy, always she thrived on the electric motion of others. When they neared bottom and parked, she said, "Come, Nate," and gripped his hand and Evaristo's and pulled them after, running, and fell, tumbling them down with her, exhausted and laughing and panting for air, in the snow, in the falling shadows, deep, which the peaks cast.

Now dark began to fill the valley, came up gorges, ravines, and only the white tips glowed and the sky threw down last light. The villa sank into the dark, a scatter of lights, scant life in the high cordillera, aglitter in this highest valley. And they retreated at last to the hotel for baths and a rest before dinner.

While Margarita was dressing, he went down to the foyer. When she came down and Evaristo joined their table, it struck suddenly that it was the first time Evaristo had dined with them—socially, as Margarita would say; he had never really thought of him as hired, a worker. And now he saw him strange—as perhaps Evaristo saw himself, sitting here with Margarita, watching himself. It was a joy to see how natural, innate Evaristo's breeding was—the tenderness in looking, which belied the hands; and a politeness, a gentility in the deeps, darks, of eyes, which implied suffering; a born sense of manners—not (he smiled inwardly) stolen.

"To your health, señor, And with thanks for all you have brought me, all." He touched glasses. "Señora—"

And Margarita—was it the isolation?—how different she looked: her hair a long fall now, her face a natural glow, so washed a look. She was reduced somehow, yet more.

"You glow," he said.

"It's the promise—of home, of going, of . . . tomorrow, I think."

"I see."

"Does that so despair you—the thought of going home?"

"I think now of nothing else—but with pain, dread, to tell you the truth."

"Then, señor, why go?"

"Oh, Evaristo," Margarita said, "you're not being realistic. He's in business. It can't go on without him."

"Why not? Doesn't it go on while he's here?"

"But he has long-range obligations. You can't run off because you've found a new place."

"But you could if you found other things?"

She was nonplussed, discomfited. "But work—for him it's the very fountain of his life. Isn't it, Nate?"

He felt Evaristo waiting.

"Isn't it, Nate?"

He was silent.

"And not love? not place?" Evaristo said. "These are *not* the fountain? A man can find work anywhere."

"Love is not a place? You can't carry with you the place of love?"

"We all do—"

"But some men grow like plants in certain places, are born to grow only there, who may even die after they discover the real place if they leave it, die even in the healed body. I've known them moving but dead, moving but not alive in their bodies. When a man knows what nourishes him, he can't do without it long and live. Sometimes he must even take it from the hand of another."

"Take it?" he said.

"If it is given."

"If it is given?" Now he was confused. Worse—Evaristo cankered him. Was he trying to tell him something again? "*What* given?"

"What's given is not said. You know a thing when you know you've received it."

"You're beyond me," he said.

"And me!" Margarita said. "Come!" She took his hand and led

him to the foyer. "Now—" She made him dance with her, though it was awkward for there were only four others in the dining room beyond and all the personnel gathered to watch; and Margarita, really not with him, ended up performing alone, performing, flung herself into a modified tango—and laughed self-consciously as they returned to the table. But, breathless, she was beautiful, her hair glimmering, her face healthy without a trace of cosmetics. The wine relaxed her, moved into her eyes; she seemed to quiver with delight.

"Whatever's got into you ought to happen more often."

"Ah, some things only happen once." She touched his hands, and he caught actually an instant's real despair, as if she would—something latent in her would—break; but she freed him, she rose, she said, "Before I have too much wine, I'm going up. This altitude gets to you. And the trip tomorrow is long. Will you be ready when the time comes, Evaristo?"

"Siempre."

"Buenas noches." She flagged to them—to all the personnel, who bowed.

After, Evaristo said, "You don't want children?"

"We've always said if the right moment comes."

"Is there such a moment?"

"We're very conditional in my country—planned parenthood, it's called."

"Here too, but that's for the limited income, no? not for everybody?"

"Ideally, yes."

"Oh, ideally! Ideal is to have them simply to see the other Margarita, the other you, there—made, in the world. Not so?"

"Perhaps."

"Perhaps, *no*. You would *perhaps*—" He chortled. "—want one every day, a little world of the *other* all around you. Then you couldn't love enough."

"You—you're amazing, Evaristo."

"Too simple perhaps and—with you—too direct. It's my life that I can't be direct with many because I'd give them ground for stealing from me. You can tell a man too much in an instant and he will use it against you—that is to steal."

"And I won't?"

"You won't."

"You know that?"

"Not even if I offered it to you to steal."

"Because if I wanted something you'd give it."

"Don't be sure."

"Why not?"

"Because what you wanted might be stealing from yourself—your own character, say."

"And a thief would worry about my character!"

"Only a real thief, a great thief, would do that. The others don't count—they're criminals. A great thief is an object of hatred because he makes you call on yourself—that is painful—and makes you responsible."

"But you said *He* was."

"He was. Why else would I hate the idea of Him? He was capable of *making* you. After His example, you must examine what you do, everything. Wouldn't that make you hate Him? Because those who accept Him, make Him responsible in their weakness and don't call on themselves, create a world where you can never escape His idea of judgment. Maybe He needed that—so He could survive against the other inside Him, who made Him do it. You see. If He were not betrayed by Himself, *He* could not have stolen this life from us, this place. He has made fools of us all, longing for another place, leading them to believe what He wanted to believe, when there is this—this wonder."

He would almost have said—it wasn't true—the wine had excited, inspired, him, but Evaristo was too still. His hands cupped the place, "this wonder," which his eyes stared into. Then he held the hands out, as if he offered what lay in them—valuable, invisible—to him. Evaristo looked into his eyes and in that glitter was the stillness of some deep assurance.

But he could respond only with silence. He gazed down into those hands. They had power; they spoke, those hands.

"*You* don't long for another place, señor?" Evaristo said finally.

"I'll long all my life now for Mendoza."

"Then you must *not*. That would be to long for another place almost as much as to long for death. And why would a man long for death? Not to be in Mendoza—isn't that death? If you could be in Mendoza, and you know that, why wouldn't you live? Why deliberately die back there?"

"Ay, Evaristo, you make it so simple."

"It's more simple than you know."

"But there are a thousand considerations!"

"So many?" He was abruptly merry, his mouth parted, the tip of his tongue at his upper lip, his head tilted—cocky. "Why not call things by their names, and so do away with them, knock them down one by one?"

"You're remarkable, Evaristo. I came to this country to escape, to rest, to take the sun, lounge and—by accident—one day I meet—" He hesitated long, meditating.

"A thief? Sí. Go ahead, say what I am. Ladrón. A good word.

A name—mine— without shame. Why do you falter?" But he was smiling. In the smile was the hand which gripped.

"No. I meet—myself."

The word halted Evaristo, stilled him—breath caught, as if by a blow.

"Forgive me, señor. I come to think too much like what I am, a thief."

"I've not known a thief—"

"No, not one, señor—but thousands? But never really *known*, eh?"

"None—but perhaps myself. You'd have that—me to know I'm the thief of myself?

"Only you will ever know that, no matter what you tell me. I can go only that far with you."

"Sí. How far can a man ask?"

"For a real thief there are no limits. He'd have even what can't be seen. There's no corner of the other's mind or heart he hasn't thought to treat as if it belonged to him—it *is* his. There's no limit to what he makes his."

"Then you're telling me no one—really—is free if the other chooses to take his freedom from him?"

"Or do I tell you this, señor—if he gives him his freedom?"

"Gives—but how?"

"In many ways. Hay maneras, sí. But he does *not* tell because it's his life. Not for nothing is he what he is." He lingered an instant over that, then rose quickly. "I go to my room. Adiós, señor." He did not look at him.

Evaristo had left him teeming, confused. He could not go up yet. He went out to walk. At once a still cold enveloped him as he crossed the great porch, descending. Below, all the villa lay silver with moon—red buildings and red earth hard silver against the soft silver snow, glowing with an aura, as if something mysterious shone through the fleshy snow. The peaks were infinite crystal towers of stillness, not a wind, nothing. He could not believe such stillness. He walked—down, and only the sound of his steps against the snow made weak wisps of sound; and when he did stop to gaze, encompass—awed at the infinite nothing of dark beyond moon, beyond stars—and listen, all was the vaguest breath about him, nearly soundless, the penetrating inward motion of cold moving, and then the sound of the throb of himself. Himself! Did you never escape from the sound of yourself—even here, where the self was nothing? where all the life of man lay in this one little valley, brought together and beating like a tiny heart in the darkness? Why did the people in those houses, job or not, come to live here at the end of earth, on the verge of nothing? To be reminded each moment of nothing? never to forget how ice, snow, sun, wind split rock, wear away the metal body of Cristo, strip the flesh of birds, animals, men from bone, and carry it all down in rivers, back over earth to lone chozas, hamlets, towns—to Mendoza. And he—where would *he* go? He too wanted to go, be part of that river, part of Mendoza—like that city, drink in the waters, feel sun penetrate him, grow— You had to keep moving, never stop. Each stop was a vantage point to leap from, go back into—if you stopped too long, there was nothing. You stopped long enough to put that Cristo there, leave it as a sign to know you had been there, could get there, to Aconcagua, go the limit—leave Cristo, a stake, or a flag so you could go on against nothing, but not to nothing.

He went in. The clerk said goodnight.

In the room Margarita lay quiet. In half-dark he stood staring at her small form under the blanket, eight years of his life—he couldn't believe!—yet estranged in the same room: they went on, for he had gone on with the business for her, for the life he had given her which had become sheer habit, then the habit of work for this habit of giving. But he could no longer live that life—it would kill; it almost had killed his spirit till he near hated the earth he never saw beneath asphalt and stone and wood, so eternal they seemed.

Looking at her, he was ashamed that she had become a reflection of all that to him, a menace, so innocently fallen into a menace which, yes, he himself had helped create—an image of his own destruction. And he wanted somehow to destroy that image of destruction—not her, not poor Margarita, but that image which encased the old Margaret he had met in the heat of romance, loved, married—and gradually buried beneath what he, with her help, had made of her. But he *had* made the move to destroy—by coming to Argentina. You had to break stillness, sheer inertia, and burst back into that motion to see where the flow would lead. He had done that. And now?

He stared at the edge of moon on the windowsill till it blinded, sight went. He lay like that a long time, suspended, till—was it?—someone called: far off, outside—

His eyes opened full, blind—he could see nothing but blinding white. He sat up. His body was cold. He touched it. Naked! He was lying in snow. With great pain he stood and reached out—he felt wind, a hard race of snow. He tried to walk. He moved blindly toward the voice. High up, far—the voice came, died, revived. All his body listened, every pore it seemed awakened and listened. And he tried to move toward the sound so high, far away, but snow and wind lashed and smat till he would scream, till he couldn't move, but would, *would*— His breath choked and he fell flat. His mouth filled with snow.

Then, close, it cried a great sound.

My name!

And he raised himself on his elbows, his arms—and crawled. There was light coming, high, with dark shadows, the dark ridge of peaks, and light spread the sky. Squinting, he saw the dark shadow ahead. It kept calling, "Nathaniel . . . " His blood quickened and he tried to crawl faster, closer, and dared to stand—"Nathaniel, Nathaniel!" And he lunged toward it—a man, half-imbedded in snow, arms raised. "Nathaniel!" He fell. "I'm here!" He gripped that arm. "I'm here." The arm was hard, icy. He drew himself close, hugged close, cleared the snow from the head and looked into that face—decayed, eaten away! It was his own. His hand froze against it. He cried out—

The cry woke him.

His hand was icy. It moved over the sheet.

"Margarita!"

Empty!

All was stillness and a far blaze of morning.

"Margaret!"

She was not in the room—or bath. He had the quick cold sensation of abandonment.

Perhaps she had merely gone down.

But at once he knew his lie: there was nothing, no toiletries, no clothing. The overnight suitcase was gone.

Gone!

Six o'clock.

He dressed. He went directly to Evaristo's room, knocked, but not the least sound came.

"Evaristo?" The door was open. The room was empty.

Downstairs, the sereno was alone behind the desk.

"Buenos días, señor." He was more than officious.

"La señora?"

"They took the international train to Santiago de Chile, señor. It left at five."

He was stunned, really stunned, for he did not know, could not unravel the strangeness.

"And oh, señor, they made arrangements for a driver to take you back to Mendoza in the car you came in."

"I see. Gracias."

"De nada."

In the emptiness of the room he was overwhelmed by the long flow of days in Mendoza—Evaristo? Margarita?—and it came so suddenly he could not hold back or sort out details in the inundation which now came with the silent thunder of light. Sun, breaking so blindly in, blazoned his mind, threw its light so painfully over the starkness of things that he nearly cried out as if in agony, but it was not agony, not agony alone, but the deep pain of knowledge imaged in the sudden, endless vista he had to look into where nothing yet lay—a vast plain, cold, clear and endless which seemed to invite, even beckon. Yet he could not move. Here, on the edge of the bed, the flood swept, kept sweeping, over—the pension, Evaristo, Margarita—the trips, excursions, the talk, absences, arrangements—passports? meetings?—and Villavicencio; and Evaristo, what he was trying to tell him that he still could not fathom. Only, he knew, he must go down, go back to Mendoza to the pension, back down, and take it all down with him—to that place.

There was a knock.

"Señor, the driver's here."

"Ya voy."

There was nothing to take, the razor and nothing.

"Antonio Romero, a sus ordenes, señor. El coche está listo."

The peaks were sharp and dark against the high morning light. Sun spread a vast brightness above. Below, the valley was growing, drawing its life from the sky. It would be long before the sun rose high enough to strike straight into the valley.

"The day begins," Antonio said. "A magnificent morning, señor."

They reached the car below, out of snow, in the villa.

"Each day will be longer and more beautiful—good, after the short days up here."

On the front seat lay an envelope.

"For you, señor."

It was not in Margarita's hand.

Antonio pulled up onto the road above the villa; it followed the inner, eastern wall of the mountain. Down. The valley deepened, and the road lay like a tube against the mountain. For a long time, staring down, where now the high ice and snow gleamed an immaculate white, the river poured in a crystal stillness, sounds grew, wind livened, even flurries from the steeps made crystal glitters high in the air.

Silent, he clutched the envelope for as long as he could, until Antonio said, "We pass Puente del Inca," and he saw the bridge and dam, the great falls plunging down, carrying all down to Mendoza—snow, flesh, stone.

Then he opened the envelope.

Acuérdese de mí.

Three words. No signature. It was the first time he had seen his hand.

Through the windshield, gorge and river and mountain, all the world shivered and rose in his vision, then settled.

Remember me.

He smiled—and then he burst into laughter so abrupt that it startled Antonio, startled even himself.

"Perdóneme, Antonio. It's that I just realized I'm going down—back to my Mendoza."

And he turned his face away from Antonio and in a confusion of agony and joy fastened his eyes on the waters.

On the Heights of Machu Picchu

la más alta vasija que contuvo el silencio
—Neruda

THEY WOULD be closer now each day—the dogs, pariahs, black and squat, their coats still carrying the mud. In the damp ground their imprints marked the stages where they'd lain, closer and closer to his hut. In his sight, blunted near blind by years of hard Andean sun and the sore winds of the puna, the dogs became Lita in a squat, or the children, or the old Indians huddled, till a voice would call from the high slopes, "Man? Old man?" Then the images returned, unceasingly dogs. And his gaze, lucid only in a certain light, would detect that they were there higher up, the Indians. Above, they would hear his sounds. Down here it was difficult to hear theirs.

Distant, the Indians were vigilant. Close, they appeared indifferent. His years in the cordillera, his own indifference, made him understand them. They knew he could not crawl very far. They knew his body by the food he left. What food they brought or threw him, the dogs fed on. The hot seasoning—*ají* in everything—made his stomach scream. He would spew. His vomit spread in ugly white flowers which stank, but did not discourage the tongues of the pariahs, which lapped.

But something stood him up firm: he knew the startle, amaze, in the Indians when he hoisted himself, reared, and stood—propped against the high ladder and easel he'd built to keep his body erect while his will drove the sinews in his arm to paint.

At the first white probe of sun under the thatch, he would drag himself across the ground to the painting, drag on his side now, dependent wholly on his arms. Not far. After Winton's last visit, when he himself could still walk, he'd built this great shelter facing the hut to keep the growing painting always in his eyes and make all his blood think. The wide shelter, with thick thatch against weather, faced half east, but one end of the painting he could move to follow and gather all day's light possible.

He halted, asink on his elbows to save straining for breath. He was tempted toward a rage of yellow daisies and blue lupine, but raised his eyes to be assaulted by the enormity of the canvas, wanting to fling himself into the thinned coca green deeps of that eye which mirrored his whole swirling universe: but no, not yet—only when made, when complete. He still ruled.

The ladder reached to where on the canvas her breast rose—stone, a mountain white with down, over which shimmered, from behind, a dawn that split her breast into a tree of ravines teeming with life.

"Helen," he murmured. The ghost of his voice fragmented the crystal air. In all the years he'd rarely uttered her name aloud. His body quaked. He farted. Nothing came. No surprise. He'd scarcely touched food, but wet dribbled hot down his thigh into the wastes his clothes held, days now.

He knew the decay. The last time Winton had come from Cuzco—or Lima?—to wheedle a painting from him, he read his decay in Winton's eyes—skin dark and broken and eaten as bark, bands of rags about bones that hung from his shoulders, and his squint in a head so thick with gray shag and beard it would topple. Winton had not wished to approach. The dealer's delicate splendor was alien. He feared smirching his white flannel by touching, sitting in the hut's defilement, chafing objects. Only the boy, the driver, touched things, carried the paintings Winton had chosen after he himself had one by one carried the "loot" from his hut into the light to reveal.

Each appearance of Winton was a journey back to the puna. Time stood an apparition in Winton, who had heard the legend of a lone painter self-isolated in the high puna and tracked him down. That last time he'd tempted, somewhat niggardly, with supplies, just as he had bartered years before for this great canvas which his eyes must have revealed his lust for—absolute desire turned absolute need. "And some money for your needs?" Winton, pseudo-generous, would tease for a painting destined for Lima or Buenos Aires or Caracas.

"Needs?" He belched a laugh. After Winton's cologne his own mouth reeked a sty. And Winton, rapid to disguise the orbit of infection, flung his glance up the high green of the montaña and plucked at a potato flower. His scented hands violated the blue petals. Poor Winton!—who would endure as art: for art.

Needs? He'd teased strips of slope into breeding. In thin ribs of earth he grew corn. He had tins of millet. He buried papas and chuños in the cold ground. He milked his goat, whose appetite threatened even the painting.

"A few random coins for exchange and charity always help with the *indios*," he said. Time had made him one of their mouths. They shared what once he'd thought sewage. "My diet's considerably reduced. My gut belts out—at one end or the other—anything with hot pepper. But it's enough, isn't it, that my mind keeps burning?"

Winton's boy had taken the two paintings to the jeep.

"I'll be back. I've been waiting years for that, your masterpiece. Don't," Winton chimed, "sell it to the Indians."

They drove off, the boy at the wheel, Winton supporting his new loves. The jeep stirred summer dust in a high camouflage which removed them—for good, if poor Winton only knew the futility of his promise to return.

They would not find him again. And he had destroyed all other paintings.

They would find only gourds, clay pots and bowls, tins with secrets of coca, orchid, jacaranda, eucalyptus. The very first years, high in the wastes, he had gathered the dead browns, yellows, ashens; collected juices of leaves, fresh petals, insects down the Urubamba valley at the jungle's edge; scraped even the backs and fine hairs of the insects; mixed colors with saps, gums, oils, at times his own urine, with paste of the guano secured from the coast or with feces of animals—miracles of color which you could say made a science. He knew now perfectly the tints and shadows of the vision.

Where in the beginning was nothing, the blank canvas, he had created the great eye, which reflected the eye it stared into, his own. In it the universe was growing from the flesh of his body and Helen's:

(Who said, "That will be fifteen cents for three days," and dropped the girl's three nickels into the library fine box with a flick of eyes to the clock—two minutes to five. As she watched the girl leave, she smelled the acrid heat from inside her own dress, an odor fresh beside the old men's breaths and feet, stale clothes, which permeated reading room and stacks. Mornings she would once brace herself against the odor, but the men had become her natural landscape, and it was the hygienic pungence of the ladies' room which now most offended.

She was impervious to mirrors but for her cleanliness. Mirrors said *scrawny, straight, flat*—all her body, castigated by asceticism, relegated to air. Bone her heart carried from apartment to library, to the zoo, along the harbor. Yet her voice she knew to be a miracle of softness. She felt the old men's eyes or hands rise in response when she'd forgotten and spoken aloud, so seldom that her own presence startled her, or when, forgetting again, she would raise her eyes and evoke an occasional "Such beautiful eyes," which would cause her to re-enter her hummingbird stillness. Well, she could not veil that last green of her eyes. Eyes were her last connection to keep her bones thriving. Less now the bones mattered, though she'd need them as long as dreams depended on bones.

The library door whisked shut and locked behind. The scent of air, outside, each day confirmed her choice of place —the west coast, San Diego with its morning mist, so like

Lima's garúa, into whose air she sent her breath south to him far down in the mountains.

She walked home, the vaguest shadow meeting herself in the anonymity of angled store windows. At her corner, Fifteenth, the woman across the way was walking her pet skunk on a chain for its relief.

In the apartment she undertook the ritual of poached egg, dry toast, black coffee, and cleaning up.

Bathed, her clothes hung up, her robe on, sealed in the efficiency for the night, she let her head dictate:

My dearest, sometimes I feel you are my son, who died that day so that he might pass into your imagination and live. Once I thought that was why, teaching each day at the orphanage school, I never did find the one child who might miraculously have been ours. But I know now it was something else. All the children would go into ours, who is in my heart, whom you would make.

The habit of speaking was in her hand, though she no longer wrote to add to the neat pile of letters, nineteen years of returned letters. There was the one reply (she'd ignored) from the second year, an airmail edged in red and white which she had used the dictionary to translate from the *administrador* himself (director? postmaster? manager?): . . . *the sadness of unclaimed and undeliverable letters . . . the presence perhaps of a North American señor somewhere in the region beyond normal habitation, the puna or altiplano? . . . desire to fulfill our maximum duties . . . lamentably . . .*

The fool! She herself knew in her heart the adobe hut, the high endless bleak waste, the verge of green below the puna, where surely he'd retreated, the eucalyptus and the jacaranda that reached in great purple cries like her own. *She* knew.

After that letter, though with an interval of missing letters, her own made rather irregular returns. The years of them grew, stretched through her university years, her late degree in library science, a teaching certificate, and the thirteen years of days in the orphanage and late afternoons or evenings in the library.

I resigned the orphanage last week. Today I closed the door of the library for the last time.

She was running down. She must see *him* through. She must know the moment when it would take all her remaining strength to cry out to him.

Today I began at last to see how our son will stand whole between us and, as we fall away, rise in some new flesh in the world we don't know. All these years it has taken us to make him eighteen and perfect. The instant he died in my womb something was born in me. It has thrived on us. In the perfect moment when you have realized him, I'll no longer need to be apart from you.

Sometimes she felt her bones could not contain the force of the crossing to him. At the library her hand had to clutch the stacks to steady her. At those moments she was all marrow. Her will stood her up and moved bones. It will not be long, she told them. I will tell you when, bones.

From his silence the canvas bloomed. His blinding face went close. Of his own sores he wrought asymmetrical flowers blighted and breeding in the perfection of jacaranda blue flesh. Out of those flowers grew ceiba, birch, eucalyptus. In their bark grew tangles of liana and strangling fig. And broom in a yellow file drove veins through sky, earth, ocean, his flesh and hers, down the stone of one breast into the sea of the other. That unending Amazonian yellow flowed silently past faces which rose from garúa, stared from sockets, mouth, heart, lungs, and filed through the viscera, all the faces he'd known and the last closest—the Indians, Winton, Padre Vicente, Lita.

Painting, he was steeped in the silence of the high puna of his first years, so vast, empty, pure it made you cry out what you were. Tough he'd been. He would close his eyes and grow dizzy with the teeming within him. Sometimes you feared to lie down flat on the earth, flat against sky, and be staked by the white steel of stars. Sometimes you felt your eyes had turned the moon-white of the puna. You came down. The body at last drove you down to vegetation and men, and to the river—you would need the waters.

Thinking the river brought him out of that silence. He leaned back on the highest rung of the ladder, listened—a quiet rush of waters (you would need the rush of waters), yes, but it was steps that had drawn him out of the silence. He turned.

"Lita?"

Far, the thing was a shrub that was moving.

"My friend," it said.

Ah—"Padre Vicente." Who would talk of God without naming. "One minute."

"You've time?" It was the padre's one joke.

Time? Time was the light his sight fed on.

"I don't know time except in your church bell—and when the wind's right all the bells of Cuzco resound—so I know it's Sunday or celebration."

"It is April, and Sunday tomorrow. . . ."

He had mastered turning and gripping the crossbars and easing down rung by rung, to avoid chafing to screams his diseased flesh. He sat on the ground and leaned. The Franciscan sank down beside him.

"You'd dare hang this painting in your church at Pisac, Padre?"

The priest laughed softly. "In the darkest corner perhaps. In His world there is room for everything."

Did the old voice reach with softer tentacles this day?

"And room in everything for Him?"

"In the heart."

"And not in every part?"

"Ah-ha! I see you haven't lost any of your powers."

"Not my head, no, or arms—yet." Though his voice had dried to near whispers. "Some chicha, Padre—if you can reach that gourd—to help me trick you to blasphemy?"

"Well, then—to defy you—yes, a few swallows. If He is in every part—" He smiled into the part that was chicha. No Winton, the saint would share the suck of his mouth at the same gourd. "—then He can be nowhere outside the world. You would have it so?"

"You came upon me once on the puna, Padre—years since. Surely you haven't forgotten that silence. Never could you hear such silence. You could hear even nothing."

"Impossible."

"It's a madness, that stillness. It overwhelms. You have to cry out." But he laughed. "Or my nanny does." Eating a twig. Dropping her wastes. He couldn't see now where the goat was. Usually in the dark his hand saw. Or his nose. But the priest did. "She's behind the hut," he said.

"And you've never felt that silence, Padre?"

"Felt?"

"It moves. Moves. And you've never painted?"

"Paint! Me? That would be only vanity in me." Humility dropped the white head.

He stared into the thin white and slick oil of the old head.

The priest's eyes rose and lifted him up, dark in them, alone. "Could I, you think?"

He didn't reply. Instead, he bent close to the priest's eyes. He gripped his hand, gripping.

The startled lids shuttered.

"No, don't move."

The man beneath black robes which refused to define turned stone for an instant.

Then he clasped the priest's other hand, gripped.

"You feel that?"

"Feel?" But the waking blood bolted, it pulled with a thrust, and the thrust throbbed his own.

"Do you feel that, Padre? Do you?"

"What?" But the eyes would burst with the straining. The priest's tense hands struggled, but he wouldn't let the hands go. He held till the heat was a burn, and wet.

"Do you?"

He felt the priest's silence, nothing else, in himself. The priest's eyes rolled up with the fear of it.

"*Do* you?"

"Yes, yes!"

Abruptly he released the hands. The old man nearly toppled.

"To paint, you have to turn against that torrent and stop it long enough to give that motion shape against its will, and sometimes your own."

He saw then the pity in the priest's eyes.

"And if you didn't?"

"Didn't?" How quickly the priest opened the abyss!

You would scream. You would never stop screaming.

Once Helen had stopped the screaming. She had come into his arms. She filled the abyss. She kept the rush back. But she had brought him the river.

"You make me fear for you," the priest said.

"There's no need, Padre."

"It will ruin you before your true time."

"Ruin? I've lived all my life among ruins, Padre. I've needed the ruins. I can't tell you the hours I've spent alone at Sacsahuamán and Puca Pucara, the baths of Tampu Machay, the Kkenco ruin. But nothing will ruin me until I finish that. I've decided."

"And after?"

"Why do you want to save me from myself?"

"Because nothing can stop that motion."

"Not even itself?"

The priest was silent.

"Or make a change in it?"

A green wind pressed quietly over the backs of the leaves.

"My friend, you play with me—always."

"Only because play is the most important thing in the world. Don't we spend all our lives playing?"

"At what cost," the priest murmured. His bones were audibly rising. "Ach, this age." His eyes roved the cordillera. "Dark comes." When it came, it surrounded abruptly, leaving a hollow vault in the sky.

"The woman is in the bush," the priest said.

"Woman?" His breath trembled.

"She's been standing there some time."

"Lita?"

She was as motionless as dark stone.

"You have family, my friend?" the priest said. Before, he had never probed the affairs of his body; it was the soul he would rescue.

"One woman only—a sister."

"Far?"

Moments, nothing was far. If the priest knew, she was standing aflame in the eucalyptus.

"There—in your country?"

"In mine, yes." Which spread infinitely, within hand's reach. He sucked it inside, whole, with the smell of the new paint.

"And you would not see her?"

In every breath of paint, see her.

But didn't each man see? And what was it Padre Vicente day and night saw?

But he could answer the priest's charity: "Our meeting, hers and mine, is all arranged."

He feigned not seeing the dark hand the priest raised over, to bless him.

"Adiós." Padre Vicente's voice thinned to a reed's.

He raised his own head to fix the priest permanently in his eye, but the black robe had already turned a dark flutter of cormorant wings.

The priest had taken up the last of his daylight. Time would come only with the morning. Soon there would be the dark timeless journey—in unfathomable night he would struggle to conceive—a river of her every hair; in the eyes archipelagoes to travel; in the flesh labyrinths, the deepest earth has ever known; Niagara terror and Iguazú beauties in the heart—

He stared at the core of the canvas, which he was filling. Above all, he had feared this last journey—to paint where all creation met, chaos held back in what threatened to break in a node through the canvas: it rose, a black fountain, a perfect and ugly black flower seething with all forms of life; the fountain bled and spilled them, drove all their beauty and ugliness through the painting, and infinitely. Where their heads met, his and Helen's, the eyes fused as one eye, which held all that was also within the great canvas eye, which reflected the eye that made it.

"Viejo?" From her mouth the word was soft. She revered his beard, its near whiteness, and respected the skin and bones he carted, if transformed. So too did the Indians respect him, if with a hatred numbed by coca and chicha.

"Lita?" He could tell where the white straw fedora gathered the light.

Above all, she had been faithful to the painting. Frequently she stood, if far, watching his universe grow.

"Here's *lote*. Eat." In dark the rich aroma of maize mush guided. He dragged, a crab, toward the hut. He sank in the path his body had grooved between painting and hut.

Beside her bowl were avocados. Padre Vicente's gift, yes. Sometimes it was guava, papaya, chirimoya. He reached, as sometimes, to pat Lita's bare foot. Her stale wool, ridden with wood smoke and oil, made an odor bitter as the llama flesh that had once saved his life.

"Palta?" She wouldn't refuse the avocado.

"Sí." Indirectly from the priest, it would be a blessing. And giving made him no beggar.

The *lote* was still warm in the clay. He mouthed the corn—for her, who would stand to ward off the waiting dogs. She knew the closeness of his journey. Was it her ritual to see he did not go empty on his way? There were days now when even her man would come—and stand far and silent—and the two boys, men themselves grown but squat—and sometimes all those from the cluster of huts above. Then would come a moment when he looked up and the clump would be gone.

He knew then Helen had stood in them.

Years before, the first time Lita had appeared near the hut, offering ears of corn, he knew Helen had sent her. Because she was shy, with a smile which defied the dumb distant daze of the Indians, her flat round face turned beautiful. She was the guardian of his painting. Nights in his hut, when he broke loose from the unfathomable dark, his hand reached out for his sister's. Thank you, Helen. O, Helen.

(On such comfortable Saturdays her custom was the great zoo in Balboa Park where she could sit on a bench under a canopy of great jungle fronds and watch the men playing boccie and write this week's letter.

I'm in the park. This simulated Amazon seems nearest to the place we said goodbye. Sometimes even now I'm walking, it seems, in Lima, sometimes Cuzco, or there by your hut with the Quechuas somewhere in the vicinity. Even the name Balboa recalls you, and so does this city that stands like Lima on the edge of the earth . . .

Here, she had written her love and curses and curses, the agony of her body, that torn child dead. *What destruction is required of us before we can understand?*

You could walk all day here in the zoo, past the poor creatures in captivity.

Sometimes I pick up a feather so beautiful that the colors demand adoration, and then there is the curse of cages, and I think of you, what's inside you that demands adoration, which is trying to escape from the cage of your body but always into another cage, your painting—and then into what cage?—as my son escaped my body into earth and the air. He walks with me here. I've watched him grow. I will him with you, who must give him his life.

She saw the son in dead leaves, the dried locusts, limp squirrels, each fallen sparrow.

She no longer feared the men who had in the years slyly appealed to her, made passes, called boldly, or those who walked here in the park who did not now want the bones she had reduced herself to.

But she couldn't resist the cries of babies and children, whom she made hers, each, all.

I carry bags of candy with me. You'd laugh to see how children flock around me, "the candy lady." I feel like St. Francis with his birds. I sit longest at the aviary, a vast cage high over trees, and am beside you. The zoo has one Andean condor high up in a lopped eucalyptus, molting and balding, pathetic, waiting. My heart goes out to it.

She wanted to tear open the cage cry Go *go go*. She'd close her eyes, but when she opened them, there were still the streaks of green blue yellow red feathers. A mynah screamed. Exotic flowers still burned from the earth.

It is that moment on Machu Picchu when you made me feel the life in green and blue, and the moving in the stone that will never stop. Never! I can feel the blood in trees now, I can feel the condor's heart in me, feel its wings, I can see with its eyes. Oh, it's all I have left—my eyes. My body's gone. My hair went scrawny years ago, You'd laugh at my gray wig—not ugly, but strange to you. And the rest of me is dried to eyes.

She stood, but blood would not move that fast. She entered a whirlpool, her hands went for the tree, but the branches which supported her were a young woman's arms.

"You're all right? Please, sit down here and rest. Shall I—can I call someone?"

She felt the soft flesh of the woman surround her bones, warm with charity.

"No, no. Someone is coming for me." These spells were almost a habit, though more and more. "I'll sit a minute and go on. You're very kind." Her hand wanted to touch the head, a blossom of gold. But she stilled her desire. In a minute the woman was gone, though her face hovered in a cluster of green leaves and darkness.

This time she made it to the aviary and gripped the wires. Though they hurt her thin flesh, she pressed her face hard against metal. Close, the odor of droppings and feathers hung in a stale vaporous air, and she wanted to pass through the cage to the other side. But not yet. Her eyes soared into blue, infinitely far. "Oh, Price," she murmured.

When she turned, her legs struggled to find the flat walk.

She had the strength—hadn't *he* given her that?—to walk to a bus stop, past the monkeys, forlorn faces and filthy flesh, *no different from the odors of years of old men in the library, retired and decaying, like all of us in one way or another, my darling*. Beside her, young yellow-green ferns sucked the old fronds dry.

"Candy lady!"

"Louie."

Six kids skedaddled after and closed in, new ones this time, nameless to her, but she opened her arms, touched their heads, laughed. The littlest girl, the blackest of hair, jerked at her dress: "Where?" she cried to the others. They surrounded. One rapped her bag. Louie said, "Stop that.

She'll give it." But two of the boys clung to her arms, heavy; one preyed at her skirt; the purse dropped. Abruptly she remembered: "The candy! I forgot it." But by then they'd pulled her to her knees; her hands gripped the bench for support. "I left the candy by the birds," she murmured, dry. "The birds! Let's go." And their little thunder of feet running beat into bones kneeling heaped on the pavement.

Her fingers surprised—their strength held, and she drew up, rested her head against them before managing a kneel and hooking her purse, then pressed one leg into a bend, held the backrest and stood—still, letting the blood careen. Trees, flowers, buildings swarmed. She did not move until they untangled. By then the bus, a great green worm, bore down. She held out her hand. It stopped, and the driver rose and reached down.

"It's been a long time!" he said, and his gentle hand almost lifted her off her feet. "You've been missing your Saturday trips."

"Yes. The library and the orphanage have kept me close." From one or the other, everybody knew her. She sat by a window. Wind, and sometimes sleep, dominated.

Sundays I used to walk along the ocean or swim and sun and lie listening to the whispers that I knew came from you—down there in the cordillera—your breath, yes, carried in the trough of the mountains and waves. The sun that touched you bore down on me . . .

The bus entered the long clear stretch at the edge of the waters. Ridges of afternoon shadows darkened the water.

When I look out, there is far, there is nothing. I'm back there with you at the beginning, for it was, was— And do you know I see the mountains so clearly, I see Machu Picchu rise from this sea, only the sea turns green, green, all the jungle is below and the muddy yellow river, that Urubamba coiling, and high are the mountains, green, so green, heavy with rolling fog and cloud that blow and fuse, and descend, and clear . . .

I'm right behind you on the peak. When we round the bend and come upon the ruins, the sight strikes the breath from us. You want to fall on your knees, you want to worship, you want—

She sees him spread his arms. He is standing with one arm in rain and one in sun. He turns to her, split with rain and sun. "I can't believe," he cries, "can't—" and catches rain, sun. Then the rain ceases, sun blazes him brilliant. "How could the Incas have built this? It's beyond belief." And *he* says it: "I've never wanted so much to worship. I could go down on my knees"—he almost does—"to what was in them." And she feels a great undertow in him, some enormity rising to break in him—can feel his will rising against it. She follows him with a fearful joy, watching.

Away from other tourists, they go through the ruins—baths, chambers, mortuaries, bedrooms, sacrificial rooms, temple. They stop at the Monument of the Three Windows. Everywhere the red Inca flower blooms like quick blood in the dead houses. "And daffodils!" They are growing on narrow ledges below. She steps down. The ledge is perilous, a nearly direct drop to the Urubamba winding below. "Do you think they're forbidden?" She turns. Price is standing above her in the middle window. She seizes the camera, but when she focuses, she is so startled by his face that she snaps involuntarily. His jaw is slack, the mouth wide, and his eyes fixed. "Price!" she cries, but he doesn't respond. She climbs back up the slope. He has not moved.

She comes between him and the window opening. "Price, what is it?" But she feels the threat of it, half knowing. His still eyes are terrible, they gaze through her—there is only her dark shadow against nothing. Then his eyes flutter with the madness of wings unable to find air—over the insatiate green forests, the peaks, endless sky.

And he is gone. He scrambles through the ruins to the ridge that crosses through the fog drifts and descending black clouds to the dark cone of Huayna Picchu. She watches him cross. Halfway he halts, his white shirt catching all the light, then disappears in the ring of dark cloud. What does he want to see from there?

She stands waiting, and after a long while he emerges. The Urubamba sinks into dark, forest and ravines go, all is a flow of darkness. Only peaks and the ruins catch a last light. Price comes down the path, the dark closing after. "Helen!" He raises his arms and she sinks with a cry against him, thrust against stone, knowing the despair of whatever he saw, clutching him against that despair and the darkness that has driven them all their lives and that at last they can turn on. "Oh, Helen, Helen—" She feels the anguish in his lips, his arms, all his body. "Oh, my love," she whispers, surrendering at last to whatever destruction and beauty may come. *Oh, my brother.*

She moaned.

The touch at her arm brought her into day.

You, driver?

Her eyes filled with the empty bus and the mouth of dark teeth which the buildings made against a sky that flowed crimson.

"You've missed your ocean," the driver said.

Missed?

She smiled. "It's always there. I see it all the time." It rushed, sounding, just under her lids. She wished his own eyes could see. But she succumbed to the arm which lowered her to the street. "You're always so considerate," she said and turned and caught him to fix his place in her. "Goodbye."

Air would have to carry her, she was that tired, and reduced.

Her own flutter of breath was all that spoke at the top of the stairs.

She let herself in, now prepared for the great splay of light which pierced from the west window, filling the sky with a blood. Yes. She raised her arms to let light flow back over. She knew the ball that was sinking under its great lid would take her down into that red sea one day soon; she would curl and lie still inside that ball and feel his hands take her up into his flesh.

She was almost prepared.

She had only to destroy her words and his photo that had stared all the years from the middle window, that shadow of a shadow of the man who was standing at the edge of a river in the mountains of Peru, waiting for her to turn in the approaching darkness and be consumed.

She tore the photo up and bagged the letters. In the hall she dropped all the words down the garbage chute.

Then came the security of shades she drew down; the dismantling of her body, clothes, wig; the ritual of bath and oil and the sheets, preparatory to the inevitable dreaming;

only her stomach vulgar with hunger, but ignored; and foul air that went through her; and a stretching out, knowing her head almost a skull. All her life stared from her eyes into darkness, waiting to be released.)

The stench of the nanny woke him. She waited as usual till he clutched her coarse hair, rapped her rump, then she went to forage. He himself ate the avocado. In his hand the clean brown pit made a perfect blind pupil. From its womb he felt the tree growing into his arm and his body and taking on the flesh of the son Helen had willed him in sleep to break through the node in his painting which bound everything whole and held back destruction. The son, and tree, that flowered and gave fruit in his head, must go back through his arms to the panting. Helen had sent the padre with this sign, which he had left in the basket.

Now he saw how it had been in his beginning, which seemed the beginning of all things—how the first impulse could not be contained and broke from its own stillness and gave everything motion and form.

Sun lay the black skeleton of his easel over the painting.

Night had restored his arms somewhat, but hoisting himself up his ladder exhausted, he cried aloud at the scabs the wood chafed and bled; he had to stop at each rung and hang, painting; he could not hold the burp of his feces or the wet dribble. He reached his brushes and the hanging pots of paint, level on the canvas with the womb he must fill, arrested an instant by a smell—not his goat's this time, different if familiar, rancid sweet oil and acrid. Alerted, he turned his head: they were in the east, dark as a herd, black against sun—all the Indians, sitting, as still as Aku-Aku or the heads of the Olmec. And he waved as a sign. Only the children waved and cried out, though he knew they all saw him. Nearer were the dogs, in a half-circle, each sitting as still and silent as Anubis, waiting.

Their presence nourished his arms, and he sank into the womb to draw out the perfect son, who began—despite the aches in his arms, his broken breath, the bum of torn scabs, and itch, and the rot of his body—to stand green and golden, a man and tree and monolith, with an eye blank too and waiting to be filled.

He ignored until he could no longer his own body, slumped forward against the frame, which had its own way of crying out in pain to stop his arms.

He would loll.

And realize abruptly that his breath had not stopped.

Or drop the brush and wait till his arm would draw out another from the cylinder he'd fashioned from guanaco hide for brushes he'd contrived from maguey and totora and the hairs of llama, vicuña, alpaca.

Or fumble with his mouth at the chicha that renewed with the strength of fire which too quickly burned out. At times Heleñ's hand touched his forehead and stifled the fever till he opened his eyes. She did not leave. She led his eyes to the son and to where wind was blowing her hair.

Or curse his arm when it would not keep up with the growth in his head, or when failing vision clouded with tears and went blind for some minutes that were forever and he moaned and shrieked at the canvas and his stinking body, which sometimes he felt was spilling back into air.

Helen came then and poured water into his mouth, down his chin, and wet his brow, but did not speak yet. Her hand restored his peace, his eyes opened to the glare but sun sharpened the canvas and his hand collected all energy with purpose—he scarce breathed, not to waste.

Her dress, brown earth now, stood close to the painting and guided his eye.

The son took on the arms of the tree and turned to stone which was living. The rivers inhabited his body, which bloomed broom and liana and strangler fig and wild orchid. And in the great eye of the son, a monumental window, stood the man on the ladder painting his eye, and the woman, still, who was beside him, and dogs, Indians, mountains, sky, all dark and brown and earthy crumbling splayed with the light breaking through them.

He dropped another brush and his arm, where it lunged after, hung down.

"Will you hand me the brush?"

She didn't answer. Instead, she took his hand and stepped into the canoa, which she had arranged with the Quechuas, for it was their moment of release, his and hers, in their journey to pierce the black heart of the jungle, the darks of the Amazon, "where you took me last night on the heights of Machu Picchu at the Monument of the Three Windows. There's no turning back for us now. What waits for us there we must find out, but together."

"No, there's no turning back," he said. The guide Marco and the Indians moved the canoas out into the current. The river-banks and ravine walls moved—past falling fuschia, cantuta, the yellow retama ("for the heart," Marco said), red air plants and gray, acacia, fig. A green parakeet streaked, and doves. There was the song of a serranita. Then the jungle closed over, wet with a thickening roof of darkness. The waters began to rush and suck. They were wet with leaping spray and a living veil of mist grew in the air. The dark smelled a rancid dank humus. The waters were too rapid and dangerous. The Quechuas balked. "They'll go no farther," Marco said. "It will take most of a day now to get back to the village, where we can get a way back to the bridge to Machu Picchu, then back to Cuzco in the morning."

"We risked the edge," she said. She stood up in the canoa at the edge of the river. From the bank he reached to lift her up.

When he did, his arm pained with the lancing of needles where it hung reaching for the brush he had dropped. For defense, years ago—the day he had fallen trapping guanaco and so for weeks had no right arm—he had taught himself the pains of painting with his left, which rose now and went on.

The sun was threatening to pass and leave him incomplete. All his strength must find way to the canvas. Day would not be stayed.

He had planned with Lita how the Indians would help him move the canvas, where the son was making his last resistance. He struggled, drawing the son out of darkness, which he himself could not yield to yet. He loved now his own stink and his pain and the heavy bones of his body, the pull of the hair at his skull, which made each breath defiant and all the air sweet, though too close at times he had allowed the threat, the thridding and churn of great waters, which the will in his arm would hold back till he gave back to the darkness more than it gave, for no man should not die exhausted.

The son stood whole now, and the painting.

"Helen," he said. He was waiting. She would touch him at last. He would take her up. She would enter him forever.

"I told you, Helen," he said. "If I sent you away I'd have you forever."

Helen?

She was so close her fragrance entered him.

He reached.

Then the ladder was tearing over all the sores of his body. Pain filled his mouth. He fell to the ground.

"Helen?"

She was standing on the balcony in the great round of sun falling—all Lima was sinking in darkness.

"Seven days," she said. "We've had seven days. All our lives brother and sister and we've had only these seven days! Oh God! How can that be? I could stay with you—forever, I could—"

One more night, the last, they would travel down into the ravages of dark before she would stand in the airport, weeping, hanging against him like his own body.

"You'd destroy us," she cried.

"*Save* us," he said. "If you stay, if I go back with you, they'll kill it."

"They they they!"

"Yes. I won't let us wallow in people's filth and blasphemy and shame. You gave me my moment, my trial and yours. There's no turning back—you said that. That would be death, the worst death of all."

"But who could I ever love now? Price, it's impossible."

"Impossible, Yes."

"Then *send* me away, but I tell you one thing—I'll be here, I'll *find* a way, and you know it."

"You'll always be with me, you'll be the only one with me. Back home every day we'd curse—not love, but each other for what people did to us. We'd be trapped and destroyed. But you wouldn't take it back? You wouldn't, would you?"

"Never. You know that."

"And I won't be destroyed. *You* understand that. I *won't*. I won't be destroyed. I'll keep what you gave me. That moment up there in the ruins of Machu Picchu I understood that Inca king Pachacutec—and all the ruins I've ever seen—why he *had* to enslave them to build his city, make that city, *make*—I knew his will. He could use their religion, yes, to defy *nothing*, yes—or he'd be nothing. Don't you see? Or there'd be nothing. He'd admit nothing."

"So you'd enslave me for that?"

"And myself!"

"Us."

"Yes. I have to fill it."

"I know I know I know. You'll never stop."

"I couldn't do it without the agony of wanting you and remembering the joy, and the madness, yes, that I must give back—into everything. But I'll want you forever. Oh, Helen!"

He clutched and she moaned in a long dry wail beyond weeping.

"Helen!"

"Señor? Señor—?" The voice drew him out of darkness. A hand was touching his mouth. Was it feeling for breath?

Helen? But his eyes still opened on light: her face held the light, *Lita*. His mouth could taste now her oil and sweat and the damp llama wool. Carmelita. He would take it all with him, inside.

Vague shadows stood behind her. There was an impatience of dogs, moving and moving against the darks of ridges.

Not far was a lashing of waters in the last light.

"You have breath?"

Enough to remind her.

She was asking for words. Or perhaps hoping against them.

He summoned: "It's time for your promise. Now. There's just time."

Her stillness was almost too long. There was the still sheen of oil on her skin. The darks in her eyes glittered. Soon her face would go into darkness.

"You promised!"

Did he have to summon the last impossible strength for that too?

But she stood and turned to the Indians.

"You!" she cried. "Take the painting."

Relief made his breath almost break.

But when nobody moved, his blood hammered the vision out of his eyes.

"Helen!" he cried. His mouth made only a hum.

"The painting! Take it down!" Lita cried, and he opened his eyes.

Their dark bodies returned to his sight, solid black stones that were moving. They lifted the painting and carried it from the shelter.

"Allá!" Lita drove them down the slope.

Helen's hand touched his. He would rise to her.

Behind, a dog howled.

(She heard the cry, and woke. She did not know she had not died yet, until she saw a river of moon was flowing through the blinds. And then, when she was standing before the blinds and drew them to, and morning sun streamed over the library reading room, she knew the journey was beginning. The dank morning, the dryness of books, and old men's stale breaths filled her, and one by one the old faces of all the years turned up to her from magazines and books and newspapers and all the faces of her children looked up from their desks, and as they passed she touched each face with her fingers.

She felt her body softer now, fleshy and not bone, larger. She was growing, and in the mirror behind Mr. Walsh, the director of the library, who was interviewing her, she sat, younger, with the thinning hair already in a bun which once in Lima and Cuzco and all her young life in New York had hung long in gold virgin simplicity, but it wouldn't do in the austerity of books and old men and children and the nunship she had declared of her life *because I couldn't bear the emptiness in your eyes—it was mine, as long as it was yours it was mine, and I wanted to fill it with love, and I did, then and now, I do now, and with hate too, years of hate that love breeds, yes, so deep that it's all pain till even the pain turns love again,* for she loved even the pain it bred, the experience was all that she had, it was theirs.

She was standing in the aisles of the classroom and touching the children's heads and their papers and scolding and laughing and playing.

And soon it was beside the brick wall of an orphanage she was standing. The cries of children had stopped her, tearing at her heart for her baby that was dead and buried. She knew she was deciding This is the day. The earth trembled in her blood. She walked up the steps of the orphanage. "I want to teach the orphans," she said. "I'll teach them how to love words so that they can tell what they mean to anyone." Mute, the man must have recognized that she would. "Frank Donovan's my name," he said. "We'll talk."

Quickly she was walking down the corridors of the university, past the men she shunned, fearing those who might blight the love all her flesh was dedicated to. She learned not to love too much what might stand between him and her.

Then there at the wall the undertakers were waiting to lower the baby's body. She was alone at the plot. The box was so small. "Nothing so small should have to go into the ground!" she cried. She was falling against the white lilac, which was blooming, but she wouldn't let the men's hands, which reached, touch her. She heard the box lowered into the ground with a whir which would pierce her heart forever.

And she would forever hate the hospital white, walls and bed and uniforms white, white. The doctor's eyes quivered. "The baby, a boy, was born dead. It had been dead for some time." All her will rose up in its fury, in stillness. Would nothing let her make? There are moments when all the blood and mind in you hate brothermotherfatherGod, and she cried it out now, *I'll make with my will. If you won't have what I breed, I'll find ways. Is that what you want?* For the first time she knew who she was. Her will would watch for the way.

When she felt the baby kick, her belly was almost too full, but it was growing smaller, and soon her stomach grew flat. She was filled with loss in New York when she stepped off the plane from Lima to go back to the house on Long Island, mother and father dead, no brother, never again now, to share that house, the sea, sky—and oh, God, how she dared not go up to bed, *not*. How could she stand all the life that remained when all her lifetime had been lived in a week? Was that what you lived?

Soon she was saying goodbye to Price, each clutched in

one body, and then she was happy with a high balcony in Lima that saw over Miraflores toward the ruin of Pachacamac, far off on the moon-white deadness of sand, and then felt the madness of his body, which drove emptiness to the brink of its own nothing. *I want a child. It will be ours, mine, to stand against all the pain of our lives, the joy of our secret, our life that is greater than wrong.* She was drawing him hard against stone, taking him away from the blank of his eye set against river and jungle and sky, taking him into her. *All our lives I've waited for this. If I can help you now, love, I don't care what happens, just to save you.* When he touched her there was meaning in stone, she understood it, it was moving, it couldn't stop, only the motion was real.

In New York she and Price were deciding to take a trip—to Peru, to the ruins of Machu Picchu, which he'd always wanted to see, far removed from Long Island so they'd ease off thinking about mother and father so abruptly dead in the auto. There was the insurance money they didn't want to hold on to, a blight, and they hadn't had each other's long company fully alone for three years because of Columbia, and they yearned for each other.

But there was father! digging out the willow whose roots threatened pipes and cistern—she ran to him and hugged him. She was filled with the fragrance of mincemeat. Mother was making pie in the kitchen, and Price was driving out from the city to be with the three of them.

In the mornings she went back day after day to the newspaper office, where old Lacey and his wife bustled to get out the semiweekly.

Don and Pete Bozeman and Eddie Brooks, so special,

from her high school class, vied for her, and after school they walked the two miles back of town—through woods, along the worn path, circling Mill Pond, over meadows—till she was too young and had to stay home after school and babysit with her little brother.

Mother and Father were so young and pretty together and laughing over the two, her with the first stories of school and Price in his high chair banging his spoon with great yawk-yawks! Now she was My little girl, my only child, and then she was being carried and set in the crib sometimes, and then something very warm, which she yearned for, she felt reach down and pick her up—My baby, my baby, we'll have a playmate for you one day—and laugh. And in a long drifting she was moving and thrumming with a tide, and caught in a coil and a whirling, taut in it, before the quiet release and a lull before fury, the rush and churn of water and fire and stone.)

Within hand's reach the Indians passed, carrying foursquare the great painting. And Lita—she followed.

He tried to thrust himself up, kneel, but fell hard against ground. He felt dirt jam his mouth and tongue, and he raised his breath. Stretching ahead, his arms dragged the tearing flesh and the clothes and his bones. It was easier when the ground pitched sharp down, and he slid, then turned to roll over, twining mountains earth sky river into one, until his body nearly split for breath. For a moment came such silence that he would ascend once more past the reed along the thin lake to the high bare waste of the puna, with no cries now of lapwings, no grebes and coots, to his patch of a hut, the purest moments of his life when there was only creation, and nothing, and, farthest away, Helen was closest.

"I'm waiting," she whispered. And his eye followed the brush of her garment over the ground and his hand reached to keep up as he dragged.

"Parad acá!" Lita stopped them. They all stood deep in dark, waiting for him.

He could hear now the waters. He felt now the beat of their waiting, but would see almost nothing where darkness left but a gray veil high over the mountains reflected in the width of the river. He had dared not move far from the banks of the Vilcanota.

His head filled with fire that would burst and consume, and his blood made a singing because her skirt moved ahead.

The damp breath of the river came up over his face. He burned for its coolness.

Somewhere behind, a flute made the sad lonely sound of a huayno.

He raised on his elbows, he thrust up on one hand, then two, and gave orders:

"Now," he shouted, but a breath, to Lita. "Hurry!" Only his arm could implore.

"Lita?"

His hand reached toward her skirt, but he slumped to the ground.

"Throw it in!" Lita cried. Yet he did not hear footsteps. He felt no tread on the ground. He knew she had not shared with them before what they must do now. Did they falter? But she moved behind them.

"Enseguida!" she said. "Throw the painting. Tiradlo! Now."

The drag of feet filled his head. He would shout! Soon nothing could deny what he gave to the waters. The river would carry the canvas down the Urubamba into the Amazon, shredded, dissolved back to humus and darkness, and then to the ocean. He knew what would lie in the sea, waiting to wake. It would be nothing. There was a flapping and struggle, grunts and panting—a long hiatus and stillness—and then came the flop of the canvas against water and a suck and a striking against boulders.

Beside him a great wail cracked the hard cold air, the worst wail of a woman in labor:

"Ayyyyyyyyyy!"

Lita stood with her hands to her breasts, her head raised to the sky. "Dios mío, Dios mío," she murmured, "O God," and the Indians murmured and brushed past him.

Almost, his own mouth would crack. "Lita, take my goat," he sputtered in dryness, and his hand this time went past the black skirt and gripped her bare foot that his lips tried to reach, but they sucked only dirt, and blindly in dark.

But the voice, soft and the gentlest his life could remember, drew his eyes to the river, where a splay of light against rock held his eyes, and a white shadow rose above. "Price," she said when his lids cloaked the pupils. But the light wedged them open. Her hand, outstretched, was not far.

It was the last act that remained.

"Helen." He said it now with all the blood and bone in him, and he could hear Lita's breath catch, he could hear many feet and the brush of bodies behind. And close, the dogs howled.

He pressed up to his elbows, thrust up on his arm, set a leg out, rose—and he stood.

The wind did not veer him. It came down dark with the river.

"Helen," he whispered, close to the bank.

There was a threshing of waters and dark glimmers.

He raised his hand, and stepped—stepped—and reached to touch hers, and sank into the waters.

The last light passed over his eyes. Cold struck his mouth open. The river filled it. *Helen,* he said in the roar of the silence, clasping her hand. Joy filled him with fire when his hands struck the canvas and he caught at his ruins. For a while they wheeled slowly together until the canvas caught on a rock, thrust him loose and down under, where a rush seized and sucked him down through a passage of sharp rocks that tore back his arms and ripped his flesh. At the rapids rock smashed his teeth and his nose. *Helen,* he cried, and his skull cracked against stone.

At Fifteenth Street the landlady found her enclosed and laid out. It was the silence that had drawn her to listen, the lack of even a flutter of feet she'd been used to from the floor above.

In the bed were thin hair and dried skin over the obvious skull, and long bones without shape, and small flesh.

You would not believe a sheet could cover so little.

She was filled with pity that one could come to so little.

And quick, after shock, to avoid too much pity, she went down and called her doctor and her minister. Better, she decided, not to mention the moment to anyone or stir up a rumor that might make for difficulty in renting after the woman was removed.

And what would come this time to fill the empty apartment? she wondered as she sat down in the silence of Sunday to wait.

Mr. Balzano

WHY DID HE keep coming here? Day after day at the nursing home he stared into this old man's face, talking and talking, with never a word and seldom a nod in return.

Besides, he was anxious to leave this town. Didn't he hate it? He had always hated it. All his life, when he could, he had avoided it, visiting his mother summers for long spells at the Long Island place rather than coming to Bristol. He was born, grew up here. He thought of his experience here as a long blight which had left an invisible scar. He thought of the town as a scar on the map of Rhode Island. His cheek burned when he thought of it long enough.

But, though his mother was buried, he couldn't leave town yet. He must unload the house and put it up for sale. He had spent a day with the antique jewelry dealer, he had had two afternoons with furniture buyers, and when word got around people piled in to pick over and haggle, vultures seeking a steal or a giveaway. He had packed what he wanted shipped to his own house. He would leave some things for the new owner to use or dispose of. He had final payments and cutoffs to arrange.

When he had shown up at the nursing home so soon after his mother's funeral, the familiar nurses, aides, administrators had been somewhat mystified. There was a preliminary startled look on their faces, then an interval's silence, then the recuperated presence, smiles warm and friendly, a so-glad-you're-here, but with questions in their eyes for his unasked response.

The old man? He had had to describe the robust old Italian, the silent drifter from the other wing, the side where the *healthy*, mobile residents lived. His mother had been in a wheelchair, with the incapacitated, of course.

Ah, Vittorio.

Yes.

Balzano.

Yes, Mr. Balzano.

They had smiled at the *Mr.* But, though they meant well, he was *not* Vittorio, he was not Vittorio for *them*, he could not *be* Vittorio to them. He was in fact Mr. Vittorio Balzano, and each day when he located him—in his room or a lounge or the dining hall or rec room, perhaps standing staring out a window at the harbor—and addressed him as *Mr. Balzano*, the man turned, enlivened, his eyes flicked alert, a fine rousing in his motions reformed his body, he sat straighter in his chair or stood taller, as if there were some recognition—of what?—and some connection—with whom? *You see?* he wanted to say to the aides. And when he heard them talking to the residents—Ed, kiss your wife good-bye, kiss her, Ed. Now take your hands out of Al's plate, Mary. Alvin, you can sit up straight, use your feet—push, push—*Don't!* he wanted to shout at all those presumptuous mothers.

His mother had fallen getting out of bed. Years before he died, his stepfather, because he was so heavy, had added a second mattress, much too high for her. From the bedroom she had dragged herself across the living room floor and through the sun porch to the front door. Luckily, children were just leaving for school and she cried out, Get help. In no time the ambulance came and took her to the hospital.

He told Mr. Balzano, The little woman I came to see every day, you know her—Ruth, Ruth Balsam. Mr. Balzano would wander through her wing, stand and stare or meander among the still ones and then wander back to his wing. He was sure Mr. Balzano would remember his mother—and *him* from his visits; so he had begun by talking of her as a point of contact, some recognition, to work back from.

Work back?

Yes. But he did not begin with his mother's death. No, he merely told Mr. Balzano she had been brought here because one afternoon—not after that first fall and a spell in the hospital, but after she had gone home and fallen again when the aide was out in the yard hanging some wash on the line. It was then, having lost some memory, incontinent and in need of more than one person to lift and change and attend her, that she had come here, you see. And from here she had gone *home*, you see. But he did not say to her permanent home. Here, they were removed almost unnoticed, most often at night—*to the hospital*, they explained, to stave off the unstavable shadow which was ever waiting behind doors, outside bedroom windows, in closets, whom their savior the doctor, on his rare visits, might exorcise or excommunicate. So he did not tell Mr. Balzano that she had been taken in dark to the hospital and one morning at three A.M., very peacefully, had died. Spring. The twenty-fifth. Almost May. You could see the forsythia breaking into still yellow fountains everywhere, and some green shoots from the earth, incautious crocuses, as if no more snow would come, it was such an unusually balmy April.

But Mr. Balzano's eyes went blank. Did he see the hollow in *his* eyes, too? Mr. Balzano must have encountered endless space in his daily travels through the two wings. What must *he* look like to Mr. Balzano—an aging man twenty, twenty-five years younger than he, a stranger, a successful painter home from Europe, a Spanish resident, who now sought him out afternoons—relentlessly, yes, who sat relentlessly facing him, who stared relentlessly into his eyes and talked as if he pursued him out of some kind of passion—hate, say—because he was propelled by something akin to hatred, a hatred for the town released by his return here and aroused by his mother's decay and death. He had fixed his emotion on Mr. Balzano the first time he had seen him; something indeterminate in Mr. Balzano, something even familiar, attracted him against his will, precisely *because* it was against his will.

In Madrid thirty-five years ago, he told Mr. Balzano, he had discovered himself. All his art training had led him to the Prado, and though in early years he had had great teachers in the United States and Paris and Oslo and Rome, it was not until he had lived daily *in* the paintings of Fra Angelico, Bosch, El Greco, Titian, Velázquez, Goya—oh, yes, especially Goya—that he had *painted his way out* of his own labyrinth into the world—yours, Mr. Balzano—found his way to confront the suffering of the world by painting the victims of the world's cruelty with a compassion equal to the world's hatred, with a respect for the terror and beauty of the irrational in him—in us, Mr. Balzano—who could hate, too. He had a reputation, he was famous, his paintings hung in museums all over the world, and magazines everywhere featured color spreads and interpretations of his work. Anyone could see in his own black paintings *why* Goya. Because Goya knew madness, he saw men live and move by madness, he knew madness provokes reason, and reason is the hand that calms the waters.

Oh, he was not boasting—he did not mean to boast—he merely wanted Mr. Balzano bit by bit to understand, he must make Mr. Balzano understand because something in Mr. Balzano the instant he had seen him had compelled. Yes. Leaving the nursing home the first day he had visited his mother, going along the corridor, he came to the rec room; the sun was burning on the sea, blazed over the floor, the air itself turned light, his vision blurred, and when it settled, that lone man stood there like a dark thing risen from the sea. The sight blunted. He confronted that face. The man stared back. Locked. But *what* gripped? what recognition? He felt wrenched. The man had no right! Bewildered, he wanted to strike, he wanted to clutch—

Now he recalled how all he had loved in his mother and all he had hated in the town seemed to rush up and center on that figure.

That face, after he had left the nursing home, kept materializing, goading, you could say. He had sat in that house bereft of his mother. Astonishingly, he was not alone—the face insinuated, he saw it, the face filled hollows. At times the man emerged and confronted him as if urging him to speak, and then *at his own will* went back inside him. He did not seem to have any control over Mr. Balzano's appearances. Was there a current, then, between them—maybe even apart from them—in which something of him and Mr. Balzano was transmitted from one to the other so that he, too, materialized in Mr. Balzano's vision? At what point, he wondered now, had Mr. Balzano first really appeared in his vision? Perhaps that curiosity, yes, had motivated him *against his will* to go back to the nursing home almost immediately after the funeral, in the vacuity which had followed his mother's interment.

But famous? From the beginning his teachers had said he possessed a touch of genius. But it was not that, no. Millions have a touch of genius, any observer could note that. In fact, to be honest with himself, his touch of genius was a small talent, but *obsession* fed, nurtured, matured it. He *knew* as he painted that he must work—incessantly. He would like to have said to Mr. Balzano, I can hear my grandfather saying, Work for the night is coming in which no man can work. Each time my grandfather said it I saw the dark like a solid wall against which I would be obliterated. But he did not want to evoke for Mr. Balzano that image of death.

Yet he was convinced—and he *could* tell this to Mr. Balzano—that an emotion akin to hatred had driven him to fame—oh, not hatred for any*body*—or was he belying himself and revealing that he hadn't quite been able to denude himself of some sentimental Christian impulse?—but for what was in us all, and in *him* deeply. And hadn't he at once felt a similar emotion for Mr. Balzano when he had stared for the first time closely into his face? If not, why would he have acted on that impulse? Why would he have been so overwhelmed that he must now find words for it? After all, he had spent all his life trying to paint the unsayable, he was trying to paint it still, he would go on trying, so why try to articulate it in words?

Mr. Balzano stared, green dark eyes which mirrored all light, caught sea and distance and all objects, still, too still. He had stared into such stillness in the eyes of snakes, rabbits, praying mantises, gulls, and into his own seething in mirrors. His body, old as it was, looked steely with the stillness of trapped energy that seethed. There is madness in us, Mr. Balzano, sometimes you have to yield to it to find out what it is, and *make* with it, shape it. Even Mr. Balzano's thick gray hair and thick brows and lashes still dark implied lusty energy, his worn face with high cheekbones and firm jaw seemed stone, the neat mustache and brief beard compelled you to a mouth youthfully full but which would not speak.

He had been a millworker and a carpenter on the side, Mrs. Beaufort, the daytime administrator said, and his wife had worked in the mill, too, until she died, and his son till the son had been killed in a machine accident. Mr. Balzano had raged. He would stand in the street and clench his fists and flail his arms and rage. Nobody ever knew when the fit would seize him. Something miraculous had happened, or simply one day he had accepted it. A thing in him had died or frozen. He had become docile, harmless. Finally they had brought him here.

So Mr. Balzano was one of the horde of immigrants who had come to this town to work in the mills, who lived beyond Wood Street and back of town to Metacom Avenue, then a neighborhood almost hidden from sight of the *Americans*. Of course, in *his* daily life, the workers who poured in and out of the cotton and woolen mill and the U.S. Rubber and the lace factory, Wops and Portygees, were beneath him, lower really than the potato famine Irish Catholics, and the Kanucks and Polacks that settled almost in equally divided areas on either side of Main Street in the next town on the bus route to Providence and whose churches were latecomers to the assemblage of Methodist Episcopal Baptist Presbyterian Congregational Unitarian. So when the myriad young Mr. Balzanos from the Mediterranean settled here, they were carefully pinned with such phrases as his mother herself used so naturally: Isn't he dark-complected?

But in the mirror *he* was, he saw. Like your father, his mother murmured. She had divorced him, but his father's image persisted in him. And the secret, silent—or inadmissible—was where it had come from, this sallow skin, olive, and such dark hair. Not from her family, oh no.

Because of the divorce, he did not know his father's side, they were a mystery. Imagine he must. But others hinted, implied, Portuguese kids he knew, or friends his mother had, the Portuguese girls Dotty and Mary, who had loved wheeling him in the baby carriage and who had *adored* his green, deep eyes and long, long, dark lashes and dark hair, his distinguishing marks in a family of blue- and gray-eyed strawberry blondes, towheads as children, who customarily turned lovely chestnut as adults—but not dark. In school the question began to come: Are you? He would shun it. *No.* English he was. *American.* Others—grown-ups—were sure: He *is.* I knew his grandmother, all his father's people. Portygee! Older, he buttressed himself. He ignored kids, adults, but burned.

In The Block, when he lived in a third-floor tenement, his mother said, We *must* get out, he's in junior high, we need to live on a better street. The Portuguese man across the hall, Marion, he dreaded to meet on the second or third-floor flights because Marion would halt, stare. And he would stare back like pinned prey. Marion's eyes were hands that might beat or caress. He did not yet know he wanted them to beat or caress. That would break the hold. And though Marion never said a word, his voice was loud across the hall as he said to his wife, The little Portygee! But *safe* behind the kitchen door, he'd let out his breath at last. He would hear Mrs. Stevens the fortuneteller open her door below and be *in on it,* too. Why, Mrs. Stevens asked his mother frequently, does he whistle all the time? He never stops whistling going up the stairs. Is the kid nervous or something? She would stick her head out as he passed her door. You stop that whistling! The sound must have marred her concentration when reading palms or tea leaves, her act. But behind the door, already he was anticipating the next time Marion would appear, afraid one day Marion *would* touch him, ohGodJesus, and he would be what he was, Portygee to Portygee. He desired to know what it was his mother kept saying he was not, what that bit of blood meant. He would later rationalize. He would figure out from the generational marriages in his father's family that his grandmother—Silva, her maiden name—must have been one-fourth Portuguese, say, and he one-sixteenth, next to nothing. Would his people never stop lying? Would *he*? Could he one day *know* and tell the truth? It loomed. It loomed in Marion.

You see, Mr. Balzano, part of me should have lived up there back of town with you, all of you. A man should not be part here, part there. A man should be everywhere. His mother and his minister and his teachers taught that, but over the years *They say, they say* creates invisible, impenetrable walls around us.

Listen, Mr. Balzano, I was forty-two before I tasted mussels. Do you know why? Because people said, the Americans said, mussels and periwinkles were immigrant food, said only Wops and Portygees followed the shoreline hunting periwinkles and mussels. That year I went to northwest Spain. I was tracing the legend of St. James's journey through Galicia. In every village and hamlet, in the cities, Santiago, La Coruña, not a meal was served without mussels—hot, cold, in soups, salads, stews, sauces. Delicious! Incredible! And in the harbor of La Coruña the ships in from sea were burdened with mussels by the thousands hanging in stalks like bananas, great clumps of black and purplish natural jewels stark in the sun; they confronted me like secret sins fattened and dredged up to eat my way back through. The mind stumbles, dragging such obstacles. *You* make me eat memory, Mr. Balzano, swallow it.

You see, in The Block the immigrants *not of our class* were on all three flights, on our very floor. My mother was not *of* them because her family had come from three centuries of *landed gentry,* yes—oh, money earned and amounted, then inherited and divided, then lost, so only land remained, plenty of that—*property poor* they became, landed gentry, or swamp Yankees. They didn't get over that—or let me. But the Army Air Force taught me in a day, and the Bomb proved forever, that we're all immigrants, yes, you and I, Mr. Balzano, and snakes roaches dogs cats alligators bats butterflies all insects all green—a universe of immigrants, Mr. Balzano.

So why should his mother want to keep moving away from *them?* For *him.* Mr. Balzano must have known, living with the Latins back of town in that pretty section, where they had duplicated the houses and the naked earth of their homelands, Portugal, the Azores, Italy, Sicily, in pink and rose and blue and yellow stucco houses where in spring appeared rows of stakes with string for peppers to climb, and Italian tomatoes for sauce, rows of endive, fennel, string beans; where men in black with black berets played their games of bocci on the hard ground. Closer to town were the block on block of three-story, three-family houses, and tenements. Three streets ran like parallel arteries from end to end of town, a block between each, but socially they were miles and dollars and blood apart. That journey from back of Wood Street to High Street to Hope Street, from the rear of town to the bright vista of the harbor, some made in years, or a lifetime, or never. By a fluke—magic to his mother—one of the Darlings distantly related by marriage rented her a historic house. It sat on the high bank of Hope Street, serene, beautiful, with a view, the slope and trees concealing Thames Street below with the mill, bars, the railroad station, the government dock, piers. All time, all space seemed to stretch before him. With what sacrifices his miracle mother achieved it, he would never know. But she *placed* him—a lie, but placed. They were part of the view. The harbor, islands, infinity were his gift: freedom.

Did you know freedom, Mr. Balzano, when you got off that ship from Sicily and touched ground? How immigrants kissed the earth in Bristol on the Fourth of July! Did *you*? Did the vision of Liberty, Ellis Island, that skyscraper city stagger? And did it tarnish with Rhode Island, this town, the mill, the harbor outside the window . . . ?

Do you dream of the Mediterranean, Mr. Balzano?

Before and after visits to the nursing home, nonchalantly he asked questions of Mrs. Beaufort, or whoever was at the desk, or a drifting aide or one of the *permanent* residents, who were always eager for an eye a mouth a hand: Nobody ever comes to see Mr. Balzano? He'd lived on Rosita Avenue, you say? What number? No family? None back in Sicily either? Brothers, you say, a cousin? They'd died there! Are there no compatriots here from his hometown in Sicily? Not a living soul. Mr. Balzano had worked day and night to send money to Sicily, and he'd saved—for the son. The wife, you never saw? Oh, yes, on the way home from the mill, a short woman, dark, in black, always mourning someone *back there*. She'd worked, like her husband, for the son.

Oh, Vittorio's the best, no trouble at all. The aides talked to him, sailed around him, touched the old shoulder.

After the second visit to Mr. Balzano, he dreaded going back to his mother's empty house, his. He found himself moving up Franklin Street to Wood to Rosita Avenue. On some few trees, early shoots were forming but Mr. Balzano's neighborhood was still waste, winter-stripped, dry. Number fourteen. A small beige stucco, surely four rooms, no more. Not homey. The usual arbor—for grapes, shade, gossip, and propping up the wooden frames with starched lace curtains stretched on pins to stiffen in the sun. Last summer's garden in dead rows, twigs in the ground, untouched. A wooden shed. No garage. Only the American link fence—no, not for dogs; like Sicily, no dogs here, only pariahs, food cost.

He dared approach Mr. Balzano's neighbors. The new one had not known him, but in the house on the right, Orazio Venturi, old too, led him into that typical Latin dark, the parlor shades drawn as if warding off the forever-threatening Sicilian sun. Venturi talked Italo-American, told him of the young Balzano—the good-looker who caroused years till he met Giuseppina of the iron hand, who handled him and the money and the son, especially after Balzano's mother and the older brother died in Sicily —*make-a him serious, change-a him*. So he and Giuseppina were like mad lovers, and then in that little house on their parcel of land they and the son closed the world out, but marched—religious Giuseppina was—to six-o'clock Mass every morning at Our Lady of Mount Carmel, weekdays straight to the mill after Mass, a ritual Vittorio stopped the day she died. After, he never came much out of the house, that Balzano, and after the son was killed turned *eremitaggio*, a hermit not even looking for another Giuseppina, though for a while women came with food, wanted to clean, wanted that man, a ring, his bed, the house, but quick they learned he was for nobody, he was for the dead, *he* was dead.

But was he?

Was there nothing in this town for Mr. Balzano? Nothing?

Well, he would know.

All he had in his pocket was an old envelope, but he made a sketch of Mr. Balzano's house.

The next afternoon he said, Mr. Balzano, I've brought you something—they were at a table in the rec lounge. At his words, a woman wheeling by halted. He laid the envelope down before him. The woman moaned.

Mr. Balzano gazed at it, long, long. Without shifting his head, he raised his eyes to him, then gazed down. Was there some connection Mr. Balzano was trying to make between him and the sketch? He said, Venturi is still next door, and his brother Dino, and the brother's wife, Lucia, though I didn't meet them. He still carves canes with wolves' heads. You remember?

Mr. Balzano's eyes left the sketch. They would not settle anywhere.

But he whispered!

Casa? Did he whisper *Casa?*

A *word*. The first true sound. A word. He vibrated with it. Not to prod, he rose. But the word had sprung between them as binding as the Mount Hope Bridge between Bristol and Portsmouth. He felt almost a malicious pleasure, *yes*, in feeling he could rouse memory, make him live. Bound. I chose you, Mr. Balzano, because . . . But perhaps he *had* no choice, perhaps something *in* him chose Mr. Balzano, perhaps something in Mr. Balzano chose *him*. He felt the sudden energy of the vengeful. He would enter Mr. Balzano. He would make Mr. Balzano spill.

When he left, he spent the rest of the afternoon and evening making quick line sketches of the Common with the Courthouse, the bandstand, the grade schools. He sketched the old Prudence Island ferry, the mill, the U.S. Rubber Company, our Lady of Mount Carmel, the Mount Hope Bridge, the castle at Poppasquash Point. Surely Mr. Balzano would recognize them. He would make the town surround him.

The next afternoon Mrs. Beaufort said, All day he's stayed cooped up in his room, no breakfast, no lunch, *that's not like him*. Her eyes lingered. Was she admonishing *him?*

Mr. Balzano was sitting on the edge of a plain wooden chair. Standing on the opposite side of the bed, he laid out the sketches one by one, starting with a view of the ferry under the bridge. You remember, Mr. Balzano, where the kids parked to make love, it was famous for that. He laughed, a little excited himself, yes, because Mr. Balzano's gaze did not once leave the sketch—the sketches. Slowly he took him through the others. Not to press too much too fast on him, he related anecdotes, brief histories: how, for example, luck saved one of the construction crew from falling to his death—that day the notorious Tonio Tedeschi sported birthday galluses as a joke, yes, but when he tripped and fell, they caught on a crossbeam and he swung there high over Narragansett Bay. How Mr. Balzano studied the mill! And he cocked his head when he said, This is *my* house on Hope Street, not far from here. You must know it, Mr. Balzano. I finally bought it for my mother. And he ended with the U.S. Rubber with its gigantic brick chimney that stood a phallus over the town.

It hooted so loudly that the ground seemed to tremble with an ejaculation. You could hear the whistle in all directions from the ferry to the reaches of the Neck and to Mount Hope and over the waters of the harbor. What could he call that sound—time? doom?—relentless, pressing him to work, *work for the night is coming*. His finger touched the smokestack in the sketch. *You* heard the five o'clock whistle. All my life I've been hearing it, Mr. Balzano. The sound's in both of us. Do you hear it *now*?

Mr. Balzano looked up abruptly, his eyes widened. He was startled at the eyes so like his own, deep green, with brown and dark little islands, and tiny planets deep in space. Then his eyes, all chaos, darted from sketch to sketch. His fingers quivered, touched, flighted, touched. He waited, wanting words, but only deep sounds came, muted bowel grumbles which merely caused his lips to quiver soundlessly.

When he rose to leave, Mr. Balzano's hands shot out and possessed the sketches, his face defiant.

They're yours, Mr. Balzano. To relax him, he laughed. I made them for you. It's your town.

And mine, he thought. I'll never see it again. Never. The house would be in the hands of his agent, Ray Boggs, and the family lawyer, Calvin Martin, so he would not have to return, ever. Thank God. But the joy was sharp, it pained. *Never*. That tolled. In the pit of him he felt a sinking, loss. Blood lamented. Why? when he hated the town—he did.

The day—it was still early—was so beautiful; and he had not, no, not *seen* the town—he'd sketched it from memory—had not seen Mr. Balzano's world or . . . his own. Had he deliberately avoided those streets, avoided facing those houses he had lived in on Woodlawn Avenue, Cottage and Burton and Wood Streets,

Shaw's Lane? Why? He would ask Mr. Balzano that question. Of course Mr. Balzano wouldn't answer—he might, there was that hope—but wasn't silence a reply? Silence would make him answer himself. Or he would be left with this passion of all his life that erupted in his compassion for those sufferers. If he could show Mr. Balzano his paintings, he wouldn't have to speak. Have to? But he *did* have to. From the moment he had confronted Mr. Balzano's face in that blaze of sun in the rec room, he knew they were standing alone bound in a silence as deep as the bottom of a sea.

Once he had begun to walk down those streets, he felt led, impelled. And so quickly had he developed the habit of Mr. Balzano's presence that he was already whispering to him, sometimes quite loud, preparing himself for his session in that room, that box, where Mr. Balzano would sit in his old world erectness, his Sicilian peasant dignity, listening.

Was he?

He took the streets as they were laid out from the farthest edge of town bordering the harbor, where once the brook from Mount Hope had run through his yard past the green cottage he'd been born in and under a bridge over the road, through the meadow across the street and to the harbor. The lower meadow was a great swamp with hundreds of wild purple iris, the higher a mass of rock outcrops surrounded by great meanders of pink and blue and white forget-me-nots. Alone, I played there, Mr. Balzano, it was all the world to me, the woods were dark and deep, I went deep in, I knew those woods—there was nothing to fear in that dark, I could have *been* a great lunar moth, I was the bark it clung to in daytime, I was snapdragons, I was the garter snakes I turned rocks to find and carry in my pockets, and trapdoor spiders, and moles and beavers and all the animals we are, I was everything, I could climb the rocks to the peak of the Mount, I could touch sky, on one side I could hold the whole harbor in my hand and the whole bay on the other or cup my hands around the enchanted city of Fall River on the far shore. . . .

That house was as far away from yours on the opposite side of town as could be, Mr. Balzano—

Well, I *went* to Woodlawn—

It was gone! No house, no brook, no meadow, the woods cut back. Only houses and houses and houses stood there. But in my head *I* saw that boy and the house, brook, meadow, woods.

Had I imagined him, Mr. Balzano? Was the boy I saw never really the one who loved to play in the brook and catch tadpoles in jars, only—infallibly—to be shoved into the water from behind by the bullies from the next block, his head pressed into the silt till he could no longer breathe and, when released, jerked up and blinked and looked around for them, only to find nobody was ever in sight they were that fast. He grew almost afraid to go into the brook, but, stubborn, he did, each time thinking, I'll get even, I'll spy them out, I'll dare them, yet always he ended up soaked, muddy, crying—but more and more crying not from shame but fury.

We moved from that green house. When you were a divorced woman, you moved. Divorce was a thing unheard of in your Catholic world then, Mr. Balzano. Oh, my mother was independent, self-supporting, valiant. And then *poor* came to mean, and *class* showed, the boy was left alone and vulnerable, and *different* came to mean, and as he grew *Portygee* came to mean. *You* know about that, you suffered *Wop*, you suffered *a section of town for Wops and Portygees*, and oh yes finally *money*. Your people saved better than the *Americans* did, imported the family from the old country better than the *Americans* did, coupled up relatives in one house better than the *Americans* did, so that one day the Italians would finally come to dominate, own and run the town, Wood Street and High and Hope, dim and tarnish and drive back, or marry—absorb? —the centuries' old names, Bradford Howe Williams Franklin Winthrop. . . .

From Woodlawn he went to Cottage Lane, where *puny* came to mean. Always any change of weather, lingering snow and slush, damp harbor air drove his *bronchials* mad. He had to sit still from *wheezing*, watch the other kids playing vigorously, years of that inactivity. Asthma. the doctors said, but only one, Dr. Bemardo —your compatriot, Mr. Balzano—diagnosed bronchial trouble, said, The boy will outgrow it in his teens. At fifteen he *did*, good strong lungs till this day, Mr. Balzano. In fact, those torturous breathings *made his lungs strong*. He benefited, that boy, from the agony, the suppressed passion which seethed in his blood, the pain of watching motion in others. But his memory was of a boy always bundled up, who lived in fear, hoping to avoid that woman he hated, that neighbor Eloise Lemaire with the *healthy* son, who deliberately *crossed the street* whenever she saw him going home from school and stared him scornfully in the face and said, *You sick again?* He wouldn't tell his mother because she would deflate with a kind of exhaustion—he could see her now, poor woman— and then inflate with fury at that woman.

But his loves saved him—books, pens, brushes turned him to the hammock under the apricot tree. Eric, the young gym teacher next door, loved kids. He must have felt sorry for him because he sometimes came into his yard and played—threw passes with him, boxed lightly, wrestled. Such activity thrilled him. He laughed, excited. His blood surged. The world beat. Wrestling one day, he was on top of Eric, Eric was startled at his sudden strength, Eric threw him off, he leaped back on, he felt a thing happening, a sensation, he clutched, Eric stopped laughing, he stared, his face went blank as a dead bulb, Eric raised him and laid him aside: Enough. Back to work. Something—he didn't know what—had happened. All his flesh different, changed. He wanted to ask—but nobody. Later the Catholic kids would say, That's why you go to church. Every Saturday *they* had to tell what they'd done that week. *Your* son did, didn't he, Mr. Balzano? But in *his* church, he couldn't, there was no priest to pave the way to God, there was no way to know if *He* heard. Besides, tell what?

And on Burton Street he knew the word *queer*. He associated the word with that time, with the pinochle and poker friends of his mother and stepfather, the Portuguese girls Dorothy and Mary, who loved to come make chocolate fudge for him, but especially the family's old friend Cooney with his built-up right shoe, a defect which "spoiled his chances" for marriage, they always said after Cooney had left. Poor Cooney. So for him Burton Street was the sound of *Poor Cooney* and the sight of Cooney's enormously thick sole which would grow in his mind and thought over the years like his grandfather's hands burned in an accident at sea till they were nothing but claws, hard bone wrenched back in such distortion that they were the perfect image of crouched spiders. But what miracles those hands performed! Independent, his grandfather had built his own house, every inch; he'd repaired broken toys, bikes, vehicles, saving them to distribute to poor kids at Christmas, and he poorer than any of them, a scavenger hunting for others. He'd collected his due from the State, he'd earned his keep with his daughter.

Burton Street was also where Randy Wills, one of the older big boys in the neighborhood, grabbed his hand and tickled his palm with his finger. He became possessed. All his strength roused, he leaped a foot higher and lashed his unathletic, untrained fist out, his sudden Samson strength struck—and Randy *fell*. He couldn't believe it. He was trembling. Across the street Randy's gang was watching, ready to ride him with names, but they went dead still, then broke into murmurs and cries. The bully ran. But *he*—never till that moment had he known physical triumph. He was giddy, but scared. He could scarcely walk to the house. At school his reputation rose, respect set in—but not for long. He soon learned how short memory is, how fickle the world.

And years later Burton Street meant Beatrice Friedman, the dark Jewish beauty of the high school class. Gaga over her, he'd walk her home. But you didn't go *in?* his mother probed. She can't let *any* of us in, he said.

All my life, Mr. Balzano, I've seen Cooney's shoe, my grandfather's hands and albino eyes, my lungs—I've painted parts. In the paintings the bodies, the parts, are composed of tendrils trying to reach, *reach*, and touch other parts. Rains of blood are falling on them, Mr. Balzano, they struggle to keep from drowning in rains of blood, the tendrils are hands in the blood, Mr. Balzano, they reach for the light, they try to grip other tendrils to keep from drowning. Some of the paintings are masses of tendrils feeling blindly, but a few, a few tendrils have developed eyes, yes, and the eyes mirror the others, yes, the eyes are the only place they can hold the others inside.

Sometimes the painting is a portrait, but when you go close, you see the face is a complex of tendrils, each separate, loose, turned *outward*. He could be you, Mr. Balzano; me, Mr. Balzano—

Then he went to Wood Street. Wood Street was The Block, Mr. Balzano, ten families in tenements, Jack's Grocery store downstairs on one side. The *world* lived there, Mr. Balzano—Italian Portuguese Irish Polish English Catholic Protestant but no Jew oh no—and Marion stared at me on the stairs, Mrs. Stevens the fortuneteller lay in wait to shout, Stop the whistling! The house was full of sounds, languages I couldn't understand, but I *could* understand the yelling, arguing, laughing, fighting, singing, playing. Years I lived there, Mr. Balzano, where *shame* came to mean. Always shame will be the little girl, Lucia, and the boy beginning to turn man. Her mother and father were out one day, alone in the house, sudden it was, we felt—we *were*—curious, or *I* was. We went into a dark closet, between clothes smelling of grease, cigarette, soap. Behind the shut door in dark I pushed her panties aside, my hand fumbled, my thing tried to know her cleft, behind the shut door in dark. I was dumb, innocent, curious—a criminal, Mr. Balzano, at twelve, and Lucia, eight. After, in daytime we avoided each other. I avoided even Lucia's glance, remembering how scared I was when she pushed my hand away and cried No no and shoved the door open and ran.

Mornings and afternoons, Mr. Balzano, as that boy grew into junior high and high, he met every day the Japanese girl, walked her to and from school. Under alien eyes they walked, and all the scorned ones in The Block, poor and immigrant and laborers, scorned the only Jap in town. Even before the war, Mr. Balzano, before Mussolini and Hitler and Hirohito, *bastard* came to mean, yes, because she was illegitimate, and in those days her *unwed* mother was stained branded shunned, so the daughter was too, ignored scorned abused, sometimes stoned, yes, till she and I stoned *them*.

In high school the boys would not let up on *small*. He was smaller than most, short, though formed well, built, though one day after gym class Tony Russo said, The guys say you got a big cock, and whipped his towel back. But the respect didn't last long. Two star athletes cornered him in the athletic ground behind the high school. One jammed him against a post, his collar caught up against his windpipe, he could hardly breathe. Starting tomorrow you bring two extra sandwiches in your lunch every day, see? His mother said, He's developed an appetite like a horse, he must be growing. And shamed, thinking of her, what she did without for him, *coward* came to mean. Seeing himself in the bathroom mirror, *Coward* he accused himself At noon they met him on the basement stairs. *Well?* He said, *Bring your own sandwiches* and stared them down. *You little fucker!* He turned and walked away, slow. He took the sandwiches home. *Ma, save them for tomorrow.*

Last, he went to Shaw's Lane. It was dusk, fast darkening. A block away from his old house, he came to a corner. It looked unfamiliar, but it was all he could do to press back a threat. He closed his eyes. A dark building materialized, snow, a sled— *No.* Shame pulsed at his temples. His cheek burned. *No.* He stood against memory.

Tomorrow . . .

But tomorrow—he felt somewhat apprehensive as he thought it—would be his last day with Mr. Balzano.

The moment he entered—as if they were waiting, watching for him—an aide intercepted to tell him the administrator would like to see him. Mrs. Beaufort? Oh, no, Mr. Cranston. And Mr. Cranston assured, We're delighted, of course, at the attention you've given Mr. Balzano; for years not a soul has come except the charities, volunteers. He sat suspended in the long hiatus as Mr. Cranston looked out on sea, sky. There's so much in a person, we never know how much the least suggestion will release. Once long ago Mr. Balzano was so . . . volatile. Oh, he interrupted Mr. Cranston, he's been docile, too docile. I'd *like* him to react. But he *has,* Mr. Cranston said. Has? Yes. There was an almost edge to his voice. Mr. Balzano has been talking almost unceasingly in his room, Italian, but we don't know what because the instant anyone opens the door he stops, and when it's left open he closes it. Mr. Balzano seems to depend . . . After you left, he walked up and down the corridors, his hands going as if they were doing the talking he didn't do, he circled the rec room, entered sickrooms, stood staring at people, circled and circled. He was all motion. He kept *at* it. We thought maybe it would help us to know if there's something, some subject, a word—you'd have to be judge—that may upset him . . . ? Mr. Cranston, I can't place a particular . . . And besides, today *is* my last visit. It would be better, Mr. Cranston said, not to say last— But, he said, then he might expect— Oh—Mr. Cranston rose—here they expect many things we don't know. If we could know— Well, forgive my troubling you, we're always concerned about our guests, and you've been such a blessing to Mr. Balzano. He extended his hand. Have a good visit, and a good trip.

Talking. Mr. Balzano?

And circling?

Was Mr. Balzano waiting for him? His visits were a precise clockwork ritual. Had Mr. Balzano's body come to expect him now?

The door was shut. He halted in the corridor. Inside, there *was* a voice, a bass chafing sound, but it ceased—at his steps? his shadow under the door?

He himself was in tumult stirred by yesterday's walk back into that time, to those houses, by the long night of reliving a thousand associations that crowded unsorted unordered unimpeded. He hadn't slept. He was tired. When he knocked and opened the door, Mr. Balzano was sitting on the bed, still as a priest, dark against the light. His lips were parted as if caught with a half-mouthed word. And he was sure Mr. Balzano had not slept either —his eyes were red cauldrons, and the lids red. Now they fixed on him, barely blinked. Almost he could not bear that gaze today.

The sun penetrated, so bright it pained. He closed his eyes.

If *he* were sitting in Mr. Balzano's place on that bed, who would come?

Mr. Balzano . . .

He sank onto the edge of the chair. Looking up, he felt like some acolyte before that unyielding face. In the air he sensed the lingering of the bass voice.

How familiar this place had become in these last days. Already he felt the wrench of breaking this new habit before he had *reached* Mr. Balzano. For he had not touched Mr. Balzano. Yet hadn't he—yes, he saw it now—quickened him? Really he didn't know what he expected, what he wanted, what he wanted from Mr. Balzano, but all week he'd felt himself inching toward him as if he had sent out invisible fingers to feel into his mouth, throat, down, down, fine tendrils that wanted to touch, grip—what?

What am I doing here? he thought.

He said, What are we doing here, Mr. Balzano?

He wanted to tell him, This is the last day. Strange, isn't it, how you creep to *lasts* and then they are sudden and then over, and so *many*. But he said, Yesterday I went to all the houses I'd lived in, Mr. Balzano. I think I went because I'd made the sketches to take *you* back to town . . . or because I started *thinking* . . . or because my *blood* . . . because . . . because I was impelled—*you* know—as if I had no control over my feet, I *had* to go where they led. I hated to, but I *yearned* to, I was torn, yes, just as I was when I saw across the rec room, standing there alone—you, Mr. Balzano.

Do *you* long to be what you hate? Do you long to *be* the rock and dust of Sicily?

He stared at Mr. Balzano's hands. He said, I went first to the house I was born in, back to that natural world— Oh, Mr. Balzano, how far back do you have to go to be happy? I loved the woods and meadows, wild rabbits insects snakes— Telling it, he felt such joy fountain in him, he was so at one with that vanished time and place, that he broke into bastard Italian—*nei boschi*, he said, with *le lepri, insetti, i serpenti*, he said. Why hadn't it occurred to him before? He hadn't spoken a word of Italian since talking bastard half-Spanish half-Italian while painting in Civitavecchia and by the walls of Tarquinia, looking out over the Tyrrhenian Sea, the same waters that surrounded Mr. Balzano's Sicilia. And he couldn't stop now. Listen, Mr. Balzano, you know The Block, I bet you knew the Romanos and the Chiricos and the Brazzis— Those names and his butchered Italian fascinated Mr. Balzano. His eyes quivered, made hummingbird darts, his fingers were restless though his hands stayed, but mostly his lips worked, mouthing his words silently.

No, he couldn't stop now. He told yesterday, *ieri*. He told that house and brook and meadow and the woods; told all the families in The Block, told Marion halting on the stairs to stare at him as he came up from the cellar with the bottle of oil for the kitchen stove, Mrs. Stevens the fortuneteller, and Lucia, *poveretta*! told Cottage Street and Eric and *small* and *puny, piccolo e infermo*; told Burton Street and Cooney's clumped foot and beating Randy Wills; told junior high and high and Portygee and *strambo, queer*;

told how one day when his mother was out the boy the kids called Harold Josephine waited at the back door, trying to lure him with his *corpo felino, le labbra tumide,* his voice *sussurando* that he had a little shack in his yard, nobody'd see them, it'd be fine, but he streaked through the door up three flights, peered out the hall window to see if Harold Josephine had gone; told jacking off in the barn behind The Block in shafts of sunlight pouring into the semi-dark through broken windows while pigeons cooed on the rafters; told his mother's saying, If I ever catch you playing with yourself, I'll burn your fingers, *bruciarsi le dita;* he told his kid fear of Catholic incense and chants and excommunication; told Jap-hate and queer-hate and Wop- and Portygee-hate and welfare-hate and his own hate for the town—mine and yours, Mr. Balzano; told it almost whispering almost incanting almost shouting, impelled by the chaotic rhythms of his own voice. He couldn't stop, no, and he couldn't tear his eyes from Mr. Balzano, he feared to. Mr. Balzano was silent, stony as judgment, even his eyes motionless on his face. And he went on telling, telling, till he reached yesterday afternoon as dark came, he passed the Common, he reached the corner of State Street and halted. Just beyond was Shaw's Lane, alongside the U.S. Rubber Co., by the great brick smokestack penetrating the sky, Big Dick the kids used to call it. Yes, halted. Because something was missing. The corner was different—

That corner. Yesterday it would not come—

Maybe *I wouldn't let it,* Mr. Balzano.

But it came now—he saw the building, its great front windows, the doorway, the two cement steps; and he smelled the meats and cigarettes and stale cartons as strong as real; and he waited, turbulent—

He slipped to the floor, he bowed his head and gazed into the floor as if *it* were visible there: the corner was a market, it was winter, there was snow on the ground, he had his sled, he was across the street from the tavern, there were two boys farther on, Hal and Carmine, throwing snowballs, they ran, he was sitting on the curb beside his sled, a man who had been standing in front of Mello's Market talking with two others crossed the street, he halted not far off and stared down at him a long time, then the man hawked, he spat, the glob of spittle struck his cheek, hot, he was stunned, he dared not move, without a word the man turned and went back, his cheek burned, he didn't touch it, he grabbed his sled, he would not run, he walked slowly up the street, he did not wipe the spit off his face till he ducked into Shaw's Lane, he had nothing to use, he wiped it with his sleeve, wiped and wiped. His cheek smarted. His mother would see his face, and his stepfather. What would he say? What was it? He felt attacked, shamed.

Saliva.

He looked up at Mr. Balzano.

Did Mr. Balzano feel the burning on his cheek?

I didn't know it then, Mr. Balzano, but *blood* knew—blood knows shame before knowledge of shame: once they shame you, you *find* reasons. All our lives there's shame. Does a thing born in us goad—to make something in us stand up against our own shame and make and *make* to retaliate for *small, puny, queer,* for Cooney's foot, for a Jap face, for *Jew, Wop*—?

You know *Wop,* Mr. Balzano, and *poor* and *broken English* and *immigrant*—

It's madness, *demenza,* Mr. Balzano, *irrazionale.*

They're afraid because *our* madness is in *them,* they don't know what to do with it so they condemn—but when they see what *we* make of it, they *recognize* it, they *claim* it. Nobody can do without madness. I put mine into my paintings. The paintings are theirs now.

Mr. Balzano. . .

There was nothing more to say, he had emptied himself, but he did not feel relieved, not cleansed, and where was the joy?

He dropped his head, exhausted. His knees ached. He was an old man talking to an old man, waiting. What did he expect? Words? Mr. Balzano's hand on his head?

He looked up into those eyes so like his own. They were nervous, riled—like *hers*. Sometimes hers were two gray moths striking at glass. He felt them battering to escape his own body.

Nothing came.

He rose. It seemed almost sacrilegious not to take Mr. Balzano's hand and say, Good-bye, I'm going—forever. But in this place every farewell must be a crucifixion. He would go as if it were the usual visit, and disappear. Wasn't that the most merciful?

But—to whom?

At the door he lingered too long. Mr. Balzano was sitting still, lost in the sketches lined along the bureau.

He closed the door.

But he bore Mr. Balzano with him through dusk, dark, through the weight of last things. He did them—called the utilities, telephone company, arranged for the hired dumpster to be picked up, told Dennie Lipscomb the junkman he could get the key from his real estate broker to pick up the bed and mattress and clear the remains out of the house.

He lay down, barren he felt, too worn to sleep this last night here. Yet in the silt of him, deep, something stirred, moved; in the darkness forms rose, materialized—bodies, faces . . . his mother father grandfather Eddie Earl Jay-Jay schoolmates and teachers McGovern Bullock Rinaldi Sisson and Lucia Marion Mrs. Stevens Beatrice Harold, so many. He did not expect the crowding: you had no control of *them*, they insinuated, willed themselves present, wandered in your head, insisted on being seen. . . . He was at the mercy of those who had waited all the years in this house, displaced now by emptiness. They approached, stood silent, withdrew, and others moved forward, close, till he *heard* them moving deep in dark, yes, heard sounds at the doors, at windows, living winds in the house, in the cellar, and creaks came, chafings, vague scuffings, then a long silence, which assured—It's my imagination, I'm tired, I'll be glad to leave—and just under his room something scraped the cellar floor.

He got up and went along the hall to the inside basement door, switched the light on, and went down the long stairs—and stood. Nothing this side, in the old rec room. There was nothing in the furnace room or the coal bin. He stood looking into the laundry and storage area behind the furnace, which his grandfather had partitioned off with crisscrossed slats. Something . . . some night creature—he sensed it—was alive there. . . .

He was gazing between slats straight into eyes. Somebody was standing by his grandfather's cot.

He went behind the partition.

Mr. Balzano was standing in that web of light and shadow.

You!

He was breathing with a harsh tear, he raised his arms, his fingers flexed as if trying to speak. The man was exhausted.

What was he doing here?

But the man was too exhausted to question. From his wing Mr.

Balzano could easily walk out at any time. How would they know?

He said, You're worn out. Sit—

Mr. Balzano's arms battered air. Nooo.

Here. Please—

Mr. Balzano sank onto the cot, heaving, his hands struggling in silent speech.

And instantly he felt he hadn't left Mr. Balzano, he was still in the nursing home, it seemed so natural, this moment he wanted Mr. Balzano here.

He kneeled by the cot.

He said, My grandfather used to rest here, it was his nook when he tended the furnace, I'd hear him talking to himself.

So close to him, in shadow, Mr. Balzano was sweating, and in the half-dark the sheen of his skin, the eyes catching the light, the sharp nose and high cheekbones and the beard, his face confounded—looked so *young*. Mr. Balzano's face looked like—he felt a surge of shame, and anger—yes, it resembled that *other* face. He closed his eyes: the man had crossed the street and stared at him and spat. He felt the stare, the quick burn of spit. His hand touched his cheek.

Him.

Could he be?

Was that face what had drawn him against his will to the dark figure in the sea of light at the nursing home?

Was that you?

His voice dropped so low that Mr. Balzano raised his head. His thick brows arched, his eyes widened, his lips parted, exposing the tongue.

Was it?

Mr. Balzano's hand rose, felt over his fingers, gripped his wrist hard, and drew him so close that he felt Mr. Balzano's breath on his cheek, he saw the wet sockets and the teeth and tongue glitter.

Mio figlio? Mr. Balzano said.

My son. The words pulsed.

Mr. Balzano gripped his wrist harder.

Mio figlio, he repeated.

Io? His own voice startled.

Me.

And at the word Mr. Balzano uttered a sharp cry, seized his other hand, clutched both to his forehead and held them tight there, with a sound half-wailing half-laughing, till releasing them abruptly, he sank back onto the cot and lay there, heaving and smiling, *smiling*.

Where did Mr. Balzano think he was?

And he— He could not contain. All he could say was Rest, sleep, and tomorrow. . .

Mio figlio.

He watched a while, waited till Mr. Balzano's breathing fell to normal.

Cautiously he rose and left him, went his way up the stairs, impelled, yes, by a curious elation. All night he lay restless, expecting *them* to enshroud him and to possess the emptiness. But none returned. Mr. Balzano filled all his sight.

Where were they?

Did Mr. Balzano's presence in the house ward them off?

Or had he imagined—?

At first light he could no longer lie there.

Not to wake Mr. Balzano, he eased down the steps, guided only by the early light through the basement windows, and crossed the cellar.

The furnace hulked dark, the great isinglass eye blank—dead, too, the dark behind it, the very air dead.

He held his breath, to listen . . . No stirs.

But before he rounded the furnace, he knew—he saw the clear gray stretch of cot—it was empty.

Gone, he cried.

The word tolled.

Had he only imagined—?

Forlorn, mystified, he was about to go back up when his foot chanced against a small white thing on the floor.

He held it up to the morning light.

That envelope! It was his own sketch of Mr. Balzano's house. Mr. Balzano *had* been here.

You! He broke into choked laughter. His joy reverberated throughout the hollow cellar.

He went upstairs. Morning filled the empty rooms, it floated and it hung still, it bared the skeleton of the house, it stood his shadow dark. He saw how flimsy are the bones of a man, or a house. Out the windows, town stood, and harbor, so strange and unfamiliar in the first fire of morning flowing down Hope Street that for a moment he wondered where he was before his vision settled, clear and clean.